Blind Fear

Blind Fear

Hilary Norman

PIATKUS

For more information on other books
published by Piatkus, visit our website
at www.piatkus.co.uk

First published in Great Britain in 2000 by
Judy Piatkus (Publishers) Ltd of
5 Windmill Street, London W1P 1HF
e-mail: info@piatkus.co.uk

A catalogue record for this book is available from the British Library

ISBN 0 7499 0518 2

Set in Times by
Action Publishing Technology Ltd, Gloucester

Printed and bound in Great Britain by
Mackays of Chatham, plc, Chatham, Kent

For Helen

Gratitude to: Dr Herman Ash; Howard Barmad; Jill Berelowitz, for sharing a little of her superb talent and sculp-ting expertise; Jennifer Bloch; Lynn Curtis; Sara Fisher for fine guidance and friendship always; Guide Dogs For the Blind – especially Carol Alexander, Shaun Basham, Joy Gilbey and, of course, her wonderful Kirk; Gillian Green, for being such a marvellous editor; Jonathan Kern (for all kinds of other marvellous things); Janet Munday and Super Trooper; Herta Norman, # 1 reader and critic now for a dozen books; Judy Piatkus, for superb advice, amongst other remarkable gifts; Otis Richards and Opus 40; Jessica Starr for her painstaking work; and Dr Jonathan Tarlow.

*

As always, all the characters, situations – and weather – are entirely fictitious.

1992

1

He had been sleeping in the crawlspace when it had started. He'd gotten into the house a little less than two hours earlier, believing it was and would remain empty for the rest of the evening because the owners had gone out to dinner with a friend and they were the kind who stayed late, who liked their food and wine and sometimes left their car at the restaurant and took a cab home. That's what the Duke had told him, that there'd be plenty of time to slip inside, take a good, slow look around and help himself.

He didn't know why they'd changed their plans, come back ten minutes after he'd begun – before he'd even had a chance to take a good look around. He didn't know why, and he didn't give a damn. He'd seen the car coming, snapped off his flashlight and looked for his best way out. Only there hadn't *been* a way out, not in those few seconds. All he'd had time to do was find a place to hide, and he knew about the crawlspace same way he'd known about the window with a broken latch; the Duke had briefed him, as always, given him all the details he'd needed for the job. So he'd found the trapdoor, wriggled down and shut himself in, and it hadn't been too bad, not too cramped, and small spaces had never gotten to him the way they did some people, so he figured he'd wait till they were all asleep and then get out. Worst case, he'd get himself some zees and wait till they went out again to work in the morning. He liked to think he was the laid-back type; he never freaked out too easily, always kept his options open, considered most eventualities.

He hadn't reckoned on a fire.

He hadn't figured some fool would set the fucking house alight, or that the ceiling in the room above his crawlspace would come crashing down, making it impossible for him to get out, or that the sounds of the smoke alarm and the fire – Jesus Christ, who knew that fire could make so much frigging *noise*? – would cover his screams so completely that no one would hear him.

He gave up screaming after a while. He knew by then that he wasn't going to make it. That he was never going to steal again, or get laid again, or eat or drink or even get *arrested* again.

He thought about the Duke. The Duke would get mad as hell at the people up in the house who hadn't heard him screaming. It wasn't really their fault, but the Duke wouldn't know that, the Duke would just go *crazy*.

Thinking about that, he almost felt sorry for them.

Not as sorry as he felt for himself, though.

Overhead, the fire roared and the alarm shrieked, and terror gripped his insides, grabbed hold of them and twisted, started him bellowing again and pounding on the roof of the crawlspace that he now knew was going to be his coffin. For a time it took him over, pitching his heart and brain and all of his body into overdrive – and then, for a few moments at least, it lessened its grip. He wondered suddenly if he was going to burn or suffocate first, and then he remembered that he might not need to find out about that because he had some horse with him – good stuff that the Duke had told him to save for a special occasion. And he guessed, with a close to last gasp of irony, that they didn't come more special than this – and he'd heard that dying was okay if you timed it so you were someplace up past Jupiter . . .

He worked fast on himself. He was an expert, but he didn't want to screw up now of all times. He didn't want to know what it felt like to fry – he didn't want that at *all* . . .

And, oh, it was so right what he'd heard about dying. Holy shit, holy shit, holy *shit*, was it ever *right*!

4

1998

2

In a dark basement of a house in a quiet side road a little way from the Glasco Turnpike in Ulster County, New York, a young female lay on a table in a twilight world someplace below natural sleep.

Her skin felt smooth beneath the Duke's right palm as he rested it for a moment on the soft, flat belly, and a little warmth drifted up out of the body, flowed, like liquid power, into the Duke's own flesh and blood, passing through his hand into his wrist and arm up to his shoulder.

The subject smelled of sandalwood.

The Duke always bathed them before.

And afterwards.

All of this young female seemed beautiful. Which made it irksome to decide which part was most perfect. Eyes closed, the Duke ran his fingertips over the head, feeling the skull compactly formed beneath fine, damp hair that had been long until the Duke had pruned it short for practicality. His fingers moved downwards, over the slender shoulders, feeling the scapulae, then down the right arm, taking and holding the hand, the miracle of each flexibly joined bone. Then the torso. Clavicles, sternum, breasts, ribcage . . .

Deftly, carefully, the Duke turned the subject over, ran a hand down the spine, counting vertebrae, admiring alignment and symmetry en route to sacrum and coccyx – then turned

7

her back over again, continuing down ... femur, patella, tibia, fibula ...

And knew that it was found.

The left ankle and foot were remarkable, the sole calloused and, therefore, externally imperfect, but the bones magnificent. Gently, with growing excitement but needing to be careful, the Duke explored beneath tendons, muscles, and ligaments, and felt a rush. He often experienced a rush when it happened. When the choice was made.

In the blackness, his sense of touch was amazingly acute. The Duke pressed harder, going deeper, needing to be certain, probing waste fibrous tissue and fat in order to properly feel and flex calcaneus, talus, cuboid, navicular, cuneiforms, tarsals, metatarsals.

The young female stirred a little, gave a soft moan.

The Duke went to work.

3

When Joanna remembered the first time she had heard of Jack Donovan, the sound of rain came into her mind. English early-summer rain rattling the windows and dripping into the bucket on the kitchen floor of Merlin Cottage while Sophia and Rufus lay close to the ancient Aga in which a shepherd's pie slowly cooked, and she listened to the unfamiliar American voice on the telephone.

'Joanna Guthrie?'

'Yes.' She had spent most of the afternoon in her dark room developing wedding photographs for a client, during which time the bucket had almost half-filled. Now, waiting for the caller to introduce herself, she watched the tiny circular ripples created in the dark water by each successive raindrop.

'My name is Mel Rosenthal. You don't know me, but Sara Hallett does.'

Sara's name caught Joanna's attention. She looked away from the water.

'You're a friend of Sara's?'

'Not exactly, but my client, Jack Donovan, is.'

'Client?'

'Let me explain, Mrs Guthrie.'

Joanna sat for a while after they'd finished talking, after Mel Rosenthal had finished explaining what it was she wanted. She felt bemused, more than anything, by the strangeness of the

9

other woman's request. And a little irritated. If it hadn't been for Sara's involvement, she knew she would simply have said no right away. As it was, she knew that ultimately she *would* refuse, but she didn't enjoy being rude; and besides, she wanted to ask Sara about Ms Rosenthal, the artist's agent from New York City, and about her 'client' Jack Donovan. There was something about that word that rubbed Joanna up the wrong way – the fact that Donovan hadn't simply picked up the phone himself to call her. So far as Joanna was concerned, it spoke against him that he was either too busy, or considered himself too important, or, worst of all, that he felt this to be a potential business transaction to be dealt with by a third party, by his agent.

Joanna got down on the floor between Rufus and Sophia, and both German shepherds raised their big heads and then laid them down again, one on each of her denimed thighs, like book ends.

'This isn't business, is it, darlings?'

Rufus, four years Sophia's senior, older but by no means wiser, grunted, while Sophia merely gazed up into Joanna's face with eyes of liquid amber.

'People like that make you wonder, don't they?' Joanna said.

She couldn't help but wonder, at least a little, about Jack Donovan. He was a sculptor. According to his agent, he was a great sculptor, but maybe she was biased. Also according to Mel Rosenthal, he was blind and needed a guide dog. All well and good, except that he wanted one of Joanna's dogs. Which might have been okay, except that Donovan lived in New York and Joanna and her dogs lived in Oxfordshire.

It had made no sense to her. Joanna had told Rosenthal that right away.

'You have a wonderful organization over there—'

'I know,' the American had interrupted. 'But things haven't worked out for Mr Donovan with them.'

'Why not?'

'A number of reasons.'

The woman's prevarication had annoyed Joanna too, though

not nearly so much as learning that not only did Jack Donovan want to put a young, sensitive animal through the traumas of long-distance flight, but also that he could not even promise a dog a normal existence at journey's end. According to Mel Rosenthal, Donovan lived part-time in Manhattan and part-time upstate, and that kind of discordant lifestyle, Joanna had quickly told her, was likely to prove too confusing for many dogs.

'That's why he's hoping,' the agent had said, 'you could bring the dog across yourself and supervise all the necessary on-the-spot training.'

'I couldn't possibly do that,' Joanna had told her. 'Aside from all the other considerations, I simply couldn't afford to.'

'Which is why Mr Donovan is offering to pay well over the odds for one of your dogs,' Rosenthal had come back smoothly, 'as well as more than covering your fee and expenses. In fact, Mrs Guthrie, he's directed me to tell you to name your own price and – forgive me for sounding crass – Sarah Hallett seems to think you're in no position to turn that kind of money down.'

Joanna did not forgive her and, more to the point, she did not forgive Sara for being so indiscreet about her private affairs to a pair of complete strangers. She didn't think, though, that she would bother to e-mail her annoyance to Sara at this exact moment, because the shepherd's pie was ready, and any second now either Kit or Miriam – her two student lodgers – would probably descend, drawn by the aroma and hoping to be invited to share.

On the face of it, Joanna had lived alone since being widowed at the age of thirty, but thanks to the lodgers she'd taken in three years ago, soon after her husband Philip's death, loneliness was not an affliction she'd had too much time or opportunity to contemplate. Except at night, in bed. She felt it then, consistently and keenly: the lack of a man's warm, solid body lying close to her – though Philip's body, of course, had been anything but solid as he'd neared the end, and he'd almost always felt cold so that she, who had in the past relied on him to warm her icy feet or hands, had become the human hot water bottle in their union.

11

*

She composed and sent her e-mail late that night, after she and Kit had eaten and washed up, and after she'd taken the dogs out for their last walk. She kept its tone mild, any irritation focused squarely on Rosenthal and *'client'*, discovering, as she wrote, that what she was most curious about was Sara's connection with Donovan.

Joanna had the utmost respect and affection for Sara Hallett who was also, she supposed, a client, since Joanna had bred and trained Sara's dog, Juno, to her rather specific needs, as well as photographing her for her three most recent book jackets. Deaf since early childhood after a viral infection, Sara, a writer of children's stories, was also partially sighted, suffering from retinitis pigmentosa, a degenerative condition likely, in time, to leave her totally blind but which thus far had allowed her to keep an increasingly narrow central field of vision. Juno, her German shepherd, was, therefore, far more constantly on duty than most working dogs, being needed to alert Sara to rings, knocks, alarm bells and other important sounds, as well as guiding her outdoors.

I was inclined (Joanna wrote in her e-mail) simply to say no and leave it at that, but as his agent claimed that this man's a friend of yours, I suppose I should ask you about him first. You must be on fairly intimate terms with him to have told him about the state of my finances. I wish you had not done that, by the way.

Sara e-mailed back next morning, inviting her to lunch, tea or dinner any time over the next four days. Not being needed until next day at the Oxford hotel where she worked as a part-time receptionist, Joanna chose that same afternoon to drive her old Range Rover the five or so miles to Sara's cottage near Shipton-under-Wychwood.

'I knew you'd be too curious to wait,' Sara said in the slow, flat, sometimes hard-to-decipher speech that was so out of keeping with her quicksilver personality. 'I knew Donovan would intrigue you.'

12

It had been a while since the friends had last met, and Joanna was quickly aware that Sara's vision had deteriorated, the tunnel through which she saw the world becoming narrower. The tell-tale lines etched around her lovely dark eyes by the effort of focusing were deeper than when Joanna had last seen her, and Sara had cut her brown hair short, in an easier to manage style. The clutter with which she had always surrounded herself had been dramatically reduced; the lovely rugs in her small entrance hall and sitting room were gone; and there were two big books on one of the end tables printed in Moon, the embossed alphabetical signs which, though larger and therefore even more space-consuming than Braille, were so helpful to blind people previously able to read. Sara was preparing, it seemed clear to Joanna, to lose what was left of her sight, and sad as that was, at least she *was* preparing, organizing what was in her power to order to remain as independent, as much the old Sara, as she had been with vision.

'You have to help Donovan,' she told Joanna now, as they enjoyed a cream tea in the sitting room, Juno draped over the sofa beside her. 'He really *needs* your help.'

'I can't help him,' Joanna said, keeping her face inside her friend's line of vision, and signing simultaneously. After years of working with blind and partially sighted people, she had learned to sign, use Moon and, to a lesser extent, Braille. 'He lives thousands of miles away.'

'Of course you can. You go there – they don't have quarantine laws.'

'Why can't he work with Guide Dogs for the Blind over there? The agent was very evasive.'

Sara smiled. 'I like Mel. She's very protective of Donovan, so she was probably wary of being too honest too soon.'

Joanna frowned. 'Honest about what?'

'About the fact that the last time Donovan tried coping at one of the training centres in New York, he got plastered and smashed up a room.' Sara paused. 'That sounds much worse than it probably was. Donovan told me he broke a chair and a flower pot, and no people or dogs were around when he did it.'

Joanna was horrified. 'He sounds ghastly.'

'He's anything but ghastly, Jo.' Sara smiled again. 'He was a mess at the time. No one admits that more readily than him.'

'Even so' – Joanna was now more against the idea than ever – 'you can't possibly think I'd even consider sending a dog across the Atlantic just to indulge a neurotic, spoiled artist. What if it didn't work out? The animal would have to come back and go into quarantine.' She shook her head decisively. 'It's out of the question.'

Sara waited quietly for a few moments, reaching out and fondling Juno's ears while Joanna spread cream and strawberry jam on to a piece of scone.

'I'm not saying you're wrong, Jo,' she said at last. 'But I would like you to hear a bit more about Donovan and then think again. I can assure you that he's neither neurotic nor spoiled.'

Joanna swallowed the piece of scone and looked back at Sara. 'Okay,' she said, and signed. 'I'm listening.'

The vast majority of guide dogs supplied to the blind and visually impaired in the United Kingdom came from Guide Dogs for the Blind. Joanna had spent six years training with and working for the organization, first with the animals themselves with the dog supply unit, then as a guide dog mobility instructor, working with applicants and new guide dog owners. But then Philip's cancer had been diagnosed, and Joanna, wanting to spend more time at home, had begun breeding the German shepherd dogs they both loved.

One thing was certain, she reflected now, driving back towards Burford, and that was that had Sara not become a writer, she could have been a top-notch sales person. According to her, Jack Donovan – a fine teacher as well as a brilliant sculptor – might not be everyone's idea of the perfect man, but no one, in her opinion, could be more deserving of Joanna's help, given that he had lost two guide dogs tragically and in swift succession. The first, a golden retriever, had died after a ten-year partnership in a house fire, leaving Donovan grief-stricken; and then his replacement retriever had developed a fatal tumour at the age of three, at which time the

14

sculptor had abandoned both work and teaching in order to nurse the dog until her death.

'Donovan was inconsolable and irrational about it,' Sara had explained after tea. 'Acted as if it was his fault they'd both died – which, of course, it was not. But it was more than two years before anyone could persuade him to try another dog. He went for retraining at one of the centres, got himself incredibly fraught and went on a binge, and after that he felt too ashamed to let them give him another chance.'

A year later, on a visit to England, Donovan had met Sara's dog, Juno, and had gone back home unable to get the remarkable German shepherd out of his mind. Ever since then, he'd taken to e-mailing Sara, asking her a thousand questions about Joanna Guthrie and her dogs.

'He's finally ready to try again,' Sara had said, 'but only with a Guthrie-bred and trained animal.'

'That's nonsense,' Joanna had told her.

'He doesn't think so.' Sara had paused. 'Donovan's not always the easiest man to get along with. He dislikes big organizations, and he sometimes drinks too much and works too obsessively – but no one – I mean *no* one – could treat dogs more sensitively or with greater commonsense.'

'Hmm.' Joanna had been moved but unconvinced.

'I wish you'd at least *consider*, Jo. I guarantee you wouldn't regret it.'

'You can't guarantee something like that.'

'I can.' Sarah had shrugged. 'I almost can, because I know Donovan.'

It had occurred to Joanna then for the first time.

'Are you in love with him, Sara?'

And Sara, who had not admitted to falling in love with anyone in all the years Joanna had known her, had smiled wistfully.

'Everyone who knows Donovan's a little in love with him.' She had paused. 'One thing I *can* almost guarantee, Jo. You'll take one look at him, and you'll want to photograph him.'

If nothing else that Sara had said had put the wind up Joanna, those last remarks had certainly done the trick.

4

SUNDAY, JUNE 28

Under cover of night and forest, the Duke stood at the side of the burial pit, glad that this part of the process was over again.

It always began and ended with perfection – but in between there was the ugliness to contend with. Too much ugliness. But the Duke had learned by now that for one kind of beauty to mutate into another, a degree of unpleasantness had to be endured; he knew and accepted that. Even so, when the detritus had gone, had been disposed of, it was always a relief.

This dark, peaceful, secret glade had served its purpose now. The grave was full, the earth sated, and the time had come to move on.

The Duke had already found a new place. Better than this one, infinitely more suitable, its natural aptness enhanced by blessed irony. No preparation necessary, waiting with open arms for the next time.

He didn't know when or where or how that time would come. He only knew that it would.

Some things were certain.

5

Jack Donovan was in his Manhattan apartment when Mel Rosenthal called to tell him that Joanna Guthrie had been in touch with a proposition.

'She thinks she may have the ideal dog for you.'

Donovan had been leaning back in his favourite leather chair in his library, smoking a cigar and listening to Jagger and the rest of the guys performing 'Brown Sugar'. Now, he picked up the remote, turned off the music, took the cigar out of his mouth and sat forward.

'Are you sure?'

'The operative word was *thinks*,' Mel told him. 'The dog she's considering is two years old, which she says is old for guide dog training by normal standards, but apparently this dog is special.'

'All dogs are special,' Donovan said.

'I don't know,' Mel said. 'I never had one.'

'So what now?'

'Now you have to go to England to meet her – Guthrie – and the dog. She says she has to assess you – whatever that means – and that she wants to observe you together for at least a week to be sure you get along. I told her you get along with all dogs, but she said it was an absolute condition.'

'She's right,' Donovan said.

'So you'll go?'

'It's a German shepherd, right? Like Sara's?'

17

'It's a German shepherd, yes,' Mel answered. 'I didn't ask if it was like Sara's. Anyway, you always say all dogs are different.'

'So they are,' Donovan said. 'Any other conditions?'

'Mrs Guthrie said it'll take three months for her to train the dog in the UK, and then, if that goes okay, she's prepared to fly over with the animal and take care of training both of you on your territory – but if she feels at any time that things aren't working out for any reason, she'll have to find Sophia another home in the US because of the rabies laws over there.'

'Sophia?' Donovan asked.

'That's the dog's name, apparently,' Mel said.

Donovan put down the phone, put the cigar back in his mouth, took a drag and leaned back in the chair, eyes closed.

'Sophia,' he said, softly.

Not too many things scared Jack Donovan these days. The bullet that had blown away his 20/20 vision twenty-four years ago had been fired in panic, so the police had later told him, by a terrified young man running away from an abortive bank heist in Philadelphia. Donovan, aged eighteen, had been running too, because he'd been late for a lecture on Brancusi, and the robber's bullet had rebounded off a stone wall before colliding with his head; hence the 'great good fortune' that more than one doctor had told him about, in that had the bullet hit Donovan's brain straight from the gun, he would have been dead instead of merely blind. It had taken Donovan – an aspiring sculptor – a long while to accept that point-of-view.

Somehow, though, he had gone on, working, living, even – as family, teachers, counsellors, friends and time helped the healing process – learning to love his life again. He'd finished school and wounded his parents by relocating to New York City, where he'd married a psychotherapist named Greta Levin and moved into her Upper East Side apartment. Within a year, Greta had pronounced him impossible to live with and had moved Donovan out and a divorce attorney in. Three relationships and two successful one-man exhibitions later, Donovan had decided that Greta had probably been right. Still

18

in love with Manhattan but claustrophobic, he had put himself in the hands of his agent, Mel Rosenthal, and had gone in search of space and fresh air in comparatively easy reach of the city.

They had found Gilead Farm almost immediately; that was, it was still referred to as a farm, but was actually twenty-five acres of land between Rhinebeck and Red Hook in Dutchess County, New York. The estate had been owned by a horse-raising man of God who had apparently been heard to say, when naming his farm, that if Gilead had been a good enough place for the prophet Elijah to live, it was more than good enough for him. Donovan had sold off more than half the land, keeping ten acres, including a bunch of barns and outbuildings and a wonderful, mainly eighteenth-century stone house. Mel and the realtor had described it to him as best they could, but he had wanted to 'see' for himself, had spent hours touching, feeling, smelling and listening – even insisting on climbing a ladder so that he could get a clearer mind picture of the two stone chimneys. And so the Jack Donovan School had come into being, and Gilead Farm had become his main base, the place where he worked and taught and could walk more than ten yards without assistance in his own fields and *not* have at least two or three well-meaning strangers coming to pick him off the ground if he tripped and fell on his butt.

Donovan accepted these days that life had been good to him in many ways. He had his sculpting, a well-established name in the art world, his students, and his two homes and lifestyles, both of which helped keep him emotionally on-track. His work lay on the farm. While he was up there, it was almost total immersion: sculpting, teaching, working side by side with Lamb and feeding off that man's particular genius and generosity. Murdoch Lambert III (Lamb to his friends), fifty-three years old, escaped from wife and WASP enclave in Rhode Island, and blessed with enough self-confidence to be willing to subsume his own talent in a blind sculptor's work.

'You know he's in love with you,' Chris Chen, the school's administrator, had once told Donovan.

19

'Nonsense,' he'd answered smartly. 'Lamb's my colleague, and if he loves me at all, it's as a dear friend.'

Donovan's New York City apartment on West Fifty-sixth Street represented a secondary, but no less significant, existence for him. For one thing, it was a place in which it was virtually impossible for him to work; a place in which he was forced, therefore, to live a more normal life. There were traces of Jack Donovan the sculptor there, a handful of his earliest works scattered inside the apartment and out on the small terrace, but there was no studio. A library of Braille and Moon books, a computer complete with voice output and linked to a Braille embosser, a state-of-the-art music system wired through to speakers in every room, a well-stocked bar (well-stocked meaning, from Donovan's viewpoint, a healthy supply of Jack Daniel's good ol' Single Barrel) and a humidor for his cigars (another unhealthy habit, but he was *not* about to even consider giving up the taste, feel, aroma or even the *sound* of them) took care of most of his needs in this particular home.

A journalist had once asked Donovan why he spent so much time in the city.

'Noise, smells and thrust,' he had answered.

He loved rush hour on the sidewalks, the pressure and small physical thrills of being surrounded by hurrying, scurrying hordes, brushing against him or knocking into him, so much more heedless of a blind man than pedestrians were in the small, civilized towns and villages upstate. He spent his city time in restaurants and fine grocery stores and bars and cinemas. He felt people's gazes of surprise when he got in line and bought his tickets, but Donovan adored movie houses, liked their individuality, the old, damp, dingy places and the swish new outfits with their ace sound systems. He would sit back in his seat, hear the hush and feel the prickle of expectation when the lights went down, and then pick his private way through thrillers or tales of love or horror, picturing the images on his own mind's screen. In cinemas, and in Manhattan generally, Donovan felt one of the crowd, though

20

he had never stopped missing his dogs. Waldo, his beloved companion for a decade, his end still too agonizing for Donovan to think about, and then Jade, his sweet-natured bitch guide for such a brief time.

He had never wanted a dog before Waldo. Back in those days he'd lived full-time in the city and hadn't liked the idea of keeping a big animal in that locked-in world of concrete, steel and glass. Besides, like many other blind people, he'd been pretty much of a champ with his long cane from the beginning, and had no shortage of friends willing to act as sighted guides – which was why he'd managed so well since Jade's death. Except that, as Sara Hallett had reminded him, his dogs had given him something no cane ever could – and then she had introduced him to her remarkable Juno, trained by this Joanna Guthrie person to be both eyes and ears for Sara.

Not many things scared Donovan these days, that was true enough. Yet it had been fear that had kept him from giving in to his need before now. He had loved Waldo and Jade, had done his best to take good care of them both, just as they had taken such devoted care of him, but they had both died and – much, much worse – they had both suffered.

'*Not your fault.*' He'd heard those words time and again from well-meaning friends, and the logical part of him had known they were right. But love and loss and guilt had little to do with logic.

He was ready to try again now, was going to fly to England and meet Joanna Guthrie and her Sophia, was going to do his damnedest to make it work out. But he was still afraid of failing another animal. Jack Donovan had let down plenty of people over the years, but people, on the whole, could take care of themselves. Failing a dog was a million times worse.

He was scared to death of that.

21

6

'So what's the verdict?' Sara asked.

'On what?'

'Don't pretend to be obtuse, Jo.'

Joanna smiled, and signed: 'Sorry.'

Less than one minute had passed since Donovan had gone upstairs, leaving the two friends in Joanna's sitting room. There had been more dogs than humans around all evening: Sophia and her mother Bella, Rufus, Juno and Honey – a labrador belonging to Frederica Morton, Joanna's Australian-born kennel manager. Kit and Miriam were both at a party, and Fred was out on a date in Oxford this evening, so Joanna was dog-sitting because Honey had taken a dislike to Fred's boyfriend and had silently chewed a large hole in the young man's tweed jacket the first time he'd come to Fred's for coffee. All the dogs but one were now sprawled contentedly around the room. Sophia was sitting at the foot of the staircase, apparently waiting for Donovan to come back down.

Joanna looked across at her beautiful two-year-old shepherd, sighed, and looked back at Sara. 'They're made for each other, aren't they?' She shook her head. 'I mean, I know trying Sophia for Donovan was my idea, but I think part of me was hoping they might turn out to be a mismatch.'

'You'll miss her,' Sara said.

Joanna didn't answer, found that she could hardly speak. She had only had her flash of inspiration about Sophia's suit-

22

ability because of the dog's extraordinary qualities. The runt of Bella's first litter, she had got off to such a shaky start that when her brothers and sisters had been sold, Joanna had decided to keep and raise the scrawny pup herself. Sophia, however, had simply been a slow developer, becoming such an intelligent, intuitive animal that one of Fred's friends – a police dog handler – had virtually begged Joanna to let him give her some special training. Joanna had permitted a little of that, but had drawn the line at handing Sophia over for actual police work, loth to risk spoiling the sweetness and calm of the young bitch's nature.

'She'd make a perfect guide, wouldn't she?' Joanna had said to Fred when she'd first thought of matching Sophia with the American.

'Bloody marvellous,' Fred had said, and instantly Joanna had wished that she'd kept her mouth shut.

Now, having observed the dog and Donovan together for most of twenty-four hours, she found herself wishing that all over again.

Her first impression on meeting him at Oxford Station had been unexpected. He looked, she had thought from the far end of the platform, more like a teacher than a sculptor, drunk or otherwise. A tall, broad-shouldered, early forty-ish, visiting American professor, perhaps, she'd decided, walking slowly towards him.

'Mrs Guthrie?' Donovan had heard her approach, heard her slow as she neared him, smelled a light, pleasant perfume blended with the unmistakable scent of dogs, transferred his folded down cane into his left hand and held out his right.

'Mr Donovan.' Joanna shook his hand firmly, took her first close-up look at the man she was considering entrusting Sophia to, and formed another instant impression of intelligence and strength. 'I hope you haven't been waiting long.'

'Not long at all.' He felt her looking at him. 'Which way?'

'May I lead?' Joanna knew better than to take his arm.

'Better had.'

He made no attempt to unfold his cane, just lightly gripped

her arm, and they began to walk towards the car park. Joanna felt the tension transmitting from his hand to her arm and knew then that he was as nervous as she was.

'Gorgeous day,' he remarked.

'Beautiful,' Joanna agreed. 'July at its best.'

She couldn't help glancing at him as they walked. That was something that often made her a little guilty when working with blind people; looking at them, watching them, seemed to take on a surreptitious, sneaky quality because she was taking advantage that the sightless person couldn't – though the blind, she well knew from experience, had sensory skills that few sighted people could match.

Donovan smelled of cigar smoke, and his lightweight sports jacket and jeans were a little rumpled from the train journey, but he was otherwise immaculate, close-shaven with fair, grey-threaded, thick hair cut short. His eyes were a cloudy blue-grey, his nose was angular, his chin strong, his mouth straight and expressive, and a narrow scar ran down the right side of his face from hairline to jaw. Sara had certainly been right about one thing. Jack Donovan would make a fascinating subject to photograph.

'Not what you expected, huh?' he remarked, after Joanna had loaded his bag into the back of her Range Rover and slid into the driver's seat beside him.

She felt her cheeks redden and began to reverse out of the space.

'You thought I'd be a wild, artistic type, ravaged by booze.' Donovan felt her embarrassment, grinned and reached across to touch her left forearm briefly. 'That was unfair of me, Mrs Guthrie. I apologize. Sara told Mel that's what you were steeling yourself to allow into your home.'

'I never told Sara that,' Joanna said quickly, as she drove out of the car park into Park End Street, then smiled. 'Not in those words, anyway. And it's Joanna or Jo, please, not Mrs Guthrie.'

'And I'm Jack or Donovan, whichever you prefer.' He paused. 'So do I make the grade? Or do I go straight to a hotel?' The questions were lightly asked, but tension rippled under the surface.

24

Joanna glanced sideways at him. 'I think I'll risk letting you in for tea. I can always boot you out later.'

'Will Sophia be there?'

There it was, Joanna saw in a flash, the nub of his agitation. He was as nervous as a young man on the verge of meeting an arranged bride. Meeting Joanna had not really fazed Donovan, other in that he knew that if he failed to meet her criteria he would almost certainly not even get to first base with her dog. Sophia was the sole reason he had flown across the Atlantic and taken the train from Paddington, and within these first few minutes of meeting him, Joanna knew that making this work out was, right now, all that mattered to him.

Their arrival at Merlin Cottage had gone smoothly. Donovan had asked questions about her home, and Joanna had taken pleasure, as she always did, in answering. She had loved their house from the instant she and Philip – both Londoners – had set eyes on it during a weekend away in Oxford. Just outside Burford and close to the River Windrush, it had originally, the local estate agent had told them, been two semi-detached thatched Cotswold stone cottages. With the dividing wall and two decrepit staircases knocked down, a single home had been created that had retained all the charm and atmosphere of the originals but now also had space for all the dogs and children that the Guthries had hoped for. The children had been a pipe dream, but the extra rooms had come in useful since Philip's death. Keen, despite the relentless expense of his long illness, to hold on to their home afterwards, Joanna had taken her part-time receptionist's job at the Oxford hotel and had decided to make Merlin Cottage pay its way, taking in Kit Down and Miriam Omaboe, her two student lodgers. Their rent, low as it was, had helped – together with the hotel job and occasionally quite lucrative photographic commissions – to keep her just about afloat.

'Omaboe?' Donovan had queried as Joanna led the way upstairs. 'That's an African name, isn't it?'

'Ghanaian – Miriam's stunning, brilliant *and* the most heavenly cook – and Kit's our resident odd-job man in his spare time,' Joanna had answered at the door of Donovan's bedroom. Actually, it was her room, being the only one with an en-suite bath; Kit, a strong, wiry, courteous and practical Yorkshireman, had insisted on taking the couch (for a small reduction in rent) so that Joanna could have his room for the duration of the American's stay. 'The place seems to spring more leaks than a colander these days, and the heating's always breaking down, but Kit keeps things going most of the time.'

'Sounds a little like Pete Szabo,' Donovan said as he paced his way through the room, feeling for walls and corners and the window. 'He's a kind of factotum and friend up at Gilead Farm, takes care of the housekeeping and gardening and most other practical things.'

'Sara says the farm's beautiful.' Joanna lifted Donovan's bag on to the bed and told him she'd put it there. 'There should be enough towels in the bathroom, and I'm afraid there's no overhead shower, just a hand thing, but if there's anything else you need, just yell.'

'I won't need anything.' He paused. 'When do I get to meet Sophia?'

'At lunchtime. Fred's out walking her and the others right now.'

'Who's Fred?'

'Frederica Morton. She manages the Nursery' – Joanna caught Donovan's quizzical expression – 'which is what we call our kennels, and she helps with the business side of things while I'm out at work.' She watched him for a moment, saw how restless he was. 'Would you like some peace and quiet, or would you like a stroll around the place before they get back for lunch?'

'A stroll, please,' Donovan said decisively.

He left his cane behind, relaxed enough to trust Joanna's guidance, and they set off at a gentle pace while she described the square garden that Philip had loved and nurtured, with its slightly overgrown lawn, flowerbeds of hybrid tea and floribunda roses, wall-trained clematis and willow trees.

26

'One of Fred's many gifts,' she told Donovan as they passed close to a clothes line, from which sheets and pillow cases blew in the light breeze, 'is persuading the dogs to pee in the beds and not on the lawn.'

'So where's the Nursery?' he asked.

Joanna smiled. 'That's all you're really interested in, isn't it? The dogs, and meeting Sophia.'

'That's not true.' Donovan stopped walking. 'Not exactly true.' His brow creased. 'Joanna, I don't mean to be rude.'

'You're not being,' she assured him. 'I'm glad she's so important to you. I wouldn't have it any other way.'

They walked on, quite companionably, past a wooden bird table and bench, both carved by Philip Guthrie, and through the corridor of privet hedges into the apple orchard, and Donovan caught the scent of dogs and knew they were approaching the Nursery which had, Joanna explained, originally been a stable house until they'd insulated and heated it for dog-breeding purposes.

'Did Philip convert this place himself?' Donovan asked, feeling his way around the building. 'He seems to have been gifted enough, judging by that handsome bench.'

'He wasn't a builder.' Joanna said, 'but furniture making was his hobby. Philip was actually an accountant by profession. He opened an office in Oxford when we moved here from London, but he was so in love with our home that he hated being away from it, so he closed down the office and began working from a room in the cottage.'

'How did that work out?'

Joanna shrugged. 'Some of the stuffier business clients who liked their accountants to function in more formal surroundings shied away, but the more creative ones – Philip had a handful of writers and music clients – loved coming to Merlin Cottage to chat about their tax returns.'

'Sounds like a good scene for you both,' Donovan remarked softly. 'You with the dogs and your photography, which Sara tells me you're very gifted at.' He paused. 'You must miss Philip a lot.'

'I do,' Joanna said. 'But things have worked out pretty well

27

for me here. I have good friends, and I love the dogs, of course.' She looked at his face. 'Speaking of which, I think Fred should be getting back about now, and she's bringing the dogs straight into the cottage for your benefit.'

The first meeting between Donovan and Sophia had moved both Joanna and Fred. They had been sitting in the kitchen when they'd heard barking and Joanna had seen Donovan practically jerk to attention, had watched his mouth grow tense and his forehead furrow with anticipation. Yet the instant the dogs had come skittering through the front door over the stone-flagged entrance hall and into the kitchen, tails wagging joyfully in greeting, Jack Donovan had been in his element. He didn't overwhelm the animals but waited patiently instead, sitting on a kitchen chair, for them to come to him, not even asking which dog was which. It was Fred – clearly smitten at first sight, Joanna judged from the flush on her normally pale cheeks – who made the introductions, while Joanna sat silently, observing, as Donovan made acquaintance first with Rufus, the most rumbustious, then with Honey, the labrador, then with Bella and, finally, with Sophia.

'Hello,' he had said, his deep voice soft and tender as the two-year-old German shepherd had sniffed his right hand. 'Hello, Sophia.'

She had stood very still while Donovan had got off the chair, crouched down on the floor and begun, with great gentleness, to feel, stroke and examine her from nose to tail and right down to the pads of her feet. It was, Joanna knew, his way of seeing the animal for the first time, and it seemed to her that Sophia sensed that, too. Always a gentle, calm dog, she was, nevertheless, still young and playful, but something about this new person was clearly fascinating to her. Perhaps, Joanna thought as he went on touching her, talking all the while – too softly for anyone else to hear – it was simply the unusual intensity of his physical scrutiny that was rooting the dog to the spot, but she didn't really think that was the case.

'Okay, girl,' Donovan said, still with that tender quality to his tone of voice. 'Okay, Sophia.'

She licked his nose. Joanna's mouth felt dry.

Donovan straightened up, felt for his chair and sat back down. He looked, for the first time since his arrival, exhausted.

'She's wonderful, Joanna,' he said, then turned to face Frederica, who was slightly open-mouthed. 'Thank you for introducing us, Fred.'

'You're welcome.'

Joanna smiled. Fred Morton had been the object of any number of young men's passions since she'd known her, Kit's amongst them. Tall and slender with long, straight fair hair, she was also immensely down-to-earth and a mistress of the put-down when any smart aleck male irritated her. Joanna had seen her with men she liked, her latest boyfriend being one of them, but she had never, until today, seen Fred smitten.

Over on the other side of the kitchen, Rufus made a sudden dive for Honey's tail, Bella barked sharp disapproval and Rufus whined.

It was, Joanna decided, time to break the mood.

'Anyone else here hungry except me?' she asked.

Donovan turned his head to her. 'Starved,' he said.

The exhaustion, Joanna noted, had been fleeting and was already gone. He looked happy now. He looked, in fact, happier than she'd seen anyone look in a very long time.

'You're right,' she said to Sara that night, after Donovan had gone upstairs to bed. 'I knew it the moment they met. They're perfect for each other in every respect.'

For a few moments, neither woman spoke. Sophia, still sitting at the foot of the staircase, got up slowly and came and flopped down close to Joanna's feet. Bella, lying beside Juno, Rufus and Honey, began to snore peacefully, her muzzle between her front paws.

'How are you going to cope with leaving home, Jo?'

'I'm hardly going to be doing that,' Joanna signed to her friend. 'If I do go, I'll only be away a few weeks at most.'

'Still,' Sara said in her slow, thoughtful voice, 'you haven't been away since Philip died, have you? Not out of the country, at least.' She paused. 'When would you plan to leave?'

'If things work out' – Joanna was being careful – 'not before late-October or early-November. Sophia's not a young pup – I'll need at least three months to complete her training here before I take her overseas.'

'You mightn't be back in time for Christmas.'

'Of course I will.' Joanna was appalled by the notion. 'Aside from anything else, you don't imagine I'd risk leaving Miriam and Kit alone in Merlin Cottage for too long, do you?'

'They're reliable, aren't they?' Sara asked.

'They're wonderful,' Joanna answered. 'But they have their studies and their own lives – I can't expect them to become full-time caretakers for too long.' She shrugged. 'And there's my job at the hotel to consider, too. There's a limit to how long they'll keep that open for me.'

Sara leaned towards her, wanting to speak more quietly. 'Donovan wants to pay you a lot of money, doesn't he?'

'Yes, but—' Joanna stopped. She never liked discussing money.

'And you do need it, don't you?' Sara persisted.

'Of course I need it.' Joanna pointed towards the sill below one of the leaded windows where the frame had let in small pools of water during the last heavy rain. 'Look at that.' She waited for Sara to turn back to face her again. 'As it is, Kit spends far too much time gluing this place together. The thatch needs doing and the heating has to have something major replaced.' She shook her head. 'I can hardly afford not to go.' She pondered another moment. 'Besides, you know how I feel about seeing a job through to the end – so frankly, if I don't go, neither does Sophia.'

'Which would leave one seriously heartbroken man,' Sara said.

'Hmm,' Joanna commented noncommittally.

'You saw how he was with her – how he is with dogs in general. He seems tuned in to them, doesn't he?'

'Even fussy Fred remarked on that before she went out,' Joanna agreed.

'Or was that just because she thinks he's better-looking than

30

Harrison Ford?' Sara asked.

Joanna gave her an intent look. 'Are you interested in him, Sara?'

Sara smiled. 'You asked me once before if I was in love with him.'

'And you said that everyone who knew him was, a little.'

Sara shook her head. 'I'm not, Jo. Not in that sense, at least. You know how I am – I like to make the most of my sight while I can – and you have to admit Donovan's easy on the eye.'

Joanna's mind summoned up the things she'd especially noticed about the man during the course of this day: his strong, long-fingered hands; the way his stance, sometimes rigid, other times relaxed, betrayed his emotions; the startling infectiousness of his big, dirty laugh.

'It's much more than looks though with him, of course,' Sara added. 'Donovan's special, Jo. I think you've already realized that.' She paused. 'And I don't think that spending a few weeks with him on his home turf is going to do you any harm at all.'

7

SUNDAY, NOVEMBER 1

The tunnel was locked inside Sara's head again, stretching from the back of her brain right to her eyes, but her lids were closed, so she couldn't see clearly. The tunnel was so *narrow*, it was like looking into the opening of a tiny black-rimmed tube, looking right into the heart of a sliver of ebony shot through with even tinier shavings of piercing silver light.

There were images inside the tube, inside the tunnel, inside her head. She strained to see them, to interpret them, but it was too hard, too *hard*. There were colours now, real, vibrant colours – red-gold strands, waving and curling as those fragments of brightness flashed through the darkness, illuminating them, and now she saw nut-brown-gold orbs, flecked with green, blinking, glittering, staring, then gone again, back into the night.

All black again now, nothing to be seen, but sensations still coming. The dark was bleak, like burial, suffocating, awful, frightening – and this time when the silver pierced through, she felt, oh, God, how she *felt* it.

Fear.

And then she heard it, too. She, who had heard nothing for decades, nothing, nothing, felt it coming, like wind, like a storm, funnelling through the tunnel in her head, rising, higher and higher, until it was too agonizing to bear.

Screaming.

*

Sara woke from her dream and lay very still, staring through her own real, living, waking tunnel up at the ceiling of her bedroom. There were stars sprinkled up there, and a crescent moon, all shimmering down at her kindly in the dawn light coming through her curtainless windows. It was, as close as human hands could manage, a painted likeness of the sky she and Michaela Rees had seen one night while camping out on Salisbury Plain years ago, around the time Michaela had been illustrating Sara's second storybook. That sky had filled Sara with such a rare sense of freedom and joy that she had never forgotten it, but it had been Michaela's idea to paint Sara's ceiling for her when her field of vision had first begun to narrow, so that she would be able to lie in her own bed and watch the heavens every single night until her last slit of sight was finally and irrevocably snuffed out.

The dream was over, but the fear was still with her.

It was abstract. They were always abstract and frustrating and often too intense to bear. Atmospheres and essences, needle-sharp sensations and impressions, sometimes impossible to read, sometimes blazingly clear.

This dream had concerned Joanna, Sara was certain of that. The red-gold of her hair, the green-flecked hazel of her eyes. The *essence* of Joanna, calm, tinged with excitement, on the brink of something.

And then that awful, sickening fear.

She lay in her bed for a long time, wondering what to do.

Joanna was leaving today. Travelling to America, on a trip, an adventure, that Sara had urged her, *pushed* her, to take.

New images flew through Sara's mind. Waking terrors about car crashes on motorways, aeroplanes falling, exploding, bodies floating in the ocean.

She sat up, perspiring, breathing too rapidly, turned her head to see the time. 6.58. Too late. Joanna had already left Merlin Cottage for the journey to the airport. Even if she had not, what could Sara have told her? That she'd had a bad dream? That it had been the colour of Joanna's hair and eyes, and that it had terrified her?

Joanna knew about Sara's dreams, they had talked about

33

them together. She believed in them, accepted that sometimes the images they contained seemed to fold themselves around a nub of something real, that occasionally they even had a presageful quality to them.

I had a bad dream. Don't fly today.

Joanna Guthrie was too earthed for that, too calm, too sensible. Even if it were not too late, even if she believed it, she would still go.

Believed what?

Sara lay back on her pillows and stared up at the heavens, growing lighter. The sound of that scream was still reverberating in her head.

With a great effort, she pushed it away and got up.

8

SUNDAY, NOVEMBER 1

Terms wholly agreed and arrangements – including two commissions (both approved by Donovan) from the *Kennel Gazette* and *Art Monthly* in place, Joanna and Sophia – guide dog-trained, sedated, crated and fully documented – made the journey via British Airways on the first day of November. Joanna, anxious to be reunited with her dog as swiftly as possible, was met on the other side of customs by Donovan – in a raincoat and, uncommonly for him, wearing dark glasses – and a big, muscular, flaxen-haired man in a fisherman's sweater and jeans.

'Pete Szabo,' he said, shaking Joanna's hand. Near giant that he was, his voice was soft and slightly lilting.

'I've heard so much about you,' she told him.

'We've all heard a lot about you, Mrs Guthrie.'

All around them, porters wheeled baggage trolleys and harassed arrivals flowed towards what looked dauntingly like a near-mob scene outside. Joanna remembered her one and only previous visit with Philip, recalled how they had touched down raring to go but how, by the time they'd endured first the hot, airless lines at immigration and then, outside the terminal building, the endless, jostling wait for an unairconditioned, jolting yellow cab, they had felt utterly drained.

'I don't mean to be rude,' she said, 'but we need to get to Cargo Building 66 to get Sophia. I hate the thought of her fretting.'

'If you can stand a little more walking, Mrs Guthrie,' Pete Szabo said to her, 'I've parked not too far away.'

'And if Pete has to try and drive it through the jams to pick us up here,' Donovan said, 'we'll all be standing here for most of the day.'

'Two things,' she said to Szabo. 'I'm Joanna or Jo, please.'

The big man smiled down at her, his eyes light brown and friendly. 'What's the second, Jo?'

'Let's get out of here,' she said.

Sophia was still a little splay-legged and bewildered, but otherwise fine and happy to see her mistress. Donovan asked Joanna if she wanted to sit up front in the black Cherokee next to Szabo so as to get a better view on the journey, but she elected to sit in the back with Sophia. *Still mine*, she thought, but didn't say, though she thought she saw from Donovan's expression that he understood her feelings.

'You're going to get plenty of time in the city,' the blond man told her, 'and Donovan figures the sooner we get Sophia out to the farm, the better for her, so we're taking Grand Central Parkway, picking up route 87 up around the Yankee Stadium and sticking with that till we get on route 9 just south of Tarrytown. Any of that sound familiar to you, Jo?'

'Some,' she said. 'Sleepy Hollow, right?'

'Right,' Szabo said.

'My husband and I went there when we were over here together a few years ago. He liked Washington Irving's stories.'

'Sunnyside was the first house Lamb made for me,' Donovan said.

'Made?' Beside her on the back seat, Sophia shifted closer until her head was resting on Joanna's lap.

'He makes – carves or models – replicas of houses or bridges or details of structures I'm especially interested in.' Donovan's tone was warm. 'I think I told you about Lamb's knack for being my "eyes". Most people do their best to describe objects or other people, and some people do a pretty good job, but when Lamb talks about a thing or a person, he won't quit till he knows I'm seeing it in my head.' Donovan paused. 'And if he doesn't feel I've really gotten the picture, so to speak, he makes me a physical model, something I can touch and get to know.'

'He sounds remarkable.' Joanna said.

'Oh, he is,' Donovan said.

Joanna had heard a little about Murdoch Lambert and his importance to Donovan, but they hadn't talked at any length either about him or any of the other significant figures in the sculptor's life. In fact, Joanna had also come to realize, Donovan had a particular aptitude for asking key questions and then using silence and patience to squeeze maximum juice out of the answer – which meant that the American had probably learned a great deal more about her than she had about him. Oh, she knew the basics about his lifestyle, had seen the photographs he'd brought with him of Gilead Farm and the Manhattan apartment, knew the names of and fundamental facts about the people close to him, but that was the extent of it. Which meant that she had just flown three thousand or so miles, and was now being driven by virtual strangers to their home, where she was to give herself over body and soul to training Sophia prior to handing her over to one of those strangers.

'Just passing the Yonkers Raceway,' Pete Szabo told her.

Joanna murmured a response, stroked her slumbering dog's head, and fought her own need to sleep, rolling over her in warming, tempting waves, trying at the same time to assemble what little she did know about Jack Donovan. She knew that he was a major success in the United States as a sculptor, that he had a pushy agent in Manhattan named Mel Rosenthal, that he smoked expensive cigars because he genuinely liked them, that he drank to excess now and again, that Sara Hallett was crazy about him, and that many other people, according to Sara, found him lovable. And then, of course, there was the one thing that had drawn Joanna across the Atlantic: Jack Donovan had fallen in love with Sophia and was one hundred and one per cent committed to making their partnership work out.

Joanna supposed – as her head lolled and her eyes grew heavy – that that would have to be enough.

She woke, startled and confused, to see a face close up at her window: a small, honey-coloured oval with large, exotic brown eyes, watching her with interest. Jolted into too-abrupt wakefulness, Joanna sat upright and stared around her, saw that she was still in the back seat of the Cherokee, still buckled in, and that Sophia too, had woken and was sitting up beside her, regarding the woman on the other side of the glass.

'Take it easy.' The woman opened the door and Joanna's seat belt released her and slid smoothly back to its out-of-use position. 'I didn't mean to scare you, Joanna.' Her full lips curved into a smile. 'The guys didn't want to wake you both. so they took the bags inside first.' She bent slightly and put out her hand. 'I'm Chris Chen, by the way.'

'Hello.' Joanna shook the woman's hand, felt it compact and cool in her own. 'I can't believe I was sleeping so deeply.' Nudged by the German shepherd, she gave her a hug. 'Better get out.'

'You've had a long journey,' Chris Chen said. 'I told Donovan he should have given you a night in the city first to rest up.'

Joanna got out, stretched her legs, and Sophia followed suit. Outside the vehicle she realized how small the other woman was. Only five and a half feet herself, she was almost a head taller than Chen, though despite her petite stature the young Chinese-American, wearing a soft peacock blue wool dress with a small, antique-looking, mother-of-pearl locket around her neck, gave an impression of strength and vivacity.

'So this is the famous Sophia. May I pet her?'

'Definitely.' Joanna smiled as the other woman bent and stroked the dog delicately between her ears. 'Sophia loves being petted.'

Chris Chen straightened up. 'That can be a problem for guides, can't it?'

'Only when they're in harness.' Joanna took her first look around, saw that the Cherokee was parked in a large paved area that had probably once been a farmyard. They were just twenty or so yards from the house that she'd seen in Donovan's photographs, and there was the eighteenth-century stone building with its grey painted shutters and pitched roof and gables and the two rugged stone chimneys that she had admired.

Sophia was wandering around, nose to the ground.

'First things first,' Joanna said, starting to come to. 'Where can she go to pee without causing offence?'

Right on cue, Donovan appeared through an open doorway. 'Any place she damn' well likes.' He'd shed the raincoat and boots he'd worn to the airport, and had pulled on a dark blue heavy cotton sweater and a pair of sneakers.

'Maybe she'd like the wild flower garden,' Chris Chen suggested.

'Sounds good to me,' Joanna said.

'Shall I take them, Donovan,' Chen asked, 'or do you want to?'

'We could all go,' he answered. 'Sophia's first pee on the farm – a veritable baptism.'

Chen smiled. 'I'll pass. I should get back to the office – working on a Sunday afternoon, please note, boss.' She turned to Joanna. 'Good to meet you both.'

'Likewise,' Joanna said.

The garden Chris Chen had proposed as Sophia's first port of call was bordered by hedges and, even in November, was a wilderness of flowers, some the kinds of weeds, lovely in their own profuse right, that Joanna often admired but that most dedicated gardeners did their best to eradicate.

'The colours are wonderful,' she said now, then winced a little at her lack of tact while Sophia danced ahead through the blues and purples.

'Don't do that,' Donovan said.

Joanna tensed.

'Don't be ashamed of talking about beauty to me – or about anything you can see.' He was very intense. 'I've told you, that's one of the gifts I prize most about Lamb – I need to see

39

things through other people's eyes. My world's dark enough without trying to banish even my memories of what it used to be like.'

'I'm sorry.'

'No need to be sorry. I had eighteen years of being able to see, Joanna, and thankfully, being an artist I went around with my eyes well and truly open, which means I have a pretty decent memory bank.' He paused. 'So if something catches your eye – which it clearly will, given your own photographic art – and you feel like sharing it with me, chances are you won't have to build a model for me to know what you're talking about.'

Joanna saw Sophia squatting over to her right, half-concealed by tall, waving grasses. 'Your garden is being baptized as we speak,' she told Donovan quietly. 'She seems to like the fact that you don't mow your grass.'

'Has she ever met a goat?' he asked.

'Not that I'm aware of.'

'Pete bought two goats at an auction a while back, lets them keep down the grass in the meadows. They're friendly enough.'

Sophia came trotting towards them, thrust her nose under Joanna's right palm, then did the same for Donovan.

'For some people,' Joanna said, after a moment, 'having lost the sight they used to have makes it worse. I can under-stand that. It must be so hard not to be bitter.'

'Bitterness just makes everything ugly,' Donovan said, softly.

Joanna looked at him curiously. 'Weren't you bitter, to begin with?'

He waited a few beats before answering. 'I was destroyed, at the beginning. I mean, I honestly believed I was finished. Better off dead.' He gave a small shrug. 'And then I found out that wasn't so.'

'Was that down to time? Or did something happen to make you feel better?'

Donovan grinned, a slow, lazy smile. 'Actually, the first thing that happened – and it was a whole series of things that

40

made me see my life was far from over. But the first thing – the first person – was a woman.' He raised his face skywards and gave one of his short, deep, dirty laughs. 'It was sex, pure and simple. A beautiful woman in my arms who still wanted me, and I could still feel that amazing, soft skin and . . .' He paused, turned his face back towards Joanna, and smiled more gently. 'I could still feel *everything*. You know?'

Joanna looked at him, saw the raptness of that single memory printed so clearly on his face, and a small shiver of something not experienced since long before Philip's death passed through her.

'Yes,' she said.

They walked on, leaving the wild flower garden, moving on through the enclosed vegetable garden in which, Donovan told Joanna, they grew their own potatoes, three kinds of beans, beets, marrows, shallots and whatever else took Pete Szabo's fancy. There was a fruit orchard that reminded Joanna of home and made her think about Rufus and Bella – almost certainly missing Sophia – and about Kit and Miriam and Fred and Honey . . . And then she remembered the thatch that needed redoing, and the heating that might not survive another winter, and the hundred-and-one leaks that Merlin Cottage had sprung over the past couple of years, and she ordered herself to put all symptoms of homesickness out of her mind and enjoy her first afternoon on Gilead Farm.

'It's getting dark,' Donovan said after a while, felt Joanna's surprised glance and explained. 'The quality of the air changes when the light goes, and the birds start their evening routines – and anyway, I checked the time before I came out of the house and I know roughly how long we've been out.'

'And my legs are telling me it's time I sat down,' Joanna said ruefully.

'You must be exhausted.' Donovan was guilty. 'Let's get back to the house – or maybe I'll just show you directly to the guest house.'

'I don't mind,' Joanna said, 'so long as I get a cup of coffee.'

41

'Don't you want tea?'

'How many cups of tea do you remember me drinking in England?'

Donovan cast his mind back. 'Coffee, dark brown, no sugar.' Again, he sensed her surprise. 'You brought in a tray that first evening when Sara came to dinner, with a milk jug and sugar bowl. I heard you pour milk for Sara and you gave me sugar, and when it came to your own cup you poured just a trickle of milk and that was it.'

'I'll have to take care not to whisper anything I don't want you hearing if you're within a five-mile radius,' Joanna said, impressed, as they turned around and Sophia came running.

Donovan grinned. 'Not too much gets by me.'

He brought them to the guest house, located between the main house and the Jack Donovan School which, he had already explained, had – like her own Nursery – been installed in large, defunct stable quarters. Dusk had been swiftly overtaken by full rural blackness as they walked back from the orchard, though the pathways, as they neared the buildings, were gently illuminated by lanterns strung from trees and walls.

Donovan escorted Joanna and Sophia into the self-contained cottage, ensured that the heating and hot water were functioning and that Pete Szabo had put away the basic groceries that he'd promised, including three kinds of dog food for Sophia to choose from – and then said he was going to leave them alone to rest.

'We'd like it if you're up to coming across for dinner,' he said, 'but if you're too bushed, there should be some pretty good sandwich makings in the ice-box, and Pete said he'd leave you some of his famous home-made potato soup.'

'What time do you eat dinner round here?' Joanna asked.

'Around seven – pretty early for you, I guess.'

'Not tonight it won't be,' she said, adding five to the hour, and thinking that soup, a hot bath and bed were more tempting than dinner in company, however pleasant.

Donovan bent, made a gentle clucking sound with his tongue, and Sophia moved to his side. He fondled her ears for a moment, then straightened up again. 'I figure she's going to be easier spending the first few nights here with you rather than come into the main house. Don't you think?'

Joanna looked down at Sophia and felt a great wrenching. 'I'm not sure about it being easier for her,' she said, 'but I know I'll be happier.'

'I figured that, too,' Donovan said, gently. He went towards the door, then turned back. 'Don't feel pressured into coming over for dinner, Joanna. It'll just be me and Pete and a pot roast, and Pete doesn't get upset if people don't show up. We're all pretty easy-going up here.'

'He seems very nice,' Joanna said. 'So does Chris.'

'And two more different characters you couldn't hope to find.' Donovan smiled as he opened the door and let in a cold evening breeze. 'And tomorrow you'll meet Lamb.'

9

MONDAY, NOVEMBER 2

Joanna woke to find Sophia on the bed beside her, long, bushy tail thumping the handstitched patchwork quilt she had briefly admired before crawling between the sheets and all but passing out.

'Good morning, my darling,' she mumbled. 'If it is morning.'

Sophia whined and edged closer on her belly, tail still wagging, and Joanna turned her head to look at the glowing digital alarm clock. It read 6.33, which meant they had both slept solidly for about ten hours.

The dog pushed at her arm. Joanna reached across to the bedside lamp switch, turned it on and gazed blearily around the room. She'd been too tired to do more than cursorily appreciate what had clearly been done specifically for her by someone, presumably the ubiquitous Pete. Flowers in three separate vases, all of them charmingly dainty; copies of the *Woodstock Times* and *Daily Freeman*; a pile of novels, half of them by English writers; and finally, the kindest touch of all, a framed photograph of Merlin Cottage with her and Fred and all the dogs in the foreground – and Joanna recalled Sara taking that a few months ago (she, too, loved taking photographs, said that because her vision had become so much like looking through a permanently narrow viewfinder, she was a natural when it came to cameras), so clearly she and Donovan had been jointly responsible for having it ready for her here.

'Nice,' she said now, softly.

44

Sophia jumped off the bed, ran to the door and looked expectantly at Joanna.

'Oh.' She got the message. 'Okay.' Slowly, she pushed back the covers and discovered that the temperature in the room was pleasantly warm, and didn't *that* make a change from the early-morning chill in her bedroom at Merlin Cottage?

Sophia scratched meaningfully at the door and gave a soft but urgent bark.

Joanna looked at the pale, pretty woven rugs on the floor, considered the probable state of her dog's bladder after the unprecedentedly long night, and got her act together.

The dawn chorus was beginning, the lanterns were still lighting the way, and the air was startlingly colder than it had been the previous evening when she'd taken Sophia on her final walk of the day. Joanna had pulled on jeans, sneakers and her favourite, ancient green cashmere sweater – Philip had bought her that sweater at Harrods long before his illness, had told her that the colour brought out the green flecks in her hazel eyes, and though it had since been darned in several places and the green had faded somewhat, Joanna regarded it as a kind of security blanket and never travelled far without it. She was glad of its warmth this morning as Sophia, already programmed after just two visits, galloped ahead of her towards the wild flower garden.

Early as it was, the lights were already switched on inside the Jack Donovan School and, as Joanna followed the path about twenty yards from the entrance, the door opened and a man came outside, a small, slim, dapper-looking man of middle age, wearing a black roll-necked sweater and black trousers. He noticed her walking, paused and regarded her, and Joanna smiled and raised a hand, ready to speak to him, but he merely nodded at her, somewhat curtly, and then walked on briskly in the direction of the main house.

Lamb, I'll bet, Joanna thought, and continued after Sophia.

She saw no one else until after she'd showered, dressed for a second time – still wearing the green cashmere for luck – breakfasted on orange juice, coffee and toast and finished the unpacking that had gone by the board the night before. Daylight had brought fine late-autumn weather with a stiff breeze that swirled toasted leaves into the farmyard outside the window of the downstairs room where Joanna had eaten breakfast and would, she presumed, spend much of her quiet time during her stay. It was a charming, open-plan yet comfortably old-fashioned area with a floral chintz-covered sofa and armchair and curtains to match, a low coffee table, a round pine dining table just big enough to seat four, a television set, radio – tuned in, when Joanna switched it on, to WKIP, a talk station – and a tiny, but practical, kitchen.

The knock on the door came at 8.35. Sophia gave a short, friendly bark and went ahead of Joanna, tail wagging.

Donovan stood on the doorstep, long cane in one hand, wearing a sports jacket, jeans and a soft grey turtleneck sweater that made – Joanna thought with a pang of something that startled her – the blue-grey of his eyes seem cloudier.

'You decent?' He smiled. 'Not that it matters.'

'I am.' She stepped back. 'Coming in?'

'I didn't want to intrude,' Donovan said, 'but Sara e-mailed me this morning wanting to make sure you guys had arrived safely. I thought she seemed anxious, so I got straight back to her and she's happy now, but I figured I should let you know.'

Sophia – who seemed aware that it was up to her, with this man, to make her presence known – pushed up against his legs, and Donovan, still outside the door, crouched low to fuss over her.

'It's not like Sara to worry,' Joanna said. 'And you're not intruding. I've just made some coffee, if you'd like a cup.'

'I'd love one.'

He stood up, came inside, folded his cane, walked unerringly over to the armchair and sat down. His orientation skills, Joanna had noticed before, were remarkable, though it wasn't the first time she'd observed blind people who had trained themselves to know every inch of their own territory. Beyond, of course, it was a different matter; the outside world

46

was unpredictable, potentially lethal, and even in a garden or small park they and their dog might know well, there was no depending on nature not to toss some alien and unexpected obstacle in their path.

'Sara said she'd had a bad dream about you,' Donovan said as Joanna poured his coffee and brought it across. 'She said she knew it was absurd of her to fuss about it, but it was obviously troubling her.'

Joanna set his mug down on the low table in front of him. 'She has odd, abstract dreams from time to time. Every now and then, they appear to be semi-psychic, which disturbs her.' She sat on the sofa, and Sophia lay down between their feet on the rug.

'She seemed fine once she knew you were safe and sound – but my computer's available any time you want to e-mail her.' Donovan paused. 'Lamb says he saw you out before first light.'

Joanna smiled. 'I thought that was probably him.'

'I don't imagine he introduced himself,' Donovan said drily.

'He probably wasn't certain who I was,' Joanna said. 'Though I don't suppose there'd be too many strange women wandering along that path at that time of day.'

'Certainly not women with German shepherd dogs,' Donovan said. 'Lamb is looking forward to meeting you, though – both of you.' He drank some coffee. 'So what are your plans for today, Joanna? Would you like to take things easy, or would you like to have Pete drive us around – or would you prefer to go someplace alone with your camera?'

'I thought you might want to start showing us around Gilead Farm,' Joanna said. 'The sooner Sophia gets familiarized, the sooner we can get started on our training.' She paused. 'You and Sophia come first on this trip, Jack – any pictures I happen to get at this stage are a bonus.'

'I was hoping you'd say that.' Donovan was pleased. 'I didn't like to impose.'

'You're not imposing,' Joanna told him plainly. 'I'm here to work with you and Sophia.'

47

'Sara told me you're very single-minded when you're working.' He smiled. 'Actually, she said you're very single-minded most of the time.'

'Are you sure she didn't say I'm pig-headed?'

'Nothing so rude.' He thought for a moment. '*Obstinate*, I think, was the word she used – but then, from what I know of Sara, she might as well have been speaking about herself.' He paused. 'Or me, come to that.'

'I expect you have to be single-minded to be an artist,' Joanna said.

'Especially a blind one?' Donovan shook his head. 'As a matter of fact, blindness makes it a whole lot easier to concentrate on any one thing – fewer distracting outside influences.'

Joanna drank some coffee. 'Are you working on something at the moment? Or isn't it like that for you? Sara seems to feel compelled to work every day.'

'That's partly because she's trying to pack in as much as she can before her vision goes completely.' Donovan's face had grown sombre. 'Sara may seem resigned to going blind, but a lot of that's to make other people feel better about her.'

'I know she's scared.'

'She's terrified, Joanna. It *is* terrifying. You learn to cope with it – you learn not to be afraid all of the time, and you also learn to use the fear when it does hit you.' He set his mug down on the table. 'Fear can cripple you, but it can also save your life, even if all it does is stop you stepping out into the street without asking for help.'

Joanna didn't speak. She was too intent on him, listening to and watching him. She knew she was doing that again – taking unfair advantage by observing him – yet she found it almost impossible to look away. There was no doubt about it. Jack Donovan was a very compelling man.

'*Everyone who knows Donovan's a little in love with him.*' Sara's words.

Her eyes wandered to his hands, to the long, strong fingers that had made him such a name in the art world, then back to his own blue-grey, sightless eyes. A new thought came into

48

her mind, startling her again the way that earlier, unexpected pang of wistfulness had.

She wished that Donovan could see her.

The familiarization of Sophia with the ten-acre world of Gilead Farm began on foot with an agreement that if one or all of them grew tired, Donovan would use his cellular phone to call Pete Szabo and ask him to pick them up in the Jeep. They walked through meadows, and Joanna and Sophia, on a regular lead for the time being, made the acquaintance of Szabo's goats; a mile and a half away, Joanna was gladdened by the sight of a half-dozen horses and ponies grazing in an enclosed field, all gentle enough, Donovan told her, to be ridden by a group of disabled children who regularly came on visits.

'I tried riding myself a couple of times,' he told Joanna, 'gave myself a hard time because I wasn't enjoying it, but then I remembered that I hadn't liked horseriding as a sighted kid either.'

'City boy?' Joanna said.

'I guess,' he agreed. 'Give me a Harley anytime.'

Once well away from the horses again, they unclipped Sophia's lead and the dog ran free, coming back regularly, initially always to Joanna, then giving Donovan a swift push with her nose before running off again. They had agreed a working plan whereby they would give the dog a few days to feel moderately at home on the farm, allowing her freedom part of that time and keeping her leashed the rest, before putting her in harness. Sophia had taken to the harness in England with an initial degree of surprise but no real fuss, her calm, trusting nature standing her in good stead as it always did. She showed apparent mild surprise again that morning when Joanna first passed the lead to Donovan, but the American's grip on her was so assured and relaxed that within moments Joanna looked down and saw, already, that she had been right, and that they were going to make a fine team.

The black Cherokee drove out to meet them within fifteen minutes of Donovan's having made his call, but it was Chris

Chen rather than Szabo at the wheel.

'Pete asked me to come,' she said as they all piled in, Donovan into the front passenger seat as the day before, Joanna and Sophia into the back. 'He had something on the stove he didn't want to leave.'

'Sounds good to me,' Donovan said.

'And me.' Joanna hadn't realized till now how hungry she was.

'Good,' Donovan said. 'So you'll come to the house for lunch?'

'I'd love to.'

'Murdoch called to say he may be running late,' Chris told Donovan.

It took Joanna a second to realize who she was talking about, and then, recalling the rather curt way he'd nodded at her early that morning, she decided that on first appearances, Murdoch suited him rather more as a name than Lamb.

'What should I call him?' she asked.

'Whatever you're comfortable with,' Donovan answered.

'Just don't expect the warmest reaction whatever you choose.' Chen glanced back with a slightly wry smile.

She was, Joanna thought, a little older than she'd first imagined, with those few extra years showing around the beautifully shaped dark eyes, but the rest of her face was taut and smooth and her hair was tied back again, as it had been the previous day, in a sleek, gleaming and enviably tidy knot. Joanna's own thick, shoulder-length, red and invariably unruly hair had, since childhood, always escaped from any kind of knot, pleat or plait that she or her mother had attempted. Philip had loved it, made lavish comparisons with Titian's heroines and begged her never to cut it short, though she had, any number of times, come close to asking Josie, her hairdresser in Burford, to crop it and have done with it.

'Chris thinks Lamb's a snob.' Donovan referred to her remark.

'He is,' Chen said, manoeuvring the Jeep expertly over a bumpy piece of track, then glancing at Joanna through the rear view mirror. 'Donovan thinks he isn't, because he left

50

his WASP family behind on Rhode Island and came to work with artists on a farm, but that just makes him an intellectual snob.'

'Losing battle,' Donovan said, mildly, to no one in particular.

Szabo had lunch ready when they arrived at the main house, but it was the first time Joanna and Sophia had set foot inside, and Donovan was keen to show them around before they sat down to eat.

'And Lamb may be a while yet,' he told Szabo.

'No problem,' the other man said easily.

The house was large and gave an impression of rugged warmth, much of it due, Joanna decided, to the materials used to decorate and furnish it, for each room they entered was almost stark, devoid of the slightest clutter. She knew, of course, that clear floor space was essential for Donovan's personal, unaided navigation, and this, unlike the guest house – which had been created for the use and comfort of others – was clearly entirely *his* home. What furniture there was, Joanna observed, was antique American, chosen, she supposed, either simply for comfort or because Donovan liked the way it felt to his touch.

Smells dominated, too, she noticed as he showed her, Sophia staying obediently to heel, into his library.

'Leather and cigars,' he said, noting her slight sniff at the air. 'And a touch of whiskey, I guess.'

'May I look at your books?' Joanna asked.

'Help yourself. Mostly Braille, some Moon.' He paused while she moved across to the shelves. 'Sara said you've studied both.'

'I find Moon easier,' she said.

'Books on tape seem to be taking over for a lot of blind people.' Donovan walked over to the small, leather-topped writing desk in one corner and checked the time on a clock that told him, in an electronic female voice, that it was 12.22. 'I still like the feel of a solid book in my hands.,'

'And the scent,' Joanna said, handling one volume of a leather-bound Braille dictionary, 'if they're as beautiful as this.'

51

There was a bronze sculpture behind Donovan, standing on the broad timber window sill. It was of a woman's head, simply, sparsely modelled, the lines pure, almost classical in style, with an intimacy about it, Joanna felt, that told of great personal meaning for its creator.

'My mother,' Donovan said.

Joanna looked at the head more intently, seeking a likeness. It was there, she saw, in the thrust of the chin, though everything about the whole was utterly feminine. 'She's lovely,' she said, and meant it.

'She was,' Donovan said. 'She and my father both died the year after I left Philadelphia and moved to New York. Frances, my mother, had one of those wildfire cancers, the kind that deliver the *coup de grâce* almost as soon as you're diagnosed, and Walt, my father, had a stroke two months later and went right away.' He turned around, put out his right hand and laid it, very gently, on the back of the bronze head. 'I guess we all hope our parents will live to ninety-eight and die in their sleep.' He took his hand away again and turned back towards Joanna. 'But at least they both went fast.'

'My parents are both still alive,' she said, quietly. 'They retired and moved from London to a place called Rottingdean on the south coast. They have a pretty house, and my mother gardens and my father goes to the pub, and I don't think they're very happy because they didn't much like each other when they were still busy and younger. I don't see enough of them.'

'They don't sound much like you,' Donovan said.

'Philip used to say that I was nothing like them in any way' – Joanna smiled – 'and I'm afraid that used to make me feel rather relieved.' She paused. 'How did you know I was looking at your mother's sculpture?'

'I sometimes feel other people's lines of vision,' he answered. 'I guess it's an energy thing. It's no special talent – don't you ever feel when someone's looking at you?'

They heard a knock, and then Chris Chen poked her head around the door.

'Murdoch's here, so whenever you're ready.'

*

52

The kitchen was a great but comforting space with ochre stone tiles on the floor, a central work station with a brass extractor hood over the stove, and a handsome, rectangular oak table and chairs located near large glass sliding doors that opened on to a small, tranquil-looking rose garden.

Murdoch Lambert, standing by the glass door, still wearing the black roll-neck and trousers Joanna had seen him in before dawn, came forward as they all entered the room, and held out his hand.

'Joanna, I presume?' he said, and smiled. 'I've been thoroughly instructed not to call you Mrs Guthrie.' His hair was silver-grey and cut fashionably short in what Joanna thought of as hedgehog-style; his speech was precise to the point of being almost clipped; and his smile, she felt, did not quite extend from his clear-cut but thin mouth to his blue eyes. 'And you,' he went on briskly, 'are welcome to call me Murdoch, or Lamb, if you wish.'

'I'm pleased to meet you. I've heard a lot about you.'

Joanna shook Lamb's hand and glanced at Chris Chen, who had moved across the kitchen to help Szabo with serving lunch. Clearly, she'd wasted no time passing on Joanna's uncertainty about Lambert's name.

'We've all heard great things about you, Joanna,' Lamb said. 'Though even more, of course, about your charming dog.' He looked down at Sophia, who stood close to Joanna's left leg, quivering with interest because of the cooking smells coming from the stove. 'Does she shake paws?'

'She has been known to,' Joanna said.

'Shaking paws is beneath Sophia's dignity,' Donovan said, walking over to the table and taking his place at the far end. 'Come sit beside me, Joanna.'

'Something smells wonderful,' she said.

'Pete's baked ham, I'd say,' Donovan ventured from his chair.

'This must be a special occasion,' Lamb said, drily.

'It is.' Szabo, wearing a red and white striped apron, lifted a large copper platter off the central work station and carried it towards the table. 'My grandfather was Hungarian, Jo, and there's Russian blood some way back, too, so I sometimes like to try my hand at Slavic dishes.'

Joanna sat, as invited, on Donovan's right, and Lamb sat on his other side while Szabo, having deposited the gleaming, fragrant ham in the centre of the table, turned back towards the work station. Chris set down two dishes, one of red cabbage, the other of mashed potatoes, and sat down beside Lamb.

'And for the other guest of honour ...' Szabo came forward again, holding something behind his back. 'I hope they meet with her approval.' He held out two ceramic dog bowls, hand-painted in rich blue, yellow and red.

'Pete, they're beautiful.' Acting on impulse, Joanna stood up, went over to him and stood on tiptoe to kiss his cheek. 'Aren't they gorgeous, Sophia?'

She wagged her tail and Szabo, face filled with pleasure, put them down on the tiled floor close to the wall and a safe distance from the table.

'Two dog bowls,' Lamb told Donovan. 'Hand-painted, primary colours. Charming. By the south wall, about ten feet from the table.'

'I know where Pete put them,' he replied.

'Fine,' Lamb said, a little testily.

'All right if I give Sophia a little ham?' Szabo asked Joanna as she returned to her chair and he began to carve. 'It's basted with cherries, sugar and mustard, so I'll steer clear of the outside.' He hesitated. 'I bake it with cloves, too. Is that a problem?'

'It sounds marvellous. Sophia usually has her dinner at around six, but I'm not sure she'd ever forgive me if I said no.'

'And with the time difference,' Donovan said, 'it's about that time now.'

'Do dogs suffer from jet lag?' Chris Chen asked.

'Given that they slumber away half their lives,' Lamb said, 'I doubt it.'

'They're very sensitive,' Donovan reminded his friend. 'Though poor Sophia has more cause for confusion than mere

54

jet lag. Discontinuity's bound to affect any creature of routine.'

Szabo finished carving. 'Humans help themselves, please.' Swiftly, he cut two slices into small pieces, picked them up with his fingers and went to deposit them in one of the bowls on the floor. Sophia was on them in a flash, and had almost devoured the ham before Szabo could return to pour water into the second bowl.

'Your sensitive creature appears not to have let it ruin her appetite,' Lamb reported equably as he took Donovan's plate, placed ham, cabbage and potato upon it in meticulously arranged portions, and returned it to its place.

'Thank you, Lamb,' Donovan said. 'Joanna, please help yourself. We don't stand on ceremony around here.'

'Nor do we eat like this every day,' Chris pointed out. 'Usually, it's a sandwich on the run, at least for me.'

'And Sophia's not *my* creature by a long chalk, Lamb,' Donovan corrected belatedly. 'Not till Joanna decrees I'm fit to keep her.'

'Doesn't your success depend on her training?' Lamb asked.

'It's not as simple as that,' Donovan said. 'Is it, Joanna?'

'Nothing ever is.'

Joanna wrote to Sara that evening by hand, in the quiet of the guest house, with Sophia beside her on the sofa. Her friend had asked her, before leaving, to write as much as possible since she cherished everything she was still able to read. Joanna had expected to manage no more than a few lines, yet at the close of what had been a long, full day, she felt restless, eager to share her experiences.

They were all welcoming, but throughout lunch I felt very much the outsider – though it did give me a chance to take a close look at them. The way the others were with Donovan, for example; the way he seems to ask for nothing, yet they seem so eager to do his bidding. Not exactly sycophantic – somehow I doubt that he'd go for that, don't you? – but I did feel that

55

Donovan seems to be the centre of all their lives.

Still unsettled, Joanna paused to make a pot of decaffeinated coffee, took Sophia for her final stroll of the night, saw that the lights were still switched on in the school and main house, then returned to the guest house and adjourned to bed to finish her letter.

Chris Chen gave me a quick tour of the school, and Lamb let me observe one of his classes. The more I see of him, the more intriguing I find him; he's small and wiry but elegant, almost graceful – he reminded me of a ballet master, moving from student to student, talking to them in his clipped, brusque way, seeming to ration his opinions some of the time, then suddenly erupting with enthusiasm or disgust.

Suddenly exhausted, she dozed off then, waking with a start to find her writing pad and pen on the floor and the German shepherd, for the second night running, on the bed beside her.

'This may not be such a good idea, you know.' She reached out to switch off the lamp, feeling the dog thump her tail. 'In a day or two you'll be expected to sleep in the big house, with Donovan and Pete.'

Was that, she wondered, trying to doze off again, what was making her feel so edgy tonight? Premature feelings of loss over her dog?

Outside, an owl's screech, loud and unnervingly close, brought understanding abruptly into relief. Her discomfort this evening was not so much related to Sophia, she decided. It had more, she realized, to do with the impression that had been slowly creeping up on her throughout the day.

Lamb did not want her here.

Everyone else had welcomed her, had been courteous, friendly and kind. And Lamb, too, had been polite enough on the face of it.

It wasn't just his air of detachment. Nor, Joanna thought, was it the snobbish quality that Chris Chen had, quite accurately, warned her about.

56

'I really think he doesn't want me here,' she said out loud in the dark to Sophia, and the dog's tail thumped again against the cover. 'He's glad you're coming, my darling, for Donovan's sake – I think they're all happy to have you. But Murdoch Lambert would much rather I weren't with you.'

It was a disconcerting thought to go to sleep with.

10

WEDNESDAY, NOVEMBER 4

They put Sophia into her brand-new harness for the first time on the third day and, apart from a little squirming around and an initial desire to try to chew at the leather, she took to it magnificently. Joanna and Donovan shared the early sessions, but Joanna noticed from the beginning that whilst Sophia reacted as joyfully to praise from her as she always had, her semi-master's low murmurs, sounding to Joanna's human ears like a man crooning to a new and fragile love, seemed to send the dog into near-ecstasy.

On Friday, their fifth day, they left Gilead Farm for their first excursion. Joanna, concerned that Donovan was simply trying to accommodate her magazine commissions, reminded him before they went out that her primary concern was him and Sophia.

'That's why we're heading out,' he replied. 'Driving around, checking out places, is how I pick up inspiration – and I see no good reason why you shouldn't bring your camera along for the ride.' He bent to check that the dog's harness was secure. 'Ordinarily, Pete drives and Lamb acts as look-out, tells me what's going on, paints me a picture of what he thinks I need to see.' He straightened up. 'But since you say you don't mind driving and talking at the same time, I think the three of us should manage pretty well.'

'You, me and Lamb, you mean?'

'I mean you, me and Sophia,' he answered.

Joanna wondered how Lamb would feel about that.

*

58

With Joanna driving another of the Gilead Farm Jeeps and needing to acclimatize to left-hand-drive and the local sign-posting, they began close to home in Rhinebeck, a compact nineteenth-century village. Travelling alone with Donovan, Joanna quickly found, was a fascinating experience. She had learned never to underestimate the capabilities of the blind, yet this man was astonishing. She might be the one driving, but he was the one showing her around.

Visiting the Delameter House, a perfect example of American Gothic, now run as part of a hotel, with Sophia walking alongside in harness and Joanna taking shots with the precious second-hand Hasselblad she'd bought two years ago in Oxford, Donovan pointed out to her in remarkable detail the gingerbread woodwork, the central gable and the lovely diamond-paned windows.

'I find it hard to believe you've never actually seen the house for yourself,' she commented as they walked into the wood-panelled interior of the Beekman Arms, the inn that owned the Delameter House.

'That's Lamb for you.'

'And your memory, surely?'

'I guess I've trained my memory pretty well,' Donovan admitted. 'I've had to.' He paused, and Sophia too stood patiently waiting. 'It's mostly a question of concentration,' he went on. 'With Lamb – and the others, too – for my human guides, I've found that all I have to do is "*see*" something one time through someone else's eyes, then add my own impressions – scents, sounds, atmospheres, whatever – and after that I have a mind picture I tend not to forget.'

'Impressive stuff,' Joanna said. 'I mean, I've just seen that house with my own eyes, yet I can almost guarantee that by bedtime tonight I'll have forgotten most of those intricate details.'

'But you'll have your photographs to remind you.' Donovan smiled. 'And before you get too impressed by my skills, don't forget what I told you about Lamb's modelling. That's one of the houses he made a replica of for me. And it's one I made a point of keeping, even though he wanted me to throw it on the fire – if you're interested, it's kept in a workshop at the school.'

'Why did he want to burn it?' Joanna asked, curiously.

'Lamb sometimes has a problem with over-modesty.'

'Really?'

Donovan smiled at her scepticism. 'He doesn't show that side of himself to everyone, but believe me, it's there. It's one of the reasons he's willing to work with me, which has been my great good fortune.'

In what remained of that day and the next, they zigzagged gently across Dutchess, Ulster and Green Counties, Joanna seeing more examples of Donovan's exceptional memory and powers of concentration. It was not, he assured her, having pinpointed with uncanny accuracy their location on Route 9 near Poughkeepsie, that big a deal. He'd been along that road more times than he could count, he explained, and had gotten a feel for speed and miles travelled, so as long as he paid attention and listened to changing sounds along the way, he found he could pretty much gauge where they were.

'But take me someplace new, or just distract me for a while,' he grinned, 'and I'm lost as a baby in a blizzard.'

They visited Hyde Park, the Roosevelts' home, where FDR and Eleanor were buried in the rose garden, then travelled north a little to the Vanderbilt Mansion, where Donovan elected to wait outside and stroll with Sophia while Joanna took a walk through the fifty-four room house. She hesitated, having glimpsed the grounds leading to the river, but Donovan pointed out to her that he had his long cane with him as well as the dog and that he had survived dog-less for the last couple of years without drowning, and Joanna, gently rebuked, went inside without another word.

'Well?' Donovan said when she found them again. Man and dog were sitting close together on the grass near the water, and as Joanna neared, focusing on the pair through the Hasselblad and taking a few shots, Sophia wagged her tail but made no move to try to leave the American's side.

'Stunning, of course,' Joanna said, sitting down a few feet away, glad of the rest. 'But too formal for my tastes. Too grand.'

'What about this?' Donovan turned his face towards the river.

'This is wonderful,' she said softly. 'Peaceful.'

'But so alive,' he said. 'Boats, birds, fish – the water

60

itself.' He paused. 'People talk about the light around here, about all the artists who've been drawn to the Hudson. Lamb does his best for me, but there are some things I guess you just have to *see*. I remember Thomas Cole's paintings of the Valley, and some of John Kensett's, too, from back before I lost my sight, but that light's one thing I really wish I could see for myself.'

It was the first time Joanna had seen real frustration in him. 'There must be many things, surely?' she said, softly.

'Sure there are.' He reached out and stroked Sophia's head. 'This lady for one.' He paused again. 'And other beauties, too.'

No matter how much he tried to convince her otherwise, Joanna knew that she was, thoughtfully and hospitably, being entertained. Not only that, with man and dog already working so well together, she was also beginning to wonder who was conducting the training – or at least who was learning more. Sitting in Schemmy's one afternoon back in Rhinebeck, for example, with Sophia under the table, Donovan began giving an unsolicited lesson in the art of eavesdropping.

'You don't need to be blind to sharpen up your senses, Joanna. Anyone can do it if they try.'

'I don't think I have any desire to,' she said drily, eating pancakes with maple syrup and vanilla ice cream.

Ignoring the irony, Donovan turned his head slowly from side to side, taking in the restaurant, which was two-thirds full. 'Okay.' He lowered his voice to a more discreet level. 'Take the couple near the window to your right.'

'I'm not going to eavesdrop.' Joanna took a quick look despite herself, saw a man, aged forty-something in a blue tracksuit with gel on his dark hair, and a woman, slightly younger, wearing the kind of overall that beauticians wore in beauty parlours.

'You're looking, aren't you?' Donovan was smug.

'I glanced,' Joanna said defensively.

'What are they talking about?'

'I don't know, and I don't want to know.'

'Don't be self-righteous, Joanna, this is an exercise.'

'They're having a private conversation.'

'She says it's too cold for ice cream,' he listened and reported.

'Donovan, stop,' Joanna said, trying not to laugh.

He concentrated more intently. 'He's just asked her if she's heard about a missing girl.'

'Donovan, stop before they hear you.'

He held up a hand to hush her, listened for another few moments, then turned his concentration back onto Joanna. 'Okay, I'm back with you.'

'I should hope so.'

He drank some of his soda through a straw. 'How're your pancakes?'

'Very nice, thank you.'

'Have you ever tried ice cream soda?'

'I have. I didn't much like it.'

'One of the great tastes,' Donovan said. 'Maybe you have to be an American to acquire it.'

Joanna put down her fork and spoon. 'So what did they say?'

He smirked briefly. 'Sure you want to know?'

'Not especially, but I know you want to tell me.'

'They were talking about a local girl who's been missing since spring.' Donovan lowered his voice. 'I remember hearing about her back then, matter of fact. Ellen Miller, from around Red Hook, just a few miles north of the farm. Her family were worried sick, but the cops thought she'd just gone AWOL. Now it seems they're not so sure, according to our window couple.'

'Poor family,' Joanna said.

'That's for sure,' Donovan agreed.

The following day being Sunday, Lamb was free from teaching and Szabo joined them too to give Joanna a break from driving. They went to New Paltz, where Donovan thought she might like to photograph the oldest street in America with original houses still standing; but as the excursion got underway, Joanna found herself more intrigued by her first chance to witness Murdoch

Lambert's gift for sharing his vision with Donovan. The others all being familiar with Huguenot Street and the rest of the town, Lamb took the opportunity of pouncing on any interesting and new, or simply transient, feature that came into view. Once it was autumn leaves being blown by the November wind into a strange conical shape; then it was the white standard French poodle that was making Sophia whine and bark; then the lean and handsome young man with closely-cropped hair – '*short and soft-looking as mouse fur*' Lamb reported – strolling with an older couple, probably his parents.

'He is good-looking,' Joanna agreed, taking a brief series of shots of the family group, aware as she did so that Lamb's sharp blue eyes were now resting on her. And then he became distracted again, and she was free to watch and listen with renewed fascination as, with each new piece of subject matter, Lamb put all his energies into transmitting the minutiae observed by his avid eyes to the blind man's hungry ears and retentive memory.

'I understand now' – Joanna told Donovan next morning when, alone again, they were back on the road under cloudy, rainy skies and heading towards Bard College – 'what you said about trusting Lamb as your finest pair of eyes. There's no way I can even begin to approach his level of concentration, or the way he seems to realize exactly what you want to know about.'

'Don't put yourself down,' Donovan said. 'And don't forget you're seeing all this for the first time, so it's a full-time job taking things in yourself without having to sift through it all to work out what might be new to me.'

'How long have you and Lamb been working together?'

'Five years, give or take. I guess we do make quite a team.'

Keeping her eyes on the road, but hearing that warmth in his tone again, Joanna felt a tug of something unfamiliar, and realized, with surprise and a hint of shame, that it was envy.

They spent an hour wandering around the splendid college campus, then backtracked, crossed the Hudson at the Kingston-Rhinecliff Bridge and headed north-west towards

Woodstock, passing a sign for *Opus 40*, which, Donovan explained, was a six-or-so-acre environmental sculpture created by a Pittsburgh-born artist named Harvey Fite.

'Amazing guy,' he told her. 'Started out studying law, quit to study for the ministry, changed his mind again to become an actor, then realized his true destiny and turned sculptor. He found a disused bluestone quarry, bought it and spent the next – and the last – thirty-seven years of his life turning it into Opus 40. It's another of those things I wish I could see for myself.'

'Want to go there now?' Joanna slowed the Jeep.

Donovan shook his head. 'Too wet today. The place officially closes between October and June. We could walk around, but all that stone can get slippery – not a great spot for me or Sophia. Though you might want to come back on a better day and shoot a few rolls.' He smiled. 'Lamb thinks Fite was a genius and Pete says he loves the carved sculptures – especially the one named *Quarry Family* – but finds the vastness of the whole work a little cold. Chris hates the place, says it has all these dark pools and places that give her the creeps – she says it'd be a great spot for dragons and evil spirits to hide out.'

'I thought dragons were benevolent in China,' Joanna said.

'Chris is a very American Chinese.'

They stayed on the farm next day. Donovan came to Joanna's door just after 7.30 to tell her that he had some urgent office business to take care of and that he'd be happy to have Sophia with him but thought she might like time alone with the dog while she still could. Joanna thanked him, but said that so long as Donovan was going to be working in a safe, straightforward environment, it was a better idea for Sophia to stay with him.

Just one more small hurt in a slow, steady series of necessary but painful wrenches, she thought a little later, heading off for a solitary walk. The morning was dry and still, but cold, and she walked at a brisk pace out into the open land beyond the school, heading for the fields.

She thought, from a distance, that she was looking at a small, slender tree waving in the breeze, but then she saw that it was not a tree but a woman, Chris Chen, dressed in a lycra catsuit of mottled, hazy pastel shades, and performing elaborate and beautiful *t'ai chi ch'uan*.

For several moments, Joanna stood about fifty yards away, motionless and watching. The other woman's hair was unpinned and hung past her waist, shining raven black in the morning sun as it gently swung in harmony with her flowing movements, and Joanna found herself recalling Donovan's remark about Chen being a very American Chinese, and thinking that he might take back those words if only he could see her now.

'Come join me, Joanna.'

Chen's voice startled her, floating, as it seemed, from the air as her body continued its fluid, strengthening exercise.

'I didn't mean to disturb you.' Joanna began to move slowly towards her.

'You haven't.' Chen came to rest and smiled. 'Do you know *t'ai chi*?'

'I practised it for a time, after my husband's death – not very well.'

The other woman's lovely oval face lifted with another smile, this one of approval. 'I've always found the Thirteen Movements healing and energizing.' The large eyes surveyed Joanna's face. 'No camera – and no Sophia?'

'She's with Donovan. He has some work to do.'

'Yes, I know. You'll miss her.'

Joanna nodded.

'Would you like to join me for a while?'

'I'd love to, but I'm not exactly dressed for *t'ai chi*.' Joanna looked down at her jeans and sneakers. 'I'm afraid I'd feel like a lead weight beside you, Chris.'

'Take off your jacket and shoes,' Chen suggested. 'The grass is dewy but not too cold.'

Joanna hesitated for just another second.

'We're quite alone,' Chen said. 'If you're feeling awkward.'

The watcher, studying them through binoculars, noted and enjoyed the contrast between the two women: the one with her dark, straight curtain of black hair, the other with her long, red-gold curls, wilder as the breeze picked up. One moved seamlessly from one movement to the next; the other seemed more tentative, graceful enough for a western woman and clearly not a complete novice but out of practice perhaps, continually checking against the more expert woman that she was doing adequately.

They raised their right legs, bent at the knees, and the watcher held them both in focus, saw that one foot was tiny, almost paw-like, the other longer and more slender. And then, moments later, the practised, effortless one moved into the more complex movement known as '*cross wave of water lily*', and the English woman stumbled and went down on her knees and, focusing on her face, he saw that she was laughing, and he stopped watching then, and turned away.

Donovan asked Joanna across to the house for dinner that evening. Pete was out, he said, but had left them some kind of casserole, and he thought it might be nice for them both to have a little quiet time at home with Sophia.

'Irish stew,' Joanna said, tasting it. 'How lovely.'

'Mutton, beef, potatoes.' Donovan smiled. 'Pete likes his food solid.'

'Does he come to the city with you when you live down there?'

'Usually drives me, but after that I'm on my own.' He chewed for a moment. 'Pete's always trying to persuade me to let him stay on, take care of me, but the truth is I like fending for myself for a change.' He grinned. 'I screw up a lot, but there's no one around to fuss and that's the way I like it.'

'That's why Sara's working so hard to prepare for when she loses the rest of her vision,' Joanna said. 'She likes her space, always has, and can't see any good reason to stop liking it just because she goes blind.'

'My kind of person,' Donovan said.

'She feels the same way about you.'

'I'm glad.'

They chatted easily for a while, talk about Sophia and Joanna's other dogs dominating the conversation as they finished their dinner at the big kitchen table, then washed up the dishes together and put them away and, once again, Joanna was impressed by his confidence and skill.

66

'Home turf,' he said, sensing her admiration. 'No big deal, so long as other people keep things in the right place. Move a stool three inches to the left and I walk into it. Put a glass where a stack of dishes ought to be, and something gets broken.'

'I break dishes regularly.'

'But you're not clumsy.'

'Not especially.'

For a moment they stood five feet apart near the cupboard where they'd been putting things away, and Joanna sensed that Donovan, on the whole so self-assured, was holding back from saying something.

'What is it?' she asked, quietly.

'I'd like to touch your face,' he said. 'To see it my way.' He paused. 'I know, pretty much, what you look like, because Lamb's filled me in.'

'Has he?' Joanna had realized, of course, that it was inevitable that Lamb would have described her to Donovan, yet somehow, right now, the idea of it offended her a little.

'You mind that?'

'Not really,' she lied.

'Would you let me touch-see you now, Joanna?'

She hesitated for a moment. 'Of course.'

Donovan moved closer, raised both his hands, then dropped them back to his sides. 'Am I making you nervous? If you'd rather I didn't touch you, that's okay.'

'It's fine,' she said.

'You're holding your breath. Just relax.'

She released the breath that she had, involuntarily, been holding, and Donovan lifted his hands again and placed them on both sides of her face. She felt their gentleness, recalled the first time he had done the same sort of thing with Sophia in Merlin Cottage, remembered how the dog had reacted with undisguised pleasure, and the memory made her smile.

'That's nice,' Donovan said, softly. 'I like your smile.'

He took less than a minute, yet in that time Joanna felt the power of his concentration and knew that the framework and texture of her head, face, ears and neck were probably now committed to his remarkable memory.

'Thank you,' he said. 'Now you'll have your photos of me, and I'll have my own picture of you.'

They moved with Sophia into the living room and sat down with a bottle of cognac and two glasses, and then Donovan lit a cigar, and they were both quiet for a while until Joanna found she could no longer contain her curiosity.

'How do I compare?' she asked. 'With Lamb's description?'

Donovan smiled. 'It's not a matter of comparison. It's a matter of adding layers. I already knew some things, partly through Lamb and Sara, partly through just being around you. I knew how tall you were, and I knew you were graceful and slender and that you have wild, curling hair and your eyes are hazel with glints of green.'

Joanna said nothing, waited for him to go on.

'By touching you, I find out all kinds of things. I'd have known, for instance, without anyone telling me, that your hair is red, because of its texture, and I know that your skin is fragile and probably pale, and I know that you use Johnson's baby soap and Lancôme make-up and First perfume.'

'I'm impressed again.' Joanna tried to sound light, though her heartbeat had quickened.

'You should be. Lord knows I've spent enough hours over the years in the cosmetics departments at Saks and Bloomies perfecting that little party trick so I can tell Chris that she's wearing Mitsouko or Lamb that he's switched from Tiffany for Men to Boss Number One.'

Joanna laughed. 'How often does that come in useful?'

'Not often,' he admitted. 'Only when I'm trying to impress a beautiful and intelligent woman.' He grew suddenly more sober. 'I've also gotten a pretty shrewd idea, just being around you, of when you're smiling or when you're sad. But the only thing I honest-to-God *really* know about you is how painful it is for you letting go of Sophia.'

'I can't deny that,' Joanna said quietly.

'I do wonder, though, if you're ever truly going to under-stand' – a vein on Donovan's temple, running parallel with the narrow scar, throbbed as he spoke – 'the depth of my gratitude to you for giving her to me.'

68

11

TUESDAY, NOVEMBER 10

Luke Schuyler, aged twenty-three, from New Paltz, was heading back to Boston, where he lived and worked these days. He made the trip frequently back and forth to see his parents whenever possible, and tended to use different routes to keep the journey varied and attractive. Today, though, he was in the mood for straight and as fast as the law and his old VW Beetle allowed, so he'd driven north on 87 and picked up the Mass Turnpike six or seven miles south of Albany, and now he was chuntering comfortably across the Connecticut River and more than half way there.

Luke was thinking about his dad's even more ancient Oldsmobile, thinking how great it was going to be when his modelling career finally started to pay off and he'd be able to buy the old guy a decent set of wheels that wouldn't let him down every time there was a nip of frost in the air.

Checking his rearview mirror just past the exit for Three Rivers, he noticed that the white panel truck with dark tinted windows that he'd first become aware of back somewhere near the New York-Massachusetts border was still behind him. He knew it didn't mean anything, knew that on a trip like this you often stayed in the same stream of traffic for miles at a time, but still, he was getting a weird kind of feeling – had felt it a couple of times over the past few days, now he came to think about it: an odd sensation that someone was watching him.

'Ego,' he said out loud, trying to shrug off the feeling.

69

His parents were probably right – they'd said more than once that he'd been spending too much time lately having his damned picture taken. He was probably starting to imagine that the whole world was looking at him.

Anyway, he thought, grinning ruefully, coasting along towards Boston, if he was honest about it, he liked the feeling.

'Hell,' he said out loud again, 'I love it.'

12

THURSDAY, NOVEMBER 12

Dear Sara,
Within the next few days, we're going to leave Gilead Farm for what I've come to think of as our 'Manhattan Trials', and I can feel Donovan's tension starting to rise again.

For myself, much as I've liked being here, part of me will be relieved to go. There's a curious atmosphere about Gilead Farm, and though it does centre on Donovan, I don't feel that it's in any great way caused by him. I suppose I'm harking back to what you said about everyone loving him. The trouble is, Sara, I think you may be right. It's more than simple admiration and willingness to help make his life run smoothly. I honestly think that everyone in this semi-commune thinks that the sun, moon and stars rise and set over Jack Donovan, and somehow that doesn't seem entirely healthy to me. Luckily, I also think he may, in part, feel the same way – he's already told me that one of the reasons he spends time in Manhattan is his need for a little independence.

Whichever ways things go in the city, we're scheduled to come back to the farm for Thanksgiving, which should be enjoyable, though I suspect that the others would rather I flew straight back to England. I know that Murdoch, no matter how polite he is, can hardly wait to see the back of me. And Chris and Pete – especially Pete – have been kindness personified, but I'm sure I've created havoc in their routines. With Murdoch, though, it's more fundamental. Because of me, Donovan hasn't been available to work,

71

and on many occasions I've been around to act as his 'eyes', and we all know by now that that's Lamb's role.

Hopefully when we do return for Thanksgiving, I'll finally have my chance to photograph Donovan sculpting. I've spent so much time with him, have observed so many of his remarkable skills, yet I still haven't seen him so much as touch a piece of clay. It's strange, to have been in the hub of this creative environment and not to have seen the man himself at work. I asked Chris Chen about that, and she answered that Donovan is an all or nothing person. Right now, she said, his 'all' is me and Sophia. I think we're both flattered.

Send me one of your e-mails soon, Sara, and take care of yourself. In the meantime, I send you this letter and my love.

Joanna.

13

They entered Manhattan's West Side on the Henry Hudson Parkway just after dawn, got on to Broadway and drove in quiet, almost surreally serene conditions to Columbus Circle, where Joanna tugged Sophia gently out of the black Cherokee into Central Park so that she could sniff about for a few minutes and relieve herself before their arrival at Donovan's apartment building, now just a few solid concrete blocks away.

'Almost home,' Szabo said from the driver's seat after they'd got back in.

'Pull up out front when we get there,' Donovan directed tersely from beside him. 'One of the guys can unload, and we'll go straight up.'

'Want me to park and come up?' Szabo asked.

'No need – unless Joanna wants you for anything.'

'Not me,' Joanna said in the back, giving Sophia a reassuring hug as the dog sat up, sensing their arrival.

'Maybe I should wait and take Joanna to the hotel?'

'We'll be fine, Pete. You go on home.'

Notwithstanding the option of a guest room offered by Donovan for the duration of her stay in Manhattan, Joanna had chosen the alternative of going to one of the nearby hotels, so that Sophia should start life in the city as it would continue – alone with Jack Donovan in his urban world. The plan was for Joanna to come up with the pair of them, check the apartment out and then take a cab, with her luggage, to the

73

Peninsula hotel a block away. It had sounded smooth enough when they'd made the arrangements, but the private angsts that had apparently been plaguing Donovan since leaving Gilead Farm had transmitted themselves to Joanna and the German shepherd during the journey, and Joanna, for one, was only too glad that it was now over.

With Sophia having proven herself the star performer upstate that Joanna had expected, they had known it was time to bring her down to Manhattan for the next stage in her American acclimatization, but Donovan was still afraid of failing with the dog, and Joanna recognized how justified his anxieties were. Just because Sophia had been calm and steady in a situation and surroundings quite closely mirroring her life in and around Merlin Cottage, that did not mean the sudden explosion around her of one of the busiest, noisiest cities in the world might not prove too much. Which was why they had decided on driving into the city at around dawn on a weekend morning, with both traffic and decibels nowhere near their dramatic height.

Donovan's building on Fifty-sixth Street between Fifth and Sixth Avenues was fifteen slender storeys of greyish sandstone with a pristine green awning over the portico, a marble entrance hall softened by concealed lighting and a small, splashing, greenery-surrounded fountain built into a bay opposite the reception desk.

While Szabo handed over Joanna's luggage for temporary safe-keeping to a young, still sleepy-eyed man with slicked-down hair named Raimundo, Donovan hurried his two guests into one of a pair of side-by-side elevators, inserted a gold-coloured key into a slot marked 'Penthouse' and turned it. Sophia shifted a little nervously, pressed closer to Joanna's side, but displayed no other sign of anxiety.

'Is she okay?' Donovan said.

'She's fine.'

'If I were on a lower floor,' he muttered, 'she wouldn't have to put up with this at all.'

'Even if you lived on the ground floor,' Joanna pointed out

74

calmly, 'there are plenty more elevators she'd have to use in this city.'

She'd told Donovan more than once previously that she was unconcerned about the problem, having taken Sophia up and down a half dozen or so times at the Oxford hotel where she worked. Looking at his face now, though, seeing the stiff set of his jaw as they rose in the steel, mirror-walled box, and the slight, but tangible, relief as the doors slid open again, she realized that nothing until now had convinced him.

'No neighbours to worry about,' she said in the tentative silence as they stood in a small, square, beige-carpeted entrance hall, and Donovan turned two more keys, one at a time, in order to open the only front door on the floor.

'Uh-uh,' he said, and stood to one side. 'Please go through.'

The doors off the hall inside were all open, and natural light was coming through from somewhere, but Donovan flicked a switch just inside the front door as Joanna walked in. It was a handsome apartment, she saw that instantly as he walked ahead into his living area: high-ceilinged, spacious and, at first glance, even more minimalist than the uncluttered rooms at the farm.

His own place, Joanna thought. Unlike the house which he shared with Szabo and his other constantly coming and going colleagues, this apartment was almost certainly one hundred per cent, undiluted Jack Donovan; a blind sculptor who did no work here, just came to the city, presumably, to check out galleries, see his agent, dine with friends – whatever a single man with a home in the countryside did when he came to Manhattan.

He showed her around, all the while paying special attention to Sophia, taking off her collar so that she would know she was staying, listening with conspicuous pleasure to the clatter of her claws on the parquet floor, giving her a drink of water in a big, brand-new, stainless steel bowl, and speaking to her in the low, warm, confidential tones he seemed to reserve exclusively for her.

'So?' he asked when Joanna had seen everything: the two

bedrooms, bathrooms, living and dining room, kitchen, library and small terrace. 'Does it pass muster?'

'It's a beautiful apartment.'

'The wall around the terrace is high enough, isn't it? For her safety, I mean.' Donovan's jaw was taut with tension again. 'I never had any concerns with Waldo or Jade, but they were Labs and they weren't into serious jumping or climbing.'

'The terrace is fine.' It was the first thing Joanna had checked out carefully, having heard horror stories of animals plunging from skyscrapers. 'Though I doubt you'll be letting Sophia out there on her own too often.'

'Of course not.' Donovan paused. 'I need you to feel good about leaving her with me, Joanna. I need to know you trust me.'

She smiled and laid her right hand briefly but firmly on his arm. 'If I didn't trust you, I wouldn't *be* leaving her with you.'

She checked in at the Peninsula, called Donovan within five minutes of being shown to her suite to thank him for his generosity and to point out that she would have been more than content with an ordinary single room in a lesser hotel.

'Don't you like it?' he asked.

'Of course I like it.'

'Do you have all you need?'

'Much more than I need.'

'Then, please, for my sake, enjoy.'

She enjoyed. They'd left Gilead Farm in the middle of the night, so the three things she felt most in need of were a shower, breakfast and an hour's nap. She had managed the first two, and was just deciding whether or not to actually get into the big bed or just lie on top of the spread, when the various phones that seemed to be fairly littering the suite, started ringing.

'I screwed up, Joanna.' Donovan sounded desperate. 'Big time.'

'What happened?' Images of Sophia lying dead on the pavement beneath his terrace flashed into her mind.

'Can you come? Now!'

She threw on the clothes she'd worn for the drive down, flew out of the suite to the elevators and, once at ground level, ran the block and a half to the apartment building. There was another man on duty in the foyer, a burly older man in uniform, with the name JERRY FEENAN printed on a tag on his jacket. He called to Joanna as she ran past the Visitors Must be Announced sign.

'Ma'am? I need to call up to the apartment.'

The rubber soles of Joanna's loafers squeaked on the marble floor as she halted and turned to look at him. 'I'm sorry – I'm here to see Mr Donovan in the penthouse.' She was breathless.

'Mrs Guthrie?'

'That's right.'

Feenan smiled at her. 'You're expected, ma'am. Mr Donovan said to go right up.' He paused. 'Everything's okay up there now, by the way.'

Joanna thanked him, bolted towards the elevators, then stopped again.

'I don't have a key,' she said. 'For the lift.'

'No, ma'am. That's okay. I'm going to call up and tell Mr Donovan that you're on your way. You just step inside Number 2 and he'll get you up there.'

She smelled the smoke as soon as the elevator doors opened. Donovan was standing in his doorway, his face chalky.

'What happened? Where's Sophia?'

'In the living room.'

'Is she all right?' Joanna passed him, good manners blown away by fear. The inner hall was smoky. 'What *happened*?' she demanded again, just as Sophia, drawn by the sound of her voice, came out to greet her. Her tail was wagging and Joanna could see that she was uninjured, but as she crouched and let the dog get close, she could feel her quivering. 'Donovan, she's *trembling*.'

'She's not the only one,' he said, closing the door. 'It was actually not that big a deal, but the smoke detector set off the

77

alarm, and it's a real high pitch, which freaked Sophia—'

'No big deal?' Joanna stood up, fright and running making her unusually aggressive. 'What was it? One of your cigars setting something alight?'

'Nothing like—'

'Poor girl.' She was down again, soothing the big animal. 'Have you opened all the windows? I take it the fire's out.'

'Yes to both of those,' Donovan said, sounding humble.

Joanna looked up at him. 'I'm sorry,' she said.

'What for?'

'I'm overreacting.' Sophia's trembling had already ceased, and Joanna stood up again. 'Is it too cold to go out to the terrace till the worst of this clears?'

'Not for me,' Donovan said.

It had not been a cigar, Joanna learned as they sat drinking coffee out on the high-walled terrace, had not even been Donovan's fault. A new, previously unused sandwich toaster had malfunctioned, resulting in charcoaled bread, peanut butter and jelly. It was clear that the sculptor was more shocked than the German shepherd. And once Joanna stopped to think about that, she realized that his shock was probably related to the fire, however many years back, that had, according to Sara, killed his first guide dog.

With the smoke almost entirely gone, they returned inside and Joanna suggested they share an early lunch. It was too soon, they agreed, to subject Sophia to the further disruption of the city streets, so they ordered in pizza and ice cream – brought up for them by Raimundo, the young man who'd been on duty at dawn – and sat on big cushions on the living-room floor so that (Donovan's theory) Sophia would feel more at home.

'Good, huh?' he asked Joanna after a while.

'The pizza's wonderful.'

'How about you, Sophia? Like yours, sweetheart?' Donovan had insisted on ordering a small, unspicy special with ham and no onions or garlic for the dog.

'I hope you're not going to make a habit of this,' Joanna said primly.

'No way,' Donovan answered. 'This is a welcome-cum-get-over-shock one time only. I know about what's good for dogs, Joanna.'

'I know you do. I'm sorry.'

'Stop apologizing.'

'Okay.' She ate another slice of her pizza, drank some Coke and looked around. As in the house at Gilead Farm, the Donovan works on display here seemed to be old – pre-big-time success – sculptures which, like the one of his mother's head, had some intimate significance. There were two larger works out on the terrace, both semi-abstracts, and here in the living room were three works: one, a striking clay cat sculpture bearing the signature *Lamb*; a bronze head that Donovan had told her on their first walk round was Walt, his father; and a medium-sized bronze female figure that he'd said was Greta, his ex-wife. Joanna looked at Greta again now, with curiosity, saw a slim, tough-looking body and a boldly shaped head with a strong nose and sensuous lips.

'Greta was a force to be reckoned with,' Donovan said. 'Too sharp for me, when it came right down to it.'

'You stayed friends?'

'We parted reasonably enough, considering she'd fallen for another man' – he grinned – 'and a divorce lawyer too, to add insult. But we haven't talked for over two years now.'

Joanna turned her gaze to the sculpture of Walt Donovan. 'What was your father like?'

'What do you get from his head?'

Weakness, she thought, but did not say, though it was true, inasmuch as the head looked soft somehow, possessed far less impact and strength than either the sculpture of Greta or of Frances Donovan, his mother.

'You're more like your mother than your father,' she hedged.

'You should have been a diplomat.'

They ate in silence for a while. The peace was companionable enough, yet it was obvious that Donovan had something on his mind. Joanna considered asking him what it was, but concluded that if it was something he wanted to talk to her

79

about, he would do so in his own good time.

She didn't have long to wait.

'I guess you saw the effect the smoke alarm had on me,' he said.

'I did.'

'You'd have loved Waldo, my first.'

'I'm sure I would have.'

'He was a real character, you know? Had a sense of humour.' He shook his head. 'Some people – the ones who've never lived with dogs – would have it that they aren't individuals in their own right, but we know different.'

Joanna said nothing.

'We were visiting with friends in Chicago, back in November of '92. Mike and Annie Scherer. Mike and I were at school together in Philly – he took up teaching, met Annie and moved west to be with her. When they came to New York, they stayed at my place, so when Waldo and I went there, they liked us to stay at their house in Rogers Park.'

Sophia, on the floor between them and sensing the shift in mood, edged closer to Donovan and thrust her nose under his right arm. For a moment or two, he murmured to her and scratched her head between her ears, then went on.

'We went out for dinner one evening, but Annie got sick, so we came home early. She went up to bed and Mike and I made a couple of omelettes in the kitchen, drank a few beers, and I pictured my way through a ball game on TV.'

Donovan told the tale simply, quietly, keeping the pain it was obvious he still felt under the surface. It had been cold for November, he remembered, even by Chicago standards, and the Scherers' heating system had been playing up, so Mike had placed an old electric heater in Donovan's bedroom to warm things up while they sat downstairs. He had never learned precisely what had caused the fire, but the heater had, according to the experts, been the point of origin. The men had smelled the smoke just before the alarm had started shrieking, so Mike had yelled at Donovan to dial 911 and then get out with Waldo while he went upstairs to get Annie out of bed. Seconds later, Donovan had heard screaming and crash-

80

ing and the wild roar of the fire itself, so he'd opened the front door, told Waldo to get out and had tried getting up the stairs to help his friends. Halfway up, yelling as he went, he heard Mike bawling back at him, telling him that he and Annie were going down their fire escape and that he should turn around and get the hell out of the house. Donovan had tried to do just that, but had lost his footing, fallen down the staircase and broken his leg. The last thing he remembered was Waldo pulling at the neck of his sweater, and then he had passed out. He found out later that the fire fighters had carried him out, not realizing in all the thick smoke that the dog was still inside. By the time Mike had told them, the ceilings had come down and it was too late.

'I came to in the hospital and no one would tell me anything, but I knew Waldo was gone.' Donovan's jaw muscles were knotted and there were tears in his eyes. 'I guess I was a bit of a basket case for a while. I remember some asshole reporter getting into my room to interview me. He claimed I told him that Waldo was more important than any person.' He shrugged, bitterly, painfully. 'Maybe I did say that – maybe I even meant it at the time, especially as I knew Mike and Annie were okay.'

Joanna looked down at Sophia, her mind conjuring up horrors about infernos and dogs, and she shuddered.

'What I didn't know,' Donovan went on, 'was that they'd found a body in the house.'

'My God.' Joanna stared at him. 'Who was it?'

'No one ever found out.' He swallowed. 'There wasn't enough left, so they said, for the medical examiner to work with. He was under the living-room floor, in a crawlspace. Mike told me they figured he was either a burglar or maybe a vagrant who'd found a place to sleep.'

'Poor man,' Joanna said, still shocked.

'Yes.' Donovan paused, stroking Sophia's fur absently. 'I guess that's why the alarm going off before, and the smell of smoke, freaked me out as well as this baby.'

'I can only begin to imagine,' Joanna said, softly.

'Don't try,' he told her.

81

14

Joanna was still in bed when the telephone rang.

'Were you sleeping?'

She smiled at the sound of Donovan's voice. 'Just being lazy, thinking about getting up for breakfast. It's a hard life.'

'Good for you.' He paused. 'There's a problem back at the farm I need to deal with. Chris has the flu and it's business, so it's not Lamb's province, which means there's no one else to handle it but me.'

Joanna sat up. 'What about Sophia?'

'Exactly,' he said. 'I know that strictly speaking she should stay with me now, but I hate the thought of jerking her back and forth this early on, so I wondered how you might feel about staying with her at my place while I'm gone?'

'When are you leaving?'

'Pete's on his way down now, but I've called Mel, and she says anything you need, any time, you just yell.' Donovan paused. 'What do you think?'

'You seem to have thought it all out pretty well,' Joanna said, drily.

'You do mind.'

'It's not ideal.' She relented. 'But of course I don't mind.' She looked around the room. 'What about the hotel? Can I check out without notice?'

'No problem there, but why bother? I don't plan to be up at the farm for more than a day, two at most, so unless you feel happy

82

staying on at the apartment when I get back . . .' He paused again. 'It's your call, Joanna. I want you to feel comfortable.'

The idea of staying at the apartment with Donovan in it sent a sudden buzz of something *un*comfortably close to excitement rushing through her veins.

'I'll keep the room,' she said.

The first four days had been challenging but satisfying, and fun, too, from Joanna's point-of-view. Her previous visit with Philip had been a five-day package deal, so this taste of Manhattan's higher living – experienced so comprehensively both at the Peninsula and wherever Donovan had chosen to take her – had been exciting.

Sophia had continued to prove remarkable in her adaptability, calmly and steadily working her way through the hustle and bustle of the crowded city sidewalks, coping with visits to Mel Rosenthal's mid-town office and a handful of Donovan's favourite stores – though taking each one of the sculptor's most regularly trodden routes at a time and repeating it until the dog was accustomed to it, was a painstaking process. Fine as any dog's instincts might be, they depended upon humans for commands, and whilst much of Manhattan was constructed in straight, easily navigable lines, pedestrian crossing was fraught with dangers for a visually impaired person, with vehicles rounding corners on WALK light that were, in any case, not backed up by audible alerts.

'On my own,' Donovan had confessed, 'I'm not averse to taking a risk now and then, rather than ask for help at every damned crossing – but with Sophia relying on me, I'd never do that.'

With guide dogs permitted by law everywhere in the city, there were few restrictions on where Joanna and Donovan could go. Fascinated by his patent enjoyment of seemingly chiefly visual experiences like going to the movies and museums, Joanna had swiftly learned to judge when the sculptor either wanted or needed assistance or sighted information and when he was happier using his own imagination and heightened senses.

Now, putting down the telephone after his call, she knew that she might have suggested that they all went up to the farm together since their work in the city had gone so well, and she'd certainly taken more than enough shots of Donovan and Sophia in Manhattan to satisfy both magazine editors. But there was the possibility that he might need to remain at the farm, and Joanna knew that once the German shepherd had coped with the transition back to the countryside, and once she herself had managed to snap those as yet elusive pictures of the sculptor at work, then her commission would be virtually complete, and she would have no good reason not to leave for England. Much as she loved Merlin Cottage and the people and dogs at home, the prospect of going home filled her with regret – and she knew by now that the regret was no longer simply due to the fact that she would be leaving Sophia behind.

That, she realized, was the real reason she had not suggested winding things up here and heading upstate with Donovan. That, and the fact that she had no wish to relinquish the few more days that they were scheduled to spend together in the city, away from Gilead Farm and all that entailed.

Strange, and not a little perverse, she thought as she pulled her nightdress up over her head, to find Manhattan less pressured than a farm.

15

Luke Schuyler had just walked into a bar not far from the Commonwealth Pier in South Boston. He'd been modelling at a catalogue shoot down at the pier for most of the day, freezing his butt off and getting ordered around, and right now he was tired, chilled to the bone, and in need of a drink.

The bar was busy and dark and one of those places that might have been anywhere, but at least it was warm from body heat. Luke caught the bartender's attention long enough to get himself a beer, then pressed back through the small crowd checking for a table coming free.

'Sir?'

Luke turned around to face the young man who'd tapped his shoulder. He wore a black T-shirt and denims and had about a dozen empty glasses clasped to his chest.

'Guy there wants to buy you another beer.' The young man gestured with his head towards a corner. 'Want me to bring it over?'

Luke squinted in that direction, but it was too dark and obstructed by drinkers to see more than the shadowy shape of a man with a white cane propped up beside his legs. His mother came suddenly into his mind, a memory of her admonishing him as a still golden-haired child against accepting candy from strangers.

'You want your beer, man?'

Luke took just another second. Fact was, he wanted another drink badly, his feet were killing him and this way at least he didn't have to fight his way back to the bar again.

Besides, what possible harm could there be in taking a beer off some lonely blind guy?

16

Mel Rosenthal lived with her partner, Sandra McGeever, in a small but exquisite apartment down on Ninth Street near University Place.

Mel was petite and energetic, with short gleaming dark brown hair, eyes vivid as black cherries, a strong voice with a New York accent more pronounced in person than on the phone, and hands that seldom ceased their gesticulating. Sandra, a cartoonist, had marmalade-coloured hair and a wide mouth, but a startlingly gentle, husky voice and a manner to match. Peaceful with one another and clearly possessed of a long-standing, contented relationship, the two women laughed a great deal and were, Joanna had quickly found, charming, easy-going companions who seemed to invite confidences.

'So, Jo, you really like him, huh?' Mel asked.

'Who?' Joanna asked, though she knew quite well.

'*Who?*' Mel scoffed. 'You know who.'

'Of course I like him.'

'Like, or more than like?' Mel pushed.

'Cut it out, Mel,' Sandra scolded.

'Cut what out?'

'Don't embarrass Joanna.'

'She's not embarrassed, are you, Jo?'

Joanna smiled at them both. 'Not in the least.'

'So answer the question. Have you fallen for him?'

'Why?' Joanna countered easily. 'Because everyone else does?'

'I thought you weren't Jewish,' Mel said.

'I'm not.'

'Answering questions with more questions is a Jewish qualification.'

Joanna smiled again. 'I'll have to check my family tree.'

She had left Sophia for three hours that Friday afternoon at Mel's office with the agent happy to babysit so that Joanna could do a little of the serious shopping for Fred, Kit, Miriam and Sara that she thought she might not get another opportunity to do once Donovan came back into the city. Coming back to fetch Sophia, Mel had invited her to take pot luck with her and Sandra at their place, and Joanna had been delighted to accept.

They were sitting now around a polished teak table, drinking beer and eating date and pistachio couscous cooked by Sandra, while Sophia snoozed on a pair of large and wondrously soft suede-covered beanbags on the floor.

'What do you make of the team?' Sandra asked.

'She means the gang up at Gilead Farm,' Mel clarified.

'I guessed who she meant,' Joanna said.

'So?' Mel urged.

'They're an interesting group,' Joanna answered carefully.

'Don't you feel they hate your guts?' Mel asked.

Sandra laughed, shook her head and forked up some more couscous.

'I wouldn't put it quite that strongly,' Joanna said.

'Of course you wouldn't,' Mel said. 'You're an English lady.'

'Mel always makes it sound as if she's facing some kind of Praetorian Guard when she visits Donovan up there,' Sandra told her.

'So I exaggerate sometimes,' Mel said. 'They're really just sentinels, I guess.' She grinned at Joanna. 'Though you have to admit it's a little like having to get past Cerberus.'

Joanna was mystified. 'Wasn't Cerberus a snake?'

'Not in Greek mythology,' Sandra explained. 'Their Cerberus was a three-headed dog guarding the entrance to Hades.'

'Not that Donovan's anything like Pluto,' Mel said quickly.

Joanna tried to keep up. 'The god of the underworld?'

'That's the guy,' Sandra said, and smiled in Mel's direction. 'And no one's suggesting Jack Donovan's anything to do with the underworld – God forbid we should dare.'

Mel drank some beer. 'It isn't his fault Lamb and the others act like they're his nursemaids.'

'According to Mel,' Sandra said, 'nothing's ever Donovan's fault.'

There it was again, Joanna mused later that night, in bed in Donovan's guest room with Sophia beside her: gender and sexual preference notwithstanding, and even if she did poke fun at Lamb's, Chen's and Szabo's devotion to the sculptor, Mel Rosenthal was clearly another borderline infatuee.

Another thing had become infinitely clearer to Joanna this evening: the reason for Donovan's artistic success. Rosenthal was the proud possessor of an artist's proof of what she had told Joanna was one of his most famous sculptures – an arm, sculpted in bronze from shoulder to wrist. It had, quite frankly, taken her breath away. It was a powerful, muscular, working man's arm, every millimetre of it telling of days spent threshing corn or chopping wood or digging soil. Joanna had imagined she could almost see the sweat glistening on it, could almost feel the muscles flexing. There had been nothing ostensibly unique about the subject, yet its impact upon her had been shatteringly strong.

Mel had observed her reaction, and had smiled, quite gently. ·

'See?' she had said, softly. 'I'm noisy, and I'm his agent, but I don't bullshit. The guy's one of the greats, Jo. Truly.'

Joanna had had no wish to argue.

17

If Luke was aware of how he came to be lying on the floor of what seemed to be some kind of truck, it no longer seemed to matter. Nothing seemed to matter in the ordinary, rational sense. Nothing seemed real. His head was spinning, his vision was blurred, he had a strange, bad taste in his mouth, and his limbs were too heavy to lift.

'Hey,' he called out, weakly, then again, with more strength: '*Hey*!' Even his own voice sounded muffled to his ears, *everything* sounded muffled, and anyway, the truck was moving, vibrating beneath and around him, and Luke had an idea that if there was anyone to hear him, they didn't give a damn.

'Oh, man,' he moaned, softly.

He knew that he'd been drugged, knew it must have been that second beer in the bar. He knew enough, in spite of the numbness, to be scared, real scared. He supposed that whoever had done this to him – the guy in the bar, maybe, or someone else – was going to do worse, given time. Luke didn't know how he was going to take that, whatever it turned out to be, didn't know too much about his pain threshold, had never had cause to find out. If it was just sex – *just* – oh, Jesus, the things he'd read about, heard about, perverted, sick things ... they hanged guys, didn't they, and tied them up with leather, and whipped them ...? Or maybe he was just going to be killed, straight out. *Just.*

The truck jolted over a bump, going faster.

If it was painful, Luke didn't feel it.

18

Joanna had just fallen asleep in the big guest room bed, Sophia already snoring gently beside her, when Donovan called.

'I woke you again.' He sounded apologetic.

Joanna struggled to sit up. 'Where are you?'

'At the farm. Just checking to make sure you're both okay.'

'We're both fine,' she told him.

'Did you have fun with Mel and Sandra?'

'Yes, we did. They're a terrific couple.' The dog lifted her head, looking quizzical, and Joanna fondled her ears.

'It looks as though I may not make it back down till Sunday,' Donovan said.

'We'll still be here,' Joanna said.

He was silent for a moment.

'I miss you both,' he said, and hung up.

Joanna put the telephone back on its hook.

'We miss you, too,' she said into the dark.

19

SATURDAY, NOVEMBER 21

In Oxfordshire, in the bedroom of her cottage near Shipton-under-Wychwood, Sara was dreaming again. In the narrow tunnel that led nowhere, shut inside her head, spinning its abstract, colourful images, unfathomable yet filled with powerful sensation. The colours were soft-hued near the start of the dream, not quite peaceful for they moved too turbulently for tranquillity, but still they were delicate, tender, early-morning shades, sent flying by an invisible wind through the world that was Sara's brain.

Sunlight pierced, briefly painful, and in her mind Sara blinked, and when her inner eyes reopened, the colours had become Joanna again, the flame of her hair and the green dusted gold of her eyes . . .

Another flare, harsher than piercing, sending painful, shrieking spangles through the tunnel, and then it was dark, darker than dungeons or moonless nights, the pitch blackness of suffocation.

She heard it again, heard it inside her head, trapped in the tunnel between her deaf, dead ears. The scream was rising, flooding, bursting with fear.

Not Sara's scream.

Joanna's.

20

Luke was still feeling no pain. Still unable to move his arms or legs, still feeling that weird, numb kind of heaviness. And fear. Much more than fear now. Terror, like a great weight sitting on his chest, clamping him down.

He was lying on something hard, some kind of table maybe, in the dark. In a house, he thought, though he didn't know for sure. Luke didn't know anything much except he was certain now that he was going to die. Soon, maybe.

He couldn't seem to speak any more, the way he'd still been able to in the truck. He couldn't see because the room he was in – *they* were in – was so fucking *dark*. He knew there was someone there with him – they'd made sure he knew that, but he still didn't know who it was. He remembered being dragged out of the truck and lifted on to some kind of trolley, maybe a gurney like the ones they had in hospitals. He'd cried out then, had asked them who they were, what they wanted – he'd still been able to speak – but no one had answered him. All they had done was wheel him from the truck into this place, and all he had seen, right above his head – because he couldn't *move* his head – was a little night sky and some branches and a stone wall and the frame of a door as they pushed him, trundled him, through.

He'd begged them to let him go, he remembered that, had asked them what they wanted with him. '*Oh, Jesus, what do you* want *with me?*' And then he'd felt a pricking in his left arm – which meant that he wasn't completely numb even if he couldn't move – but they'd definitely given him some kind of a shot, because next thing he knew he'd been on this table, and he still didn't know what they wanted. And maybe – probably – it was better that way.

Someone had started touching him a while back. Luke hadn't even realized that he was naked until then, had no memory of being undressed, wasn't sure if he'd been naked in the truck or not. He thought they must have bathed him, because his own odour had changed – he could still smell, he didn't *like* the smells in this place – and now there was a scent of sandalwood soap rising off his body, and he always recognized sandalwood because it had been his grandma's favourite and he'd always given her that kind of soap for Christmas and she'd always acted surprised and happy, as though it was the biggest treat of the year.

Luke had tried thinking about his grandma, conjuring up her warmth and gentleness, when they – *he?* . . . *she?* . . . *it?* – had begun silently examining him. His mind had begged, shrieked, for them to stop, but his voice had stopped working, had gotten jammed up somewhere in his throat, and all that came out was a kind of moaning. He had thought at first that they were going to rape him, sodomize him, but nothing like that had happened; it had felt more like a doctor's hands on him – and *see?* He could feel the hands, he *could* feel, God help him – *God help me* – and the hands kept coming back to his left leg. 'Great legs, Luke,' he remembered one of the models on the catalogue shoot telling him yesterday – was it only yesterday?

Something changed in the room when the hands touched his leg. Something . . . a quickening of breath. Excitement, maybe. *Something.*

Terror exploded like a bomb in Luke's chest.

He knew now, he really *knew*, that he was going to die.

They moved away from him, in the dark. He heard something, small sounds, metallic and duller, movement quickening.

Three seconds later, as the first little rubber-feeling, rubber-stinking, plug entered his left nostril, pushed till it jammed tight, Luke knew exactly *how* he was going to die.

In his mind, he flailed, hit out, kicked out, wept and screamed. In reality, as the second plug blocked his right nostril, all that moved were his eyes, bulging, his mouth, gaping, gulping air out of the blackness, and his chest, contorting.

They moved away again. He heard a click, and the light came on.

Luke screwed up his eyes against the dazzle, blinded by it – and then, slowly, like a young child too filled with dread to look at something scary, he opened his eyes.

And saw.

And even if they had not closed his mouth and sealed that up, too, suffocating him, Luke Schuyler's final thought was that the terror would probably have killed him.

21

Hardly anyone was getting mugged in New York City these days. So said Mel Rosenthal and Sandra McGeever and, when Joanna thought about it later, she remembered Jack Donovan saying much the same thing, too. Certainly practically no one had *ever* been mugged – even in the bad old days before 'zero tolerance' – walking along Sixth Avenue on their way back from Central Park towards Fifty-sixth Street on a Saturday afternoon in the company of a full-grown German shepherd dog.

They had been out and about for half the day, during which time Joanna had, amongst other things, collected contact sheets and negatives from the photo lab Mel had recommended, and though she had taken a quick look through the sheets at the lab, Joanna was now looking forward to spending the evening back at the apartment studying each shot through her own magnifying glass.

The man (she assumed it was a man, though she never saw him, never had a chance to see *anything*) weighed into Joanna from behind just as she was looking up at the late-afternoon-lit skyscrapers soaring on both sides of the avenue as far as the eye could see. She fell diagonally, reeling from the pain in her back, striking her face on the concrete and pinning Sophia to the sidewalk. She saw proverbial stars, felt the man's hand first wrenching her shoulder bag away, then ripping the wedding ring from her finger, and she heard poor Sophia, trapped partly by the weight of her body and partly by the lead still wound twice around her wrist, barking, snarling and yelping in her frenzy to escape and help Joanna.

'Me and Deborah Kerr,' she told the young, bespectacled intern named Sam Golitzen, who was stitching up a cut on her forehead in the emergency room at St Clare's Hospital on West Fifty-second Street.

'Deborah Kerr was there?' He looked bemused.

Joanna managed a ghost of a smile. 'Both looking up?'

'You've lost me.'

'Not important.' She was trying, unsuccessfully, to keep her mind off what he was doing to her poor wounded skin. 'Just an old movie. Deborah Kerr was looking up at the Empire State Building when she got knocked down, and I was looking up at all the lights on Sixth Avenue when . . .'

'When you got rolled,' Sam Golitzen said succinctly. 'Sorry,' he added as she flinched.

'Are you *sure* my dog's all right?' It was the third time Joanna had asked that particular question.

'I told you,' the intern said patiently, 'they said she's fine.'

'Why can't I see her?'

'Keep still, please,' Golitzen said. 'You can't see her because this is a human hospital.'

'But Sophia's a guide dog. I thought guide dogs are allowed everywhere in the city by law.'

'You're not blind,' Golitzen pointed out.

'But you're sure she's all right?'

'Far as I know.'

'Could we forget about the dog for just five minutes?' Officer Barbara Mendez of the New York Police Department suggested – like Sam Golitzen displaying a more than reasonable degree of patience as she tried, for the fourth time, to take down the details of Joanna's loss.

'I'm sorry, officer. I'm just anxious to get to see her.'

Joanna was perfectly aware that she was being a nuisance, but this policewoman had told her that so far as she knew

97

Sophia had been taken to the Animal Medical Center on Sixty-second Street, and if Joanna had been concerned before, now she was terrified, for the dog and for Donovan.

'You can go see her just as soon as they know if your X-rays are okay, Mrs Guthrie,' Officer Mendez said. 'So if we could please get back to your being robbed . . . you're sure all he got was your wedding ring and your purse?'

Joanna forced herself to cooperate, and found that concentrating on the crime itself made her feel no better. 'It was a shoulder bag,' she said, 'quite old, but leather, and it contained most of the work I've been doing for a photographic assignment over the past two weeks.' That thought made her feel slightly sick.

'Any cash?'

'About seventy dollars, and my credit cards and travellers' cheques – and my passport, which I had with me because I was cashing some cheques.' A new realization and fresh alarm struck her. 'The keys to the apartment were in there – I hadn't thought.'

'This is Mr Donovan's apartment?' Mendez verified. 'And he's out of the city until tomorrow?' She made a note. 'Was his address in the bag?'

Joanna's mind sifted through the contents. 'Yes. Yes, it was.' Guilt swamped her. 'There was a letter in the bag with that address and Donovan's address upstate.' She tried to get off the bed, but felt suddenly dizzy.

'You shouldn't get up yet, ma'am.'

Joanna wasn't sure now that she *could* get up. 'Can you send someone to the building, please, officer? There's no one home. The thief might be there now.'

'I doubt that, ma'am.' Barbara Mendez checked her notes. 'At that address, I guess there's a doorman?'

Joanna thought about the redoubtable-looking Jerry Feenan. 'Yes.'

'They're generally pretty careful who they let in.'

'But you will check it out?'

'We will.' The officer paused. 'And you're sure you can't tell us anything about the man who did this?'

Joanna shook her head, winced, put her strapped right hand up to touch her head and winced again, this time from the pain in her wrist. 'He came from behind. I didn't see a thing.'

'And he didn't speak to you?'

'Not that I heard.'

All Joanna remembered hearing – all that was reverberating now, over and over again, in her head – was the sound of Sophia's distressed yelping beneath her on the concrete pavement.

If the mugger had made any attempt to gain access to the building on Fifty-sixth Street, Joanna learned when she and Sophia returned to the apartment early on Sunday morning, he had failed. By the time a distraught Donovan arrived just after nine, the two assault victims were comfortably ensconced in his living room.

'We're fine,' Joanna reassured him the instant he came in. 'Both of us. We're snuggled under a blanket on your sofa. Sophia's wagging her tail – I'm sure you can hear it.'

'I hear it.' Donovan stood tentatively in the doorway, lines of worry creasing his brow. 'Raimundo just said it's a good thing I can't see your face.'

'My face is fine. Come on over, Sophia wants you to pay court.'

He didn't move. 'Is she really okay? Tell me the truth.'

Joanna understood. 'She's not jumping down because they gave her a little sedative and she has a few bruises on her side from where I fell on her. That's all.' She made her tone firm.

Donovan folded down his cane and came across to the sofa. Sitting cautiously on its edge, he was greeted by whines of contentment and a substantial licking, in which he indulged himself for several moments, rubbing his face against the dog's fur and examining her tenderly, before he was satisfied enough to sit up straight again.

'Now please tell me about yourself.'

'I have a few cuts on my face. I had some stitches on my forehead, which I did not particularly enjoy. My back is sore. I have bruises on parts of my anatomy which I would not show

99

you even if you *could* see, and I have a sprained wrist, which hurts, but is not a serious injury.'

Donovan sat silently for a moment. 'May I feel your face?'

'You may.'

Joanna remained motionless while he ran his fingertips lightly over her skin, lingering briefly on each cut and scratch. The idea flashed through her mind that he was about to kiss her small wounds, but he did no such thing, merely located them with that delicate touch and then stopped.

'I am so sorry,' he said.

'What for?' Joanna asked.

'For what happened to you both.' He paused. 'Did you lose all the negatives?'

'Except for what's still in the camera. I didn't have that with me.'

'I'm sorry,' he said again.

'Hardly your fault.' She paused. 'I'm sorry for causing you such trouble. I should have known better than to carry your address in the same bag as your keys.'

'Frank Esposito's changed the locks,' Donovan said. 'He's the super.'

'I know.'

'And Jerry Feenan's told everyone to watch out for anything suspicious.'

'He told me when we got back.'

'So there's no trouble, is there? Not for me, anyway.'

Donovan's calm lasted for little more than an hour. Having dispatched Joanna to bed, leaving Sophia to sleep off her sedative on the sofa, he went into his library, where he sat smoking for a while, listening to Ella Fitzgerald and Hoagy Carmichael, whose voices usually served to tranquillize or lift him. Not this morning. This morning, the more he thought about what had happened – the more he tried *not* to think about it – the more agitated he became.

Finally, just before noon, he knocked on the door of the guest room and went straight in.

'Joanna, are you awake?'

100

He heard the rustle of sheets and the changing rhythm of her breath.

'I am now,' she said.

'Sorry.'

Joanna looked at the clock. 'High time I was awake.'

'You need your rest.'

She saw the look on his face. 'What's wrong?'

He came a little further into the room and stopped, his bearing stiff and unnatural. 'I think it's time you and Sophia went back.'

'We are going, aren't we?' she said. 'For Thanksgiving.'

'I mean, to England,' Donovan said.

Joanna sat up, startled. 'Why?'

'Before anything worse happens,' he said. 'To either of you.' He took a breath and went on rapidly. 'It isn't as if I can't cope without a guide dog – and you know I vowed I would never endanger another animal.'

Joanna stared at him. 'This is because I was mugged?'

'Of course.'

'But it had nothing to *do* with you.' She got out of bed, wincing a little, picked up her dressing gown from the chair near the dressing table and put it on. 'Sophia was with me, not you.'

'You were both in Manhattan *because* of me,' he said. 'You were walking alone in the dark because I went away and left you both here.'

'We have muggers in England, too,' Joanna reminded him gently. 'Even in Oxfordshire.' She walked towards him, stopped a foot away. 'You may as well stop this right now, Donovan. I won't have it.' She tried to brighten her tone. 'Other considerations aside, I have all that photography to reshoot.'

'What if you're wrong? About my being bad luck for Sophia?'

'I'm not wrong, and I never heard such foolishness. You're made for each other. We both know that.' She paused. 'Besides, I wouldn't dream of putting her through another flight, let alone quarantine, and neither would you.'

'I guess not.' A faint smile stretched his lips.

'So no more of this nonsense?'
The smile creased his face with small lines.
'What?' Joanna asked.
'You sound so British,' Donovan said.

By the end of the day, the sculptor's irrational guilt had vanished and unreasonable anger had taken its place, vented as it was against the NYPD who had dealt with Joanna sympathetically but, it was true to say, impotently. With nothing to go on, no description and no witnesses – first a sergeant, then a lieutenant pointed out to Donovan – the chances of getting either the mugger or Joanna's belongings were less than slender.

'Like it's your fault the bastard shoved you from behind,' Donovan said to Joanna over a Chinese take-out in the living room.

'Please stop seething. It's not their fault either.' Working chopsticks with her injured right wrist was proving troublesome, but using her left hand was altogether impossible. 'And it's bad for your digestion.'

'Want me to feed you?' he asked.

She shook her head. 'Are you sure you're blind?'

'No, I just invented the bullet in my head so beautiful women would feel sorry for me.'

'And then be amazed by your skills.'

'You got it.'

She managed to transfer some noodles and beanshoots from her bowl to her mouth. 'I'll have to go to the British Consulate, about my passport.'

'No rush.'

'So you don't want to get rid of me yet, after all?' Joanna smiled.

'Not just yet,' Donovan said.

Twenty-four more hours passed relatively uneventfully. Having emerged from the mugging with a sense of mild elation, because she had escaped from assault and robbery relatively unscathed, Joanna now began feeling after-effects.

102

Her injuries were trivial but hurt nonetheless, yet more annoyingly than that, she felt suddenly unwell and generally distressed. She knew she was not physically ill, recognized that her symptoms were probably some low-grade post traumatic thing, but the loss of her wedding ring and (another loss that had not at first registered) the two small – but equally irreplaceable – photographs of herself with Philip that she'd kept in her wallet, made her feel not just sad, but also unaccountably insecure.

'You need chicken soup.' Donovan had insisted on cancelling her reservation at the Peninsula so that he could take care of her, and was now trying his hardest to spoil her.

'I do not.'

'You need more rest.'

'I need to pull myself together,' Joanna said.

'You've had a shock.'

'Nonsense.' She sounded much brisker than she felt.

'Did anyone ever tell you you're a hopeless case?'

'Several people, several times.'

She received, via Donovan's computer system, a strangely anxious e-mail from Sara, wanting urgent confirmation that all was well with her. When Joanna responded with a lighthearted account of the mugging, she got back an oddly euphoric e-mail from her friend. Sara was, of course, she wrote, sorry about what had happened to her, but compared to the awful disquiet that had haunted her since having another of her bad dreams, the news that Joanna had merely been mugged – rather than murdered or killed in some awful accident – struck her as bordering on splendid.

Glad to be of service in making you feel better, Joanna typed back ironically, late on Monday evening. Please don't have any more dreams for a while.

The first of the telephone hang-ups occurred five minutes later. Donovan picked up in the library just as Joanna was switching off the computer on his desk.

'Hello?' he answered, waited a couple of moments, then hung up.

'Wrong number?' Joanna asked.

'I guess,' he said.

The same thing happened five more times through that night. Joanna heard the ringing on the extension in her room. After the third time, she got out of bed and found Donovan in the kitchen, just pulling a quart of ice cream out of his freezer.

'Want some?' He prised off the lid and sniffed the contents. 'Toffee and pecan.'

'I'll settle for tea,' Joanna said.

'Sit down, and I'll make it.'

'I think I can manage to make a cup of tea, thank you.' She picked up the kettle, filled it under the tap and only just managed not to grunt with pain.

'Wrist bad?'

'Not so bad.' Joanna put the kettle back on the stove and lit the gas. 'Does this happen often?'

'The hang-ups? No, not often.'

'Think there's a connection with the mugging? Your number was in the bag.'

'Probably coincidental.'

'Probably,' Joanna agreed.

It was Jerry Feenan's report next day – after their return from a gentle city training session with Sophia – about a florist with an anonymous delivery for Joanna trying to slip past security in order to gain entry to the penthouse floor that finally tipped the balance for Donovan.

'I'm going to call an FBI guy I know up in Albany,' he told Joanna that evening as they were sharing some sushi at a nearby Japanese restaurant, with Sophia lying under the table. 'Get him to check out a few things.' He registered the surprise in her silence. 'The NYPD aren't going to do much on the strength of a few hang-ups and a *maybe* bogus flower delivery.'

'I don't suppose there's much they can do,' Joanna reasoned. 'Anyway, surely we're going back up to the farm tomorrow, and Mr Feenan seems on top of things here.'

'All true,' Donovan said. 'But I still don't like that delivery having your name on it, and Tom Oates – the FBI agent – is a pal. He showed up for some lessons at the school two years back after a surgeon told him sculpting might be fine therapy for a hand injury.'

'Was he any good?'

'At sculpture?' Donovan shrugged. 'Not especially. But he had a good time, and he was fun to have around the place – even Lamb liked him.'

'Goodness,' Joanna said. 'That *is* a seal of approval.'

Donovan poured sake into their small cups. 'Why do you believe that Lamb doesn't like you?'

'It's hard to say.' Joanna tried to give an honest answer. 'He's been perfectly pleasant to me. It's just a feeling.'

'He certainly respects you.'

'That's mutual,' she said steadily.

'But you don't like him, do you?'

She took a second. 'No. Not a great deal.' She paused. 'I do like the fact that he's such a good friend to you.'

'I'm not sure if I could cope without him.'

'I think you'd do well enough.'

'I wonder,' Donovan said.

He called the FBI's field office in Albany early on Wednesday morning before their next session with Sophia, learned that Special Agent Oates was on long-term sick leave, then tried his home number and found the agent there and going stir-crazy. He wasn't sick, Oates explained to Donovan, but in the latter stages of recovering from a broken leg.

'In the line of duty?'

'In a manner of speaking,' Oates replied. 'My car blew a tyre and went off the road down near Rensselaerville and I got a little banged up.'

'So I guess you're out of commission?'

'Depends what for.'

Donovan told him. Oates said it so happened that a neighbour was leaving for Thanksgiving in New York City in less than an hour's time, and he'd been asking Oates to join him and his family.

'I don't want you coming down because of this,' Donovan said.

105

'I won't be,' Oates assured him. 'I just needed something to get me kick-started out of here, that's all.'

He was in the Fifty-sixth Street apartment by one p.m.

'Good to see you, Donovan.' He turned to Joanna and shook her hand. 'And to meet you, Mrs Guthrie. I'm sorry you've had such a bad time here.'

'Just a few bad hours,' she told him. 'The rest has been delightful.'

If she hadn't been intent on finding out what he had to say professionally, she knew she would have been itching to pick up the Hasselblad and start shooting. He was a remarkable-looking young man – too young, she thought initially, and somehow too touchingly good-looking to be a federal agent, or at least her notion of what an FBI man ought to look like. His skin was unlined and smooth as polished wood, his dark eyes and hair seemed to shine in the light, his cheekbones were high, his ears flat, his nose curved but small. In his off-duty casual clothes, his right leg still heavily strapped and using a single crutch, he appeared to her slim as a boy, almost too vulnerable for her to conceive of him being placed in the kind of potentially dangerous conditions his title indicated. And yet, watching as he sat, straight, still and alert in one of the armchairs, listening first to her account of the mugging, and then to Donovan's meticulously recalled list of minor events that had succeeded it, Joanna observed Oates's quiet concentration and the keenness of his gaze and saw that he was, indeed, both older and sharper than she had first thought.

'I shouldn't imagine there's much cause for concern,' he said when Donovan had finished speaking. 'But I agree with you that there's no sense taking chances.' He looked across at Joanna. 'I take it you don't know of anyone who might have sent you flowers?'

'Not here in New York,' she said. 'And certainly not anonymously.'

'Still,' Oates said, 'it could be innocent.'

'The delivery boy tried to get up to our floor,' Donovan pointed out. 'And if it was just some kind of mistake, how come he dumped the flowers and ran when the doorman tried

106

to stop him?' He paused. 'Tom, I wouldn't be concerned if that bastard hadn't taken Joanna's passport—'

'He didn't set out to steal my passport,' she interrupted. 'It just happened to be in my bag with the other things.'

'Still,' Oates said again. 'It never hurts to take a few precautions. This city may be safer than it was, but the crazies haven't sunk into the sewers, and there's no guarantee that a Manhattan mugger might *not* take a side-trip upstate if he thought he was on to a good thing.'

He promised to have a word with one of his city colleagues to see if there was anything more to be done locally on the case – though he doubted it – and told Donovan that he, or one of the agents in the Bureau's satellite office in Kingston, would find a way to keep tabs on Gilead Farm, especially for the duration of Joanna's stay.

'Wouldn't it be less trouble for everyone,' she asked just before Oates left the apartment, 'if I simply went home now? We've covered all your regular routes here, haven't we?'

'What about your magazine commissions?'

'I don't want to disrupt your whole life for the sake of a few photographs.'

'It's pretty disrupted anyway,' Donovan pointed out. 'Whether you stay or go, the mugger still has my addresses.'

'And you don't have a passport,' Oates reminded her.

'I'm told that I can get a one-way travel document from the British Consulate if it's urgent – and I could go back to the hotel right now.'

'You could,' Donovan said calmly. 'Except that you're still bruised, and you can't do much with your right hand, so you'd be a whole lot better off coming back to the farm with me and Sophia till you're stronger.' He played his trump card. 'And what *about* Sophia? She's just getting over one trauma – do you think it's fair for you to run out on her before she's properly settled back at the farm?'

Joanna looked down at the dog. There was no arguing with the fact that she had been staying noticeably closer to her since the mugging.

'I know when I'm beaten,' she said.

22

Thanksgiving Day at Gilead Farm started out gently and easily. Mostly, Joanna observed – once she and Sophia had come across from the guest cottage to the main house two hours before dinner was scheduled – the morning appeared to be a pre-prandial fest of cooking, tasting and sipping.

'What can I do?' she asked Donovan and Pete Szabo in the kitchen.

'Nothing,' Donovan told her.

'Pete, please, I'd like to help with *something*.'

'You can taste my soup.'

'*Your* soup?' Donovan raised an eyebrow.

'Our soup,' Szabo allowed.

'Who's cooking this dinner?' Donovan wanted to know.

'Whose recipe is this soup?' Szabo enquired politely.

Hastily, Joanna found a spoon, dipped it into the creamy, fragrant, pale butterscotch-coloured liquid, blew on it and tasted it. 'That's gorgeous.' She let the flavours establish in her mouth. 'Pumpkin?'

'Of course,' Donovan said.

'What does it need, Jo?' Szabo asked.

'Nothing,' she answered. 'Absolutely nothing.'

Joanna had seen Donovan working in his kitchens both here and in the apartment, but she had never witnessed him working on any kind of major dinner. Watching him today, she was more impressed than ever by his unafraid, hands-on approach, and his extraordinary adeptness – though equally impressive, she decided after a while, were Szabo's methods of assisting him. If until now Joanna had occasionally found Szabo a trifle servile around his easy-going boss, on this occasion they made a perfect team, treating each other with candour and respect as they chopped, sliced, seasoned, tasted, basted and stirred.

'Did I just screw up?' Donovan asked whilst carving patterns in tomatoes.

Szabo went to take a look. 'Sure did.'

'Shit,' Donovan said.

'You want to fix it or shall I?'

'Do we have enough left for me to chance it?'

'Not really.'

'You better do it.'

No pretence, no fakery, Joanna thought, sitting pleasurably back, as ordered, watching and listening, her only task to keep Sophia clear of their feet and the oven and stove.

'Is Chris over her flu yet?' she asked after a while.

'She called this morning,' Donovan answered, checking roast potatoes by smell, feel and taste. 'She hopes to make it. She hasn't missed a Thanksgiving dinner yet.'

'How many years has she worked here?' Joanna asked.

'About five, I'd say, give or take.' He closed the oven door.

'She came the year before Lamb,' Szabo supplied.

'What about you, Pete?' Joanna asked.

'Me?' The big man smiled. 'I've been here forever.'

Thanksgiving was, Joanna knew, not an occasion for exchanging gifts, so it was all the more touching when, soon after they'd sat down in the huge open-plan living room for a pre-dinner drink (Donovan and Szabo having whipped off their aprons and donned jackets and ties), Chen, Lamb and Szabo all presented Sophia with gifts of welcome.

'For her real homecoming,' Szabo explained. 'Now that it's decided.'

'Though I think we all knew from the start that things would work out,' Chris said. She seemed well-recovered from her illness, as chic as ever, wearing a soft violet-coloured wool dress, her hair pinned up again, the mother-of-pearl locket that usually hung on a chain around her neck, now attached to a comb holding her French pleat in place.

'Not that it hasn't been a joy having you here to smooth the way.'

Joanna glanced swiftly at Lamb's face as he said that, but found no apparent irony there. There was, she decided, a quite disarmingly shabby elegance about the man today. His short silver-grey hair was immaculate, and he was dressed in almost unrelieved black again: black roll-neck fine wool pullover under a splendid, aged-looking black velvet blazer with a burgundy handkerchief in his breast pocket. Joanna recalled thinking, observing him teaching, that he had looked more like a ballet master than an artist; today he seemed every inch an old-fashioned actor.

The first two gifts – a soft woollen rug from Chris for Sophia's bed, and a splendid beef marrow bone from Szabo – were both charming, but Lamb's offering, wrapped in tissue paper for Joanna to open on the dog's behalf, left her speechless, moved and not a little ashamed.

'It's magnificent, Murdoch.' She stared at the neck chain in her hands, each link hand-worked in yellow gold and signed by him on the back of the identity disc that bore the engraved name *Sophia*. 'I don't know what to say.' She shook her head. 'It's one of the most beautiful things I've ever seen.'

'Just a token of my gratitude,' Lamb said, and for once the blue eyes were filled with real warmth. 'I know how much your Sophia is going to mean to Donovan.'

Joanna took the chain over to where Donovan was sitting. 'Here,' she said, and put it in his hands. 'Isn't it exquisite?'

'I know it is.' He held it briefly, then gave it back to her, a small smile tugging at his mouth. 'See?' he said softly.

They sat, for the special occasion, at the dark polished oak table in the dining room: another uncluttered but handsomely proportioned room with a carved wooden chandelier overhead

110

and large windows giving plenty of natural light. The table had been laid with fine silver and crystal and damask napkins, and the day beyond the windows was clear and fine, yet unlike the rest of the house, Joanna found the room slightly oppressive.

'This is a day when most people choose to go home to their families.' Donovan stood at the head of the table before the first course, holding a champagne flute. 'Those of us here today may not be blood relatives, but I think we've become about as close as any real family.' He lifted his glass. 'Happy Thanksgiving, my very dear friends.'

Murdoch Lambert, seated to his left, rose to his feet, and Joanna, sitting on Donovan's other side, noted that his cheeks were a little flushed. 'And to you,' he said, and embraced the other man before sitting down again.

'God bless us all,' Szabo said, from his end of the table.

'Amen.' Chris Chen, on Joanna's left, looked pointedly towards the white porcelain tureen in the centre of the table. 'Now who's going to ladle out the soup before we all starve?'

As dinner progressed, Joanna became aware again of the subtle but palpable competition for Donovan's respect and affection. She was also aware, almost from the first course onward, that the sculptor was drinking far more than she had previously witnessed, having started before the meal with malt whisky and now working his way through glasses of Châteauneuf-du-Pape.

It was, she came to realize, a deliberate act on his behalf.

'I'm checking with you now, Joanna,' he said soberly while they were still eating turkey with butternut squash, potatoes, brussels sprouts and home-made cranberry sauce, 'to see if you're going to object to my hanging one on?'

'You don't need to check with me,' she said lightly, though startled by the question. 'It's your party.'

'And you're my guest,' he said, steadily, 'and I don't want you to think that I wouldn't stop drinking right now if you believed it might affect the way Sophia was going to be looked after.'

111

Joanna smiled. 'Sophia's not a child. There are four of us here to walk and feed her – that should be about as much looking after as she's likely to need.'

'I've already checked with Pete, and he's going to be standing by,' Donovan told her. 'Just so's you know.'

He maintained a good façade for the remainder of the dinner, drinking steadily but continuing to talk, laugh and joke with the rest of them, the alcohol building in his bloodstream not manifesting itself in any untoward or remotely unpleasant way. And then, as soon as the last dishes had been removed from the table, he lit a cigar, stood up, left the dining room without a word, and did not return.

It was Chris, a while later, who picked up on Joanna's discomfort. 'This probably seems a bit bizarre to you – Donovan going off like that, I mean.'

Murdoch Lambert, too, had now left the room, and Szabo was in the kitchen commencing the clear-up, so the two women were, for the moment, on their own.

'Does it happen often?' Joanna asked.

Chris shook her head. 'This is work-related.' She read the confusion in Joanna's expression. 'Murdoch's been holed up in his workshop most of the time since you both went to the city – you know they've been collaborating for the past few years?'

'I know that,' Joanna said, 'but that's all I know.'

'They do tend to keep things pretty much under wraps,' the other woman explained. 'All I know is Murdoch's been itching for Donovan to get back, and if Donovan's letting off steam today, that means he's ready to start work on whatever the new project is.'

'I've been looking forward to him getting around to sculpting,' Joanna said.

Chen shrugged. 'We all knew he wouldn't be working until Sophia settled down. That was part of the deal, wasn't it? That he should devote himself completely to your training plan?'

'Which he has,' Joanna agreed.

'You wait and see, Joanna. Once his hangover's worn off, Donovan will shut himself into his studio at the school, and no one will set eyes on him for days on end.' Chris paused. 'I know you're planning on photographing him at work, but the fact is, if you were hoping to do that in a hurry, you're likely to be disappointed.'

23

TUESDAY, DECEMBER 1

Chris Chen's prediction had proven accurate, compounded by the fact that after Thanksgiving Day Donovan had kept Sophia close to him virtually twenty-four hours of every day. Joanna had seen the pair from time to time, and often the sculptor made a point of having a few words with her, told her that the instant he felt ready to have her in his studio she'd be the first to know, and Sophia greeted her each time with her usual passion, yet still Joanna felt abandoned. Her 'student' had graduated and had no more need of her. Her beloved dog had a new master who took her to work with him and walked her in his fields and took care of her needs. It was what Joanna had intended, yet it hurt nonetheless.

Suddenly, her whole situation seemed frustrating. If she had not needed to find a way of replacing all the work that the mugger had stolen, Joanna thought she would certainly have gone straight back to New York City, chivvied through her replacement passport and made the break without further ado. But though she had volunteered to go home during their conversation with Special Agent Oates, she did hate the idea of letting down the two magazines – not least because doing so would almost certainly rule out any future commissions for her. The problems were, first, that she did still feel quite battered and sore, and second – and far more crucially – that Donovan at work had unexpectedly turned into a Donovan out of her reach.

She e-mailed Sara on Tuesday evening, too restless to settle down to hand-writing a letter.

All those instants-in-time lost because, as you know, there's never any point trying to recreate spur-of-the-moment natural situations. All those early excursions alone with Donovan, and then with Lamb and Szabo; there were shots that I could never have used for the magazines, Sara, but I should so much have liked to have kept them for myself – Lamb's expressions at certain moments, for example, when he so clearly resented my being there. Nevertheless, the photographs are gone for good, which means I have no real alternative but to wait for Donovan to emerge from this initial bout of work.

The trouble is that, as you well know, I've never been too good at hanging around for anyone.

Any irritation she had been beginning to feel about Donovan's elusiveness vanished next morning after Pete Szabo knocked on her door with a courier-delivered parcel for her.

'What is it?' she said, looking at the brown paper-wrapped package.

'Search me,' Szabo said, as he left. 'Only one way to find out.'

Intrigued, she tore off the paper and found a short hand-written letter from Kit and Miriam, folded around a smaller package wrapped in corrugated paper.

Dear Joanna,

Jack Donovan was in touch with us, explaining that you'd lost two photos of yourself with Philip and asking if there were any pictures here that we could make copies of for you to carry around with you while you're away. We picked these two, and hope we made the right choices.

Merlin Cottage is fine, and Bella, Rufus, Honey (oh, yes, and Fred, too) all send you their love. As do we.

Take better care of yourself, please, and blessings to Sophia.

See you whenever you're ready.

Miriam and Kit.

*

Joanna unwrapped the corrugated paper and found a small leather wallet which, upon opening, became a double photograph frame holding a miniaturized copy of the wedding photo that lived in the sitting room at Merlin Cottage and another – of her and Philip on a wet and windy weekend in the Lake District – that usually stood on the dresser in the kitchen at home.

Donovan, who had not experienced the pleasure of looking at a photograph for the past eighteen years, but whose sensitive antennae must have picked up on the pain of her small loss after the mugging, had organized this for her so that she would not be unhappy for the remainder of her stay.

She could hardly be angry with him now.

Having found it impossible to get to see Donovan for the rest of that day, Joanna made do with using the Brailler in Chris Chen's office at the school on Thursday morning to compose a short, but painstaking, note of thanks.

'You're not bad with that,' Chris told her.

'I'm very slow,' Joanna said.

'You could have just left me a message for him.'

'It would have been easier,' Joanna admitted. 'But he went to some trouble for me, so a note seemed more appropriate.'

'I guess you mean the photos from home?'

'You know about them.'

The other woman smiled up at her from her desk. 'Of course.'

Lamb was walking towards the school from the car park as Joanna was leaving.

'Good morning, Murdoch.' She waited for him in the doorway.

'Something I can do for you?' It had turned colder and wetter, and he wore a raincoat and a hound's-tooth checked slouch hat that made him look like a city tourist.

'Perhaps.' Joanna looked at his damp, impatient face and realized that prevarication would simply make him more bad-

116

tempered. 'I wondered if you would mind my sitting in on one of your classes?'

'Would this be to sculpt or to take pictures?'

'Both, if you or your students have no objection.'

'Have you ever sculpted, Joanna?'

'No.'

His cool eyes appraised her from beneath the down-turned brim of the hat. 'I take it this is just distraction from sitting around waiting for Donovan?'

It was hard, under that gaze, not to feel like a chastened schoolgirl.

'I do find myself at a looser end than I'd expected,' she managed to answer evenly, 'and sculpture-wise, I suspect I have no talent. But I would be genuinely interested in making some kind of an attempt.'

Lamb nodded. 'Come at noon,' he said.

She hadn't noticed the model before, set as it was on a table in a far corner of the large room; it was the model of the Delameter House that Donovan had told her about, its accuracy and intricacies every bit as remarkable as he had described. She would have liked to examine it and compliment Lamb on it, but it seemed inappropriate. There were eight students at work – *real* students, Joanna thought self-consciously as she settled herself on the stool that Lamb directed her to, placed her loaded Hasselblad carefully down on the floor beside the stool, and then pulled a neatly pressed oatmeal-coloured smock over her head. Five were women, the youngest about nineteen, she guessed, the oldest somewhere around seventy-five, and the three men were all in the retirement age bracket. All but one of the women, a thirty-something with frizzy wild bottle-yellow hair and panda-ringed eyes, exuded enviable tranquillity, but the panda woman seemed almost as frantic as her hair as she worked on what might, or might not, have been a man's head in clay. One of the men, a shaggy, stoop-shouldered yet somehow heroic-looking type, appeared to Joanna's untrained eyes to be hugely talented as his large hands moulded, stroked and

117

probed, transforming an unformed lump of clay, even as she watched, into an early but unmistakable female head and shoulders.

'This is Joanna Guthrie,' Lamb startled her with a sudden, belated introduction, 'a visitor from England who'd like to take some photographs of us at work if we don't object. Do we?' There was a general murmur of assent and he smiled. 'Apparently we don't. Joanna says she wishes to try her hand at sculpting, though she claims to have no talent. Time will tell.'

The oldest woman in the group, sitting on a stool just a few feet away from Joanna, grinned at her from a beautifully weathered, fine-boned face surrounded by snowy, naturally waved hair. 'Typical Lamb intro, hon,' she whispered. 'We're none of us ever sure if he's quite the curmudgeon he makes himself out to be. He really can be almost kind, you know.'

Reluctantly, Joanna remembered the chain he'd made for Sophia.

'Yes,' she said. 'I do know.'

He was not kind to her, not at least during the class, but as time passed and Joanna learned how infinitely harder it was than it looked to mould clay into any kind of remotely satisfactory shape, she did nevertheless find herself somewhere on the borders of enjoyment. She was a practical woman accustomed to manual work, but usually, of course, when she worked with her hands, it tended to be around living, breathing, receptive dogs rather than lumps of material. As the first session wore on, she confirmed what she had told Murdoch Lambert, namely that she had no talent, though she was already beginning to understand why so many people found handling clay therapeutic.

'I feel like I'm back in kindergarten,' she confided in her neighbour, who was named Alice Munro, 'playing with plasticine.' She glanced around to make sure Lamb wasn't too close. 'I'm just feeling guilty about wasting clay.'

'No need,' Alice told her. 'Unless you become devoted to your mess, Lamb will recycle it.' She laughed at Joanna's face. 'I'm sorry. My children are always telling me I'm too blunt.'

118

'Don't be sorry,' Joanna assured her, 'I may not be a sculptor, but I can recognize a mess when I see one.'

'I guess that's not helping.' Alice gestured towards Joanna's no longer strapped, but still bruised, wrist.

Joanna smiled. 'Actually, I don't think it's made any difference at all today.'

'What happened?' Now Alice was eyeing the stitched cut on her forehead. 'Boyfriend or accident?'

'Neither. I was mugged.'

'Around here?' The older woman looked startled.

'No. Don't worry,' Joanna reassured her. 'In New York City.'

'Now that's no big surprise.' Alice went on working, her hands sprinkled with brown age spots, but as deft as they were long-fingered. 'Do you get many muggings in London, Joanna? I'm leaving for Europe in a couple of weeks' time.'

'More than we'd like,' Joanna admitted. 'Though I live in Oxfordshire, not London.'

'Oxford must be quite a glory,' Alice said.

Joanna smiled, and felt a small prick of wistfulness. 'Yes,' she said. 'It is.'

It had, she thought, carefully removing every trace of debris from her hands before allowing herself to pick up the Hasselblad, to be rewarding to find that one could create something fine rather than (as she had done) turn one blob into another. But, she decided, as she began to watch the group and teacher through her lens, at least she knew how to laugh at herself, and it had certainly been relaxing.

'I hope you didn't find that too intrusive,' she said to Lamb, after she and Alice Munro had exchanged telephone numbers and the rest of the students had cleared up and gone.

'Not too much,' he replied, not unpleasantly. 'The space was available and, as Alice told you, your clay can be reused.' He smiled slightly. 'You're quite a good sport, aren't you, Joanna?'

'Thank you, Murdoch.'

'All this waiting around must be awfully tedious for you. I'm surprised you don't just give up and go home.'

That's more like it, she thought.

'I'm not big on giving up,' she said.

There was no sign of Donovan inside the school, and the door that she believed led to his personal studio was closed, but she did come across Pete Szabo hunched over in a workshop hardly bigger than a cupboard and not very much larger than himself, and was surprised to find that he, too, was a sculptor.

'That's wonderful, Pete,' she said in real admiration, looking at the small but remarkably lifelike pair of entwined figures coming to life beneath his big hands. 'I didn't know you were an artist, too.'

He shrugged modestly. 'Strictly amateur.' He was wearing a T-shirt and a pair of khaki shorts, apparently not feeling the cold.

'Really?' Joanna said. 'It looks fantastically good to me.'

'If you don't believe me, Jo,' Szabo said, 'ask Lamb.'

'I don't think I'll bother,' she said. 'He's just been almost nice to me. I think I'll quit while I'm ahead.' She paused. 'Is the room at the end on the left Donovan's studio?'

'Yes.'

It was apparent that Szabo did not want to continue with his work while she was there, and though Joanna had a strong urge to photograph him – she saw some sort of piece unfolding now, in which everyone who came near Gilead Farm seemed infected by creativity – she sensed that a request would not be welcomed.

She turned her thoughts back to Donovan.

'I know he doesn't like being disturbed,' she said, 'but I was wondering when he was going to take Sophia out for a walk.'

'No way of finding out,' Szabo told her. 'He locks himself in and he won't answer, not for anyone.'

'I didn't know he was quite this obsessive.'

'Dedicated,' Szabo amended.

Joanna knew a rebuke when she heard one.

24

'They got another missing person in the valley,' Special Agent Gary Poole said to Tom Oates as they ate coffee and jelly doughnuts at Svensen's Diner, about half a mile from the FBI area headquarters on the south side of Albany.

Poole and Oates had been colleagues for the past three years and good friends for almost that long. Oates had been scheduled to return to duty on December 1, but the surgeon who'd operated on him had declared that his leg was not healing as well as anticipated and that there was a possibility he might, therefore, need more surgery. The waiting was driving Oates nuts, and Poole was doing what little he could to ease his pal's tedium by keeping him informed about Bureau business.

'I heard,' Oates said. 'Guy from New Paltz.' He licked sugar off his fingertips. 'What's that make it? Four in the past year?'

'This one's a model.' Poole raised an eyebrow. Physically, he was the antithesis of his colleague, a solid bull of a man who loved to eat and drink too much and showed it, while Tom Oates could put away just as much food and still stay slim as a whippet. 'Name of Schuyler.'

'Luke Schuyler,' Oates magnified. 'Living and working out of Boston. Went missing a few days before Thanksgiving, never showed up for the holiday at his parents' place in New Paltz.'

'You sure you're off sick?' Poole queried.

'It was in the *Record*,' Oates said. 'I can still read.'

They ordered more doughnuts and went on talking about the latest disappearance. Schuyler's parents, they gathered, were getting fiercely frustrated with the local Sheriff's offices, and the Boston police department's refusal to take seriously their concerns about their son's safety. The problem, Oates and Poole were both aware, was that Luke was twenty-three years old and entitled to take off on a whim; besides which, the young man's work as a photographic model seemed to indicate to some people that Schuyler might be the kind of flaky character not to consider his parents' concerns.

'Which is bullshit, according to the parents,' Poole said. 'They say that Luke was always coming back and forth, that he'd been staying with them ten days or so before he went missing, that he never missed Thanksgiving or Christmas with them.'

'And if he is mixing with weirdos,' Oates considered, 'that might just have made him a perfect target for some sonofabitch.'

Officially, the case – if there even *was* a case – was not a federal matter, but with an apparent rash of unsolved disappearances spreading over the Hudson River Valley area, the FBI office up in Albany and smaller satellite offices were keeping appraised of the general situation. The first comparatively recent disappearance to arouse the wholehearted interest of the law (others had gone missing from the area in the past; men and women choosing to leave their lives and families without giving forwarding addresses were not all that uncommon, after all) had been that of a female aerobics teacher from Troy; the second, a sixty-year-old male farmer from a hamlet near Hurley in Ulster County; the third, another young woman, a dance student from Red Hook. And now there was Luke Schuyler, plucked out of thin air in Boston, Massachusetts, but, according to his parents and friends, still firmly rooted in New Paltz, New York.

People did go missing from time to time, the Schuyler family had presumably been told; husbands went out to buy cigarettes and never came back; mothers asked their sisters to mind the kids while they went to night school, and months later it turned out they'd been with their lovers or just gone off someplace else because they couldn't endure their lives any longer. And young people – especially young men with questionable lifestyles in big cities – went off without telling their mothers and fathers where they were going.

'Still, this almost has a pattern,' Tom Oates mused over his third cup of coffee. 'Three young people with super-fit beautiful bodies.'

Poole looked at his watch and got ready to go to work.

'Pity about the one old farmer to screw that up,' he said.

25

SUNDAY, DECEMBER 6

It was Sunday afternoon before Joanna saw Donovan again
while she was out for a stroll with her camera. She had, till
this moment, been feeling distinctly out of sorts, beginning to
grow impatient with her own company, but now she stopped,
fascinated, about two hundred yards away.

He was with Lamb and they were playing ball near the field
where the two goats were kept. Sophia was in harness but
lying down out of harm's way, observing, her head moving
back and forth as the ball spun through the air. Joanna knew
that it must have been tantalizing for the dog, but still she lay
patiently, biding her time, not even getting up at the sight of
her former mistress, just wagging her tail and remaining
where she had been told to remain.

The two men were tossing a tennis ball to and fro.
Sometimes Donovan caught one-handed, other times he used
both hands, but he caught every single ball thrown at him,
before tossing it back. Another prime example of Murdoch
Lambert's patience and meticulousness combining with
Donovan's hyper-developed senses; Lamb threw unerringly,
appearing to vary the angle and curve of each throw, and the
blind man, presumably hearing and feeling the flight through
the air of each successive approach, caught with uncanny
accuracy. It was, Joanna suspected, another of their party
tricks, but that knowledge detracted not at all from the impression it made.

She waited until it was over, until Lamb had collected the tennis ball, bade Donovan farewell and then turned, with a slight nod in Joanna's direction, back towards the school.

Right, she thought, and made her approach as Sophia was returning to the sculptor's side, tail wagging furiously.

'Hallo, strangers,' she called from twenty yards away.

'Hi there.' Donovan raised his left hand in greeting, allowing Sophia, though in harness, to give her customary exuberant welcome.

'I was watching the ball game.'

'I know.'

'You make quite a team.'

'It's good exercise for my senses,' he explained. 'We started out putting a bell in the tennis ball and went on from there.' He gripped the handle of the harness and began walking, and Joanna fell in beside him and the dog. 'Everything okay with you?'

'Fine,' she answered.

She had made up her mind, while watching and waiting, to launch straight into a fresh request for a photo session, but now that Lamb had gone and the ball play was over, she felt that Donovan had already re-immersed himself in that other, presumably creative, world in which she was not welcome.

'How are the bruises?' he asked after several moments of walking in silence. 'I hear they're still colourful.'

Lamb's report, Joanna assumed. 'They feel better than they look.'

'And the wrist?'

'Better, too.'

'That's good.'

The words were polite but he seemed absent. *Now or never*, she decided.

'Donovan, I hate to pressure you . . .'

'But you want to know when I'll be up for being photographed?'

They both paused to allow Sophia to urinate in the long grass, and a pair of magpies flew raucously overhead.

'I thought you might have forgotten.'

'Not at all.'

125

'It's just that time's passing,' Joanna went on, 'and the fact is I can't stay here forever – and I would prefer to go back to the magazines with something.'

He looked startled. 'You're not planning to go home yet, are you?'

'I'm starting to think I should.'

'You can't.'

'I'm not sure I could persuade the Consulate to issue an emergency document now that I've waited so long, but if I get in touch with—'

'You misunderstand me,' Donovan interrupted. 'I mean, you can't go just like that.'

Joanna bristled. 'Of course I can.'

He walked on silently for about three seconds, then stopped again. 'Please don't go.' His whole face was tight with tension. 'Please, Joanna.'

She was bewildered. 'Why not?'

'I don't want you to. Not yet.'

'But you're working.' She was still confused. 'You've hardly found time to say three words to me since Thanksgiving.' She paused. 'I'm not complaining. I know how much time you've already allocated to me – I know you must have been longing to get back to work. I just thought—'

'*No.*' He shook his head again, more vehemently this time. 'You don't understand.'

'You're right. Obviously I don't.' She looked down at Sophia. Not having been told to '*wait*' or '*stay*', the German shepherd was standing alertly, and the twitching of her ears told Joanna that she was not enjoying the sudden tension between them. 'Donovan, let's go on walking. For Sophia.'

'Sure.'

They went on a little way. The day had started out brightly but clouds were gathering, their slate-grey, solid appearance threatening snow.

'Let me try to explain something,' Donovan said after a while.

'By all means.'

'Generally, when I'm here at the farm, work is pretty much all

126

I do. There are three kinds of work: sometimes I teach – though not, as a rule, when I'm sculpting – sometimes I have to *make* myself sculpt, to keep myself functioning even when there's no inspiration.' He ran his left hand through his short hair as he walked. 'And then there's the real thing. The work that grabs you by the throat and the gut, the stuff that drags you in and drives you on and won't let you loose till you're through.'

Joanna waited for a moment. 'Is that what's happening now?'

'Yes, and no,' Donovan answered, and stopped walking again. 'You want the truth, Joanna?' He went right on. 'This should be one of those times – it's one of those pieces that I want to work on, that I *need* to work at until either I drop or I feel I've got it right. It should be the way it always is, more necessary to me than food or sleep or water.' He paused. 'But the truth is, it isn't that way, and I'm not exactly certain why, and it's driving me a little crazy.'

'So the ball game was partly to relax you?'

'I guess.'

'And the last thing you need is me and my camera.'

'I'm afraid that's true.'

They walked on a little way further and then, one more time, Donovan stopped and turned to face her. 'Could you stand to hang in just a while longer, do you think, Joanna?' He looked hopeful, younger than she'd ever seen him look. 'Please?'

It was hard to imagine turning him down when he looked like that.

Truth is I don't want *to turn him down.*

'Yes,' she said. 'Of course I can.'

'Thank you.' He paused. 'Tom Oates hasn't been around, has he?'

'Not that I've noticed. Were you expecting him to be?'

'Not necessarily,' he said. 'I guess he has some local guys keeping a watch on the farm.'

'Why do you ask? Have you been getting phone hang-ups here?'

'No. Nothing like that. All quiet. Just wondering.'

127

*

Joanna went to Chris Chen's office just before ten on Monday morning. 'Are you very busy?' she asked from the doorway. 'If you are, tell me, and I'll disappear.'

The other woman beckoned her inside. 'Come in, Joanna.' She rose from behind her paper-cluttered desk and walked across to where a glass filter coffee jug had a fresh brew slow-dripping into it. 'Have a cup with me?'

'I'd love it.' Joanna came in and sat down in the single visitor's chair. 'Another beautiful outfit,' she said, looking at Chen's soft turquoise knitted trouser suit. 'You have wonderful dress sense, Chris.'

'Thank you, Joanna.' She waited for the coffee to stop filtering through, then poured from the jug into two white china mugs. 'How do you take it?'

'Dark brown, no sugar, please.'

Chris brought the mugs over and set them on either side of her desk. 'You have natural dress sense too.' She sat down.

Joanna laughed. 'Natural's probably the right word. I just get up in the morning and pull on whatever's close to hand and comfortable.'

'But you've chosen great clothes to begin with,' Chen said. 'With that red hair and pale skin, it could be easy for someone with poor taste to choose badly.'

'Thank you.' Joanna sipped her coffee, which was good and strong.

'So what can I do for you?'

'Donovan's work.'

'What about it?'

'I've been hoping for an opportunity to photograph some of it, but I've seen so little. One remarkable piece – a man's arm in bronze. Mel Rosenthal had an artist's proof at her apartment and she let me take some pictures, but the negatives went with the rest.'

'I'm sure Mel would let you take some more.'

Joanna nodded. 'Still, I'm hoping to see others.'

'They're quite a rarity.' Chris elaborated. 'Donovan's bronzes are usually cast in editions of nine, with two artist's proofs. The proofs can be either the first or last piece cast, or sometimes both – some people prize the last because after that the mould is destroyed. More commercially minded sculptors will have editions of more than nine, of course – sometimes thirty or fifty, even a hundred or more. A Donovan these days could be sold for huge sums of money, hundreds, perhaps even thousands of times over, but in the serious art world, nine is the accepted edition.'

'I didn't know that,' Joanna said. 'Donovan's told me very little.'

'You've had other things to talk about.'

'I suppose so.' Joanna paused. 'Mel was going to show me another of his famous pieces at the Museum of Modern Art, but that room was closed for some sort of renovation so the only other sculptures I've seen are the ones here and at the apartment.'

'Mostly older pieces,' Chen said. 'Before he got famous. With so few on the market, they're almost all sold, except for any artist's proofs he keeps for himself, and, of course, his clay and plaster originals – and even I don't know where Donovan stores that private collection.' She put down her coffee cup. 'I can show you some photos of his works, if you'd like, mostly in catalogues – and I'm sure you could have copies of those, though that won't really be what you're after.'

'Not for the magazines, no,' Joanna said. 'But personally, of course I'd like to see them.'

For the next twenty minutes, she browsed through the collection of catalogues and loose photographs, many of them different angles of the same pieces. It wasn't like seeing the real thing, lacked the impact of the physical, three-dimensional work Mel had shown her, but it was still a good enough way for Joanna to comprehend the artist's amazing gifts.

'He was always terrific.' Chen explained, looking over Joanna's shoulder, the by now familiar scent of Mitsouko drifting from her, 'but this is the series that really turned him into such a giant.'

Like the arm she'd already seen, each sculpture was of a

129

different part of the human body, life-sized and exquisitely accurate. A hand . . . a fragile foot . . . a female leg, knee bent . . . another arm, this one with the feel of an athlete's, a tennis player's serving arm, perhaps, she thought, almost hearing the power thwack of a ball off a professional racquet . . . each bronze piece seeming to embody not just flesh, blood and bone, but also muscles and tendons and the lines and blemishes of living.

More than ever, she ached to see Donovan at work.

Since the weather was fine, she borrowed a Jeep that afternoon and drove across the river and north-west to Opus 40, the huge environmental sculpture Donovan had pointed out to her on one of their early excursions. She remembered him saying that Lamb thought Harvey Fite, its creator, had been a genius, and that Chris Chen hated the place because it gave her the creeps. Joanna walked around the monolith on the central pedestal and moved from one sweeping terrace to another, shooting sections from different angles, knowing that she would never be able to do justice to the whole because her photographs would be too fragmented, and thought that she could understand both their points-of-view. The sculpture itself took up six and a half acres, the grounds surrounding it covering more than eighty, wooded with maples, white pine, sumach and ash trees. The whole thing was vast, intriguing and striking, some of it undeniably beautiful, some of it too cold and somehow daunting, perhaps because of the season. But most of all, for as long as she wandered around Opus 40, Joanna felt awe at Fite's breadth of vision and tenacity, and that in turn led her back to thinking about Donovan and what he'd said about his own work grabbing him by the throat and refusing to release him till it was done.

She ate supper alone that evening in the guest house. Szabo had telephoned at around seven to ask if she wanted to come across for dinner, but Joanna thought she had heard a touch of relief in his tone when she declined, and she understood that well enough, thought what a bore it must be to have a guest

130

permanently needing to be considered.

At around eleven, she went for a stroll. She missed Sophia badly at times like these, became aware that in the course of her ordinary life she seldom went out without at least two dogs in tow – and that, at least, would be a joy worth going home for, she told herself now, as she wandered aimlessly towards the wild flower garden, looking up for stars and finding only clouds. The snow she had anticipated yesterday had not come, yet it was colder tonight, damper. Still, she found herself enjoying the earthy nighttime scents and countryside sounds, like the screech owl that had startled her on her second night at the farm – an old friend now, she thought, like the horses and the goats out in the fields. *Animals again*, she registered wryly as she left the garden on her way back, for she'd known the humans at Gilead Farm for the same length of time and could not begin, she realized, to regard them as friends.

Though there was only one person here she was interested in forming a real friendship with, wasn't there?

'Friendship?' she said out loud in the dark.

Who was she trying to kid?

She was walking along the path that ran parallel with the school building when she heard the new sound. A faint cracking, from somewhere behind her. She paused, then went on. It came again, duller, halting her. It was out of place, somehow, not the sound a nocturnal animal might make scurrying in bushes. More like a human tread.

Joanna turned around, peering into the darkness, and suddenly shadows that had moments before seemed familiar and unthreatening took on new shapes and meanings. A tree bending blackly in the light wind looked like a huge monk stooping his cowled head, arms limp and gnarled, hands clawed . . . waving grasses growing where the land rose in a small hillock seemed like the taunting, shimmying tendrils of some sleeping giant's head . . .

'Get a grip,' Joanna told herself, and turned away from the garden. That was the kind of self-tormenting shadow game young children played lying sleepless in their tiny beds, the kind that transformed teddy bears into monsters and gave them

131

nightmares. Look long enough at anything in the dark, she reminded herself as she walked more rapidly on towards the farmyard and guest house, and it could become alarming.

She heard another sound. Two sounds, actually, coupled together. That tread again, and breathing.

One more time she stopped.

'Who's there?' Her voice sounded tinny and scared.

No one answered, but the breathing continued.

Joanna ran, a good, solid, sprinting run, skidding briefly on a patch of damp, decaying leaves, but staying on track, the big house up ahead of her in the distance, lights on and welcoming, but the guest house, her own place, empty but with its own lockable front door closer at hand.

She reached it, fumbled for the handle, opened the door, stumbled over the threshold, slammed the door behind her and turned the key in the lock. She had left one of the table lamps switched on in the far corner, and now on impulse she moved to it swiftly, turned it off, then slipped back to the front window, crouching low so that she could look out without being seen.

There was nothing out there. Nothing human or animal. A branch in the middle of the yard stirred in the wind. A scrap of something smaller – a piece of paper perhaps, or just a leaf – lifted off the ground and dropped back.

Nothing else.

Joanna stood up straight, walked back across to the lamp, switched it on and looked around the room. Everything was as it had been, snug and pleasant and normal.

'What was *that* all about?' she asked herself.

She felt like a fool.

26

Alice Munro was trying her best, but failing miserably, to coax her sick old Mustang back to life at the side of the road. They were only a few miles from home, but it was dark and damned cold, and this was *not* the end she had envisaged to the pleasant afternoon she'd spent in Millbrook Village, browsing through antique shops for gifts for her English cousins.

'Not the end at all,' she muttered, kicking the front nearside wheel with her white sneaker and then swiftly administering an apologetic pat to the aged car's roof. 'But frankly, old friend, I do not need another big repair bill.'

It was ironic in a way. Off and on for the past several days, Alice had been plagued by the foolish, but uncomfortable, sensation that someone had been watching her. Being a woman of sound and practical mind, she had told herself each time it had happened to pull herself together and stop imagining things. Right now, though, just when she *needed* someone keeping an eye out for her, there was no one, and the drivers of the handful of cars that had passed her and the Mustang – hood up so that any fool could see they were in trouble – had all ignored her and driven right on by. So much for the old-fashioned, courteous values she liked to think people up here still possessed. She recalled her shock at hearing about the nice British photographer's mugging before she'd gone on to explain that it had happened in New York City, not around

133

here. If Joanna Guthrie had asked if anyone would stop for an old woman at the side of the road in these parts, Alice would have laughed and said, sure they would.

'Huh,' she said now. '*Huh.*'

She wasn't sure what to do for the best. She was in pretty good shape for a woman of seventy-six, but still she didn't relish the idea of walking home to Schultzville, not in this cold.

'Someone's bound to stop soon,' she told herself, stamping her feet and blowing on her gloveless hands. *Foolish old woman, leaving home without gloves in December*.

From somewhere around the next bend in the road she thought she heard an engine being started, and stood very still, listening and hoping. And then, sure enough, headlights were coming towards her and Alice stepped out into the road and raised her right arm.

The white panel truck drew closer and slowed right down. Alice tried to peer through the windows to see who was driving, but it was too dark, and anyway, the windows were the black, tinted kind that famous people had on their limousines – except that this *was* just an ordinary truck.

Frankly, Alice Munro was too damned cold to care if the driver of this particular vehicle was a rock star or a plumber or the President himself. All she cared about right now was that he or she was a nice enough person to give an old woman a ride home before she caught pneumonia and had to waste her ticket to England and those nice gifts for her cousins.

The truck came to a halt, and the door began to open.

A decent human being, at last.

Alice gave a sigh of relief.

27

Joanna had been talking to Pete Szabo in the kitchen of the main house that afternoon, asking if there was anything she could do to be of use, when first Lamb had telephoned from the school to ask Szabo to come across and help him with a project, and then, just moments later, Chris Chen had hurried in asking him to drive to Kingston to pick up some urgently needed art and stationery supplies.

'I can go, if Murdoch needs you, Pete,' Joanna had volunteered.

'No way, Jo.'

'Why not? I'm available and it's too late for me to take photographs.'

'But your back's still sore,' he argued. 'and your wrist. You shouldn't be carrying supplies.'

'I'm feeling much better.'

'I don't know,' Szabo said. 'I don't think Donovan will like it.'

'Donovan won't know.' Chris rolled her eyes heavenwards. 'Honestly, Pete, you're such an old fussbudget. We're not asking Joanna to stack crates. If she wants to help, let her.'

She took Chen's Volvo Estate into Kingston, picked up each item on the administrator's meticulously worded list, had the young man at the stationery store help her with one heavy cardboard box of sundries, and then, errands completed, enjoyed an early supper at a pleasant family-run diner.

Pleasure ground to a halt suddenly and almost violently a mile and a half from home, just inside Gilead Farm's south perimeter boundary, when one of the Volvo's rear tyres punctured, and Joanna only just managed to keep the car on the track.

'Blast,' she said, waiting for her heart to stop pounding.

She opened the glove compartment, found a torch, got out of the car and walked around to find the tyre beyond hope. Getting the key from the ignition, she opened the back, in search of the spare, then glanced around.

'Of all the places,' she said, softly. This had to happen on the darkest, loneliest stretch of road on the whole journey.

Joanna had changed a few tyres in the past, but this time she got not much further than lifting the jack and spare out of the back of the vehicle before pain wrenched through both her back and wrist and she knew there was no possible way she was going to get the job done without really damaging herself.

The walk back might not have been so unsettling if it had not been so unremittingly dark, or if the road had not been so hemmed in by tall spruces and white pines, every single one of them creaking and rustling in the rising winter wind. Or if Joanna had not been so spooked just two nights earlier after her walk in the wildflower garden.

As it was, by the time she got back to Gilead Farm on this occasion, Joanna was exhausted, in pain, jumping out of her skin at every flap of a wing, and once again – almost worst of all – feeling like a prize idiot.

'*I told you so*,' she waited for Szabo to tell her, just as she waited for Chris to demand to know if her Volvo was intact. But neither of them did any such thing. They were both as upset for her as any old friends might have been; sensitive, gentle, not fussing overly but taking care of her nevertheless.

'What about the car?' Joanna asked Chris after she had insisted on helping her back to the guest house and making sure she had everything she needed. 'I should take you to it.'

'No, you shouldn't,' she said firmly. 'It's just a car. Pete can get to it in the morning and change the tyre. You said it's not in the middle of the track, right?'

'Right.' Joanna was relieved not to have to go out again.

'So it's posing no danger to anyone else.'

'I did lock it,' Joanna said.

'You told us, and I already told you, it's just a *car*.' Chris smiled. 'I'll bet you were scared out there, all alone on that dark road?'

'I was,' Joanna admitted. 'Which isn't like me – it isn't as if I'm not *used* to walking on country roads at night.' She paused. 'I think it was just . . . coming so soon after the other thing.'

'The mugging still shaking you up?' Chen was sympathetic.

Joanna shook her head. 'It was something else – nothing, really. Probably just my imagination getting the better of me.' She saw the other woman's exotic eyes, watchful and waiting. 'I went for a stroll in the wild flower garden late on Monday evening, and I heard something . . .'

'What kind of something?'

Joanna shrugged. 'Nothing worth talking about. As I said, I'm almost sure I was imagining things, but I did think, for just a few minutes, that someone was following me.'

She slept late next morning and was only just making her first pot of coffee of the day when Szabo and Chen came to her door.

'So what's wrong?' she asked after they'd all sat down with a cup.

The two visitors exchanged glances.

'Pete didn't want to worry you,' Chris began, 'but after what you told me happened on Monday night, I thought you ought to know.'

'Know what?'

'It's no big deal, Jo,' Szabo said, easily, 'but I noticed when I was changing over the tyres early this morning that the one that blew had a cut in it.'

'Slashed,' Chen said.

Joanna was startled. 'It seemed okay when I left Kingston. Wouldn't I have noticed?'

137

'Not necessarily.' Szabo looked at Chen. 'It only looked so bad because it was driven so far with a cut in it. Real slashing would have flattened the tyre right off.' He looked back at Joanna. 'We told the local police about it. They agree with me that it's probably just kids. They said there've been a heap of tyres let down in the area lately.' He paused. 'What exactly happened the other night, Jo? Chris said you thought you were imagining things.'

'I think I must have been,' Joanna said.

'But you are *sure*?' Chris asked. 'Because if you're not, we should tell the police or Agent Oates about it. After all, we know your mugger got the address of the farm.'

'I'm sure what happened the other night had nothing to do with him,' Joanna insisted. 'I really do think it was just my imagination.'

'Or is that your British stiff upper lip talking?' Chen asked gently.

'Not at all.' Joanna was firm. 'I admit I was spooked – perhaps the mugging did leave me more jittery than usual. But that's all it was.'

'Certain?' asked Szabo.

'Definitely.'

Joanna saw Donovan that afternoon: just one of those brief glimpses of him emerging from the school with Sophia, out of harness, both heading towards the house. Joanna was close to the window when she first noticed them and came right up to the glass as they passed, hoping for an opportunity for a word. But though Sophia saw her, wagging her tail and skittering a little, Donovan made no sign of being aware that Joanna was there, and she was left with a feeling of renewed disappointment and confusion as he walked on.

Thirty or so minutes later, Lamb came to call.

'I feel I should be clutching a bouquet,' he said as he came into the sitting room. 'As it is, I bring only sympathy for your ordeal.'

'I'm fine, Murdoch,' Joanna said briskly, closing the door. 'Getting more embarrassed by the hour, but otherwise

138

absolutely fine.' She paused. 'Won't you sit down? Can I get you something to drink?'

'I can't stay.' He regarded her. 'I had dire reports of you staggering back to Gilead Farm barely coherent or able to stand.' He seemed amused. 'I'm happy to see they were grossly exaggerated.'

'Apparently.'

'Even so,' he went on, 'your visit to the United States does seem to have been unduly peppered with bad experiences, doesn't it?'

'I wouldn't say that.'

'That's very brave of you.' He paused. 'As I said, I just came to offer my sympathy for more unpleasantness.'

'Thank you.' She felt suddenly ungracious. 'Truly, Murdoch, it's kind of you to take the time. I know how busy you and Donovan are.'

'Donovan's certainly working up a storm,' he agreed. 'I'm merely trundling along in his wake.'

'But you are collaborating, aren't you?' Joanna asked.

Lamb's eyes cooled. 'Merely as his assistant, nothing more.' He began to turn away, then paused. 'On the subject of Donovan, I wonder if I could ask you to do me a great favour, Joanna?'

'If I can,' she said.

'Don't mention the tyre incident when you speak to him.'

'I haven't spoken to him since Sunday.'

'I only ask,' Lamb continued, 'because he's at a critical stage of work, and any disturbance could be detrimental.'

'Of course,' she said, evenly.

'Thank you.'

He turned towards the door, then halted again and turned back. 'You will tell me if there's anything I can do for you, won't you? If you've had enough bad luck, for instance, and want to get back home, I'll be glad to help with your arrangements.'

It was her turn to be amused. 'More kindness, Murdoch,' she said wryly.

'Just being hospitable.' He opened the door.

139

'I have no plans to leave yet,' Joanna told him, 'but I'm sure I'll be able to manage when I do.'

'I'm sure you will.' Lamb went out into the darkening afternoon. 'But if you change your mind, the offer's still there.'

28

She was in bed when she heard the sound, shortly before midnight.

Scrabbling.

She lay still, listening, wondering if it was an animal outside, hoping she wasn't starting to let nerviness become a habit.

Jumpy Jo.

She heard it again, only this time it wasn't so much a scrabbling sound, more of a bumping. *Not animal.*

She tensed up, trying to gauge whether it was coming from outside or inside the house. For five or so more seconds there was nothing. Then it came again.

She reached for the bedside lamp and flicked the switch.

Nothing. No light.

'Shit,' she said, very softly, into the dark.

She took another moment to debate her options, trying not to panic. She could stay put, do her best to ignore the sounds, but that might just make her a sitting duck, and the only objects in the house that she thought might double as defence weapons were all downstairs. She could try the other lights in the house, hope that the failure of the bedside lamp was just a dead bulb and that a houseful of glaring electric light might scare off the intruder – but on the other hand, she wasn't sure she *wanted* to scare him off. What she wanted was for him to be caught and for this nonsense to stop.

'Down you go,' she murmured, and wished that Sophia were with her.

Silent on bare feet, holding firmly to the banister rail as she crept downstairs, she played with her next batch of multiple-choice questions: get to a phone and alert Donovan or Szabo – but she didn't know the number by heart and didn't want to switch on the light or waste time looking it up; get to a window and start screaming – but that would produce the same result as setting the house ablaze with light; or deal with the situation herself.

Great, she thought, gritting her teeth as she chose the last.

She stopped at the foot of the staircase, listening again. No breathing sounds. No sense that anyone was in the house with her. That had happened to her once in Merlin Cottage when she'd come home and surprised a burglar – she had known the instant she'd come through the door that he was in there.

At least that meant that this intruder was outside.

She considered, one more time, simply letting him stay there while she ran back up to bed and pulled the covers over her head. And then she moved silently to the fireplace, plucked a poker out of the brass pot beside it, trying not to rattle the other fire irons, and padded towards the front door, wondering if anyone in the main house would even *hear* her if she had to scream.

All this thinking about screaming, she thought as she raised her left hand to unlock the door, gripping the poker in her right. *I'm not even sure if I know how to scream – I don't think I've ever screamed in my whole life*.

She opened the door, stepped out two feet, and saw him – a large moving shape to her left.

She raised her right arm, then swung the poker down, catching the man hard on the shoulder. He gave a deep yelp of pain and shock as he fell, then grabbed at Joanna's left ankle, making her drop the poker and bringing her down with him – and she did scream then as she went, the high-pitched noise only dying in her throat as she hit the ground and her own pain took over, momentarily, from fear.

142

'Holy *fuck*!' the man said, still gripping her ankle.

Joanna waited to feel worse, for him to punch her or knife her or . . .

Her brain went numb for a second. She didn't want to know.

'Joanna?'

She hadn't even registered till then that she'd screwed her eyes tight shut.

The man let go of her ankle.

Joanna opened her eyes, saw his shape looming again as he sat up – and then moonlight struck his face.

'Agent Oates?' Her voice was hoarse.

'Uh-huh.' He held out a hand. 'You okay?'

She nodded, though truth to tell she didn't know, couldn't seem to run that kind of physical checklist yet, was too relieved – too mortified – to do anything much more than stare at him.

'Are you?' she asked.

Tom Oates felt his left shoulder with his right hand and grimaced. 'Nothing busted. No thanks to you.' He shook his head, getting up. 'I just got rid of that damned crutch, and now you're trying to break my arm.'

'I'm sorry.' Joanna began sitting up, let him help her to her feet. The pain in her back growled at her and her wrist complained. 'What on earth were you *doing* out here? I thought you were the mugger.'

'That's a relief,' Oates said. 'I'd hate to think you knew it was me.' He watched her face, noted her discomfort. 'Don't you think we might be more comfortable inside?'

She nodded, took a couple of shaky steps towards the doorway, then stopped and turned to face him. 'You haven't answered my question. What were you doing out here?'

In the moonlight, Tom Oates's face seemed younger and even finer than when Joanna had first seen him in Manhattan.

'I've been watching you.' His voice was low.

Joanna felt her stomach clench. 'What do you mean?'

'Pete Szabo called me yesterday, thought he should bring me up to date on what had been going on. I figured I should take a look around the farm—'

'And keep an eye on me.'

'You're angry,' Oates said.

'Yes.' Joanna realized it was true – she was exceedingly angry.

'You knew Donovan had asked me to keep a check on things.'

'I'm not a *thing*,' she said. 'If you'd knocked on the door or telephoned to let me know what you were doing, then I wouldn't have been given the fright of my life and almost killed you with a poker.'

'You only hit my shoulder.'

'I wasn't aiming for your shoulder.'

'Great,' Oates said.

Joanna felt her back twinge again and became aware for the first time that she was shivering, which was hardly surprising given that she was standing outside in a December night-chill wearing a man's shirt and nothing else.

'Would you like to come inside?' she asked, still crisply.

'It might be an idea,' he answered. 'Unless you want pneumonia to add to your problems.'

She went inside ahead of him, turned the light switch experimentally, and saw the overhead lamp come on. 'That's a relief.'

Oates came in, limping slightly, and closed the door. 'What is?'

'When I heard you outside, I switched on my bedside lamp and it wouldn't come on.' Joanna shrugged. 'Must have been the bulb.'

'Want me to take a look?'

'I know how to change a lightbulb.'

'I'm sure you do,' Oates said easily, 'but just in case.'

'There's really no need. The sounds I heard were you, which makes the lamp coincidental.'

'You're the boss,' he said.

Joanna watched him for a moment, saw him flex his shoulder and wince a little, and felt a pang of guilt.

'How about some tea?' she offered.

144

'I could use something.'

'Something stronger?'

He smiled at her. 'Tea would be fine.'

Joanna started towards the galley kitchen, then stopped, abruptly aware again of how little she was wearing. 'Do you mind waiting while I pull on a sweater, Agent Oates?'

'Tom,' he said. 'No, I don't mind waiting.'

She went up the staircase with an odd self-consciousness, a feeling that the FBI man was looking at her bare legs as she went, though when she glanced down from the top, he was over by the window, looking out.

The light switch for the small landing was to her right. She flicked it and it did its job. Growing calmer by the second, she went into the bedroom, doing the same with the overhead lamp in there. Amazing the way light seemed able to do that, to dispel creeping fear or unease.

Donovan has to live in the dark all the time.

It wasn't the first time Joanna had registered that, yet now, as she went to the chest of drawers and wardrobe and pulled out a pair of jeans and a sweater, the bleakness of the thought seemed to strike home even more forcibly. Donovan compensated, she knew that, had his remarkable coping mechanisms and his talent to help him through, just as Sara Hallett would have her courage and her storytelling to help her bear her total blindness when it came.

I don't know if I could bear it, she thought, zipping up the jeans and dragging the sweater over her head. Staring into blackness day and night, dependent upon the kindness of strangers, struggling for self-reliance.

The bedside lamp caught her eye, and she walked across the room, intending to check it out.

Her right hand moved towards the switch. And stopped.

It had not been a question of a dead bulb.

There was no bulb.

'No, I didn't switch it on before I went to sleep, but yes, it was most definitely working yesterday evening,' Joanna told Tom Oates downstairs as she waited for the kettle to boil.

'So you've no way of knowing if the bulb was there or not when you went to bed this evening?'

'No,' she said, trying to stay patient, putting tea bags into mugs, 'because I knew I was tired enough to go straight to sleep when I went to bed, so I turned off the overhead light and never looked at the bedside lamp.'

'Good,' Oates said.

Joanna turned to look at him, realization dawning. 'Even I'm not paranoid enough to be worrying that someone crept into the bedroom and unscrewed the lightbulb while I was asleep.' She turned back to pour the boiling water into the mugs. 'Tom, the only other person to come into this house tonight has been you.'

'Okay,' he said, gently. 'I just didn't want you getting scared again.'

She picked up the mugs and carried them over to the coffee table. 'I'm not scared now, just a little puzzled that someone's been in my bedroom during the course of the last twenty-four hours, unscrewed a perfectly healthy lightbulb and not replaced it.'

'Maybe it wasn't healthy,' Oates suggested reasonably as he sat in one of the armchairs. 'Does anyone come in here to clean up?'

'Not that I know of.' Joanna sat on the sofa. 'If there was a problem, Pete Szabo would be the one to come over and fix it.'

'Why don't we ask him if he was here today?'

'It's the middle of the night,' Joanna pointed out. 'And it's only a lightbulb – hardly worth waking everyone up for.'

'Everyone?' Oates queried.

'Pete or Donovan.'

'I'm kind of surprised we haven't already woken them.' Oates grinned as he sipped his tea. 'Your scream was pretty loud.'

Joanna made no comment, though the thought had certainly passed through her mind too. She'd wondered before unlocking the front door if anyone would hear her if she had to scream, and she most certainly *had* screamed, and no one

146

from the main house had come running. Which meant, presumably, that no one had heard. Which was a little strange, considering Donovan's extra keen sense of hearing. Surely, if he had heard, he would have come over?

'Sophia didn't bark,' she said.

'Is she a good guard dog?' Oates asked.

'She's a German shepherd,' Joanna said. 'And she's still enough my dog to bark if she heard me screaming.'

'Maybe she and Donovan aren't home?' the agent suggested.

'He's been working all hours,' Joanna said, 'but I'd have thought they'd have heard from the school house, wouldn't you?'

'Lights weren't on in there when I passed earlier.'

'Donovan doesn't have much use for lights,' Joanna reminded him.

Oates left a while after that. Joanna had allowed him to roam around, checking all windows and the lock on the front door, and before he departed he went so far as to suggest that he get someone in to dust the bedroom and lamp for prints.

Joanna laughed at the notion. 'For a lightbulb?'

'A missing lightbulb that contributed to scaring you half to death.'

'Don't let's exaggerate, Tom.'

'Okay,' he said, 'but you did say you'd had the fright of your life which was why you tried to kill me with a poker.' He paused to look her over. 'Is your back okay now, by the way?'

Joanna flexed it a little. It was sore, but she didn't think any more harm had been done by her tumble. 'I'll live.'

'I guess I brought you down pretty hard.'

'Yes, you did.'

'You did hit me pretty hard, first.'

They both smiled, and then Oates wished her a good few hours' sleep, told her to lock up behind him, and was on his way. Joanna remembered then that he'd said he'd been having a look around the farm, and she hadn't got around to asking him if he'd found any cause for concern.

147

She supposed he had not, or else he would not, presumably, have left her alone now. If, of course, he *had* left her alone. Maybe he was still out there, still keeping an eye on the guest house. She'd been angry when she'd first discovered that he had been watching her, but that was only because she hadn't been consulted.

Now, as she turned out the downstairs lights and went back up to bed, she found – if she was honest – that the notion was surprisingly comforting.

Oates, Donovan and Sophia showed up the next morning soon after ten. Joanna greeted both men, let them in, then spent several moments caressing the dog who, judging by her yelps of joy, was as happy at the reunion as her former mistress.

'I've missed you so *much*,' Joanna said softly into one of the big pointed velvety ears, and Sophia whined with pleasure and nudged her arm with her nose, demanding more. 'But where were you when I needed you?'

'We were in my studio.' Donovan, six feet away, heard what she'd said.

Joanna looked up at him from her crouched position and said nothing.

'Sound-proofed,' Oates said, reading her thoughts.

'I had it insulated a few years back,' Donovan explained, 'when I found that all the hubbub the students made was disrupting my work. I sometimes have music playing while I sculpt, and I guess I miss being able to open the windows and hear the birds, but I can't stand other people's noise, so I've had to compromise.'

'Wouldn't it have been easier to build yourself a studio someplace else on the farm?' Oates asked him. 'An acre or two away from the school, maybe?'

'In some ways,' Donovan answered, 'but I like being on the premises.' He looked in Joanna's direction. 'The school has a certain atmosphere. Haven't you felt it, Joanna?'

'There is an energy in the building,' she admitted.

'But that's why we didn't hear you scream last night.' Donovan shook his head. 'Lamb made me put in an alarm

148

system in case of fire, but other than that, I guess I'm really cut off when I'm working.'

'That's why Sophia didn't bark either,' Oates said.

'What did you think, Joanna?' Donovan asked her quietly. 'That we heard you and didn't come?'

Joanna stood up, and Sophia trotted back to Donovan's side.

'I didn't think anything much at the time,' she said. 'I was too busy trying to get my breath back after Special Agent Oates's rugby tackle.'

Donovan smiled. 'I heard about the poker. Nice job.'

'You could have warned me,' Oates told him. 'I didn't know that Englishwomen shoot first and ask questions later.'

They talked for a while over some coffee. Oates had brought Donovan up to date on the tyre incident and Joanna's sense of being watched on Monday evening, and the sculptor's concern was evident as he asked her about both episodes. Still mindful of what Murdoch Lambert had said to her about Donovan's work being at a critical stage, Joanna made light of both things.

'Besides, with Tom keeping such a close eye on me,' she told him, 'I don't have much to worry about.'

Donovan turned his head towards Oates. 'You still think there's any reason to keep an eye on Joanna? If the tyre was just local kids . . .'

'Probably not,' Oates answered easily, 'but it wouldn't hurt.'

Joanna caught something behind his tone. 'Why not? If we all agree there's no connection to the mugging, and that I've probably been imagining things—'

'I never said you were imagining anything.' Oates paused. 'You heard noises outside last night.'

'I heard you.'

Oates seemed about to speak, then stopped.

'What?' Joanna prodded.

'I didn't make any noise.'

'You did. I heard you.'

'No,' Oates said. 'Whatever you heard, it wasn't me.' He gave a small smile. 'Maybe it's my Native American roots,

149

but one of the things they like about me at the Bureau is that I'm a real silent tracker. If I'd made those sounds you heard, Joanna, I'd admit it.'

'And you don't think I imagined them?' She was almost hopeful.

'Let's say I don't have you down as the hysterical type.'

'What exactly are you saying, Tom?' Donovan had been silent through their exchange, but now there was real tension in him. 'That someone else was skulking around this place in the middle of the night?'

Lying near his feet, Sophia grew restless.

'I'm saying I'd rather not rule out the possibility,' Oates answered.

'Did you find any evidence? Any tracks?'

'No.' The agent paused and looked at Joanna. 'I talked to Pete Szabo. He says he didn't touch your bedside lamp yesterday. He says he hasn't been inside this place for a couple of days, and then you were here with him.'

Joanna didn't speak for a moment. The connotations of what Oates was saying were disturbing, to say the least, yet in spite of that, what they were dealing with seemed so slender, so *trivial*; a couple of noises outside at night and a missing lightbulb.

'It's hardly a federal case, is it?' she said, at last, and managed a smile. 'Isn't that the right term?'

'It's probably nothing at all,' Oates agreed.

'I don't like it,' Donovan said. 'Not putting it all together.' He paused. 'Maybe I should quit working for a while. Sophia and I could come back to the city and—'

'No.' Joanna's tone was firm. 'You have to keep working.'

'I don't have to do anything,' he said sharply.

Sophia sat up, gave a small whine.

'What about my photographs?' Joanna reminded him.

'To hell with the photographs,' Donovan said. 'If there's some guy hanging around, I want to get you off the farm.'

'Not without my photographs,' Joanna said stubbornly. 'I've waited over two weeks, and I'm not going home without them.'

150

'We can go to my studio now.' Donovan stood up, and Sophia followed suit. 'You bring the camera, we can shoot a few rolls, and then we can go to the city.'

'That won't do,' Joanna said.

Tom Oates sat, quiet and amused, watching them both.

'Why won't it do?' Donovan asked.

'Because I need to shoot you while you're working, and if we go there now, you won't really *be* working, you'll just be pretending to, and the pictures won't be any good.'

'Who are you all of a sudden, Annie Leibovitz?'

'No,' Joanna answered steadily, 'but that doesn't mean I don't take a pride in my work. Besides, if the photos aren't any good, the magazines won't pay me.'

Donovan sat down again and Sophia flopped back on to the floor, resigned. 'So what do you want to do, Joanna?'

'I want you to go back to work, get right into it again, as you were. And then, as soon as you can bear to have me in there with you, let me know.' She smiled. 'After that, I'll pack my bags, go back to Manhattan, get my passport, do the rest of my Christmas shopping and go home.'

'And till then,' Oates said, 'can you cope with having me around?' He smiled. 'Not all the time, just now and again.'

'Don't you have better things to do?' she asked him.

'Not till I'm told what the doc wants to do about my damned leg.'

'Why don't they have you on desk duty?' Donovan asked.

'Not good for the knees, so I'm told.' Oates looked from one to the other. 'So, people, do we have a deal?'

Joanna wondered, after Oates had left and Donovan and Sophia had gone back to the studio, if she had imagined the flicker of jealousy passing across Donovan's face towards the end of that conversation. She also wondered about her own response. It was not in her nature to accept protection from anyone. The kind of aid that she could somehow reciprocate – the sort that Kit gave her at Merlin Cottage, or the favours that she and Fred Morton did for one another – were fine. But agreeing to let a man, a virtual stranger, keep watch over her for what still seemed to be no substantial reason, was not the type of thing Joanna could normally tolerate.

Donovan hadn't liked the idea, either.

You're losing it, Joanna.

Perhaps she was. Perhaps too much idleness and the strangeness of Gilead Farm were affecting her. Neither Donovan nor Oates had given the slightest indication that they were attracted to her. On the contrary, one man had been spending the past two weeks locked up away from her, and the other – younger than her, probably by several years, and of such fine looks that he probably had gorgeous young women queuing up for his attentions – was simply bored by enforced time off, and helping out a friend.

It was as well, she decided, that she'd pushed Donovan towards a conclusion. A couple more days for him to work alone, then an hour or two with her and her camera in his inner sanctum, and she would leave, just as she'd said.

29

SUNDAY, DECEMBER 13

Oates was getting ready to leave his house up near Kinderhook to go and meet Gary Poole for brunch at Svensen's and a round-up of last week's Bureau news, official and social, when his telephone rang.

'I need a raincheck, Tom. We just got word of a big one.' Poole's voice lowered a notch. 'Some kind of burial pit down in a forest near Bearsville.'

Oates felt the flesh on the back of his neck creep. 'Pit? How many?'

'Don't know that yet. Three, maybe four. State Police are on the job – word is their own mothers wouldn't know them.'

For a moment both men were silent, aware that if these remains were ultimately traced to local residents, the sense of tragedy, shock and loss would reverberate for many miles around.

'So is the consensus that the remains might be linked to our missing persons?' Oates wanted to know.

'We're waiting on the M.E.'

'But if it is, we might be going in.'

'*We* might be,' Poole replied. 'You won't.'

'Gee, Gary,' Oates aid, 'thanks for reminding me.'

30

On Sunday afternoon, Joanna had been writing to Fred Morton and trying, but failing for the third time that week, to reach Alice Munro (her neighbour at Murdoch Lambert's sculpture class ten days before) on the telephone, when Tom Oates had called to invite her to dinner.

'Fact is, I'm being left out of a big investigation because of my leg, and I could use some cheering up.'

Joanna had been surprised but pleased, glad of the chance to get to know a little more about the young FBI man.

Besides, what else did you have to do tonight? she asked herself wryly as she got changed for the evening. *Find someone else to write another letter to while you hang around for Donovan?*

Even in the crowded dining room at the Beekman Arms that evening, Joanna could see that Oates, in a dark suit and tie, was the absolute winner in the good-looks stakes. Over prime rib and baked potatoes, she asked about the Native American heritage he'd briefly alluded to on Saturday morning.

'Only one-quarter,' he told her. 'On my mother's side. According to my grandmother, we're descended from a Californian tribe rooted someplace north of San Francisco.'

'Is that where your family still lives?' Joanna asked.

'My mom and dad and my brother and two sisters – I'm the youngest – all live around Los Angeles. My brother's a

154

computer analyst, one sister's a nurse and the other has four children.' He paused. 'My grandmother died two years ago. She was the fount of all knowledge on the subject of our Indian heritage.' He grinned. 'I used to love hearing her stories.'

'She sounds great.' Joanna took a sip of wine. 'No one else in the FBI?'

Oates shook his head. 'Dad was an engineer – he had to take early retirement because of back trouble. My mother teaches part-time. I grew up on a diet of crime fiction and movies, had a yen from way back to join the police – then my grandmother told me that Native Americans needed more representation in the FBI, and after that joining the Bureau became my goal.'

The conversation switched to Joanna's life and background, and she found herself touched by his genuine interest as she told him about Philip and Merlin Cottage and her friends at home.

'You miss your husband a lot, don't you?' he remarked gently.

'Not the way I used to, but I still think of him every day.' She contemplated that for a moment. 'It's a little different now that I'm away from Merlin Cottage. At home, I tend to feel Philip in every room, because that's where we lived together. Since I've been here, I've still thought about him, of course – about the things he would have liked doing if he were with me – but he's less of a presence.' She paused. 'I suppose that's just time.'

'It's like that for me too,' Oates said quietly.

Joanna looked at him, surprised. 'You lost someone close?'

'My girlfriend, Lisa.' The dark eyes grew softer. 'We only lived together for three years, but it felt like losing a limb, a physical part of myself.'

'She died?'

'She had an ectopic pregnancy – we didn't know until it was too late. We'd talked about children, figured we'd get married a year or two down the road, then try for a family.' He

155

smiled. 'Lisa wanted at least three kids. She was a kindergarten teacher.'

'I'm so sorry,' Joanna said.

Oates nodded. 'Like they say, shit happens.'

They were quiet for a time, eating apple pie.

'So what's the investigation you're missing out on?' Joanna asked, finally.

'Not much I can tell you.' He leaned forward, lowered his voice. 'Except we've had a spate of missing persons in the valley this past year.'

'I think I heard about one of them.' Joanna frowned, remembering. 'A young dancer? From around Red Hook, I think.'

'Where did you hear about her?'

'Donovan and I were in an ice cream parlour, and a couple were talking about her.' She paused. 'Is she still missing?'

Oates nodded. 'Along with three, maybe four, other people.'

'All from around here?'

'Most recent was a guy from New Paltz – but, yes, all from the valley.'

Joanna remembered going there during her first week at the farm.

'I don't suppose you've heard anything around Gilead Farm or the school that might relate?' Oates asked. 'Any students upped and vanished without explanation, anything of that kind?'

Alice Munro came fleetingly into Joanna's mind. But not answering the telephone a few times hardly constituted a disappearance – and anyway, Alice had mentioned a trip to Europe, so maybe she'd muddled the dates and Mrs Munro had already gone.

'Joanna?' Oates prompted her.

She shook her head. 'No one I know of. Presumably you've asked Donovan or Chris Chen?'

'Oh, sure,' Oates said easily, then leaned back again. 'Coffee?'

'Please.'

156

She watched him order, declined his offer of brandy, and then he turned their conversation to the lighter subject of the differences between Christmas traditions in New York and Oxfordshire. Joanna answered his questions, allowed him to lead her away from the implicit darkness of what he'd been talking about minutes before; yet all the while, she had a sense of unfinished business on his part, of his having embarked upon something – she wasn't certain what exactly – but then having thought better of it and veering away again.

She was not certain why, but that both intrigued and disturbed her.

31

The knock at the door came while Joanna was still clearing the fog from her brain with her first caffeine hit of the day. She checked that the belt of her bathrobe was decently fastened, and opened up to find Chris Chen on the doorstep.

'How do you *do* that?' Joanna asked impulsively.

'Do what?'

'Look so good this early in the morning?' Joanna smiled. 'I'm sorry, Chris. Please come in.' She stepped back, and the other woman, petite in yet another close-fitting powder blue wool dress seemingly dusted with her by-now familiar Mitsouko, stepped smoothly past her into the room.

'It's not so early,' she said. 'I was out more than an hour ago. I thought you might come and join me.' Energy seemed almost to spark off her.

'For *t'ai chi*?' Joanna was rueful. 'I'm afraid I'm getting lazy.'

'Late night with Agent Oates?' It was Chen's turn to smile.

'Not many secrets at Gilead Farm, are there?' Joanna went to retrieve her cup from the kitchen counter. 'Can I pour you some coffee?'

'I can't stay, Joanna. I just came to deliver a message from Donovan. He says that if you're ready to take your photographs, he's happy for you to join him.'

'Really?' Joanna was startled. 'When?'

'Today. If you can spare the time.'

158

Joanna found no irony in the other woman's face. 'I'll just grab a shower and get dressed, and then I'll be across.'

'I'll tell him.' Chen moved back towards the door, then paused. 'I guess this means you'll be leaving us in a day or two?'

Joanna smiled again. 'I think you'll all be glad to see the back of me.'

'Not at all,' Chen said.

Once Sophia's greeting was over and she had returned to her place – an ample wood-carved bed against one wall (handmade, Donovan told her, by Lamb) lined with what looked like a pure cashmere rug – Joanna set down her equipment case and portable umbrella reflector.

'Feel free to look around,' Donovan told her.

'I can't believe I'm finally here.'

It was, for the most part, as she had imagined it: stark, uncluttered and workmanlike. She remembered a visit she had paid with an old boyfriend many years ago to the studio of a sculptor friend of his, recalled that his space had been crowded with pieces of work and the tools of his trade. That kind of atmospheric jumble was, of course, out of the question for Donovan, to whom order was of such vital importance. One side of this good-sized rectangular room was shelf-lined, each length of wood neatly stacked with the tools and ingredients of the sculptor's trade, with spaces between each item to make it easier for him to identify, swiftly and accurately, what he needed at any time. There was a large wooden table, its surface bare but for a set of old-fashioned scales and an unlabelled bag of something that looked to Joanna as if it might be a kind of powder, and there were two workbenches, one with a wood surface, the other marble, both with height-adjustable metal legs and movable parts.

Something stood on the surface of the wooden workbench, covered with a snowy white cloth and standing about eleven or twelve inches high.

'Is that the new work?' She experienced a kick of excitement.

159

'Yes,' he answered simply.

She went on looking around, noting the sound-proofed window that Donovan had told her about; the glass looked thick and tinted, the kind one could see out of, but not *into*. From where she stood, Joanna could see a copse of bare-branched beech trees, a pathway on the far side, a good patch of sky – blue today, crisp winter azure with scarcely a cloud. While she watched, a magpie flew to join its mate on one of the trees and she saw its beak open and close, heard in her mind, but *only* her mind, its raucous cry, and found it disturbing to realize that Jack Donovan had elected, while in this place, to render himself deaf as well as blind.

'Is the silence getting to you?' he asked, startling her.

'A little.' That, too, was disturbing at times, she thought – his ability to read her thoughts.

'Lamb says it's like working in a bank vault.' Donovan smiled. 'Or in a coffin, I remember he said one time, in one of his darker moods.' He inclined his head towards the dog, who lay in her bed, watching them both. 'It's not so silent now that Sophia's here, of course. I hear her breathing, turning around, getting restless every now and then.'

'She certainly looks relaxed.'

'Is she resting her head on the edge of the bed?'

'Yes.'

'Lamb rubbed the edges very smooth, knowing she'd have to spend so many hours in it.'

'That was very kind.' Joanna noticed a Bang & Olufsen unit on one of the higher shelves, glanced around and located two slim speakers. 'And you have music when you need it.'

'Let's have some now,' Donovan said. He walked across to the wall of shelves, reached up to a rack of compact discs, felt their Braille labels, extracted one and inserted it into the CD player above his head, and in less than a second a Chopin prelude flowed sweetly into the room and wrapped around them. 'Better?'

'It's your studio.'

'I'm fine.'

Joanna looked down at her case, then glanced around,

trying to gauge where best to set up her lighting, super-conscious of the need to be as unobtrusive as possible.

'It's okay, Joanna,' Donovan said. 'This isn't going to be a performance for the sake of your camera. The work started to come together a while ago, so once I get back to it, you'll have the real thing. If I hadn't thought I was ready, I wouldn't have asked you to come.' He moved towards the wood-topped workbench, pulled out a stool, stained and clay-splattered. 'I figure the Chopin should help act as a buffer between my work and yours, just in case your clicking disturbs me.'

'Now I really feel like an intruder,' Joanna said.

'You're no intruder.' Donovan sat down on the stool. 'There's another of these tucked in against the wall where the shelves end,' he said, 'but I expect you'll want to move around while you work.' He paused. 'Joanna, you're my invited guest and my very valued friend.'

'Thank you,' she said.

'Don't thank me. After what you've done for me, I think I'd let you photograph me day and night for a week if you really wanted to.' He grinned. 'Though I imagine an hour or so will be more than enough.'

'I imagine it will,' she said.

She asked him to wait while she set up her minimal equipment, organized her lighting, checked her meters and took a few test shots, explaining that she was keen to record the instant when he uncovered his work-in-progress.

'After that, I'd like you to try and forget I'm here.'

'Easier said than done,' he said.

Joanna paused in the midst of checking a lens for specks, conscious of dust flying around the studio.

'I'm not referring to your work,' Donovan said, gently.

Joanna felt the heat on her cheeks, and went on checking.

So fascinated was she that when he did remove the white cloth from the stand on his workbench, Joanna almost forgot to photograph the moment. The sculpture was of a foot: a

161

remarkable female foot, a dancer's, she decided, standing on half-toe.

'That's perfect,' she said, though she'd vowed to be silent.

'It's nowhere near that,' Donovan told her.

He set to work, and from then on her own task became a kind of dance for her as she switched between the sculpture itself, Donovan's constantly moving hands, his face, rapt in concentration, and the rest of his body, shifting, angling, hunching, leaning back. He kept his eyes closed while he worked, giving him the appearance of a man moving through some kind of intense dream, and though he sat, all the while, on his stool, the act of sculpting seemed to flow through his entire body. Joanna moved quietly around him, taking picture after picture, the tall, broad-shouldered man in his clay, plaster and paint-stained navy blue guernsey and jeans, short hair greyer than usual from the light coating of dust which clung, too, to the faint fair stubble on his jaw and to the scar on the right side of his face.

She shot in monochrome, predominantly in close-ups, working swiftly but more smoothly than usual despite her eagerness, with no real sense yet of how long it would be before either she or Donovan had had enough. For a time, she switched her focus to Sophia – switching to a wider angle lens to incorporate both man and dog – sharply aware that this was, in a sense, the first time she had been able to judge how remarkably the German shepherd had taken to her new life and partnership. Out and about on the farm, in the house and further afield, she was, as Joanna had expected her to be, a contented companion and admirable guide, but here, in this place of work, in her new master's most crucial environment, Sophia seemed more at peace than Joanna had ever seen her. She lay almost motionless, yet not sleeping, simply waiting patiently, watching Donovan, almost seeming to be absorbing the ever-increasing other-worldliness of the atmosphere in the studio.

'Amazing, isn't she?'

It was the first time Donovan had spoken since they'd begun.

162

'She's watching you the whole time,' Joanna told him softly.

'Uh-huh,' he said, and went on working.

She changed the lenses again and returned her attention to the new sculpture itself. To her untrained eyes, it had seemed almost perfectly formed when he'd pulled off the cloth, yet Donovan's fingers had been far from satisfied and now, even as she watched and clicked the shutter repeatedly, slowly moving around the artist in a semi-circle, she saw veins and tendons and even calluses coming into being, saw tiny bones appearing through clay flesh; and not since taking her first intimate photographs of Philip could she remember feeling so stirred, both physically and emotionally, by any subject.

The Chopin came to an end, but neither Donovan nor Joanna missed it. Even without the music, the starkness had disappeared, melted into the ether, and now there was a kind of magic in the air.

'How're you doing?' he asked suddenly, his voice low in the silence.

'I'm doing wonderfully,' she said, and snapped his profile, capturing, she hoped, the intriguing blend of weariness and elation now emanating from him.

He leaned back, away from the sculpture, stretched both arms up over his head in a great V, and then stood up. 'Favour?'

Joanna stopped shooting. 'Of course.'

'Take a break and sit for a moment.'

'I'm okay.' She felt too energized to stop.

'I know,' he said. 'But I want to see your face.' He sensed her hesitation. 'I'm being selfish. I want to see the effect of my work on you, if you don't mind.'

'I don't.'

He moved aside so that she could sit on his stool, and then, as he had that time in early November and again after the mugging, Donovan moved closer and touched her face with both his hands. For a moment, Joanna tensed, then relaxed again, letting him know – *wanting* him to know – how she felt.

163

She wanted him to touch her. More than anything.

'Oh, my,' he said, after a moment, his fingers on her temples.

He took his hands away.

She wanted to cry out.

He didn't move away from her.

'Joanna?' His voice was very soft.

'Yes?' Hers was even softer.

'Favour number two.'

'If I can.'

'Touch me?'

She felt her stomach clench, felt another stirring, old and almost forgotten. She wondered, for the briefest moment, if she might have misunderstood him. *Maybe his shoulders ache; maybe he needs someone – anyone – to rub them.* But she knew that wasn't it at all.

'Joanna?' There was urgency in his voice, in his face.

She put up her right hand unsteadily, touched his left cheek and closed her eyes. His skin felt smooth, warm. She moved her palm down a little way, felt the tracing of where his shaven beard began. She opened her eyes, saw that now his were shut again.

The yearning in his face stunned her.

'Jack?' She said his name uncertainly. Like everyone else around him, she had, till this instant, called him nothing but Donovan.

'Don't stop.' His voice was so quiet it was scarcely audible.

She put up her left hand and closed her eyes again, wanting suddenly to know – as if she *could* know – what this was like for him. She ran her fingers over his temples, felt the scar, traced its length, became acutely aware, as she neared the corner of his mouth that with just a tiny sideways move she could reach his lips.

She took both hands away.

'Don't stop,' he said again. 'Not now.'

There was a kind of buzz inside her head, spreading like liquid heat down through her body and limbs. It had begun with the shoot itself, and physicality had become an essential

164

part of that, giving her strength and energy – but what was happening to her now was very different.

Not a good idea, Joanna.

She raised her right hand again, let it hover close to, but not touching, the lower half of his face. The urge to brush over his lips was intense . . .

You know what'll happen if you do that.

She did it anyway.

Donovan opened his eyes, and they were beautiful eyes, Joanna thought, not dull at all, almost like a clear winter sky deprived of sunlight, and if she hadn't known better she would have thought they were gazing right into her mind.

She started to move her hand away, but he gave the smallest of moans and grasped for it, caught her wrist, pulled the hand back to his mouth and pressed his lips to its palm, and now it was *her* turn to moan, for it felt almost as if he'd scorched her skin, and the heat already percolating inside her was simmering again, travelling lethally downwards. She tried telling herself to pull away, but it was too half-hearted to be any kind of command, and anyway she didn't have the slightest *wish* to pull away.

And Donovan knew it.

His arms found her, pulled her to him, drew the camera and its leather strap up over her neck, set it down carefully on the marble-topped workbench and held her again. And Joanna knew now where the heat had come from. It had come from *him* – his skin, his flesh, felt hot to the touch. Their mouths met and they kissed, gently for a second or two, but the voltage was too overpowering for either of them to settle for that, and the kissing became deeper, hotter, hungrier, until mouths and tongues were no longer enough either. She felt his hands on her waist, felt him pulling up her sweater, felt him shudder as he touched her bare back, and she was already gasping. She had never known anything like this, not with Philip, not with anyone in her whole life, until now, *now*, and she didn't say a word – neither of them spoke, there was nothing to say, nothing that could add to what they were feeling. Donovan unhooked her

165

brassière, and Joanna didn't stop him, had no more thoughts in her about wisdom or folly, and her own hands were tugging at his navy blue guernsey, and oh, God, the skin on his body was hot, too, like a man burning up with fever. And then she felt his hands on her breasts, and she cried out, just a mindless cry of pleasure-pain, and she heard Sophia stirring in her bed, but she didn't turn away to look at her. All she saw, all she wanted to see, was Donovan's face, every muscle taut with wanting, with *needing*. And then he was pulling at her jeans, and she was unbuckling his belt, and it occurred to her for just an instant that perhaps they should leave the studio, go to the guest house – but there was no time, no question of stopping now for either of them.

'Oh, Christ,' he said. 'Oh, dear Christ, Joanna, are you sure?'

'That I want you?' Her laugh sounded harsh with desire.

They were both naked now, holding on to each other as if survival depended upon their not letting go. Joanna was torn between pressing her body as close to him as she wanted it to be, and drawing back a little way so that she could see him.

'There's no bed,' Donovan said, abruptly, huskily. 'Don't you mind?'

'Just don't stop,' she answered.

Even as she said the words, a warning voice was nudging at her, urging her to step back, grab her clothes from the floor, get out before things could get out of hand.

They're already out of hand.

And she did not want to step back.

And then it was too late.

Afterwards, at first, it was almost exactly as Joanna might have hoped it would be – had she allowed herself to think about it at all. They lay together, entangled, sweaty, scarcely able to breathe, on the cashmere rug they'd stolen in the midst of the wildness from Sophia's bed, and Donovan held her close enough for her to feel his heartbeat, and she was gripped

166

by an urge to weep and laugh simultaneously.

'I know,' he told her softly. 'Oh, I know.'

'I can't believe it,' Joanna said, a few moments after that, as reality began to permeate. 'On the *floor*.' She laughed, a small, embarrassed laugh, already in need of reassurance and disliking herself for it. 'So Bohemian.'

'I'm an artist,' Donovan said, simply. 'I did consider the table, but I thought you might have found that sordid.'

First doubt assaulted her, like a worm wriggling between them. He had taken time, even if just a second or two, to calculate, whilst she had been scarcely capable of coherent thought. *Fool*, she told herself now, for at least he had been considering her finer feelings . . .

Sophia stood up, stretched, got out of her blanketless bed and wandered across to sniff at them with her cold, wet nose, whining a little, and they both laughed and caressed her for a moment. And then, suddenly, almost abruptly, Donovan pulled away to sit up, and Joanna was left lying on the floor, feeling horribly, painfully exposed and abandoned.

'Sophie needs to go out,' he said, by way of explanation.

'We'd better get dressed then,' Joanna said, thinking they would all go together.

Donovan stood up. 'Will you want to go on working when I get back?'

Joanna watched him locate the white cloth and cover his sculpture, and felt so thrown that she could hardly speak.

'Let's see how things go,' she said quietly.

'Sure,' he said.

They both pulled on their clothes quickly after that, and Donovan made a point of coming to her and kissing her, swiftly and gently, on her mouth, but the sense of shock and loss stayed with her. And the instant he left the studio with the dog, she folded down her umbrella reflector and packed the rest of her things into her equipment case, and told herself that so far as her magazine commissions went, she had more than enough material to work with.

And then she, too, left the studio.

*

167

However unsettling Donovan's abrupt departure had been, it did not occur to Joanna – at least not for the first few hours of that long afternoon – that he would neither call on her nor pick up the telephone to speak to her before the day was out. His work – that remarkable piece of sculpture – would, she realized, come first – *had* to come before most things, she could actually understand that now. But then again, what had gone on between them this morning surely didn't come under the heading of '*most things*'.

Not to me, anyhow, she thought, making yet another pot of coffee as the final scraps of light went out of the day.

The situation was patently absurd, she decided, taking a cup back to the sofa and turning on the TV. She had decided against borrowing a car and driving to Kingston to have the morning's films processed in case Donovan thought *she* had taken their lovemaking too casually. She'd even chosen not to take a simple walk all afternoon in case they bumped into each other and he thought she was engineering an encounter.

You're behaving like some absurd ingénue, she rebuked herself. But then again, she reflected wryly, sipping coffee and staring unseeing at Channel 13, she could hardly be said to be exactly experienced when it came to sexual matters. A few dabblings before meeting Philip, then years of marriage and fidelity, then virtually nothing at all. Till now.

Till she had made love on the floor of a sculptor's studio.

She remembered how she'd felt in the immediate aftershock. Even now she still didn't know whether to laugh or cry.

'Laugh,' she decided, out loud.

Anything else would be a complete waste of time.

At 8.45 that evening, she telephoned the house and left a message with Szabo asking Donovan to phone or call on her some time before midnight because she had something pressing to tell him.

The knock on the door came at 11.35.

He stood in the doorway, Sophia at his side.

'Come in,' Joanna said.

168

'We're on our way to the wild flower garden,' he said. 'Needs must.'

'All right,' she said.

'Pete said it was urgent. Are you okay?'

A slap in the face could not have brought Joanna to her senses more swiftly. Defence mechanisms aroused, her voice emerged steady and cool. 'I just wanted you to know what I've decided.'

'About what?' Beside him, Sophia whined, and Donovan reached down to fondle her ears.

'You don't need me any more,' Joanna said. 'Sophia could not be more settled if she'd been born here.'

He straightened and stood quite still. 'I guess that's true enough.'

'So, as I said on Saturday,' Joanna went on, still superficially calm, 'I think it's time for me to make plans for going back home.'

'If you must,' he said.

She looked up into his face, attempted to read his inner reaction to what she had just told him, but if he felt anything at all, it was unfathomable. *No going back.* She took a quick breath. 'I'll go to the city on Wednesday morning. I'll take the train.'

'No need for—'

'I'm quite fond of trains.' She felt her heart-rate speeding up – the conversation was becoming intolerable. *One more chance to make this more bearable – or at least more civilized.* 'If you're available for lunch or dinner tomorrow, I'd like to repay some of your hospitality.'

'I don't know.' A pair of frown lines deepened between his eyebrows.

'No problem,' she said coldly.

'Joanna—'

'It's perfectly all right.' She was crisp. 'I do understand about your work. It is very remarkable.'

'You don't understand at all,' he said frustratedly.

'You'd better take Sophia to the garden.'

She closed the door, leaned against it, waiting, listening.

169

Only when she heard him walking away, did she allow herself the freedom of tears. And even then, remembering the acuteness of his hearing, she wept very softly.

32

The Duke, having disposed of the superfluous remains of Alice Munro, had kept all that was needed.

The old woman's right hand.

Now, in the safety of the dark basement of the silent house in the quiet side road near the Glasco Turnpike, he examined it. It was an excellent specimen, all the more interesting for the changes that age had wrought: skin wrinkled and brown-spotted, joints a little swollen, but the fingers long and fine, probably still nimble and capable to the end. The Duke had learned to appreciate the complex structure of hands: eight wrist bones, five metacarpals, five phalanges – tendons surrounded by synovial sheaths, short muscles; two arteries, easily drained . . .

Alice Munro had been an active, quite handsome woman for her years.

But her hand was all the Duke needed.

33

The telephone roused her early.

'Joanna, it's Tom Oates. How're you doing?'

'I'm doing well, thank you. How's the leg?'

'Getting there.' He paused. 'Could you have dinner with me again?'

Her eyes were barely open. She had a headache, and her spine hurt.

That's what making love on the floor does for you three weeks after a mugger shoves you in the back.

Come to think of it, she wasn't entirely sure this morning which had wounded her more – the mugging or yesterday's events.

'Joanna? Are you okay?'

'Fine.' She paused. 'I'm going to be leaving tomorrow, Tom, so tonight won't really be possible. I have packing to do and—'

'Lunch then.'

'I'm not sure.'

'I would like to see you before you go.'

He sounded earnest. Joanna pictured him, remembered his warmth, the niceness of him. Perhaps, given her bruised emotions, an hour or two with Tom Oates might be exactly what she needed.

'Are you up to a bit of a drive? Only I'm hoping to meet up with a colleague for a while this morning, get an update on

172

some things, so I might not make it down to the farm. And I'd really like to show you my place, give you lunch here, if you don't mind.' He paused again. 'You might want to bring your camera – I live about a mile outside Kinderhook, which is a pretty neat place.'

He lived in a tiny old stone house about a mile outside the village. The whole ground floor area measured no more than thirty feet, with a slightly sloping stone floor and a low, timbered ceiling. It might easily have been claustrophobic, but Joanna found it charming. It was also plain from the careful way he'd laid his small dining table and from the good aromas emanating from the pans on his stove, that Oates had gone to a lot of trouble over their lunch.

'I'd have been happy with a sandwich,' she told him.

'I was taught hospitality by my grandmother.' He took her coat and hung it on a hook near his front door. 'A lady drives forty miles to visit me, there's no way I'm going to offer her a sandwich. Anyhow, it's only chilli.'

'It smells good.' Joanna paused. 'What I could use after the drive is the bathroom.'

'Up the stairs. Watch out for the uneven treads – the place is pretty old.' Oates said. 'Lunch should be ready by the time you get back down.'

She realized that she had opened the wrong door and was about to shut it again when something inside the room caught her eye: a grotesque mask, attached to the wall beside some kind of costume.

'Found my weirdo collection?'

Oates's voice behind her made Joanna jump.

'Sorry.' He put out a hand and touched her arm, then removed it again. 'That was what Lisa used to call it. Come take a look.'

He stepped past her into the small room and Joanna followed, gazing around in fascination. Every inch of wall space was occupied by one of the most unusual accumulations of photographs, prints and other artefacts she had ever seen.

'Native American?'

'Only partly. Have you heard of shamans?'

'Heard of them, yes,' Joanna said, 'but that's about all.'

He showed her around – limping hardly at all today – and explained that the collection related to shamanism in general, many of his photographs and prints depicting Siberian, Turkish, Manchurian and Eskimo shamans in costume, some decorated with human ribs, arms and finger bones, others with snakes, frogs and other creatures. Oates had begun collecting the items, he said, some years after his grandmother had first told him family legend had it that one of their ancestors had been picked as a shaman – a young man said to have magic powers.

'Fundamentally,' he explained back downstairs over their bowls of chilli, 'shamans were ecstatic figures believed to have powers to heal the sick and communicate with the world beyond. They would assist with births, marriages and deaths—'

'Like priests,' Joanna said.

'I guess, except that some shamans were good guys, which meant they did business with good deities, but others dealt with evil spirits.' Oates served Joanna with brown rice and put some on his own plate.

'You said that one of your ancestors was chosen. Do you know why?'

'Hard to say exactly. This is all legend, remember, but selection was certainly very bizarre.' Oates's eyes gleamed even more darkly as he warmed to his subject. 'They liked picking guys with some kind of physical or mental flaw, but the big question was whether or not the "*chosen*" had extra bones in their bodies. According to legend, they would put the young men—'

'Was youth part of the package then?' Joanna asked.

'I guess so. Often they were just pubescent, and had to be tortured into agreeing.' Oates ate a forkful of chilli and drank some water. 'Anyhow, the story was they would put these poor guys into extended trances or sleep.'

'Drugs?' Joanna queried.

'Almost certainly,' Oates agreed. 'Many Californian

174

Indians back then were heavily into narcotics.' He dabbed his mouth with his napkin and went on. 'So while the shaman candidate was sleeping, the spirits were asked to "cut up" his body and count his bones to see if he had one extra.' He grimaced. 'Problem was when it came to our personal family shaman – according to Grandma – someone must have had a little too much Jimson weed or whatever it was they were using, because they cut up the poor kid for real. Which meant, I guess, that no one ever got to find out if he would have become a good or bad shaman.' Oates grinned. 'End of story.'

Joanna laughed. 'I can't say I'm sorry.'

'It was a little gruesome, I guess.' Oates cleared away the dishes and brought out an apple pie that had been warming in the stove. 'So do you really have to go home?' he asked, setting it down with two plates. 'It seems so sudden.'

'Not really,' Joanna said casually. 'My work's finished. It's time.' She watched as Oates cut a steaming slice of pie and laid it on her dish. 'Though I'll probably be in the city for a few days at least.'

'The passport,' he remembered. 'And shopping.'

She nodded. 'Pre-Christmas Manhattan does sound tempting.'

'Will you stay at Donovan's apartment?' Oates gave himself some pie and spooned thick cream on to Joanna's.

'I don't think so.'

'Do you have a reservation anyplace? The city's likely to be jammed.'

'I'll find somewhere,' she said, quietly. 'I don't need much.'

'Are you okay, Joanna?'

'Of course,' she answered.

'Only you don't seem yourself.' Oates looked at her intently. 'Has something else happened?'

'Else?' Joanna felt her cheeks colour slightly.

'Any more incidents? Stalkers, slashed tyres, whatever?'

'No,' she said, relieved. 'Nothing like that.'

'So why the rapid exit?' he persisted.

'I told you,' she said, evenly. 'My work's done. It's time.'

*

The watcher, parked far enough away along the road to remain unnoticed, saw them through his binoculars as they left the small stone house and drove, in tandem, into Kinderhook. He kept his distance as Oates showed Joanna around and then, on parting, gave her a card.

'We'll speak before you leave the country, won't we?' he said as they stood beside the borrowed Cherokee.

'Of course we will.'

'I've written down all my contact numbers,' he told her, 'including my colleague's – his name's Gary Poole – in case you have a problem locating me.'

'You've been so kind to me.'

'You're a lovely person.' Oates grinned. 'And I've always been a sucker for a redhead.'

Joanna smiled at him and thought, not for the first time, that if she were an artist, she'd want to paint or sculpt his head. 'May I take your photograph, Tom?'

'I'd be flattered.' He hesitated again. 'And if I take one of you, would it be too much trouble for you to mail it to me?'

They took their pictures, and then Joanna got into the Cherokee. 'Any news on those missing local people?' she asked him.

His eyes grew perceptibly blacker. 'Nothing good.'

'How awful,' she said. 'For their families.'

Oates nodded. 'I'm really going to miss you, Joanna,' he said, softly, and closed the door.

She adjusted the seat belt and started the engine.

'It's been a real pleasure knowing you, Tom. I hope we meet again.'

Oates stepped back on to the kerb.

'I have a feeling we will,' he said.

Joanna was back at Gilead Farm by four o'clock, where she spent the next two hours packing, cleaning the guest house and calling hotel reservation services. Oates had been right about the city being jammed at this time of year – it seemed every-

176

one else had the same idea about Christmas shopping in Manhattan.

Just before six, she walked across to the school. As she had hoped, Chris Chen was still at her desk.

'I was wondering,' Joanna began, 'if you might have a list of New York city hotels and phone numbers. I'm heading back down in the morning, and I'm afraid I didn't realize how difficult it was going to be to find a room this time of year.'

'No problem.' Chen closed down the document on her computer screen and leaned back in her chair. She looked tired this evening, with faint shadows beneath her lovely eyes.

'Are you feeling all right?' Joanna asked.

Chen took a tissue from a box on her desk and wiped her nose. 'Just getting another cold, I think.'

'Would you rather I came back for the list later?'

'No need. I already booked you into the New York Hilton.' Chen paused, seeing the question mark in Joanna's expression. 'The Peninsula's full, but I have a contact at the Hilton. I hope that's okay for you?'

'Of course.' Joanna shook her head. 'I'm just startled by your efficiency. I only told Donovan late last night that I was leaving.'

'And he told me first thing this morning.' Chen dabbed at her nose once more, then tossed the tissue into the basket at her side.

Another small hurt twisted inside Joanna. She hadn't realized he'd been that eager to have her gone.

'It wasn't Donovan who asked me to make the reservation for you, Joanna. It was Murdoch's idea.'

Joanna blinked. 'Really?'

'He seemed to think you'd be happier in a hotel than back on Fifty-sixth Street. "More secure" were his words, as I recall.' Chen shrugged. 'I can never be sure when I'm going to see Donovan next, so I figured better safe than sorry.'

'Murdoch was right, anyway,' Joanna said, getting back her equilibrium. 'I'm grateful to you both.'

Chen fingered the computer mouse on her desk. 'So will we get a chance to meet again, Joanna? Or is this it?'

'I'm planning on taking a morning train, so this probably is it.'

The other woman stood up and shook hands. 'It seems quite sudden,' she said, 'but I guess with Donovan working all the time . . .'

'As I told Tom Oates earlier,' Joanna said, with a touch of briskness, 'I've done all I can so far as Sophia's concerned, and I've taken the photographs I needed for my commissions, so there's no reason to stay.'

'And it hasn't all been happy, has it?' Chen said, gently.

Joanna smiled. 'Most of it has.' She turned to go, and then, at the office door, she paused. 'Is Murdoch around, do you know? I'd have liked the chance to say goodbye.'

'I think he's working with Donovan this afternoon,' Chen answered. 'Though it's hard to be sure.' She paused. 'Hard to be sure of anything on Gilead Farm, as you've come to learn.'

Joanna did not see Lamb that evening, but calling in on Pete Szabo, she found him adamant that he was going to drive her down to the city next morning.

'Nothing to do with Donovan asking me to,' the big man told her, seeing she was about to argue with him. 'We've become friends, haven't we?'

'I hope so,' she said. 'But I still don't see any need to put you out when I'm perfectly happy to take the train.'

'Please, Jo.' Szabo sounded almost humble. 'Let me do this one last thing for you. Think of it as doing me a favour, if you prefer.'

Joanna shook her head but smiled, beaten. 'If you put it that way.'

Szabo beamed. 'I do.'

They arranged to leave at nine a.m. Shortly after eight, growing ever angrier with Donovan but determined not to be deprived of taking her leave of Sophia, Joanna walked over to the school, found the front door open, marched straight on down to the sculptor's studio and knocked on the door.

There was no answer. She knocked harder. Still nothing.

178

Finding herself suddenly close to tears of frustration, Joanna turned around to leave and saw Lamb standing a few feet away in the corridor, dressed in a black parka, the hood covering his hair.

'It's snowing,' he told her. 'Quite hard. It's as well you're getting on the road early.' He paused. 'Our leader not answering?'

'I'm not sure if he's in there. I wanted to say goodbye.'

'He's in there all right,' Lamb said. 'But he's been more or less incommunicado since Monday night.' He came a little closer. 'Don't be too upset, Joanna. It's Donovan's way, I'm afraid.'

She felt her jaw clench. 'It's all right,' she said. 'Though I am a little upset not to see Sophia.' She managed a shrug. 'Perhaps it's best.'

'Perhaps it is,' Lamb said, quite kindly. 'I'm never quite sure about farewells myself.' He paused. 'How long do you plan to stay in the city?'

'I'm not sure. A few days.'

'And then sweet home.' He smiled. 'I must say, Merlin Cottage sounds a most attractive place. I'm sorry not to have seen it.'

'Perhaps you will someday,' Joanna said.

'Who can say?'

At 8.45, Szabo showed up to collect her bags and stow them into the back of the Cherokee.

'Are you sure you want to drive in this weather?' Joanna asked.

'This is nothing.'

'If you want to leave now, I'm ready.' *The sooner the better*, she thought. The quicker she escaped Gilead Farm, the sooner she could use some city energy to start shifting the painful wedge of bitterness inside her.

'I'll be a little while yet, Jo,' he said. 'Okay with you?'

'It's up to you, Pete.' She paused, looking out at the heavy sky. 'I just don't want to have to worry about you driving back later on dangerous roads.'

179

'You don't have to worry about me.'

'If you say so.'

He took the bags and closed the door behind him, and Joanna was left to kick her heels disconsolately. What she wanted to do – what she might have done had Donovan deigned to answer the door earlier – was to give him a piece of her mind. Even forgetting the fact that they had become lovers less than two days earlier, his failure to speak to her after all these weeks – after all the things he'd said to her about gratitude for Sophia . . .

'Not that I need his gratitude,' she said out loud, gazing out of the window at the fine gauze of snow now falling.

But it would have been nice.

He arrived with one minute to spare, at 8.59. Sophia was beside him, and he was carrying a large brown paper-wrapped package. He looked wretched, tired, standing on the step outside the door, coatless, snow falling and frosting his hair.

'This is for you, Joanna.' He handed her the package. 'It's the reason I'm so late.' He paused. 'Also the reason I didn't answer your knocking earlier.'

'I see.' She took the package. It was heavy.

'You're angry.'

'Disappointed.' She didn't want to invite him in, but the dog was another matter. 'You'd better come in. I want to say goodbye to Sophia.'

They came inside, leaving the door open. The snow on Donovan's eyebrows melted and trickled down his face, but he made no attempt to wipe the moisture away. Joanna put the package on the coffee table and knelt down. Sophia, sensing tension, came and leaned against her legs, and the animal's warmth and weight almost undid her.

'Chris told me about the hotel reservation,' Donovan said. 'I've asked her to cancel your room.' He went on before she could speak. 'I know it's cavalier of me, but I really want you to have the apartment for as long as you need it. Manhattan's a big hassle this time of year, Joanna, believe me. This way,

180

you'll have Jerry Feenan and the guys to get you cabs and take in packages for you.'

'I was planning on paying for the hotel myself, Jack.' She sounded icy. 'Please ask Chris to phone back and rescue the room.'

'I'll ask her,' Donovan said, 'but I'm afraid they're likely to be booked out.'

Joanna felt a fresh wave of anger at being manipulated. 'If that's the case, I'll leave for home just as soon as I get my new passport from the embassy.'

Silence reigned.

'Sorry doesn't really cover the last couple of days, does it, Joanna?' Donovan said, at last.

Joanna hugged Sophia closer. 'I suppose it'll have to.'

He felt her sadness, knew it had far more, right now, to do with the dog than with him. 'I'll step outside and wait,' he said, 'leave you two to have a few moments.'

'Thank you,' Joanna said. 'We shan't be long.'

She looked up, saw such pain in his face that she almost relented. *No point, Guthrie.*

'Can you manage, Jack?'

'Of course I can manage,' he said quietly.

He went out and shut the door behind him. Joanna let go of Sophia and sat down heavily on the floor. The dog sat, too, watching her with her liquid amber eyes.

'I'm not going to cry.' Joanna spoke softly. 'If I start, I probably won't be able to stop, and that won't help either of us, will it?' Sophia gave a low whine. 'You're going to be very happy here, you good, beautiful girl. And I know I don't have to tell you to take good care of him.' The dog got up, came closer. 'And you know that Bella and the others will look after me.'

She allowed herself one more long moment, pressed her face against the animal's coat, fiercely swallowing down the threatening tears. And then she stood up again. 'You're the best dog I've ever known, Sophia,' she said.

She opened the door. Sophia went out ahead of her, directly to Donovan, waiting by the Cherokee, while Joanna put on her parka, took a last look around, then picked up her shoulder bag and the brown paper package.

'Ready now,' she said, stepping outside.

They were all assembled, she suddenly noticed: the whole Gilead Farm coterie standing in a line in the snow – '*Donovan's Praetorian Guard*', as Mel and Sandra had referred to them. Szabo, wearing a tomato-coloured ski jacket and black knitted hat, came forward right away, took the package from her, put it into the back of the Cherokee with her bags. Then Chen, neat and slender even in her own turquoise parka and already looking back to her usual vital form, stepped out of the line and held out her arms to Joanna.

'I'm going to miss having you around,' she said, hugging her swiftly. 'And I won't be the only one.'

'I'll miss you too, Chris,' Joanna said, quite moved.

Chen stepped back, and it was Lamb's turn.

'May I kiss your cheek, Joanna?'

'Of course, Murdoch.'

He leaned closer. The kiss, Joanna registered, felt a little like being brushed by an icicle. 'Poor you,' he murmured against her ear, 'getting your farewell after all.' He drew back. '*Bon voyage*,' he said in his normal tone.

She smiled at him, and as if they were soldiers falling out after a parade Lamb and Chen moved away and Szabo got into the Cherokee and started the engine, leaving only Donovan and Sophia.

'You'll catch pneumonia,' Joanna said, quietly, 'if you stand about any longer without a coat.'

A vein in Donovan's temple, close to the scar, throbbed. His face was pale with cold. 'Will you forgive me, Joanna? I need you to forgive me.'

'There's nothing much to forgive,' she said, quietly.

'If I come to the city in a day or two, perhaps we could talk about it?'

'Nothing to talk about, Jack.'

'Will you let me come anyway?'

She let her eyes linger over the white, tired face. 'I can't really stop you, can I?' she said, her own voice weary.

182

He put out his right hand and brushed it briefly against her hair, and she noticed that his fingers were trembling slightly. 'I'll take care of Sophia.' His voice was hardly above a whisper. 'I won't let you down in that, at least.'

'I know you won't,' Joanna said and went quickly around to the open passenger door of the Jeep. 'Go inside, Jack.'

'You be careful in the city,' he said.

Joanna got in and slammed the door.

'Can we go now, please?' she said to Szabo.

'Sure.'

They began to move forward.

She did not look back.

Szabo was so extra-gentle with her on the early part of their journey that Joanna wondered if Donovan might have spoken to him about what had gone on between them.

'It won't be the same without you around,' he said, about an hour into the ride. 'We're all going to miss you.' He paused. 'Even Lamb.'

'I doubt that,' Joanna said. 'He's been angling for me to leave for a while.'

Szabo shrugged. 'He respects you a lot, Jo.' He paused again. 'If he isn't exactly sorry you're going, it's only because he feels he has to protect Donovan – Lamb gets wary of anyone he thinks might cause him pain for any reason.'

'Why should Murdoch imagine I'd want to hurt Jack?' She was bemused.

Szabo shrugged again. 'It's what happens sometimes, isn't it?'

Joanna didn't see much point in arguing with him. 'I'd say that everyone at the farm seems almost over-protective of Jack.'

'We like taking care of him.'

Joanna noted the defensiveness in his tone. 'He's very lucky to have you.'

Szabo kept his eyes on the road ahead. 'We think we're the fortunate ones.'

Another of Mel's comments came back to her: '*Like having*

to get past Cerberus.' She smiled ruefully. She'd got past, much good it had done her.

'Can I ask something of you, Jo?' Szabo said a few minutes later.

'Of course you can, Pete.'

'If he does come down to see you before you leave—'

'I think it's unlikely,' she interrupted. 'I shan't be staying long.'

'But if you do see him again,' Szabo persisted, 'please be careful. As you say, you're leaving, after all.'

'That's right.'

'So no sense messing with the man's head any more than you already have.'

A flash of anger seared through Joanna.

'I don't mean to offend you, Jo,' Szabo said.

'You didn't,' she said, stiffly.

There was little conversation after that for the rest of the journey, but one thing was clearer in Joanna's mind than it had been before. She had known from the outset that Murdoch Lambert had not wanted her in Jack Donovan's life, and over the past few weeks there had been moments when she'd been uncertain about Chris Chen's feelings too, though latterly the other woman had seemed quite warmly disposed towards her. But Pete Szabo had been the most welcoming to her from the first; she had actually come to think of him as a friend, yet now, suddenly, it seemed that here was one more person who would be glad when she finally boarded her 747 for England.

Cerberus, she thought again. The three-headed dog guarding the entrance to Hades or, in this case, Gilead Farm. Lamb, Chen and Szabo.

She stared straight out through the windscreen into the steadily falling snow, wondering if it would be heavy enough to obscure the first, always stirring, sight of Manhattan.

Concrete, glass, steel, and thousands of strangers.

Such a prospect had never seemed more welcome.

34

She had insisted they stop at the New York Hilton to check on availability before driving on to the apartment but, as Donovan had predicted, they had no room for her and were waitlisted right through to the New Year. Irritated as she was, Joanna had to admit that Jerry Feenan's welcome, combined with the handsomely decorated Christmas tree in the lobby, had warmed her through a little and helped her to bid Szabo farewell with less awkwardness than she'd been afraid of showing. He could not entirely help, she decided, watching him hand over her possessions to the equally welcoming Raimundo, being one of Donovan's sentinels. Pete Szabo was simply the modern equivalent of the old family retainer; there had been no malice in those words spoken on the journey.

I shall buy him a gift and send it to him before I leave, she decided as she let herself into the penthouse apartment with the set of keys handed to her by Feenan. In fact, she would buy them all gifts – even Lamb.

The apartment was hushed, dark, and redolent of its owner, and Joanna spent several minutes opening every blind and window, letting in daylight and air and trying to eradicate the aroma of cigar – not because it was either strong or offended her, but because it reminded her of *him*. It was snowing here, too, though looking down at the narrow cross street fifteen stories down, Joanna could see that at least during the busy daytime hours there was no likelihood of it settling, except in

185

the parks. Central Park in the snow would, she imagined, be a delight. *Not without Sophia*, she reminded herself masochistically, and her sense of loss returned with a vengeance.

'Unpack,' she told herself, then remembered her passport. She ought to contact the British Embassy in Washington right away (she could hardly ask the Manhattan-based consulate for emergency papers after so long a delay) to find out exactly what was needed, not to mention organizing herself a flight home, which might (given that London was at least as popular a tourist's city as New York) prove far more difficult than she had allowed for.

Tomorrow, she decided.

And saw the brown-paper package in the corner of the living room.

She was, after unpacking the gift, grateful to be alone, since she could never have found any possible way of concealing its emotional impact upon her. It was a small – less than life-sized – sculpture of her head. A Donovan original, uncast, in smooth white plaster. It was a very different creature from the other works she had seen, with little of his extraordinarily lavish attention to minute detail; this piece had clearly been swiftly rendered by a man who had never seen Joanna as others did. And yet it was breathtakingly true to her – to her *essence* – in a way that even the most brilliant photograph could never be.

She sat back on the floor and gazed at the sculpture. Her heart was beating fast, and her stomach was clenched tight. Donovan had told her, when he had handed her the package, that it had been the reason he had not responded to her knocking at his studio door.

You don't understand, he had said late on Monday night.

And Lamb had told her that he'd been incommunicado since that night.

She understood now. She had been so certain it had been the dancer's foot to which Donovan had returned straight after their wild hour in his studio and which had driven all thoughts of her out of his mind. When instead it seemed likely now that

186

he had abandoned his work-in-progress to bring all his energy and concentration and all his magnificent talents to *this*.

A sculpture of Joanna Guthrie.

'Oh, God,' she said out loud, and all her shame seemed to reverberate through the empty apartment. 'Oh, *God.*'

She composed herself sufficiently to telephone Gilead Farm. Chris Chen told her that it was not possible to put Joanna through to Donovan since he was working and had asked not to be disturbed.

'I really do need to speak to him, Chris.'

'I'm sorry, Joanna, you know the score.'

She promised to pass on the message, but as Joanna put down the receiver she had the distinct feeling that the other woman had already withdrawn. However warm Chris had seemed prior to her departure just a matter of hours ago, now that Joanna had left the farm, it was clear that the proverbial shutters had already been pulled down against her.

She tried to focus on trivial things; unpacked the clothes she felt she might need in the next few days, ironed those that were wrinkled and hung them away in the guest room. The emptiness seemed to yawn around her and the still lingering twin scents of cigar and dog made it even more painful.

She decided on escape for a while, took the elevator down, smiled back at Jerry Feenan's salute, assured him she didn't need a cab, and, turning left out of the building, headed towards Fifth Avenue. It was still snowing, though more lightly, and having chosen her long beige Jaeger coat as being more suitable to the city than her hooded parka, she knew that it was only a matter of time before her hair turned frizzy from melting flakes. *I could buy a hat.* The idea of purchasing a hat in Manhattan – something lighthearted that she could wear at home when she wanted to remember these sleek, chaotic streets – pleased her and took her mind off Jack Donovan, and she turned right into Fifth, walked five blocks, admired the vast tree at Rockefeller Center, many storeys high, and went into Saks.

She lasted just over an hour and a half: the first five minutes spent conquering panic because of the crowds, the next forty-five devoted to trying on a variety of headgear, the next twenty-something paying for her final choice, and the rest of the time engaged in attempting to find a seat on which to sink down on and drink a cup of coffee, before giving up and escaping back on to the street.

It was still snowing. Joanna found a suitable piece of Saks window to use as a mirror, unfolded the tissue paper surrounding her purchase, yanked off the price tag and pulled it over her head. It was the kind of hat which could be worn jauntily as a beret or tugged down as a cap to cover her ears and most of her hair, a cashmere and mohair mix knitted in glorious multicolours, of which emerald green, poppy red, peacock blue and violet dominated. In the store window, Joanna's reflection – softened by snow and misting and the constant movement around her – gazed back at her: a woman in a classically cut long coat with a mass of curling red hair crowned by a veritable rainbow-coloured cloche. She looked, Joanna was surprised to note, almost jubilant. She presumed, at first, that it was the hat. Then, turning around and noticing a group of jolly Santas on the far side of the street, she decided it was simply the atmosphere.

Then she remembered the sculpture and, hot on its heels, making love with Donovan on the floor of his studio, and knew it was something else.

Something else entirely.

There were no messages on Donovan's answering machine when she got back, and that evening, eating a bowl of fettucine and drinking a glass of chianti, loneliness struck again with a fierceness she had not experienced since the period following Philip's death. On one hand, there was a degree of comfort that stemmed from being surrounded by Donovan's possessions; on the other, Joanna knew that being here, in his home, was merely prolonging what was now bound – whether he came to Manhattan before her departure or not – to be a very painful ultimate farewell.

Joanna had always had great respect for other people's

privacy, yet tonight she found herself unable to resist the temptation to roam around the apartment, even going into Donovan's bedroom and bathroom. She had grown accustomed to the practical starkness of both his homes, yet these two rooms seemed almost ascetic in character. Donovan might come down to Manhattan for pleasure, and he might indeed be a man with a liking for occasional excess, yet these rooms, Joanna felt, reflected above all the fact that they were inhabited by a blind man at least for the most part on his own. Having become used at Gilead Farm to seeing him surrounded by protective friends, suddenly this relative barrenness made her aware of the isolation that Donovan had surely, all too often, to experience.

This is doing no good.

She left the bedroom, poured herself another glass of wine and, hoping to take her mind off her growing emotional turmoil, settled down for a while in Donovan's library. Braille, as always, was a great challenge, but she did become absorbed for a while in the books on anatomy and osteology, understanding now rather more how vital the study of human bones and musculature had to be to the sculptor's meticulous work.

There was a handwritten inscription from Lamb beside the frontispiece of one of the most handsome books: *To my very dear friend, this small gift – and anything else I can contribute. Always. Your ML.*

Joanna returned the book to its place and wandered back into the living room, and there was Lamb's signed clay cat between the bronzes of Walt Donovan and Jack's ex-wife Greta. Murdoch Lambert, ever-present, even here.

Yet she hadn't seen a sculpture *of* Lamb.

And here, on the coffee table, was her very own Donovan head.

Joanna raised her glass to it, then turned to face the cat. Something heard in a score of American films slipped into her mind.

'Eat your heart out, Murdoch,' she said.

*

189

The whole of the following morning was spent on the telephone to Washington, and at the British Airways office on Fifth Avenue, trying to find a flight home. The problem was that all the planes to London with available seats seemed to be flying in the next couple of days, and Joanna was highly unlikely to have her new passport by then, especially given the busy season.

Back on Fifty-sixth Street, she didn't notice the man in the raincoat until she stepped beneath the canopy of Donovan's building.

'Tom.' She was startled. 'What are you doing here?'

'I told you we'd see each other again,' Oates said. 'Do you mind?'

'Of course not.' Joanna smiled at him. 'As a matter of fact, I couldn't be more delighted.'

'Lousy morning?'

She shrugged. 'Annoying. Nothing that a cup of coffee with you couldn't cure.'

They walked to a coffee shop on Sixth, a hectic, noisy place with an eclectic menu where they stood for a while waiting for somewhere to sit, before being given a window table for two.

'What are you doing in the city?' she asked again.

'I had some business to take care of.'

'How's your leg?' She paused. 'Your limp's almost completely gone now, hasn't it?'

'It's getting better every day,' Oates agreed. He held up two crossed fingers. 'Looks like it may not need more surgery.'

'That's wonderful news,' Joanna said.

The waiter brought them coffee, followed swiftly by Oates's corned beef on rye and Joanna's tuna salad sandwich, and for several moments they both ate hungrily, talking easily like old friends, and Joanna was relieved to find that in spite of the fact she felt certain by now that Tom Oates did consider her attractive, there was no discomfiting sexual tension between them.

'Any more word on the missing people?'

'Why think of them now?'

'I don't know,' she answered quietly. 'It's just stayed with

190

me, that's all.' She paused. 'Maybe it's this season. I was thinking how dreadful it must be for their families, not knowing what's happened to them. I can't imagine anything much worse.'

'Except maybe finding out the truth,' Oates said softly.

Something inside Joanna grew chilled. 'What's happened?'

'You don't want to know,' he said.

'I suppose you're not meant to talk about this,' she realized suddenly.

'Not really.'

'Then of course you mustn't.' She paused. 'I apologize for asking.'

He came to a decision, glanced around, leaned in towards her. 'They found remains.' His voice was so low it was hard for her to hear. 'Identification's taking a while, but it looks bad.'

Joanna's flesh crawled. 'Are we talking about murder?'

'Without a doubt.' Oates sat back a little. 'That's all I can tell you right now, Joanna. I shouldn't have told you that much.'

She looked at him with sympathy. 'I don't know which must be harder for you. Working on something like this, or not being allowed to work on it.'

'I know what you mean.'

They were the last words spoken on the subject that day. The waiter came to clear their plates and offer them dessert, but their appetites had gone, and as much as they both tried to lift the mood by talking about lighthearted things, the awful word *'remains'* seemed to hover over them like a dark cloud.

Oates did smile again, just before they parted outside the coffee shop, when Joanna mentioned her difficulties with a homeward reservation.

'So we may get to hold on to you a while longer?'

'Only till I get the passport,' she said. 'Then I'll start calling around *all* the airlines – I may have to consider flying via some other European city.'

'If you fly via Rome,' Oates told her, 'you have to buy two seats.'

191

'You have a thing about Rome?'

'With the right person,' he said.

She laughed. 'I promise to let you know if I have to fly to Rome.'

'Deal,' he said.

She felt sufficiently energized after their lunch to tackle some of the Christmas gift shopping she'd promised herself she was going to do before she went home. She had already decided on books all round for Lamb, Szabo and Chen; something arty and upmarket for Murdoch, a fine cookery book for Pete, and perhaps, if she could find such a thing, something beautifully illustrated about *t'ai chi* for Chris. As for Jack, she had no idea yet what to buy – she knew, of course, that present buying was not supposed to be competitive, but what, after all, could possibly compare with his gift to her?

I'll know it when I see it, she decided as she walked into the Rizzoli Bookstore on West Fifty-seventh Street. And certainly, she did find the perfect book for Szabo in the shape of a tome devoted to Russian cookery, each recipe ascribed to a region with anecdotes to match. Lamb's gift was, as she had known it would be, harder to be sure of. She was briefly tempted by something titled *The New Neurotic Realism Book*, but settled instead for a book about Luca Della Robbia, deciding that the Renaissance was a safer bet than the contemporary world of sculpture. (Donovan might choose to believe that Murdoch had very little ego, but Joanna still had doubts on that score.)

Finding nothing suitable for Chris Chen, Joanna emerged from the bookstore and, finding herself in the mood for some window browsing, she headed east on Fifty-seventh, crossing Fifth Avenue, and continuing on past some of the glossiest and most appallingly expensive boutiques and stores she had ever laid eyes on. *Too much*, she decided, and turned left on to Madison. Memories assailed her: first, of the early Manhattan training walks she and Donovan had taken with Sophia along this gentle but sophisticated avenue; and then recollections from longer ago of how Philip had liked the higher reaches of

192

Madison, closer to the Guggenheim.

Somewhere high above, past the skyscrapers and helicopter flight paths, the sky began to cloud over and darken. *Fifty per cent chance of precipitation*, Joanna remembered the weatherman saying that morning on television. Rain, probably, she thought, though she hoped for more snow.

Walking towards her about a block away but on the same side of the street, an old lady with bluish-white hair and wearing a dark mink coat stumbled and almost fell. Reflexively, Joanna hastened towards her, then slowed her pace again, seeing that a man in a dark coat and fedora had stepped out of a boutique to go to her aid. He was holding her arm, and the lady, seeming composed and unhurt, was thanking him and drawing away and now the man turned in Joanna's direction and strolled on, pausing again beneath the canopy of an apartment building.

Murdoch Lambert.

Joanna halted for a second, then walked more swiftly towards him. Lamb was speaking to a uniformed doorman, the two men appearing to be sharing a joke, and then Lamb disappeared inside the building. She reached the canopy, peered into the interior, but saw no sign of him.

'Help you, ma'am?' the doorman enquired.

Joanna turned to face him. 'The gentleman who just went in.'

'Yes, ma'am?' His cheeks were ruddy from cold.

She looked back inside the high-rent building. 'I wanted a word with him – with Mr Lambert.'

The doorman glanced in the same direction. 'Looks like he's gone up.'

'Did he happen to say he was going to be long?'

'He did not.'

Joanna detected slight disapproval. She smiled at him. 'I don't suppose you can tell me who he's gone to visit?'

'No, ma'am, I don't suppose I can.' The doorman was scrupulously polite. 'If you wanted me to, I could ring the apartment and have a word – if you'll give me your name.'

Joanna hesitated. She could just imagine Lamb's reaction to

193

being disturbed by her. And why should she want to? Because they were such good friends that she hated to miss an opportunity to see him while he was in the city? Hardly.

'It's all right,' she told the doorman. 'I don't want to bother him.'

'Would you like to leave a message, ma'am?'

She pondered that for a moment, saw no harm in it. 'All right,' she said. 'When Mr Lambert comes down, just tell him Mrs Guthrie saw him going inside and said to send good wishes.'

'Mrs Guthrie,' the man repeated. 'Very good, ma'am. I'll leave a note for him,' he added, 'in case he doesn't come back down this afternoon.'

Joanna thanked him and turned back the way she'd come. She had meant to stroll further, gaze into some more windows, perhaps visit a private gallery or two, but somehow, seeing Lamb had put her off her stride.

The doorman's last remark had thrown her somewhat too. Why should a visitor not come back downstairs after their visit was over? Unless Lamb was not a visitor?

She mused about that, passing a pretty children's clothing boutique. She did not recall Donovan or anyone else saying that Murdoch Lambert had a place in the city. Come to that, she still had no idea, even after all these weeks, where Lamb actually *did* live when he was upstate.

None of your business, she told herself while waiting for the WALK sign at Sixty-first Street.

Yet still, her curiosity was piqued.

Thoughts of Lamb and whether or not he kept a home in Manhattan were wiped from Joanna's mind when the telephone rang less than two minutes after she had walked back into the penthouse apartment.

'Finally,' Donovan said.

'Have you been trying me?' The warmth that filled Joanna had little to do with the excellence of the central heating system.

'About five calls, and that's just today.'

194

'Did you leave messages?' She wondered if perhaps she hadn't mastered the workings of his answering machine.

'You know I don't like speaking to machines.'

'I didn't know that,' Joanna said, and thought again how little she *did* know about him. 'Anyway, I'm glad you've found me at last. Did Chris give you my message?'

His hesitation was brief. 'I don't think so, but there was quite a stack of stuff waiting for me when I got out of the studio.'

At least, Joanna thought wryly, loyalty at Gilead Farm stretched both ways. Chen clearly had *not* passed on the message she'd left after she'd opened his package and seen the sculpture. She remembered the other woman's comparative coolness when she'd talked to her.

'Joanna?' Donovan prompted. 'Are you still there?'

'I was just thinking about your gift,' she covered.

'Did you like it?'

'I don't think that "*like*" really describes how I feel about it.'

'You do like it.' Pleasure coloured his tone.

'It's the loveliest present I've even been given,' she said softly. 'And it isn't just the piece itself, but the fact that you spent so much time – that you interrupted your real work—'

'It was what I wanted to do,' Donovan cut in gently. 'After we . . .'

Joanna smiled at his sudden awkwardness. 'Made love?'

'Yes,' he said. 'Suddenly it was all I wanted to do – *had* to do. I'm just not sure that I did you justice.'

'Believe me, Jack,' she told him, 'it did far more than that.'

There was another small silence.

'I could come down to the city tomorrow,' he said, 'if you have no objection?'

'I'd like that very much.'

'Do you have a flight booked yet?'

'Not yet, no.'

'Okay,' he said. 'Then we'll see you tomorrow sometime.'

'We?'

'Just me and Sophia,' Donovan said.

'I was hoping you meant that.'

195

*

Less than two hours later, Joanna was carrying her dinner of chicken salad and a glass of white wine from the kitchen into the living room when she tripped over her Rizzoli bag of books, dropped the tray and stumbled against the unit housing the two Donovan bronzes and Lamb's own sculpture. She heard the sound of smashing even as she was still holding on to the unit, trying not to fall – and she knew, without looking, that though she'd dropped a plate and glass, the sound that had just pierced her like a small axe through her solar plexus was the awful scrunching of the clay cat.

'Oh, hell,' she said out loud, hardly daring to look.

She forced her eyes down on to the floor. The sculpture seemed, at first glance, to be in four pieces, partially coated in chicken slices, the tail end soaked in wine.

'Oh, bloody, bloody hell,' she said.

She got down on her knees, trying to avoid the shards of glass, but all her real concern focused upon the cat, or what was left of it. Looking more closely, she realized, to her surprise, that there was, in a sense, far more of it than she might have expected. She had learned, during her single class at the Jack Donovan School, a little about the armatures, usually made of wire, that formed a rough 'skeleton' for many sculptures. All the more startling, therefore, to discover that this cat's skeleton appeared on first inspection to be made out of what looked almost like real bones linked together with wiry thread.

For several more moments, Joanna gazed at the broken segments, marvelling at intricacies she had not imagined could lie inside a piece of sculpture.

'So much work,' she murmured.

Wrecked by her.

If Lamb had disliked her before, she could only begin to imagine how he would feel about her when he learned about this.

196

35

'Accidents happen, Joanna.'

'The plate and glass were an accident, Jack – this is a disaster.'

'You didn't cut yourself?'

'No, I told you.'

'You didn't hurt yourself again when you fell?'

'I didn't really fall, just stumbled.'

'Then it's no disaster, is it?'

Joanna looked wretchedly down at the four pieces of clay cat that she had laid out on the softest cloth she could find on Donovan's small dining table.

'I doubt that's what Murdoch will say.'

'He'll be okay about it.'

'Has anyone ever smashed one of your pieces?' she asked.

'Originals get damaged all the time at the foundry.'

'Has anyone ever totally destroyed one of your pieces?' she persisted.

'This isn't totally destroyed, Joanna.'

'You're not answering my question.'

Donovan smiled. 'No, they haven't.'

'So you can't say how you would feel, can you?'

'I guess not,' he admitted.

Joanna had drawn him directly to the breakage almost as soon as he and Sophia had come through the door of the apartment, while the dog was still in the midst of her joyful

197

greeting. Having scarcely slept all that night, she had known by then that she would get not a single moment's peace until she had confessed to her crime against Murdoch Lambert and the world of art. Donovan had reacted with calm and perfect manners, but Joanna thought she had detected a fleeting flinching of his facial muscles when he had first laid his fingers on the wreckage, almost as if the feel of such a badly damaged work of art had caused him physical pain.

'Actually though,' he said now, tenderly examining the pieces, 'I think this may be fixable.'

'How can it be?' Joanna was disbelieving.

'To some degree, it could be. I know a guy upstate who performs near-miracles with breakages like this.'

'You have to let me pay for the repair.'

'Sure.' Donovan located the ends of the soft cloth and began wrapping the pieces carefully.

'Perhaps you should give me his number,' Joanna suggested.

'What for?'

'I don't trust you to send me the bill.'

'Why don't we wait and see what he says?'

'Okay,' Joanna agreed. She took a breath. 'Is Lamb at the farm today?'

'I think he has classes. Why?'

'I'm going to call him – tell him what I've done.'

'No need for that.'

'Of course there is.' Joanna grimaced. 'Anyway, I want to do it while I'm feeling braver.'

She stood up to go to the telephone, but Donovan reached out and gently grasped her left hand.

'I have a better idea. Why don't I tell Lamb I knocked over the cat?'

Joanna made no move to free her hand. 'Because you didn't.'

'So what?' Donovan smiled. 'I'm blind, Joanna – blind men bump into things all the time.'

'You don't, and Lamb knows it.'

'I do when I'm drunk.'

'You hardly ever get drunk.' She still stood there, liking the feel of her hand in his. 'This is silly, Jack. I'm not a child – I don't need protecting from Lamb's anger.'

'He won't be angry,' Donovan said. 'Lamb's a far less egotistical artist than you can possibly imagine, Joanna.' He tugged gently at her hand, drawing her closer. 'Besides, what I'd like to do now is change the subject.'

'I really ought to call him.'

'Later.' Donovan's voice was suddenly deeper, huskier. 'After I finish telling you how much I've missed you.'

Joanna closed her eyes, felt him pull her hand up to his lips. She didn't trust herself to speak.

'You missed me too, didn't you?' he asked.

'A little.' Her voice was scarcely above a whisper.

'Show me?'

Behind them, Sophia shifted and whined.

'She's still wearing her harness,' Donovan said.

'You should take it off her.'

'In a moment.' Donovan pulled her down so that she was sitting on his knees. 'After I check out what I'm going to take off you.'

He let go of her hand and ran both of his very lightly over her sweater, lingering hardly at all over the curve of her breasts, yet that slight touch was more than enough to cause them both to inhale sharply, simultaneously, in sudden, intense desire.

'Angora and lamb's wool,' he said, huskily, and his hands moved downward. 'Woollen skirt.' He smiled, finding her stockinged thighs. 'Short.'

'Jack,' she said.

'Uh-huh?' He went on feeling.

'Why don't you go and take off Sophia's harness so she can relax?'

'And then?' he asked.

'And then we're going to bed.'

It had been all hunger the first time, in the studio, their minds and bodies blown away by the wildness and sheer, glorious discomfort of falling down on to that hard floor and taking each other.

This was immeasurably different. The hunger was still there – heightened, even – but this time they were both conscious of having time and space as well as the luxury of a comfortable mattress. And, for Joanna, there was the fascinating sensation of being made love to by a man whose whole existence was ruled out of necessity by his own senses. No one had ever touched her or explored her as he did. He caressed her, lavished kisses on her, *all* of her; but beyond that, *way* beyond it, he seemed to be tasting her, inhaling her ... He spoke to her in gentle, wondering whispers as he made his discoveries. He knew precisely where she had dabbed her perfume, knew where she'd dusted baby powder that morning ...

'What colour's this?' He murmured the question, brushing her pubic hair with his mouth. 'Darker than your hair? Lighter?'

Joanna smiled at the ceiling. 'A shade darker.'

'And the insides of your thighs ...' His mouth moved down. 'Mm ... Milk or cream? Tell me. I need to know.'

She told him they were pale cream, and then, fighting the temptation to lie there simply lapping up every moment, every touch of his fingers or tongue, she began to love him back.

'Do you know,' she asked him, twining herself around him, 'how wonderful your hands are?'

She took his left hand, ran her lips along his knuckles, then kissed the index and middle fingers and took them a little way into her mouth, sucked them gently and heard him groan. She released the hand and brushed her lips along his arm and up to his shoulder, let the palm of one hand feel its curve and muscles, then continued down over his chest.

'Tell me,' he said, 'how I look to you.' There was, for one brief instant, a sense of desolation in his pause. 'I haven't seen myself for so many years.'

Joanna bent over his abdomen and kissed it. 'I'm embarrassed to tell you how you look to me,' she whispered. 'Maybe I'm too English.'

200

'Please,' he said. 'Please, my darling Englishwoman, tell me.'

She raised her chin and looked up towards his face, allowed her eyes to take their time. 'Beautiful,' she said, very softly. 'You look beautiful to me, Jack Donovan.'

The last time, in the studio, he had entered her quickly, almost roughly – it could not have been any other way that day, had been part of the madness, and she had loved it, *loved* it. But this time he came into her smoothly, deliberately, with long, measured strokes, thrusting deeply but gently. And even down there, in the private recesses of her body, Donovan seemed to understand exactly what Joanna needed, the way she was formed. She felt he was moulding himself to her, felt for a while that she was one of his sculptures – or maybe they were *both* a part of the same new creation, melting into each other, being joined. He sought secret places and found them, so that Joanna cried out, screamed softly, bit his sheets, arched violently against him, drew him in further, deeper, feeling herself consumed, *imploding . . .*

And the rest of the world fell away and disappeared.

They stayed in bed for a long time, holding each other loosely in the unique peace-haze that comes only after the best kind of lovemaking. They talked, of everything and nothing in particular, touching on subjects like birds coming to rest briefly on blades of verbal grass, pecking around for a few moments before flying away again. Joanna told Donovan about Oates's unexpected appearance and the lunch they'd shared, and she was both amused and gently pleased by the jealousy that tautened her lover's face.

'He's probably still doing what you asked him to after the mugging.'

'I asked him to keep an eye on you,' Donovan said. 'So far he's taken you to dinner at the Beekman Arms, cooked for you at his house, and now he's lunching you in Manhattan. Hardly standard FBI procedure.'

'He's on sick leave.'

'Maybe it's time he went back to work.'

Joanna changed the subject. 'I saw Lamb yesterday, too. On Madison Avenue.'

'Couldn't have.' Donovan ran his right index finger over the length of her nose and dipped down to the indentation over her mouth.

'I did. He was going into an apartment building.' She reached for his hand, pulled it to her mouth and kissed it. 'Does he have a place in the city?'

'Lamb? Of course not.' He rubbed his left cheek against her hair. 'God, your hair smells so *good*.'

'All of you smells good,' Joanna said.

They kissed, a long, gentle, but still passionate, kiss, and then Donovan turned her over on to her side and pulled her close so that her back was against his chest. 'Spoons,' he said. 'I guess this is one of my favourite rest positions because you can't see me any better than I can you.'

She experienced a pang of sorrow.

'Don't be sad,' he said, quietly.

'I'm not,' she said. 'Not really.'

'I can't remember ever being happier.'

A flood of warmth suffused her, then dissipated as she remembered that she was on the verge of going home to England. *Don't think about that*, she told herself, and turned her thoughts back to Lamb.

'I'm sure it was Murdoch I saw,' she said. 'He looked very elegant, wearing one of those wonderful old-fashioned hats – what do they call them? Fedoras. Does he have a hat like that?' She bit her lip sharply, realizing she'd asked a foolish question.

'It's okay.' Again, he read her mind. 'Lamb almost always runs his clothes by me. He likes my approval.' Donovan smiled. 'He's usually pretty acerbic when I get something wrong in my own wardrobe.'

'So it might have been him?' Joanna persisted.

'I guess so.' Donovan snuggled closer. 'What's the big deal?'

'No big deal,' she said. 'It's just that I assumed he was visiting someone, but then the doorman said something that

202

made me wonder if he lived there. And I realized that I don't know where Murdoch does live, even upstate.'

'He has a cottage a few miles from the farm, north of Hyde Park.' Donovan yawned. 'What say we grab a little nap?'

'Sophia's going to think we've deserted her.' They'd closed the door of the bedroom against her.

'She'll be fine,' Donovan murmured.

For a moment, Joanna felt his arms draw around her even more tightly, and then his grip relaxed, and she knew he was asleep.

I'm wide awake, she thought. *I don't even want to sleep.*

And then, seconds later, she, too, was gone.

Both in the mood for what Donovan called 'easy but alive', they caught a cab that evening down to lower Manhattan and found themselves and Sophia a table at the Ear Inn, a bar that served hamburgers, soups and salads, frequented by local writers and poets who sometimes gave readings. This evening there were no speakers, but there was jazz in the background, there were customers playing backgammon and cribbage, and Guinness was flowing freely.

'I thought this might make you feel at home,' Donovan said after they'd ordered their burgers, 'so maybe you wouldn't feel the need to rush back quite so soon.'

Joanna smiled. 'I've hardly been rushing.'

'But you're still planning to leave.'

'I have to.'

'Why?'

'It's home. It's where I live.'

'At least stay for Christmas.' Donovan spoke as if the thought had just leapt into his head. 'They can do without you at Merlin Cottage until then, can't they?'

'I'm sure Kit and Miriam can do very well without me,' Joanna said. 'But it's not fair to expect Fred to manage alone for much longer.'

'I'm not talking about much longer,' Donovan persisted. 'Christmas is only a week away.' He picked up his beer glass and took a drink. 'You could stay for New Year's.'

Joanna laughed. 'If I can't get a flight out of here, I may very well have no choice but to stay.'

'Suits me,' he said.

Their burgers came and they fell to eating for a while.

'There's something I've been wanting to ask,' Joanna said between french fries. 'Where does Murdoch fit into your work?' She paused. 'I know how important he is to you as your "eyes", and I know about his models, but I had the impression that he plays a greater role than that.'

'Oh, he does.' Donovan gave one of his wry smiles. 'Lamb still really bugs you, doesn't he?'

'Only inasmuch as I know how important you are to one another.' She took a sip of light beer. 'I'd like to understand more about how your life works, Jack. If you're prepared to tell me.'

'No reason why I shouldn't.'

He ordered himself another drink and told her. How he had first met Murdoch Lambert III at a Manhattan party and how the other man had shown him some samples of his own work.

'He was a fine artist,' Donovan said, 'but his greatest talent was for sculpting bones. He'd started out with animals – used to persuade veterinarians to let him examine their deceased patients' skeletons. Then, when he was ready to graduate to humans, he made deals with poor med students and arranged access to ancient remains in museums so he could study them.'

Lamb, he explained, had kept, in his former Rhode Island home, an ex-med school skeleton, making it his business to learn how to sculpt each part until he'd worked his way right through the whole human system, creating anatomically perfect resin replicas.

'That explains the bones in the cat sculpture,' Joanna said.

Donovan grinned. 'Did you think they were real?'

'They certainly looked it.'

'That's how good he is. And that was why, when he came up with his new idea, he brought it to me.' Donovan drank some Guinness and wiped a touch of froth from his upper lip. 'My "flesh and blood" on his "bones" was how he put it.' He paused again. 'You know what an armature is?'

'The wire foundation for a sculpture.'

'Lamb figured it might be interesting to see if building, say, a leg or a foot, could be improved if we replaced the regular armature with an accurate piece of "skeleton".'

'Which he would make?'

Donovan nodded. 'His idea was that we should choose a subject, plan it through, after which he would create the bone structure for that subject, and then I'd take over. What worried me was that if I agreed, then Lamb's own work was going to be buried inside mine. I didn't think that credit alone was enough – his work needed to be *seen*.' He shook his head. 'Lamb didn't care about that – he didn't even *want* credit. What counted, he said, was what we achieved together. I tell you, Joanna, I've never met another artist, gifted or otherwise, with so little ego and so much generosity. Murdoch Lambert really is the consummate artist. All that mattered to him then – all that still matters – was the end result.'

'And it really worked out.' Joanna couldn't help but be impressed.

'Just as he believed it would.'

The two men, Donovan continued, had begun going about their world together, the sighted man seizing on the beautiful, the striking, the unusual, and describing it in minute detail to the blind artist. Then, at some later date, Lamb would present Donovan with his foundation for their next combined work, after which the third aspect of Lamb's brilliant imagination would emerge.

'He would give me these amazingly intricate resin bones to feel and become familiar with, and he'd say: "This is the arm of a farm labourer." And then he'd remind me of a man we'd seen working in a field months back' – Donovan's face was rapt, even in the retelling – 'and he'd remember every single detail about the guy, and it would all come to life for me.'

'I think I may have seen a bronze of that sculpture.'

'In Mel and Sandra's home?' Donovan smiled. 'That's the one.'

205

Their food had gone cold. Joanna toyed with the remains of her burger, passed some of it down to Sophia, lying quietly under their table, then neatly placed her knife and fork in the centre of her plate.

'I've wondered, now and again,' she said, carefully, 'if Murdoch loves you.'

'I think he does,' Donovan answered, steadily. 'So far as it goes.'

'Is he *in* love with you, do you think?'

He smiled. 'Chris told me once that she thought he was.'

'And what did you tell her?' Joanna asked.

'That she was wrong. Lamb and I have never been anything more than friends and co-workers.' He paused. 'I'll admit it concerned me for a while that there might be some kind of hero-worship in our relationship, but I came to realize that was just *my* ego bragging. Lamb knows his own worth, Joanna. We're both sculptors, we both have our own separate gifts which we've found a way of sharing. Together, we create a whole that is simply finer than anything we might produce separately.'

'You make it sound so practical,' Joanna said.

'It is,' Donovan agreed.

They walked several blocks with Sophia before they found a cab to take them home, and on the way back Donovan urged Joanna again at least to consider staying for Christmas, if not the New Year festivities. They necked for a while in the back of the cab, the big dog getting between them and making them laugh so much that the driver cast frequent glances back at them as he drove, and then, when they reached the apartment, they wasted no more time and went directly to bed.

'How long can you stay?' Joanna asked him at around three in the morning.

'I have to go back tomorrow – today.'

All the contentment that had been wrapping itself around her disappeared. 'Today?'

He heard her disappointment, felt her body tense against him. 'It was tough enough taking the one day.'

206

'I'm sorry to have broken your creative flow.' She edged out of his arms.

'I wanted to be with you.' He was dismayed.

'And you have been.' She felt suddenly wretched, used and unreasonable, and her natural reflex was to punish him. 'So now you can hurry on back to work.' She tried swallowing her anger, but failed. 'What's your ideal timetable now, Jack? Am I supposed to stay on here in your flat, do the rest of my Christmas shopping and then trot up after you to dear old Gilead Farm for another happy holiday dinner with the family?'

Donovan didn't say anything.

'I'm sorry, Jack,' Joanna said stiffly. 'I'm just being selfish.'

'Not really,' he said. 'But if you're trying to make me feel like a worm, you're succeeding.'

'That's something, I suppose. Not much, but something.'

There was another silence.

'Now I really don't know what to say,' Donovan said. 'If I say I want to stay another day or two, you'll think I'm patronizing you, and if I go back to work, you'll think I just came down for a quick fuck.'

'No, I won't.' She sat up a little way, wrapping the upper sheet around herself against the slight chill in the room. 'All right, maybe I will think that.' She hesitated. 'Jack, I'm not really used to . . . It's been a long time since I had a relationship.'

'It's been a while for me too.'

Her first instinct was to disbelieve him. She said nothing.

'Has there been anyone for you since Philip?' he asked.

'One man, *very* briefly,' she answered, 'and that was out of a mutual kind of misery.' She smiled ruefully. 'Not a great recipe for success.'

'No,' he agreed. He found her left hand and gripped it. 'If I said I hadn't hoped, when I came down, that we might go on with what started up at the farm, I'd be a damned liar. But mostly, I couldn't stand the idea of just not being with you again.'

207

She waited a moment or two. 'I'm glad you came.'

His tension was palpable in the darkness. 'Joanna, will you at least *think* about staying for Christmas? We don't have to be at the farm, if you'd rather not.'

'I'm sure Pete makes a beautiful Christmas.' She felt ashamed now for her outburst. 'I wouldn't want to spoil that for you or him.'

'If you agree to come,' Donovan said, quietly, 'you'd make it for me.'

'Do you ever stay in the city for the holidays?' she asked.

'Not since I found the farm. But I would, if that was what it took to make you stay.' He paused. 'Hell, I'd come to England, spend it with you at Merlin Cottage if it weren't for quarantine. I don't want to leave Sophia behind.'

'Of course you don't. I wouldn't want you to.' Joanna lay back down against the pillows. 'Go home today, Jack. Forget what I said. I'll think about Christmas.'

'Are you sure?'

'Absolutely.'

He was hesitant. 'It's not so much creative flow, you know – it's the whole process. It's not great to leave it for too long.'

'And you've already broken off twice for my sake.'

He gripped her hand more tightly. '*My* sake,' he said.

36

He woke her with coffee and toast on a tray in the morning, impressing her as he always did with the confidence of his movements on home territory.

'How long have you been up?' It was semi-dark in the room, the blinds still closed, but she could see he was dressed in a heavy sweater and jeans.

'About a half hour.' He bent and kissed her hair, then her mouth. 'Sophia's getting antsy. I've put on her harness, so we're heading out.'

'I could come with you,' Joanna said.

'You stay put,' he told her. 'Enjoy the breakfast, relax. We'll be a while, maybe go to the park.'

'Be careful.' She winced. 'Do you hate that?'

'Having you care about me?' He shook his head. 'I don't hate that at all.'

He left the room. Joanna lay back for a moment, luxuriating, and then, deciding she needed the bathroom, set aside the tray and got out of bed. Walking across to the windows, she opened the blinds. It was snowing. Looking down fifteen floors, she saw that it was snowing hard enough for people to be wearing hats, down coats and boots.

'Jack,' she called, wanting to alert him. 'It's practically a blizzard!'

She heard the outer door open and close and hurried out of the bedroom into the hallway. 'Jack,' she called again,

209

opening the front door.

The square outer hallway was empty, the elevator already on its way down.

'Damn,' she said, softly.

About to turn back, she noticed the indicator over the elevator showing that it had bypassed the first floor and gone down to the basement. She paused, wondering if he'd made an error, watching to see if it would go back up to the lobby, but instead, after a moment or two, it went to the third floor.

Joanna went back inside. Presumably there was an exit from the basement. Anyway, Donovan might have said he liked knowing she cared about him, but she didn't think he'd take kindly to her rushing down to check on his well-being when he'd just left her breakfast in bed.

She was in the small kitchen, washing up her plate and coffee cup, when she heard them returning. She wiped her hands on a towel and went into the hall to meet them just as Donovan was removing Sophia's harness.

'Hello, gorgeous.' Joanna stooped to pet the dog. 'Good walk?'

'Great,' Donovan answered.

Joanna put her arms around the German shepherd and found her fur hardly damp. 'I tried calling after you when you left because of the snow.'

Donovan hung the harness on its hook. 'It wasn't so bad. Takes more than a few snow flakes to stop us, doesn't it Sophia?' The dog wagged her long tail and went to his side. 'So.' He rubbed his hands. 'Have you thought about Christmas?'

Joanna straightened up. 'Yes.'

'And?' His face was tense.

She had not decided until that instant, had gone on vacillating all through breakfast and her shower, but his expression clinched it for her. Joanna was in the process of falling in love with an attractive, fascinating man, and, even if it was inevitably going to end in separation and tears, if there was one thing Philip's death had taught her, surely it was to make the most of happiness while it was on offer.

'Joanna?'

She walked over to him, touched his right arm. 'I'd like to stay.' She paused. 'And I'll be glad to come up to the farm, at least for Christmas Day.'

If there were any serious doubts lingering at the back of her mind, the look on his face was enough to reassure her that she had made the right decision.

Less than one hour after Pete Szabo had arrived to collect Donovan and Sophia (Donovan having packed Lamb's broken sculpture in his bag, insisting again that Joanna thought no more about it, at least until they knew the extent of the damage), Tom Oates telephoned.

'Thought you might like to know I'm back at work as of Monday.'

'Tom, that's great news.' Joanna was delighted for him.

'It'd be greater if the reasons for them getting me back weren't so grim.'

She remembered what he'd told her on Thursday. 'Have they made those identifications?' She paused. 'Don't answer if it's inappropriate.'

'They made them.'

A strange need to know more about this horror assailed her, though she wasn't sure why it should. 'Is one of them the girl from Red Hook? The dancer?'

He took a moment. 'Looks that way.' He paused. 'Officially, it's still under wraps, but press and TV have been circling like vultures, so you'll probably be reading at least some of the grisly details by tomorrow or Monday at latest.'

She felt her stomach twist. 'Grisly?'

Oates sighed. 'There was some mutilation involved. You don't want to know more than that.' He took another instant. 'Joanna, you never did hear about anyone else going missing, did you? Anyone connected with the Jack Donovan School, I mean, or with the farm?'

Alice Munro came back into her mind.

211

'Joanna?'

She told him about Alice. 'But she said she was going to Europe, so I probably confused her departure date.'

'She was quite an old lady?' Oates queried.

'In her seventies, I'd say.' Joanna's skin prickled.

'No one fitting that description in the group,' he said swiftly.

'Thank God.' She paused. 'Why did you ask me about the farm again?'

'No special reason.'

He was lying. Joanna realized that, and wondered why, when he had been so straightforward with her about the rest. Awareness of the lie brought awkwardness into the conversation as solidly as a third person stepping between them.

She changed the subject, not wanting to challenge him.

'Jack came down with Sophia for a day,' she said. 'They just left a while before you called.' She paused. 'I may be staying for Christmas.'

'Here?' Oates asked, slowly. 'Or will you go back to Gilead Farm?'

'I'm invited to the farm.'

'Oh.' He paused. 'That should be fun.'

Another lie. Joanna wanted suddenly to end the conversation.

'How about you, Tom?' she asked. 'Any plans for Christmas?'

'I'll probably be working. Good thing, I guess, after so much time off.'

The call ended at last, with a few more words exchanged about staying in touch, but Joanna knew there was something on Tom Oates's mind that she hadn't been able to make sense of, and that both puzzled and irritated her.

It might, she thought, have been a simple case of his being jealous of Donovan. Except that he'd told the first lie before she'd mentioned Jack's visit and her decision to stay for Christmas. Joanna felt guilty for not having told him the rest, for not clarifying, right there and then, that there was no longer any question about it, there *was* something going on between her and Donovan. If Oates was interested in her in

212

that way, it was entirely wrong to keep him dangling, and she had never been a woman who enjoyed playing games of that kind. Yet at the same time, whatever *was* happening with her and Jack, it was still early days, and she would have felt wrong talking about it.

In any event, she consoled herself, she would be going back to England before too much longer, and Oates would be back at the FBI, doing his awful, ugly work, and so for him it would almost certainly be a case of out of sight, out of mind.

Murdoch Lambert's sculpture was next on her agenda. No matter what Jack had said before his departure, Joanna still believed he might tell Lamb that he had broken it, and she was determined to pre-empt that if possible. Being Saturday afternoon, however, tracking him down before Donovan might be tough.

She tried the school's number, presuming that the machine would pick up and she would leave a message for Lamb to call, but Chris Chen answered in person.

'How's it going, Joanna?' She sounded warmer than last time.

'Well, thank you, Chris. Working overtime again?'

'You know how it is.' Chen paused. 'Good time with Donovan?'

Joanna had almost forgotten how little got past her. 'He's on his way back as we speak.' She paused. 'I don't suppose Murdoch's in today, is he?'

Chen said that he was not. Joanna asked if she happened to know if he was in New York City, and the other woman said no to that, too, though she sounded somewhat mystified by the question. Joanna explained about having thought she'd seen Lamb entering the building on Madison Avenue, and Chen pointed out that, as Joanna knew, Murdoch tended not to confide in her.

'Do you want me to give him a message when I next see him?' Chen paused. 'Might not be till Monday.'

Joanna thought for a second, then decided to rid herself of her burden right away, rather than sit it out. 'I'm afraid I had

213

a small accident and broke one of his sculptures.'

'Which one?'

'The clay cat.'

'Oh, my,' Chen said, discouragingly.

'I think that Jack may be going to tell Murdoch that he broke it,' Joanna pushed on, 'but I prefer to take responsibility for my own mistakes.'

'Is it irreparable?'

'Jack thought perhaps not, but since it was in four pieces, I didn't believe him.'

'Then if I were you,' Chen said wryly, 'I'd let Donovan take the rap.'

'I'm sure you wouldn't, Chris,' Joanna laughed.

'Don't be so sure.'

37

Tom Oates had sat for a while after ending his call to Joanna, mulling things over in his mind and trying to figure out exactly what was bugging him. Aside, that was, from the fact that he was now almost certain that the Englishwoman with the pre-Raphaelite hair was in love with Jack Donovan.

The other thing that was gnawing away at him had something to do with the people up at Gilead Farm. One of them, in particular. It was nothing to get het up about, really, nothing more than a moment in time that had lodged in his memory the way thousands of such trivial instants had a habit of doing.

Still . . .

He called Poole, found him at the office. 'I know I'm back in Monday, Gary, but I need you to run a couple of checks for me.'

He heard the familiar sound of Poole's chair scraping across the floor, heard him rummaging around his always cluttered desk.

'Hit me,' his friend said.

Oates went with the lesser query first. 'Woman name of Alice Munro, from Schultzville. Joanna Guthrie's been trying to call her but getting no answer, though she thinks she may be on vacation. Probably nothing at all.'

'Next?'

'Murdoch Lambert.'

215

'Lambert?' Poole paused. 'One of the guys at Gilead Farm?'

'The one Donovan calls his "eyes",' Oates affirmed.

'Why the check?'

'Just one of those niggles, you know? I saw his own work one time, while I was taking lessons at Donovan's school. He was making bones.'

'Bones?' Poole's voice sharpened a notch.

'Uh-huh. Nothing to get excited about – a lot of artists sculpt bones, so I'm told.' Oates paused. 'It was just that I remember I was real interested, maybe because of my own collection, you know? So I tried talking to him about them, asked if I could touch them, but Lambert froze me out big time.'

'Maybe just a temperamental arty-type, protecting his work?'

'Maybe.'

'But it felt like more to you,' Poole said.

'Maybe,' Oates said again. 'Maybe not.'

38

Donovan telephoned before dawn on Sunday morning.

'I know it's too early for you,' he said right away, 'but I was afraid I'd miss you if I left if any later.'

Joanna was too sleepy to bother pointing out to him that if he'd remembered to call the previous evening, he wouldn't have faced the problem. 'At home,' she said, 'I'd probably be in the Nursery giving the dogs their breakfast.' She stretched and stifled a yawn. 'New York is making me lazy.'

'Good for you,' he said.

She peered around the still-dark room. 'I'm in your bed, Jack. Do you mind?'

'So much I may never change the sheets.'

Joanna smiled.

'Go back to sleep,' he said.

She remembered the broken sculpture. 'Did you talk to Murdoch yet about his cat?'

'Thought I told you not to worry about that.'

Mild irritation scratched at Joanna. 'I spoke to Chris yesterday and told her what I'd done.'

'There was no need for you to do that. I told you—'

'Please stop telling me what I should or should not do,' she said swiftly.

'I apologize,' Donovan said. 'When are you coming up?'

'I'm not sure.'

'Don't get mad at me again, Joanna.'

'I'm not.' She softened her tone. 'I didn't say I wasn't coming, just that I'm not sure yet exactly when. I have some more shopping to do . . .'

'Only I'm heading back into the studio now, and there are some things I need to do before you get here.'

'What kind of things?'

'None of your business.'

'Don't buy me anything, Jack, please,' she told him. 'The sculpture's the best gift anyone could ever give me.'

'Did I mention gifts?' He paused. 'There is one thing I would like to know before you come, if you don't mind thinking about it.'

'What's that?'

'Would you object to sharing my bedroom?' He hesitated. 'Or should I ask Pete to clean the guest house?'

Joanna didn't need to think about it.

'Tell him he has one less chore to do.'

Donovan took a moment before he said, softly: 'Thank you.'

'You're welcome.' A memory of him beside her, *inside* her, flashed into her mind. 'Thank you for asking.'

'I'd never take you for granted, Joanna, whatever you might think of me.'

'I'd never let you,' she said.

She dozed for a while, then, finding herself suddenly too restless to lie around any longer, she took a shower, dressed, toasted a muffin, brewed coffee and ate her breakfast in the living room. She sat on the sofa listening to a talk station on the radio and taking sidelong glances, from time to time, at her very own Donovan plaster head which she had, the previous evening, placed in the centre of his dining table. The sight of it warmed her, filled her with the kind of glow she had not experienced since Philip had presented her with the oak bedstead he'd carved in honour of their marriage.

Thoughts of the days to come flowed through her mind: images of American Christmases stacked up over the years courtesy of endless repeats of *It's a Wonderful Life* and

218

Norman Rockwell's paintings. A man on the radio talked of more snow forecast, and her mental pictures of Gilead Farm became romanticized, with images of Sophia, out of harness, playing in snowy meadows, digging her muzzle into the cold white stuff and then taking off in sheer exuberance while Joanna and Donovan walked arm in arm behind her.

The telephone rang. Joanna stood up gladly, hurried to answer, certain it was him calling back, perhaps unable to settle to work, perhaps egging her on again to decide exactly when she was coming.

'Joanna?' *Not Donovan.* 'It's Tom Oates.'

'Hello, Tom.' She tried to keep the disappointment out of her voice. 'What can I do for you?'

'I have a question for you that may seem odd.'

Joanna carried the phone over to the sofa. 'What's the question?' She sat down.

'What do you think of Murdoch Lambert?'

Joanna's fantasy Christmas glow disappeared. 'Why do you want to know?'

Oates hesitated briefly. 'I saw something of him while I was trying my hand at sculpting a couple of years back. I found him a tough kind of a guy to get to know.'

'You're not alone there.'

'He was a good teacher, no question – but when it came to asking him about his own work, he shut up tighter than a clam.'

Joanna, having nothing to offer and still puzzled, kept silent, wondering where exactly the conversation was heading.

'I recall one time' – Oates kept his tone casual – 'I walked in on him in a workshop at the school while he was working on one of those bone sculptures of his. Have you seen one?'

'Not exactly.'

'What does that mean?'

Joanna winced. 'Jack had one of Lamb's pieces here in the apartment, and I knocked it over and broke it a few days ago.'

'I'll bet that pissed Lambert off,' Oates said drily.

'I'm sure it will – I don't know if he's heard yet.'

'Was it one of those bone pieces?' Still casual.

219

'Yes and no,' Joanna said. 'It was a clay sculpture of a cat – very fine, so you can imagine how I feel. But when it broke, I saw that it was built around what looked like an actual cat skeleton. Jack explained to me that Lamb makes these amazing resin bones.'

'Would you know the difference?' Oates asked.

'Between resin and real bones? Evidently not. Though I probably would have if I'd looked more closely.' Her curiosity returned. 'Why the questions?'

'Probably no good reason at all,' he answered.

'Which means you're not going to tell me.' She frowned. 'Is it personal, or is it work-related? Can you tell me that much?'

'I can't tell you anything at all, Joanna, except . . .'

'Except what, Tom?'

'I'd be happier if you'd stay away from Murdoch Lambert.'

'I'd be delighted to stay away from him,' Joanna said frankly, 'but since I'm going back to the farm for Christmas, that's not likely to—'

'I'd rather you didn't go back,' Oates said bluntly.

'Why not?'

'I can't tell you that,' he said again.

'Then you certainly can't tell me where I can or cannot spend Christmas.'

'I guess I can't,' he admitted quietly.

'Tom, do you suspect Murdoch of something?'

'He's not a suspect.'

'That's not exactly what I asked you, is it?' She was growing exasperated.

'I guess not.'

'For heaven's sake' – her annoyance was growing again – 'what are you trying to tell me?'

'I don't know. Probably nothing. I'm almost certain the guy's nothing more than socially awkward – maybe a little on the eccentric side.'

'Almost certain,' she repeated.

'That's right.'

'And on the strength of that, you expect me to change my Christmas plans?'

'I didn't say that, Joanna.'

'No, you said you'd rather I didn't go to Gilead Farm.' She gave him no further opportunity to say anything. 'Well, that is where I'm going, probably on Tuesday, maybe Wednesday at the latest. So unless you have anything *real* that you want to share with me, I suggest you keep your non-suspicions to yourself.'

'I'm just trying to take care of a friend.'

'Friends are honest with one another.'

Tranquillity gone, she paced around the apartment for five minutes, then seated herself at Donovan's desk and pounded the computer keys for another fifteen or so, composing a long overdue e-mail to Sara Hallett. It was, she was aware even as she typed, a not wholly truthful picture that she was sending to her friend. Joanna was glad to share intimate confidences with Sara that she would not have dreamt of sharing with another living soul, but something within her chose to block off the note of unease that Tom Oates had just injected into her contentment. She told Sara, instead, about the slightly less recent ups-and-downs, and about her decision to go back to Gilead Farm for Christmas to be with Donovan.

Sara's response came swiftly.

Yet again, I understand a dream I had about you two nights ago. Wondrous colours and images, loaded with sensuality. Oh, my dear friend, all I have to say is: follow your instincts. Mine, for what they're worth, say go for it! You already know what I think about Jack Donovan. (Though your rather Special Agent sounds charming, too – the proverbial embarrassment of riches. And no one deserves it more than you.)

So far as Christmas is concerned, don't even think about us folks at home. And if you feel Donovan's pals at the farm may not be too thrilled to have you back again, all the more reason to go, as I see it.

Newly encouraged, Joanna put on mascara and lipstick, brushed her hair, picked up her Jaeger coat and her new in-case-of-snow hat, made certain that she had her two credit cards and front door key, and caught the elevator down to the first floor.

Until she saw Jerry Feenan, she had fully intended to go straight out to embark on the remains of her Christmas shopping, all the stores being open even though it was Sunday. But seeing him behind his desk, for once apparently at a loose end, Joanna suddenly remembered the other, smaller matter that had briefly perplexed her yesterday morning.

'Good morning, Mr Feenan.'

'He had already jumped to his feet. 'Good morning to you, Mrs Guthrie. Can I get you a cab or are you walking?'

'Walking, I think – at least I will be.' Joanna had not known until that very instant that she was going to lie to the man. 'I just wanted to ask you about the basement.'

'Yes, ma'am?' Feenan waited.

'I may have got this wrong,' Joanna said, feeling her way, 'but I think that Mr Donovan was going to show me something down there before he left yesterday, but then we ran out of time and . . .' She let her sentence trail off.

'You mean his storage room,' Feenan said, easily. 'Would you like to go down there now, Mrs Guthrie?'

Storage room. That made sense, at least. Joanna experienced a sudden and intense wave of guilt. Why on earth was she being so underhand?

'Ma'am?' The doorman prompted her. 'Mr Donovan's told me that his place is yours for as long as you're in the city, so I'm sure it's fine for me to let you in if you'd like.'

Joanna looked at him. 'Thank you,' she said. 'I would like that.'

Her sense of guilt magnified as Feenan made a call to Raimundo to ask him to mind the door for him, then he unlocked a drawer in his desk, removed a medium-sized steel key, re-locked the drawer and walked with her to the elevators.

'Are you enjoying your stay, ma'am?' he asked her as the left-hand lift opened its doors and she went in ahead of him.

'Very much, thank you,' she answered.

'It's a grand time to be in New York City.' Feenan pushed the button for the basement. The doors slid shut and they descended. 'Been doing a lot of shopping, I suppose?'

'Of course,' Joanna said. 'So many wonderful stores to choose from.'

'Yes, ma'am.' The elevator stopped and the doors opened onto a gloomy, stone-walled hallway. 'Perhaps I should go first,' Feenan suggested, and stepped out ahead of her. 'It's this way, Mrs Guthrie.'

He turned to their right, following a dimly lit corridor with dark green painted doors on both sides at regular intervals. It smelled damp, and Joanna wondered about cockroaches and, perhaps, rats. *Serves you right*, she told herself as Feenan turned left at the end of the corridor before stopping at another green door, marked B9 in black paint.

'Here we are.' He inserted the steel key into the lock and turned it. 'Mr Donovan generally likes to be alone when he comes down here, ma'am – I know what a special place this is for him. Would you prefer me to wait outside, or will you be okay bringing the key back when you've finished?' He noted her swift look back along the corridor. 'The way to the exit's marked, ma'am, but if you're nervous . . .'

'No, I'll be fine,' Joanna said quickly. 'You said exit – is there a way out to the street from down here?'

'Yes, ma'am,' Feenan answered, 'but it's for emergency use only.' He opened the door, leaned in a little way, found a light switch to the left, and flicked it on. 'I should have said elevator instead of exit.'

'That's fine.' Joanna's cheeks felt hot. 'Thank you again, Mr Feenan. I'm sorry to have put you to so much trouble.'

'No trouble at all.' The doorman smiled down at her. 'Anything for a good friend of Mr Donovan's.'

He stepped back to allow Joanna to enter, placed the key into her hand, told her to take all the time she needed, and walked away. Joanna waited a moment or two as the sound of his footsteps receded, then closed the door and turned around to face the room.

I shouldn't be here. Almost on delayed reflex, she began to

223

turn back, then stopped. Surely, if this storage place were strictly off-limits, Jerry Feenan would not so readily have let her in and, moreover, left her here all alone.

'Just looking,' she murmured.

The room looked and felt cavernous and eerie. The light that Feenan had switched on was of a low wattage variety, casting no more than a pale glow over the place. Joanna took four slow steps forward, halted again, her breath catching in her throat at the uncanniness of what lay ahead of her.

It was like stepping into a surrealist painting. Human limbs and body parts growing out of the concrete floor in a grotesque, twilight world.

Sculptures.

Joanna felt her heart racing, had a foolish urge to bolt.

'Steady,' she said, softly.

She moved forward slowly, stepping cautiously among the works, and as she came closer to the first row, the initially horrific impact of the collection began to fade, her pulses calmed, and a new brand of excitement began to flow through her.

These were Donovan's originals. The clay and plaster works sculpted by the artist before casting. Perhaps all of them – though she had no way of knowing that – each enclosed, she saw, now that she was closer to them, in a transparent case. She stood motionless, gazing around at sculptures she had, to date, seen mostly reproduced on glossy paper in the photographs and catalogues that Chris Chen had shown her.

The female leg with bent knee . . . There it was, one row back, the curve of the knee chipped a little, presumably damage wrought by the casting process that she had heard about. And in the first row, closer to the wall, the remarkable athlete's arm that had so impressed her – though here, lying in its glass box on the ground with no supporting plinth to help the illusion of life and vitality, it seemed to Joanna to smack of desolation and almost, bizarrely, of death.

She turned away from it, stepped carefully further into the forest of clay and plaster remains that were, she realized, a veritable treasure trove in artistic and financial terms – and

224

there was the farm labourer's arm that Mel Rosenthal had shown her, and that Jack had talked about on Friday evening.

She remembered what he'd told her about Lamb's talents for seizing on the fascinating, describing them to him and then, later, bringing him his resin bone structures for their latest project.

'This is the arm of a farm labourer.' Lamb's words to Jack upon presenting him with the foundation for this very sculpture. Joanna recalled what Jack had said about Murdoch remembering every single detail about a man he had seen just once working in a field. From Jack's view-point, it was a magical, near-miraculous gift, the very thing that had made all the difference to his work, to his standing in the art world. From Joanna's, right now, looking down at the original piece of work, it seemed suddenly a rather macabre skill. She wondered, abruptly, if the farmer in the field knew, had given permission for his arm to be recreated, or if he might have objected had he known.

Why should he? she decided briskly, noting again all the same touches of brilliance that had taken her breath away when she'd seen Mel's bronze proof. The farmer would probably be flattered, even honoured, to be plucked from obscurity by a great artist.

Except, of course, that it had not *been* Donovan who had spotted him. Murdoch Lambert had done the plucking. A man apparently fixated by bones; a fixation that had, clearly, somehow disturbed, perhaps offended, Tom Oates.

Joanna remembered Tom's own collection, the Eskimo shamans in costumes decorated with human ribs, arms and finger bones. Hardly a squeamish man himself, yet Murdoch Lambert's recreation of human remains had certainly triggered a highly negative response in him.

Why?

Suddenly, Joanna wanted, *needed*, to get out of there, out of that dim, dank-smelling place filled with its oddly cadaver-like treasures. She moved swiftly, cautiously, back towards the door, opened it first, before switching off the light, afraid of being left in the darkness even for a second. Outside again, she turned and locked the door securely and felt a brief sense of relief, before the secondary eeriness of the dungeon-like basement corridor got to her, and she walked, as fast as she could without breaking into a run, to the elevators.

'Everything okay down there, Mrs Guthrie?' Jerry Feenan was all smiles as she handed him back the key.

'Fine, thank you.' Back on ground level, in the marble lobby with the fountain, everything *was* fine, and Joanna felt idiotic for the moment of funk that had driven her out of there so abruptly.

'Guess you'll hit the stores now?'

She had almost forgotten that that had been her original intention when she'd first come down from the penthouse.

'I guess I will,' she answered, and then decided that if she was starting to include Americanisms in her spoken English, her return home to Merlin Cottage and normality was probably well overdue.

Tomorrow morning, she decided, walking out into the refreshing cold of Fifty-sixth Street, she would begin making a fuss about her passport, after which she would do everything possible to find herself a seat on a flight home between Christmas and New Year.

Jack Donovan or not – love affair or not – she was a responsible woman with a business of sorts to run, a house and a part-time job to go back to. Anything more that might or might not develop between them would simply have to survive her crossing back over the Atlantic. After all, all they really had in common thus far was their love of Sophia, a certain mutual admiration, and sex.

And sex – even it had been of the variety that made meltdown a genuinely comprehensible word – was not everything.

39

Some time in the early hours, Joanna woke in Donovan's bed, conscious of a persistent and vivid image that felt as if it were well on its way to burning a hole in her brain.

The dancer's foot Jack had been sculpting the morning she had photographed him in his studio . . . the morning they had become lovers.

And hot on the heels of that image, another recollection, more recent: Tom Oates telling her on the phone about the discovery of the body of the girl from Red Hook. The dancer who'd gone missing in the spring.

'*There was mutilation involved.*'

Joanna sat up in bed, clutching at Jack's sheets.

What was she *thinking* about?'

She sank back against the pillows. Clearly, the visit to the basement room had unsettled her more than she'd realized. Which served her right for poking her nose into dark places that were none of her concern.

And yet she *did* know what she was thinking about.

'*This is the arm of a farm labourer.*' Murdoch Lambert's words to Jack upon presenting him with a perfect set of replicated resin bones.

Resin, Joanna reminded herself.

'*Would you know the difference*?' Tom Oates's question about the bones she had discovered inside the broken cat sculpture.

227

And that, she realized abstractedly, was the question that was vexing her now, vexing and sickening her.

Would *Jack* know the difference? Could a blind man, however acute his other senses, tell the difference between exquisitely duplicated resin bones and the real thing?

Answer: probably not if he was not *seeking* a difference.

Besides, by the time it came to working with the bone armatures, they would have been wrapped in a thin coating layer of gypsona – Jack himself had told her that. Though that had not been so in the case of the cat.

'For God's sake,' she said out loud, and sat up again.

It was only four in the morning, but any further sleep was, she now knew, out of the question, so she might just as well get up and make coffee.

And wait.

Ludicrous as it might seem, she knew exactly what she was waiting for.

She was waiting to telephone Tom Oates on his first morning back on duty in order to ask him one specific question.

What, precisely, had he meant when he had mentioned that word?

Mutilation.

40

At ten minutes past six am, Tom Oates was already driving his Chevy into a space in the car park outside JC's Diner off route 9 halfway between Kinderhook and Albany. Breakfast, he figured, would set him right; he'd been awake since four and edgy as a rattlesnake, which he thought was probably due to first-day-back tension – though Oates knew that work generally acted as a kind of tranquillizer on him; he was a guy, he supposed, who liked knowing his place and role in the world. That, for him, was the FBI, which had, of course, made the past idle weeks so tough on him.

That, he guessed, too, was why Joanna Guthrie – who was so utterly unlike Lisa or any other woman he'd ever fallen in love with – had gotten such a grip on his mind, or maybe even his heart. That, presumably, was also why he'd started getting fixated by Lambert and his bone sculptures.

Better soon, he figured as he killed the engine and opened his door. By 7.30 he would be at his desk getting the latest word on the mass murders from Gary Poole, as well as the results – if any – of the checks he'd asked him for on Alice Munro and Murdoch Lambert. And soon after that he'd be up and running, a member of his team again, and all the calmer for it, all the more *earthed*.

Though he was certainly far from being earthed right now, he decided, walking from the Chevy around the back of JC's towards the front door, or else why would he be feeling the kind of unpleasant itch running down his spinal column that he usually experienced when there was something badly wrong? He felt, God damn it, as if someone was watching him – and it was not the first time in the past couple of weeks that he'd felt it.

Oates stopped, leaned closer to the clapboard wall at the side of the diner, two feet from the vending machine that sold sodas and candy, and took a good, long look around the car park. Still early, so there were no more than five cars and a white panel truck to check out; no drivers or passengers in any of them, though it was hard to tell with the truck, which had tinted windows.

He felt that itch again.

'Fuck's sake,' he muttered under his breath.

All he wanted was a decent breakfast, some good crisp bacon rashers, a few pancakes and two cups of strong coffee – and then to get back to his real, working life.

He took another look towards the panel truck.

The itch got worse, like it was pressing on a nerve.

He glanced at his watch. 6.14. Plenty of time.

If it itches, he could remember his father telling him, *scratch it*.

'So go scratch,' he said.

41

She waited until one minute after nine o'clock to make the call, having dug around in her half-filled suitcase to retrieve the card that Oates had given her.

'Special Agent Oates, please.'

'Not in yet,' a male voice answered. 'Who's calling?'

'Joanna Guthrie.' She glanced down at the card in her hand, saw that she'd used his direct line. 'When do you expect him in?'

'An hour ago,' the man told her. 'This is Gary Poole, Mrs Guthrie – Tom's mentioned you to me. Is there something I can do to help, or would you rather I take a message?'

She left word asking Oates to return her call. When, an hour later, she'd heard nothing, she tried again. Told, this time by a female voice, that Oates was still unavailable, she left a second message.

A few minutes after eleven, having paced, cleaned her Hasselblad and every other item of photographic equipment she had in the apartment, and finally unable to stand any more waiting, she went into Donovan's library, sat down behind his desk and telephoned the number one more time.

Poole answered again, discerned her agitation and enquired once more as to how he might help her. Joanna considered for a moment.

'I had a question to ask Tom.'

'Try me instead?' Poole suggested.

'About the murders you're investigating.' Joanna realized suddenly that she might be making trouble for Oates. *Too late now*. She went on. 'Tom didn't tell me much, but . . .'

'But?' Poole urged gently.

'He used the word "mutilation".'

'Uh-huh,' the FBI man said noncommittally.

Go on, she urged herself, having come this far.

'There was a girl from Red Hook.' Joanna paused. 'Tom said it was only a matter of time before the media got hold of the story.'

'He was right.' Poole let her off the hook. 'She made the local news last night. Her name was Ellen Miller.'

Joanna took another minute, composing herself, feeling her heart racing.

'What is it you want to know, Mrs Guthrie?'

'She was a dancer, wasn't she?'

'Yes, she was.'

'A ballet dancer?'

'That's right.' Poole waited patiently.

Joanna swallowed. 'What did Tom mean by "mutilation"?'

'I can't tell you that exactly.'

'I thought you said it made the news?'

'Her death was mentioned, nothing more.' Poole's tone toughened up a little. 'Why exactly do you want to know?'

'I'd rather not say,' Joanna evaded.

'If you have any information, Mrs Guthrie, you have to tell me.'

'I don't have any information.' *Just a feeling*. A terrible feeling, growing stronger by the minute.

'Does it have something to do with Alice Munro?' he asked.

Joanna was startled. 'Has something happened to her?'

'Not so far as we can ascertain.' He paused. 'You're asking these questions for some good reason, Mrs Guthrie. Unless you tell me what it is, I can't give you an answer.'

Joanna stared, unseeing, at the shelves of books along the library walls. She, too, toughened up. 'Unless you tell me what Tom meant about mutilation,' she countered, 'I can't give you my reason.'

Poole recognized the impasse and took a gamble. 'A part of Ellen Miller's remains was missing.'

Joanna felt suddenly sick. 'Which part?'

'Why don't you tell me which part you think it was?'

'Please, Agent Poole, just tell me.'

'I show you mine, you show me yours,' he reminded her.

'Was it her foot?' she asked. 'Her right foot?'

'How did you know that?' he asked tersely.

Joanna hung up.

Stood up.

Closed her eyes, saw again the beautiful foot coming to life beneath Jack's fingers. Clay becoming flesh and blood.

Over one of Lamb's partial skeletons.

She left the library and ran to the bathroom.

She went out a little later, passing Raimundo in the lobby with no more than a nod, seeing but noticing nothing as she walked up to Fifth and turned right, slipping between shoppers and business folk, sliding past Santas and windows displaying mega-priced jewels and clothes and other unaffordable gifts. It was a world of concrete and bustling humanity, some set-jawed, some laughing, and most of all it was a world of *noise*, yet Joanna heard none of it, saw none of it, felt almost disembodied, as if she had been cut loose from normality and was floating someplace above it.

Yet she knew where she was heading. MOMA. The Museum of Modern Art. Back to the room on the first floor that had been closed off when Mel Rosenthal had first tried to show her one of Donovan's most celebrated works.

Open today.

She knew it even from the doorway. Chris Chen had shown it to her in a photograph. Titled '*Youth*', it was the shoulders and back of a young boy. No front to it, to him, simply a blank expanse of bronze. But the perfection and detailing of the lad's rear view, the impression of youthful strength and flexibility, were remarkable.

Joanna stood for a long time. Others came and went, looked for a few moments or with no more than a passing glance,

233

before moving on. One man, himself old and needing a stick to lean on, let out an involuntary sigh of wistfulness for something long since lost. One of a pair of teenagers, straggling behind a school party, remarked contemptuously about the blank that was the front of the boy's torso that it reminded her of a boy called Gordon.

Joanna's own eyes traced the rippling line of vertebrae visible beneath the bronze flesh and muscle. Who had he been? she wondered and then, swiftly, fiercely, amended: Who *was* he?

And then her mind returned again to the dancer's foot.

And she left.

She knew, arriving back at the penthouse, what she was going to do. She was going back to the basement, to Donovan's storage room. Other possibilities, easier in some ways, certainly infinitely less hateful, fought for top place in her mind as she made coffee, drank half a cup, washed it up, wiped up the ring her cup had made on the counter . . . all delaying tactics, of course, she knew that too.

What she wanted to do, more than anything, was to call Jack. *And tell him what*? That she had invaded his privacy, that she had listened to Tom Oates's questions about Murdoch Lambert, his great friend, and that she had put two and two together and made about a thousand.

'It's all too *ridiculous*,' she told herself, pacing the living room, passing Walt Donovan's and Greta's implacable bronze faces over and over again. It really was – of *course* it was.

Yet wasn't there – hadn't she thought from the very beginning that there was – something a little sinister in the air up at Gilead Farm? And hadn't Mel and Sandra more or less confirmed that to her? And Tom?

And Special Agent Poole had given her the answer she had feared he would give her. About poor Ellen Miller.

'Oh *God*!' Sickness twisted in Joanna's gut again as she ceased her aimless pacing and went in search of her camera and film. She refused to ask herself why she needed the Hasselblad, refused to contemplate the possibility that she might be gathering evidence.

The telephone rang just as she was slipping the loaded camera into its leather case and hanging it around her neck. *Jack*? She started towards it, then halted. It continued to ring.

She answered it, her right hand shaking a little.

'Hello?'

'Mrs Guthrie, it's Agent Poole.'

'Yes?' Her breathing was ragged. She wished she hadn't answered.

'I've been trying to reach you.' He paused briefly. 'Mrs Guthrie, I have two questions for you, and please don't hang up on me again.'

'All right.'

'When did you last speak to Tom Oates?'

Joanna frowned. 'Yesterday. Why?'

'You asked your questions earlier.' Poole was brusque. 'Here's number two. Why did you ask about Ellen Miller's foot? What do you know?'

She didn't answer.

'Mrs Guthrie, you must know that withholding information from a law enforcement agency is a serious offence?'

Still she said nothing.

'What are you not telling me?'

She took another moment, all the hideous uncertainties sifting in her mind.

'Mrs Guthrie, *talk* to me.'

'The trouble is, Agent Poole,' she said at last, 'I honestly don't know that I have anything real to tell you – I'm probably not withholding *anything* . . .'

'Maybe not,' he said, 'but something's worrying you.'

'Yes,' she conceded. 'But I need a little more time before I can talk about it.' She paused. 'I would like to talk to Agent Oates.'

'Not possible at this time.'

She couldn't take any more. 'Then I'll call back later,' she said, and put the phone down again.

She was already at the front door when it began ringing again.

She could hear the ringing continuing as she stepped into the elevator and started her descent.

235

*

It took several moments' persuasion before young Raimundo agreed to give her the key from Jerry Feenan's desk drawer. She had Mr Donovan's permission, Joanna assured him, and if he checked Mr Feenan's records, Raimundo would see that he had given her the keys only yesterday.

'My problem is,' Raimundo said, holding up the key, 'that Mr Esposito – the super – has gone home, and I cannot leave the lobby, and there's no one I can call right now.'

'That's fine,' Joanna told him calmly. 'Mr Feenan left me there alone yesterday. I'll just let myself in, and then I promise to bring you back the key as soon as I've finished.'

A silver-haired old lady was entering the building and Raimundo's attention was split two ways. Joanna took advantage and held out her hand. 'You'll have it back in no time.'

He gave her the key.

42

It had been eerie the last time she'd entered. This time, in the first seconds after turning on the dim lighting and closing the door, Joanna took in the sculpted body parts and her temporarily highly strung mind flicked through biblical references to Gehenna and Sheol and other hellish places.

'Rot,' she said aloud, and the sheer commonsense of that word seemed to settle her and give her courage. *Courage*. She scoffed silently at the notion that she should even think of needing such a commodity in what was, when all was said and done, just a storage place.

In fact, she decided, as she stepped forward again towards the first row of transparent boxes housing their precious cargo, the real courage was going to be needed after this was over, when she would have to face Jack Donovan and confess the ludicrousness, the sheer *offensiveness*, of what she had been thinking.

And what she was about to do.

She walked around, moving carefully. Now that she had decided on this course of action, she felt bolder, determined to rid herself of her crazy suspicions once and for all, so that she could move on.

Go home. Home was the only place she would be able to move on to after this, since Jack would certainly never forgive her, and she could not, in all conscience, blame him for that.

She stopped in the centre of the room, surveying the scene

237

around her, trying to remain detached, objective. She took in each sculpture, noted works she had not taken in on her last visit. Over to the right, in one of the larger cases, was the original – a work in plaster, not clay – of the MOMA piece, '*Youth*'. A kind of awe overtook her for a moment, along with a fearsome guilt.

But then she remembered Ellen Miller, and determination returned.

She had to choose, and swiftly. *Get it over with*.

She focused harder, searching for something that might, just feasibly, be considered a lesser piece, though that, she realized full well, would be a moot decision on her part, probably flawed and certainly arrogant.

Nothing obviously 'lesser' sprang into view, but starting to move around again, Joanna counted three separate sculptures of arms: the magnificent athlete's, the farmer's, and another; that, she fancied, staring down at it, of a young woman. It lay in repose, already partially damaged by casting, lacking the muscularity and strength of the other two, yet with a vitality of another kind, the soft, smooth fleshiness of young womanhood.

Joanna knelt beside the case, taking care that her camera did not swing and do harm. Looking more closely, even in the poor light, she could make out traces of downy hair, skin pores, tiny creases and blemishes. Its lifelike quality stunned her, brought fresh, hot shame pouring over her like lava. How could she *do* this?

She reviewed her options. There were only three other courses of action open to her. She could tell Jack, leave it in his hands, risk wounding him deeply for perhaps no good reason. She could tell Gary Poole, who would, together with Tom Oates and the other involved agencies, bring all the horrors of a murder investigation down on Jack's head, almost certainly futilely. Or she could leave here now, get her passport and ticket and go home to England without explanation or resolution.

Whereas acting now, here, alone, could finish it.

Joanna stood up, looked around, saw what she needed. A

238

small, axe-like implement on the wall beside the glassed-in fire alarm point near the door.

She walked across, took off her coat – she had put it on to appear, if necessary, as if she was going out – and laid it on the ground with her camera, then reached up, withdrew the tool from its bracket, and stepped back carefully through the small field of art works to the woman's arm.

She knelt again, laid the axe on the stone floor, then, for the first time, touched the case around the sculpture. It was, she realized immediately, plastic rather than glass. She placed one hand to either side, and tried lifting it experimentally. It was not fixed and lighter than it appeared; it would, she supposed, need to be easily removable in order for a blind artist to be able to view his past works.

'Here goes nothing,' she said, raising the case and placing it safely in the space to the right of the sculpture.

From somewhere beyond the room, she heard the sound of men's voices.

Joanna froze, her hands in mid-air, ready to put back the case if she had to.

The voices receded and disappeared.

Joanna exhaled, slowly. And reached for the small axe.

Jack will never forgive me for this.

Yet she had to know the truth.

Aiming for the section of the sculpture already the most damaged, she brought down the point of the tool with a short, swift blow. The outermost part of the clay, treated with varnish of some kind, was pierced, but insufficiently for her to see into the heart of the piece. She raised the axe again, then brought it down.

The clay fragmented, sprayed outward and fell with a soft clatter to the floor.

And she saw the outline of the bones in their gypsona wrapping.

Joanna put down the axe, crouched lower, inserted her right hand and scratched at the fine layer of plaster of Paris with a fingernail. It resisted, so she retrieved the axe and used its point to scrape it away. And then she set the tool down again, bent her head and peered more closely.

Please, God, let them be resin.

They looked real.

She reached in and touched the two long arm bones, drilled through and joined with wire, much as the cat skeleton had been. *Radius and ulna.* She remembered the time when Philip had broken his arm on a cycling trip in Norfolk. A compound fracture, they had pronounced in the ambulance as she had sat beside him on the way to hospital in Norwich; one of the men had asked Joanna if she was the queasy type, and she had said not as a rule, and then he had shown her the snapped bone sticking out through poor Philip's skin. She remembered it now with great clarity, the different layers, hard and spongy, the blood vessels and the marrow. And she remembered, too, having seen much the same thing with one of her pups when it had broken a leg and she had stayed with it in the vet's surgery.

You have to look.

Gritting her teeth, Joanna got hold of the radius with both hands and noted right away that it felt fibrous; more so, she thought, than resin was likely to feel.

She snapped it.

Not resin. Different, of course, from the living bone in Philp's arm, but not resin. Definitely not.

She withdrew her hands and stared at them for a moment, unseeing. She felt very ill. She had the most urgent desire to run, but that was, she realized, out of the question.

This was evidence. It needed to be safeguarded.

She stood up. Her legs felt weak. She walked across to where she had left her Hasselblad on the ground. Her hands were trembling as she retrieved it, fumbled with the leather case, hung the strap back around her neck. Her skin was damp. She moved back towards the clay and bone remains.

It wasn't so bad once she was looking through the lens. She could pretend that she was working, doing a job for someone else. She supposed, as she took her photographs from various angles, that she *was* doing that, because she would, before long, be handing her film over to Tom Oates or Agent Poole . . .

240

'Oh, God,' she murmured, letting the camera drop on its strap, its gentle weight smacking against her breasts. She could hardly bear to contemplate what she was doing, what she was intending to give to the FBI.

These were still Jack's sculptures. No matter what she or Tom suspected Murdoch Lambert of doing – and what *was* that, precisely? Using real human bones and pretending he had made them, which would mean that he had been duping a blind man and, presumably, breaking some law appertaining to human remains?

'Bastard,' she said, securing the camera case again. *'Bastard.'*

Whatever Lamb had or had not done, this arm and all the other sculptures down in this place were Donovans. He was the artist behind them, no one else, not in the eyes of the art world. Lamb hadn't wanted credit for his part in their collaboration, she remembered Jack telling her. He had never known an artist with such little ego, he'd said, heaping praise on his friend.

'Friend,' Joanna hissed into the air, and her anger fuelled her energy, gave her strength to take the next step.

She had no bag with her, but she did have her Jaeger coat. She went to retrieve it from the floor near the door, brought it across, laid it down on the concrete and lifted the half-broken sculpture on to the lining. She was breathing rapidly, shallow, almost painful breaths, her pulses were racing and she had the beginnings of an ugly headache. She looked back at where the work had been; a litter of fragments, clay, gypsona, wire and bone remained to be cleared up. Having photographed it in situ, on film that would be logged with date and time, she was anxious to leave nothing behind. If either Raimundo or Jerry Feenan or the superintendent came down to see that all was well they were unlikely to check every individual item, but if they did notice an empty case, so long as there was no sign of breakage they might assume that Donovan had removed one sculpture for his own means.

Joanna checked her watch. It was ten minutes to two. She thought she had probably been down here for a little over half

241

an hour. If she took much longer, the young and conscientious Raimundo would probably come down in search of her.

She finished the job swiftly, checked for fragments one last time, put the plastic case back in position, then wrapped the woollen coat securely around the whole, straightened up and tucked it, in a large, unwieldy ball, under her left arm.

It was done. For better or worse, it was *done*.

She had an idea it was almost certainly for worse.

She went straight from the basement to the penthouse, deposited the coat on the sofa and the camera on the coffee table, then sank into an armchair. A new thought had struck her on the way upstairs, and her mind was in a worse turmoil than before.

Lamb's cat. Donovan had been so decisive about taking it away with him, to have it repaired. She had asked him about it when he'd called early on Sunday morning, and he had told her not to worry about it. And now she was wondering – she could hardly bear to *think* such a thing, but she couldn't seem to help it – whether he had taken it away to be fixed. Or disposed of.

'Dear *God*,' Joanna said aloud, jumping back out of the chair, reeling with shame. It was a revolting, impossible thing to be contemplating – after all, it wasn't Jack whom either she or Oates suspected. It was Murdoch Lambert and his bones. It was Lamb who provided the armatures, the supposedly resin skeletons for Donovan's works, who had done so for years, whose special gifts had, according to Jack, made so much difference to his success. '*Lamb's genius*', he had called it. And oh, dear Lord, what if that 'genius' had been providing Jack Donovan with real human bones?

Maybe even the bones of murdered people.

Joanna began pacing again, her mind struggling to analyse what little she knew about Murdoch Lambert III. A strange, dislikeable man, unquestionably, apparently devoted to Jack, perhaps even in love with him. Sufficiently in love, maybe, to consider this a kind of great, unpurchasable gift?

But if that were true, how could Jack not have *known*?

Gypsona wrapping or not, he had told her about the wonders of Lamb's resin bones, which meant that he had to have felt them at some point prior to their being wrapped.

Joanna's legs turned to jelly, and she sank back into the armchair.

Perhaps Lamb had presented Jack with one set of resin bones and then tricked him by wrapping the real remains in gypsona before work had commenced?

She was floundering, and she knew it.

If she sat here much longer, thinking about this, trying not to look at her winter coat all bundled up on the sofa, she thought she might go crazy. And if the object of the last part of that whole appalling exercise had been to hand the evidence over to Tom Oates or Gary Poole, then she might as well make that call now.

She stood up slowly, walked across to the telephone, then stopped.

The key. If she didn't return it to Raimundo soon, its loss might attract unwelcome attention. She checked her watch. Not yet two-thirty, so there would be plenty of time to make the call when she came back up.

She didn't really look at the man standing on the far side of the lobby, his back to her, when she emerged from the elevator. She saw Raimundo behind Feenan's desk, saw his smile broaden as he noted the key in her outstretched right hand . . .

'Hello, Joanna,' a familiar voice said. 'I was hoping to find you home.'

She turned slowly, fighting to stay on-balance. 'Murdoch. What a surprise.'

'A nice one, I hope.' His blue eyes almost twinkled.

He had on a dark coat and was holding a fedora – exactly what he had been wearing last Thursday on Madison Avenue, which Donovan had claimed had been impossible.

She managed a smile. 'What brings you here?'

'Christmas shopping – what else?' Exuding joviality, he held up three bags, two from Bergdorf Goodman, one from

Doubleday. 'But having virtually finished, I thought I'd come and see if you'd like a ride back up to the farm with me – even if I am a day early.'

Behind his desk, Raimundo gave a discreet cough, and Joanna froze.

'I think he wants that key,' Lamb said helpfully, looking at her hand.

'Of course.' Feeling her face flushing slightly, Joanna turned and quickly passed it over.

'Thank you, Mrs Guthrie.' Raimundo beamed at her. 'Everything okay down there?'

'Fine, thank you.' She turned back to Lamb, determined to cover. 'I won't be ready to go back to the farm today,' she said, 'but I was thinking of going out for a cup of coffee.'

'Without a coat?' Lamb glanced over his shoulder. Snow was falling.

'Looks like we gonna have a white Christmas,' Raimundo said happily.

'Indeed,' Lamb said. 'Actually, Joanna, I'd love some coffee, but I'd rather come upstairs to the apartment, sit in comfort.' He grimaced. 'My legs, you know? All that shopping.'

Joanna felt badly rattled. 'I'm not sure if I have any decent coffee left, Murdoch – that was why I was going to go out.'

'No problem.' He began to walk towards the elevators. 'I'll settle for a little peace and quiet after the hubbub.' He paused. 'If you don't mind, that is?'

'No.' Joanna took a deep breath and followed him. 'Of course I don't mind.'

They were halfway up to the penthouse when she thought of the bundled-up coat on the sofa and her face grew hot again.

'All right?' Lamb asked.

'Fine,' she answered.

She unlocked the door and went in ahead of him, her movements smooth, her manner, she hoped, easy and at least relatively normal.

244

'I'll just clear some of this mess.' She swooped on the coat, held it close to her so that no fragments would escape and fall, turned and smiled at Lamb, standing a few feet away. 'I spilled something on it earlier,' she explained, already on her way out of the living room. 'It'll have to go to the cleaners.'

'Why not give it to the boy downstairs?' he called after her. 'These people all know the best experts.'

'I'll probably do that,' Joanna called back over her shoulder.

She entered Donovan's bedroom and put the coat carefully down on the bed. She thought about finding a bag to roll it and the ruined sculpture into, but she didn't want to risk taking another minute and having Lamb walk casually in on her, so she left it there on the spread and closed the door behind her.

'I'll just go and see about that coffee,' she said, brightly, looking into the living room – seeing that Lamb had removed his own coat and draped it over one of the dining chairs, the fedora planted on top – then ducking out again and going to the kitchen.

'May I come along?' Lamb followed.

'Of course.' She made a small show of opening the cupboard in which Jack kept his coffee beans, taking down the jar and peering into it. 'That should be enough.' She took down the grinder and shook out some beans.

'Shouldn't you give that coat to the boy now?' Lamb said.

'No rush.' Joanna fixed the top of the grinder and pressed down to start the action, grateful for the piercing noise that made conversation impossible at least for a few seconds. *All you have to do is give him a cup of coffee, then get rid of him.* The grinding done, she found filter paper and the small glass pot, transferred the coffee into the paper, then filled the kettle and set it to boil.

'Won't be a minute,' she said.

'I'm in no hurry.' Lamb smiled at her. 'Aren't you leaving for the farm tomorrow?' He saw her confusion. 'Your coat,' he explained. 'Only I know that the best dry cleaners can do the job in a few hours.'

Joanna managed to smile back at him. 'I don't think I'll be

coming till Wednesday. Too many things left to organize.'

'You will be coming though, won't you, Joanna?'

The kettle came to the boil. 'I wouldn't miss it,' she said.

'Donovan's so excited you're going to be with us for the holiday.'

She made the coffee, set the pot on a tray with milk, sugar and two cups and saucers, and carried it all into the living room. Lamb strolled after her, then, as she put it down on the table beside her camera, wandered around the room, very much at home.

'Black or white, Murdoch? I'm afraid I can't remember.'

'No reason why you should,' he said pleasantly, sauntering towards the windows.

Joanna poured, left his black, added a splash of milk to her own and sat down in one of the armchairs. She reached for her cup.

'Donovan told me what happened to my sculpture.'

Lamb was still facing the large picture windows. Joanna put down the cup again rather than risk spilling her coffee.

'I'm so sorry about that.'

Lamb turned around. 'There really was no need for anyone to lie about who broke it, you know.'

'I agree with you,' Joanna said steadily.

'I knew right away that he was trying to protect you. Donovan doesn't go around breaking things. He's more graceful and adept around his homes than most sighted people are.'

'You're absolutely right.' Her voice grew a little crisper. 'It was my clumsy accident, which I wanted to tell you about immediately, but Jack put me off because he thought he might be able to have it repaired.'

'I doubt that will be possible.' Lamb walked across the room, sat down on the sofa and picked up his cup and saucer.

'I was afraid of that.' Joanna paused. 'I wish I knew how to make amends, Murdoch.'

'The piece had little financial worth, if that's what you mean.'

Joanna thought about the clay cat's skeleton, thought about what lay in the bedroom wrapped in her coat. It was almost impossibly hard to reconcile this calm, impeccably mannered conversation with the wild suspicions that had been flying around her mind when she'd carried that coat upstairs in the lift. Perhaps she might, after all, be a hundred miles off the mark.

'I thought it was very fine,' she said, then, suddenly emboldened, added: 'And I could hardly believe how intricate it was.'

The blue eyes were no cooler than usual. 'You saw my little cat's innards, I take it?'

The telephone rang. Temporarily reprieved, Joanna stood up to answer, heart beating too fast. 'Hello?'

'Gary Poole, Mrs Guthrie.'

'Yes.' Her heart rate accelerated. 'How are you?'

'Wanting to know what you have to tell me.'

Her palms felt damp. 'Nothing special.'

'I need you to understand something, Mrs Guthrie.'

'What's that?'

'If you've found out anything that might possibly be connected with the homicides we've been investigating, you may be putting yourself in danger by not confiding in me right now.'

Joanna said nothing. On the sofa, Lamb sipped at his coffee and then leaned back, apparently comfortable and entirely at ease.

'One more thing,' Poole went on, his tone harsh. 'Agent Oates is now almost seven hours late for duty, he's not answering his phone at home, nor is he picking up on his cellular.' He paused. 'You told me that you last spoke to him yesterday.'

'That's right.'

'What did you talk about?'

He asked me what I thought of Murdoch Lambert.

'Could I call you back a little later?' Joanna caught Lamb's eye and raised her eyes heavenward, as if she were being trapped in conversation by someone unwelcome or dull. 'It's just that I have a visitor, and I'm being very rude to him.'

'Who is it?' Poole's question was sharp.

'As soon as I can,' Joanna said.

247

'You can't talk, right?'

'That's right.'

'Okay, listen to me,' Poole said swiftly. 'I'm going to be out of reach for the next two to three hours, but I'll be calling in for messages, so you go right ahead and call, okay? Have you got that, Mrs Guthrie?'

'Yes, of course,' Joanna said, and put down the phone. 'I'm sorry, Murdoch.'

'No problem,' Lamb said, easily.

She was halfway back to the armchair when he spoke again.

'What were you doing in the basement?'

Joanna thought her heart had stopped.

'My laundry.' She remembered seeing a sign down there for residents' use.

'Really?' Lamb paused. 'Is Donovan's washing machine broken?'

'I don't like using it for my personal items.'

'I've never heard of a laundry room being locked up.'

Joanna said nothing.

'The key you gave young Raimundo,' Lamb said. The blue eyes grew colder, the mouth thinner. 'Does Donovan know you've been down in his store-room?'

Attack back.

'Does he know you're here in the city giving me the third degree?'

'Not yet,' Lamb answered.

Joanna stood up. 'To be honest, Murdoch, I've a great deal to do.'

'Perhaps I could help you with something?' All pleasantness again.

'No,' Joanna said, firmly. 'Thank you.' She said a swift, silent prayer. 'But if you don't mind, I would like to get on.'

'I take it you'd like me to leave?' He remained seated, looking up at her.

'I would. As I said, I have things to do.'

'You could work around me,' Lamb suggested. 'Donovan likes me to feel free to use this apartment as a home base while I'm in the city.'

'Oh?' Joanna's entire body felt stretched to the limit. 'What about your place on Madison Avenue?'

Something behind his eyes flickered. 'What place is that?'

Stay even. 'I saw you going in there last Thursday. I left my good wishes with the doorman.'

Lamb nodded and smiled, very slightly. 'Not my place. A friend's.'

'Jack didn't seem to know that you'd been down here that day.'

Another shifting behind the eyes. 'Jack – as you now call him – prefers not to know every move I make, Joanna. He values the independence of his friends almost as much as his own.'

'I'm sure he does.'

At last, Lamb stood up. 'Thank you for the coffee.' He walked slowly over to the dining table, picked up his hat and coat, folded the latter over his left arm, and turned back towards her. 'You can telephone your friend back now.'

'Yes,' Joanna said.

Lamb started to move towards the door, then paused beside the coffee table. He looked down at her camera, still in its leather case. 'Been taking interesting snapshots, Joanna?'

'They interested me,' she answered. 'I doubt they'll greatly excite anyone else. You know the sort of thing.'

He looked right into her eyes. 'I expect I do.'

Joanna turned and walked ahead of him out of the living room and to the front door, praying that he would follow.

He did. She opened the door.

'Once again,' he said, smiling, 'thank you for your hospitality.'

'It was just a cup of coffee, Murdoch.'

'Yes,' he said.

He went out through the door, then turned once more. 'We'll see you in time for Christmas, then, Joanna? Shall I reassure Donovan of that?'

'I'll tell him myself.'

She closed the door, resisting the temptation to turn the key and slide home the two bolts at top and bottom, knowing that he was still out in the square hallway. She waited for the sound of the elevator's arrival, for the doors to open and close again. She suspected, suddenly, that he might have a key of his own, both for the penthouse floor and for the apartment itself. It was the first time she had felt unsafe in Jack's city home. She thought about moving to a hotel, wondered how swiftly she could, once she began making a real fuss, get out of the country.

The sound of the elevator had faded away. Joanna thought of opening the door again to check that he had really gone. Instead she locked up thoroughly and then, possessed by a sudden attack of paranoia, wanting to see him actually leaving the building, ran back to the living room and opened the glass doors leading to the small terrace.

Snow was still falling, had settled in the corners and on the parapet. Joanna placed both hands in its chilled softness and leaned over to see below, momentarily dizzied by the combination of flying white flakes and height.

She held her breath, waiting.

What if he wasn't intending to leave? What if he was, at this moment, persuading Raimundo to give him the key to room B9? Or what if Jerry Feenan was back, and Lamb was telling him that she had gone down without permission, and perhaps they were both, even now, going down to see that all was well, and even if Feenan or Raimundo didn't notice the missing arm, Lamb surely would . . .

He emerged from beneath the canopy, putting on the fedora and stepping out, in his meticulous style, clearly mindful of slippery concrete beneath his feet.

Thank God for that, at least.

He stopped, and again Joanna ceased breathing. And saw him look up.

For an instant, she thought of ducking and escaping, but instead, with a final spurt of bravado, she raised her hand and waved at him.

Lamb lifted his own right arm in what looked almost like a small salute.

And then he carried on walking, to the corner of Fifth Avenue, where he turned right and, almost immediately, vanished from sight.

43

In Oxfordshire, Sarah was having another Joanna-dream, the tunnel in her head a kaleidoscope of the autumn colours that always made up Joanna in the narrow but infinite mind's eye of her slumbering state.

It was early evening and she was at home in her bed. She knew that even in the midst of the dreaming because this sleep of hers was an unnatural one, forced by the raised fever of influenza – and maybe that was why, as the colours became increasingly fiery and painful, Sara was conscious of trying to push them away, of trying to escape from the tunnel. It was too hot, too asphyxiating. She wanted desperately to wake up before it choked her, dragged her deep inside itself, like a black hole in space sucking up everything in its path . . .

She recognized the blackness, knew, even in the dream, that she'd been here before – *it's just a dream, only a dream* – but the heat was cooling, vanishing into the darkness, and now the tunnel was freezing, and the water was all around her – *black, stinking water* – and she knew that she was drowning, dying . . .

It closed over her, flooded into her ears and eyes and nose, filling up the spaces in her head and body with blackness – and she was Joanna now, entirely Joanna—

As she opened her mouth to scream.

And let the icy wet darkness come rushing in.

*

Sara woke up, sweat pouring, heart pounding, staring up, seeking the stars on her ceiling, finding none, total blindness panicking her, paralysing her . . .

Only night.

She struggled up from the pillows, reaching for the light switch on her bedside lamp, and the narrow tunnel of her vision was still there, thank the Lord, the stars still sprinkled above, the wardrobe still straight ahead. All present and correct, all right in her small, ever-shrinking world.

Except that it wasn't all right.

Something was happening to Joanna. Something terrible.

Just your fever.

Sara pushed aside her duvet and swung her feet to the floor. The room spun. Her head throbbed and her face burned.

Just the flu. Nothing more than that and your neurotic brain.

Her throat hurt as she swallowed.

Sara groaned, and got back into her bed.

44

Alone again in Donovan's apartment, Joanna debated her options. Agent Poole had told her to leave a message for him – but what should she *say*? If she told the FBI about the bones in Jack's sculptures, even if they shared her mistrust of Murdoch Lambert (and Tom Oates *did* share it, she knew that much, but he, according to Gary Poole, was now on the missing list), their main focus of investigation was still bound to be Jack Donovan, the man she had fallen in love with.

Her greatest quandary was not knowing whom she could trust at this moment. She could not, after all, be entirely sure about Jack. He was brilliant and very brave and a wonderful lover and devoted to Sophia, but the sculptures now weighing so heavily on Joanna's imagination were primarily and undeniably his; it was *Donovan*'s name, not Lamb's, that tantalized the art world and sold to the big spenders. And it was Donovan who kept those originals – those macabre, appalling clay and plaster originals – in a store-room in his own apartment building.

For heaven's *sake*!

She shook herself out of that line of thought. Every instinct she possessed was telling her that Jack was the innocent party in all this – whatever '*this*' turned out to be. Yet still, if it came down to doing what she most wanted to do – telling him what she had found and voicing her suspicions – Jack was so intensely fond of and grateful to Lamb that she couldn't be sure he'd even believe her. After all, he'd known and worked with the other man for years and known her for a matter of weeks.

Joanna threw away the coffee she'd made for Lamb and made fresh, hoping caffeine might clear her muddled thoughts. Who else was there to put her trust in? Those relationships up at Gilead Farm were all so intertwined, so intense and strange. Lamb, Chen and Szabo, all orbiting around Donovan, their sun. She wasn't even one hundred per cent certain about Tom Oates: so attractive, so gentle for an FBI agent, with his charming little home and that bizarre collection of shaman memorabilia ... more bones there, too, Joanna remembered, which probably meant nothing at all, yet made her shudder just picturing them again.

But Tom was missing now, too. One less person to turn to – one more to feel uneasy about.

She wandered around the apartment, holding her mug of coffee.

Mel Rosenthal sprang suddenly into her mind. Mel had been kind to her, grateful to her for coming through with Sophia. She, too, adored Jack, but at least her entire existence did not revolve around him, at least she had an actual, close relationship with another human being. *Mel will listen to me.* She would listen and then give her some sound, down-to-earth advice, and of course she would be shocked, perhaps dismissive, maybe outraged by her interference, but Joanna thought that Mel would also possess the objectivity to differentiate between fact and wild hypothesis.

Which I seem to have lost the ability to do.

'You just caught me,' Mel said when Joanna called her office. 'I was about to go home, catch up with some paperwork there.'

'I'm sorry – if you're too busy ...'

'You said you need to talk.' The agent was as acute as always. 'What's up, Jo?'

'Nothing I can talk about on the phone.'

'Now I'm really intrigued.' Mel took a beat. 'Forty-five

255

minutes too long? Time for me to get home and kick off my shoes?'

'That would be great.'

Joanna's next quandary was whether or not to take the 'evidence' with her. Removal of the broken sculpture from Jack's home, she decided, might be construed as actual theft – besides which, she had the film in her camera that could be developed at a one-hour lab if Mel needed some kind of physical proof to be going on with.

She checked the time again. Already after four, and with the snow still coming down out there, the traffic would be heavy and cabs hard, if not impossible, to find, which meant the subway was her best bet for getting to the Village. She went into the guest bedroom, pulled one of her bags out of the wardrobe, took it into Jack's bedroom and, with the greatest care, placed the coat and sculpture into it and zipped it up.

Not much of a hiding place if Lamb did come back.

Nothing I can do about that, she decided, put the bag into the back of one of Jack's wardrobes, then swiftly changed into her favourite green cashmere sweater and jeans, pulled on her boots, grabbed her parka, shoulder bag and the Hasselblad, and headed for the front door.

The phone rang. She stopped, rigid with indecision. Poole, or Oates, perhaps. Or just a call for Jack.

Or Mel, calling to change the arrangements.

She went to answer.

'Hello?'

'Hi, beautiful.'

His voice sent a brief rush of warmth shooting around her system, then tension pushed it back out.

'Hello, Jack.'

'Who were you expecting?'

'What do you mean?'

'You sounded tentative.' He paused. 'You okay?'

'I'm fine. I was just going out, that's all.'

'Let me guess – more shopping?'

256

'Probably.' Joanna bit her lip. 'How are you? How's the work?'

'Not as focused as it ought to be. Your fault.'

'Mine?' Her stomach contracted even further.

'You're distracting me, Joanna. When are you coming? Tomorrow?'

'I hope so.' There was no way she could bring herself to wreck the warm anticipation in his voice by even broaching the truth. 'Provided I get everything finished today.'

'Please do,' he said.

See if he knows Lamb was here, a voice in her head nudged her.

She took a breath, preparing.

'I'm sorry I couldn't come back with Murdoch today.'

'Murdoch?'

'He was here.' Joanna kept her tone casual. 'He'd been shopping and thought I might be able to ride back up with him.'

'I didn't know.'

She believed him. 'Probably a last-minute idea.'

'We miss you.' Donovan paused. 'Sophia and I miss you like hell. We can't wait to spend Christmas with you, so call the minute you know your schedule. I'll leave word with Chris and Pete to tell me, even if I'm in the studio.'

And that, Joanna realized as she hung up, her emotions more awash with conflict than ever, was almost tantamount to special dispensation from the Pope.

45

'You look like hell,' Mel said, opening the door almost an hour later.

'I took the subway and got lost.'

'Come in and fall down.'

Joanna came in, handed over her parka and sank, as she'd been bidden, on to a soft armchair, carefully lowering the shoulder bag containing the camera and film onto the rug beside the chair. The combination of safe arrival, warmth and the genuine welcome of those smiling black cherry eyes gave her a sudden urge to burst into tears which she barely managed to resist.

'So what's up, Jo?' Mel was wearing a snug grey track suit and fluffy pink socks. Clearly, Joanna's delay had given her more than enough time to get cosy after work. 'No, don't tell me – not before you have a drink.' Mel peered down at her. 'Cognac? You look like you could use something strong.'

'Just a small one, please.' It might be heavenly to escape into an alcoholic fog for once, but what Joanna needed most, she was all too aware, was a clear head.

Mel brought her a cognac, then sat down with a glass of red wine on one of the big suede-covered beanbags on which Sophia had lain the last time Joanna had visited.

'I'm sorry to have descended on you in this way.'

'Don't be,' Mel said. 'Have a drink, take your time, then talk.'

'It's a very bizarre story.' Joanna cupped the glass in both hands. 'And I'm hoping that, at the end of it, you're going to tell me I'm being incredibly melodramatic.'

Mel regarded her from the floor. 'You don't strike me as the melodramatic type.' She drank some wine and shrugged. 'Then again, what do I know?'

'How's Sandra?' Joanna had so much liked the woman with the marmalade-coloured hair, yet she was relieved to find her apparently not at home.

'She's good,' Mel said. 'She had a meeting at Condé Nast this afternoon. I guess she'll be a while yet.'

'Especially with this weather and all the traffic.'

'You want to talk about traffic or you want to tell me what's on your mind?'

Joanna smiled at her bluntness, took a sip of cognac and then a deep breath. 'You're obviously aware of the way Murdoch Lambert contributes to Jack's sculptures?'

'Sure,' Mel said. 'His bones.'

'Did you know,' Joanna asked slowly, 'that he uses real human bones?'

'To study from, sure.'

'He uses real human bones in the actual sculptures, Mel. In the originals Jack works on.'

'No way,' the other woman said, dismissively.

'I've seen them.' Joanna paused. 'I don't think – I can't imagine – that Jack knows what's going on.'

'If it was true,' Mel said flatly, 'then he would know.'

'Not if Lamb wrapped the bones in gypsona before giving them to him.'

'Donovan's shown me Lamb's work, Jo.' The agent smiled, 'They're uncannily accurate replicas, but I promise you they're not real.'

'He may show Donovan resin bones at some point in the work process,' Joanna forged on, 'but what he brings him to work around, after they've been covered in gypsona, are not resin.' She paused. 'I've taken one apart.'

Mel stared up at her. 'Say again?'

'One of Jack's originals.'

259

The other woman's eyes narrowed. 'You've been in the basement?'

'Yes.'

'Does Donovan know?'

'Not yet.' Joanna took another sip of cognac. 'The point is, Mel, I cracked open one of the originals—'

'Jesus Christ,' Mel said.

'—and I broke one of the bones, and it wasn't resin.' Joanna looked right into the agent's disbelieving face. 'I know what real bones look like.' She took another deep breath. 'I think Lamb's been duping Jack into using real human remains, Mel, and that's quite bad enough.' She paused again. 'But what I'm really scared about is how he may have obtained those bones.'

Mel put down her glass on the floor, suddenly too shaken to hold on to it. 'What do you mean by that?' she asked quietly.

Joanna told her. About the way the first suspicions had been floated her way by Tom Oates. About Lamb's clay cat and Donovan's unexplained visit to the basement, and her own deceit in letting Jerry Feenan believe she'd been invited to view the storage-room. About the missing persons up in the Hudson Valley area and the discovery of the bodies. About the dancer's body being found, minus her right foot. And about the awful, nagging, steadily growing sense of dread – magnified by the knowledge that Jack was currently sculpting the right foot of a female dancer – that had led her back down to room B9 and to the clay arm she had deliberately broken.

For what seemed like forever, after she had finished speaking, Mel sat motionless and silent. And then she reached for her wineglass and drained every last drop from it.

And set it down again.

'Okay,' she said.

Joanna said nothing, just waited.

'I'm glad – I *think* I'm glad – you came to me. Obviously you need help with this.' Mel took another moment. 'I guess I have to say that I can imagine Lamb might be capable of doing something pretty perverse.' She shook her head. 'I'm talking about using real bones – not the murder thing. That's just too bizarre for words, Jo. Surely you realize that?'

260

'Of *course* I realize it,' Joanna said. 'I want nothing more than to have someone show me that what I've found has nothing to do with that dancer or those other people. It's the FBI putting things together, Mel, not me.'

'I know,' Mel said, then grimaced. 'You have an idea how I feel about Lamb and the whole scene up at Gilead Farm.'

'I do,' Joanna said.

'I've never liked the man. I've met him any number of times, and I still don't really know him at all; he's a punctilious smart-ass, and what humour he does show is usually at someone else's expense.' Mel paused. 'But the guy seriously worships Donovan, and I find it real hard to believe he'd do anything to harm him.'

'But he hasn't, has he?' Joanna spoke quietly. 'My understanding is that Jack's greatest successes have come about since he and Lamb joined forces.'

'What are you saying? That he's been doing it all *for* Donovan. Not duping him at all, as you first suggested, just helping make him a star?' Mel puffed out her cheeks and exhaled her breath, then rose unsteadily from the beanbag cushion. 'Wasn't there a guy in England a while back who got caught using human bones for his sculptures?'

'That was very different,' Joanna said. 'All he did was acquire the parts illegally to make casts of them. His sculptures had no actual bones in them, and there was certainly never any question of his having killed anyone to get the bones he worked with.'

The phone rang, and Mel went to answer it in her study. The respite was relief for Joanna, who leaned back in her armchair and closed her eyes, trying but failing to empty her mind.

'Sorry about that,' Mel said, returning.

Joanna opened her eyes and leaned forward again.

'Okay.' Mel sat down on the sofa. 'Want my take on all this?'

'That's why I came here,' Joanna said.

'Fine.' Mel scratched her head, hardly displacing her short dark hair. 'I don't believe for one single moment that this has anything to do with murder.'

261

Joanna remained silent, listening.

'Maybe, just *maybe*, Lamb has found some creepy way to use real bones, but I honestly think you've been blowing up whatever questions this Agent Oates asked you. Lamb probably rubbed him up the wrong way like he does most people.' Mel's eyes narrowed again, this time in concentration. 'What exactly did the other FBI guy – Poole? – say that got you so all-fired up?'

'He more or less confirmed to me that Ellen Miller—'

'The dancer?'

Joanna nodded. 'That her right foot was missing.'

'You said more or less.'

'He didn't deny it, Mel.'

'And that's it?' Mel paused. 'And because Donovan's latest work is a dancer's foot, you've concluded what exactly? That Murdoch Lambert killed Ellen Miller back in August just so he could bring Donovan the perfect bones to build on now?'

'I haven't concluded anything.' Joanna's face was starting to burn.

'Or are you saying that Donovan and Lamb are in it together?'

'*No.*' Joanna was emphatic. 'Of course I'm not.' She stood up and walked, still holding the glass, towards a wall bearing some of Sandra McGeever's bold black and white cartoons, then turned around. 'Do you think I don't know how far-fetched this all sounds?'

'I guess you do.' Mel's eyes tracked her. 'You seem like a reasonably sane person to me.' She grinned slightly. 'Or you did.'

Joanna wasn't ready to smile about anything. 'But Jack's talked to me about what he calls Lamb's "genius" and the difference it made to his work – *and* he told me about Lamb refusing to take any credit for his contribution.'

'Which Donovan thinks is pretty damned saintly,' Mel said.

Joanna returned to the armchair and slumped down. 'Agent Poole warned me that if I knew anything about the murders, I might be in danger. And less than a minute later, Lamb was

262

asking me why I'd been down in the basement.'

'But he left you alone. He didn't hurt you or even threaten you?'

'No.' Joanna paused. 'But I felt threatened all the same.'

They both sat quietly for several moments.

'I guess I need to see for myself, don't I?' Mel said, finally. 'It's not that I don't believe you, Jo, but you have to understand I have an enormous vested interest in Donovan's work. Not to mention that I've loved and respected the guy for many years – and that's before Lamb came along.'

'Of course I understand.' Joanna glanced down at her bag. 'You have two choices. I took photographs of the broken sculpture and the bones, and I brought the camera and film with me.'

Mel looked at her wristwatch. 'It's past six. Even if we find one of those one-hour places still open, they're probably going to make us wait till tomorrow.' She eyed the bag on the rug. 'I don't suppose you brought the real thing with you, too?'

'I wrapped it up in my coat and put it in a suitcase in a wardrobe at the apartment. I didn't fancy taking it on the subway.' Now Joanna managed a smile. 'And I thought you might decide I'd stolen it.'

'Is that supposed to be worse or better than smashing it?' Mel enquired.

Fresh distress overwhelmed Joanna. 'I don't know.'

'It's okay.' Mel stood up again, came over, bent and put her arms around Joanna's shoulders. 'I know how tough this must have been on you.'

Close to tears, Joanna drew back and looked into the other woman's face. 'Jack and I have become very close.'

Mel straightened up. 'You're in love with him.'

'Is it that obvious?'

'It was obvious a month ago when you came here last – Sandra realized it instantly.' Mel smiled again. 'And that was before you stopped calling him Donovan, the way the rest of us do.' She checked the time again. 'So, how are we going to do this? Do you want to come back there with me, or will you trust me to go alone?'

'If I didn't trust you,' Joanna said, 'I'd hardly be here.' She thought about it. 'Frankly, I could live without going back there just yet, but Jerry Feenan or whoever's on the door might not let you in.'

'I know all the guys on the door,' Mel assured her. 'But it might be an idea for you to call, let them know I'm coming and that I'll have your keys.'

'Don't you want me to come with you?'

'You're exhausted, Jo. You stay here – unwind a little.'

'It does sound tempting,' Joanna agreed.

'You deserve it,' Mel said.

It was almost an hour before she telephoned. 'Traffic's unbelievable, but I finally made it here.'

Joanna was wrecked with tension. 'Have you seen it?'

'What's left of it, you mean.' Mel was trying to keep it light. 'I don't want to say much now, but there's no question we have a lot of thinking to do.'

'Is that supposed to make me feel better or worse?'

'I think you should consider staying with us for the night.'

'I thought perhaps I ought to go to a hotel.'

'What for? We have the space and Sandra won't mind.'

Just the thought of finding and checking into a hotel was a strain Joanna knew she could do without. 'If you're sure.'

'That's settled. What do you need from here? We have clean toothbrushes and most stuff.'

Joanna considered. 'Clean underwear?'

'Tell me where.'

Joanna told her.

'Meantime' – Mel went on taking over – 'what you should do is relax while you can, maybe take a hot bath? There's some great aromatherapy oil in the bathroom, and clean towels in the closet next door.'

'I'd rather do something useful – maybe make dinner for you and Sandra?'

'We'll order take-out later.'

A question was burning a hole in Joanna's brain. She had to

ask it.

'How much trouble do you think Jack may be in?'

'Please God, none at all,' Mel said.

'Amen to that,' Joanna said.

46

The water was bluish with white foam caps, lapping around and over her with tender satiny fingertips, lulling her with warmth and fragrance . . . geranium and rosewood with a hint of almond, she thought she'd read on the handwritten label, though after the day she'd been through, Joanna suspected she mightn't have cared if the bottle had contained squeezed-out tea-bags. Warmth and comfort were all that mattered to her right now, and the temporary ability to shut her eyes and blot out the real world.

'Whatever that is,' she murmured to herself.

She heard the front door.

'Hello, Mel,' she called out lazily. 'I'm in the bath.'

No response.

She opened her eyes and sat up, sending ripples up and down the bath. The bathroom door opened, and Mel looked in.

'How're you doing, Jo?'

'Wonderfully,' Joanna said. 'I'll be right out—'

'You stay exactly where you are.' Mel was firm. 'I bought some great herbal tea from a store on Eighth Street' – she said ''*erbal*', the way many Americans said the word – 'and I thought we should both have a cup while we figure out what to do next.' She paused. 'If you don't mind?'

Joanna lay back again. 'Not one bit.'

'Better top that up with more hot,' Mel advised. 'The oil works better if the water's really steaming.'

'I'm starting to feel very guilty,' Joanna told her. 'You're running around after a long day's work, while I laze around in your bath.'

'The last thing you need to feel is guilty,' Mel said.

Joanna was just reaching to turn off the hot water tap when Mel returned with one tea cup. 'Where's yours?' she asked.

'In my study.' Mel bent to give her the cup carefully, handle first. 'I just remembered one or two chores I have to finish before we start our brainstorming.'

'Anything I can help with?'

'Not a thing.' Mel's cheeks were pinker than usual, as if she had been running. 'You just drink your tea and relax while you have the chance. I'll be with you soon as I can.'

She went out, closing the door softly behind her.

Joanna sniffed the contents of the cup. It smelled vaguely of camomile, maybe bergamot, with something else. *Nothing ventured*, she decided, and took her first sip. *Not too bad.* She drank some more and settled back to soak.

Mel had directed her to relax while she could.

She had a feeling that was probably sound advice.

From beyond the bathroom door, something choral and pure and even more soothing than the bath water began to play . . .

Voices woke her from her doze, penetrating through the music but too faint to hear properly. The radio, Joanna thought vaguely, or television . . .

She had never felt so relaxed.

Too relaxed.

She sat up slowly, noticing that she'd placed the cup on the side of the bath. Her mind was muzzy, her limbs felt heavy. The water had cooled to just above tepid. Time to get out before she wrinkled or fell into a real sleep.

She tried to reach the bath plug. Her right elbow struck the tea cup, which fell noiselessly on to the carpeted floor. Muzziness became wooziness. A chord of alarm began to strike, but almost instantly faded out . . .

You should get out now. The thought came quite calmly.

The voices reached her again. Female and male. *Mel and* . . . ?

Joanna started to get up, water dripping off her body, the splashes seeming to magnify and echo inside her head. She put one leg over the side of the bath, felt the carpet, soft and reassuring, beneath the sole of her right foot, then the left . . . Her head was spinning. She reached for the bath towel that she'd hung over the heated rail . . . The bathroom tilted . . . She caught sight of her face in the mirror, saw that she was very white, and then that, too, distorted as her legs gave way.

From the floor, she heard the voices again, coming closer. She tried to call Mel's name, but no sound came out of her mouth. Scraps of conversation drifted through the narrow gap at the base of the door.

'. . . for her own good . . .' *The man.*

Then Mel, her voice raised, upset, words indistinguishable.

'. . . calm and quiet till Donovan can . . .' The man again. Clipped.

Lamb.

They were arguing. Mel said something inaudible, then, louder, in anguish: '*Jesus*, Murdoch!'

Joanna couldn't see properly now. Her eyes were fogging, and she wanted to rub them clear, but she couldn't seem to lift her arms, and she was cold, terribly cold, lying there naked and wet on the floor.

She moaned, *thought* that she moaned, but maybe she was imagining things or dreaming, because she still couldn't hear her own voice, not even her own breathing . . . Maybe it was all just a dream, and any moment now she'd wake up in bed back at the apartment or maybe even at home in Merlin Cottage . . .

Not a dream.

The world turned thick and muddy and deafening.

And wound down to zero.

47

When she woke again, she was still lying on the floor – *a* floor – but there was no rug now beneath her; it was hard and cold and *moving*, and that, together with the sounds around her, told her that she was in some kind of vehicle on the road, and though it was dark – *blind* darkness – she was sure she was entirely alone – blind, *empty* darkness.

Sit up, she told herself.

She couldn't move. Her limbs felt even heavier than before, weighted down. Her head was whirling dizzily, there was a bad taste in her mouth, her tongue felt thick.

'Help me.'

The words came out – she could *hear* them this time, muffled, as if she were shouting into a wad of cotton wool. The vehicle carrying her was moving quickly, the floor vibrating beneath her, and every movement jarred her, yet there was no real pain.

Not naked.

Someone must have dressed her; she felt cloth against her skin. *Felt*, thank God – her body was leaden, she registered, but not numb; she was not, at least, paralysed. The cloth felt thin and silk, like pyjamas, maybe, but she couldn't move her hands to check, couldn't lift her head to look down at herself – and it was, in any case, too dark to see. Oh, God, she hated this blackness, it made her think about the way life was for Jack all the time. She remembered thinking the same thought

269

the night the bulb had vanished from her lamp in the guest house at the farm. *Not vanished*, she thought now. *Taken*.

'Why?' her muffled voice asked the dark cold air, but no one answered, and who the hell cared, anyway, if a lightbulb had been taken? *She* had been taken now, hadn't she? She had been drugged and taken from Mel's place and put in this vehicle ... van ... *truck*? ... it sounded like a truck ...

Her mind was functioning with awful clarity. She knew that Mel had brought her tea – *'erbal tea*, damn her – *damn* her black cherry eyes. *Why*? Was it because when Joanna had been unburdening herself to her – Jack's agent, Jack's friend, another one of his great, good friends – she had unwittingly been telling Mel things she already knew about? Or was it because Mel had simply found her story too impossible to believe? *But she went to Jack's apartment and saw for herself.* Or maybe Mel had seen the bones in the sculpture and believed Joanna all too well, and all the ramifications, for herself as well as for Jack – his career crashing, perhaps her own with it – had scared her enough to call in reinforcements?

Lamb.

And now what?

Joanna might not be feeling physical pain, but she was certainly feeling fear. Dread. Nothing more than that, not terror exactly. This was all too unreal for terror; the dream-like sensations that had gripped her in Mel's bathroom were still with her, protecting her from the potentially unbearable. She had an idea that that might come soon enough, but for now, at least, whether it was self-preservation or the drug in her system, the fear was being held at bay.

For now.

48

'You have to call Donovan.'

'I can't.'

'You *have* to, Mel.'

Sandra had come back to the Washington Mews apartment about two hours after Lamb's departure with Joanna, to find her partner – usually confident to the point of opinionated – in a state not far from gibbering.

'You want me to call him on the phone to tell him that his whole world's a fucking *sham*?' Mel's eyes were rounder than ever with guilt and fear. 'That I just helped the sonofabitch he thinks is his best pal dope the woman he's probably in love with?'

'Uh-huh.' Sandra's wide mouth was set tight as she held out their black cordless phone. 'Go on, Mel.'

'Lamb was being so *candid*.' Mel raked her short hair with her right hand as she paced distractedly back and forth across the living-room floor. 'I'd just found the broken sculpture, and then there he was in the apartment, telling me that no, Jo wasn't exactly nuts, just overreacting like crazy—'

'You told me.' Sandra was implacable. 'Now tell Donovan.'

'Oh, Jesus.' Mel sank miserably on to one of the armchairs. 'How could I have been such a fucking idiot?'

'I don't know, Mel.' Sandra thrust the phone right at her. 'Make the call.'

271

'Shit.' Mel shook her head violently. 'Shit, shit, *shit.*'

'I'm sure Joanna feels the same way,' Sandra said drily.

Mel gave a sigh and held out her hand.

'Good girl.' Sandra headed for the kitchen. 'I'll make coffee.'

Mel hit one of her speed dial numbers and waited.

'Gilead Farm.'

'Pete, it's Mel.' She sent up a silent prayer. 'Is Joanna there, by any chance?'

'Joanna's in the city.'

Mel sagged. 'I need to talk to Donovan.'

'He's working, Mel.' Szabo was friendly as always. 'How've you been? It's been a while.'

'I've been good.' She paused for less than a beat. 'Listen, Pete, you have to get me through to him now.'

'You know better than that, Mel.'

'It's an emergency,' she said starkly.

'What kind of emergency?'

'A private kind. His, not mine.' She paused again. '*Now*, Pete.'

The waiting took forever. Mel got up and paced some more, sat down, got up again, trying to blot out the memory of how sick Joanna had looked when Lamb had half-carried her out of the apartment.

'Mel, what's up?' Donovan sounded tense.

She filled him in, telling it all as swiftly yet completely as she could bring herself to. Lamb had simply shown up at Fifty-sixth Street, she said, nearing the end, had told him that Joanna was right up to a point, but *only* up to a point, that yes, he had done a couple of questionable things to obtain real bones for Donovan's sculptures, but that the rest of Joanna's claims were absurd and dangerous for them all – especially Donovan – which was why Mel had thought she was doing the right thing by going along with him about the sedative.

'What sedative?' Donovan's voice sounded way beyond shaken.

'He had some powder with him.' Mel held tightly to the

272

phone and gritted her teeth before going on. 'He said it would calm Joanna down until we could get her to you at the farm. He came back here, and told me to put it in some herbal tea.'

'You drugged her?' Now his voice was soft and lethal as plastique.

'I gave her the tea,' Mel admitted. 'He seemed so *plausible*. I'd already told Jo I thought she was way off base trying to link the bones with those murders – Lamb just convinced me I was right.'

'Where is she?' Donovan asked. 'Where's Joanna now?'

'I don't know,' Mel said wretchedly. 'They left over two hours ago. Lamb told me he was taking her to the farm, and I believed him, but now I'm not so sure. I mean, the roads might be jammed up because of the weather, but ...' Her voice grew shriller with fear. 'What if Jo was right, Donovan?' He said nothing. 'Donovan?'

'How could you, Mel?'

'I'm so sorry,' she said. 'I could cut off my own arm, I'm so sorry.'

'Feel free.'

'Maybe he *is* bringing her to the farm.' She knew she was clutching at straws.

'Somehow I doubt that, don't you?' His irony was cutting.

'What should I do now?'

'I think you've done enough.'

'I have to do something.'

'Stay put.'

'But maybe I could—'

'Just stay *put*, Mel. If Lamb contacts you, make sure he believes you're still on his side and try to find out where he's taken Joanna.'

'Couldn't I make some calls for you?'

'No calls.' Donovan's voice was like a whiplash. 'Keep your phone line clear and stay there. If you hear from him, find out what you can and leave word with Chris or Pete. Can you manage that?'

Mel shrank from the violent sarcasm in his tone. 'Sure,' she said, and added, swiftly: 'Call me when you find her? I'll be going nuts till I hear.'

'Forgive me if that doesn't fill me with compassion, Mel.'

49

Szabo did not respond to Donovan's yelling as he came into the house, swishing his cane, Sophia behind him out of harness, but Chris Chen was in the kitchen, dressed in pale blue slacks and sweater, pouring coffee into a mug as they came in.

'Pete's not here. Can I help?'

'Where is he?'

'I'm not sure. I was working overtime – he was here when I came in a while back, then he went off someplace.'

'What about Lamb?'

'I haven't seen him.'

'When *did* you last see him? Has he called?' It was a struggle for Donovan to stay even relatively calm. 'Chris, this is important.'

'Why? What's happened?'

'I'm not sure, but there may be some trouble.'

'What kind of trouble?' Chen waited a moment, saw indecision on his face, and her dark eyes narrowed a little. 'You know, Donovan, I think you might put a little more trust in me after all these years.'

'This has nothing to do with trust, Chris. I need to find Lamb, and he's not answering his phone. Do you have *any* idea where he might be?'

'I might.'

'Where? Chris, please, I don't have time for games.' Donovan's jaw was clenched so tight his teeth hurt.

275

She thought for a moment. 'What about his other place?'

'What other place?'

'The house near Mount Marion.'

'*What* house?' Donovan's frustration was growing by the second.

'He didn't tell me about it either,' Chen reassured him. 'I was out driving a month or so back, and I saw his car turn off on to a dirt road leading to this old stone house – somewhere between Mount Marion and High Woods.'

'Is it a friend's house?'

'Maybe. Though I saw him letting himself in with a set of keys.'

'Could you find it again?'

'I guess.'

'Let's go.' Donovan, cane extended, was already on his way out through the kitchen door, Sophia behind him.

'Are you going to tell me what's going on?' Chen asked.

'On the way,' he said. 'Come *on*.'

'Am I allowed to put on my coat?'

'Just step on it.'

'You don't have a coat on.'

'Fuck my coat,' he said near the front door.

'What about Sophia's harness?'

'No time,' Donovan said. 'I have my cane, and you can guide me.' He realized he was barking orders and that his normally easy-going administrator didn't like it. 'Please, Chris. This really is urgent, you don't mind, do you?'

'It'll be my privilege,' she said drily.

50

The truck had stopped a few minutes ago, and the back had been opened up, icy air rushing in. Joanna had called out to whoever was there, but they hadn't answered, and now they were dragging her by her feet, and strands of her long hair were catching on the floor as they dragged, and she knew there ought to have been small smarts of pain, but she couldn't feel them.

'Murdoch, is that you?' she cried out in her thick, drugged voice.

They didn't answer, went on pulling at her.

'Talk to me, please,' she begged. 'Whoever you are, *say* something!'

The hands let go of her feet, slid beneath her, one arm under her buttocks, the other beneath her upper back, lifting her, and Joanna cried out again in new fear, and now there was fresh, freezing air on her face, and she stared wide-eyed into a new, changed, more open darkness, but still she could not see – there was nothing, no one, *to* see. They – *he? she?* – laid her down again . . . another hard surface, but not a floor . . . moving again, but not a vehicle this time . . .

'What's happening? Why are you *doing* this to me?'

Wheels . . . trundling . . . She was on a trolley, maybe one of those gurneys they used in hospitals. She could hear breathing, and footfalls on grass or maybe snow . . . It *was* snowing again – still – she could see feathers descending out of the

277

black, and thank God she *could* still see, had not gone blind
... *Jack, where are you?*

The sound of the footfalls and rolling wheels altered as they moved on to stone or ice. Joanna could see a little more now, her eyes adapting to the less infallible blackness of night ... She saw outlines of trees as the trolley passed them, saw something fly overhead – an owl perhaps, or a bat – *do they have bats here in winter?* – and then they stopped. She heard new sounds: keys clinking, being fitted into a lock and turning, a door opening. The gurney jolted and rattled and was pushed through the doorway – and now it was total blackness again.

Not the farm. Some other place.

Joanna was still unable to move, still heavy as lead, but the fear was growing, building, and now it *was* terror, she realized, rising through her body into her throat, choking her, suffocating her ...

Back to zero.

51

'Why are you driving so *slowly*?'

'The snow's getting thicker – we don't want to have an accident.'

Donovan, in the passenger seat of Chen's Volvo estate, was hunched as far forward as the constraints of his belt would allow. 'How much further?' He shook his head in frustration. 'Damned snow always screws up my bearings.'

'Not too far now, Jack.'

In the back, Sophia whined, catching the tension, and Donovan twisted around, reached back to caress her. 'Take it easy, sweetheart.'

The car skidded a little and Chen changed gears.

'Why're we slowing down?'

'You felt the skid,' she said.

'Just a little *skid* – Pete drives twice as fast in a blizzard!'

'Perhaps you should have waited for him,' Chen said, evenly. She glanced at him, saw him battling to keep his temper. 'Patience, Jack.'

'That's the second time you've called me Jack,' Donovan noticed, and was unsure why he should have felt it mattered.

'Big moment,' she said, softly. 'Big night.'

He felt something then, heard a shift in her voice and tone, and knew he had offended her, and that surprised him, too, for she was not the type to be so easily upset. 'I shouldn't be yelling at you, Chris,' he said. 'It's just this thing with Joanna.'

'I know. You've explained.'

'I'm grateful to you,' he said. 'Just anxious to get there.'

'Sure you are, Jack.'

She recognized his uncertainty.

And smiled.

52

Joanna's first conscious emotion when she came to again was dread.

She knew she was still lying on the gurney, but she thought that the person – maybe Lamb, maybe not – who'd brought her here had gone.

She had thought the truck impossibly dark, but this was worse. Inky black, cold and dank. *A cellar?*

She could hear something. Wind, from outside. And something besides . . .

Breathing. Steady and deep. *Someone else.*

'Who's there?' Her voice was clearer than it had been, fear making it sound thin and high. 'Who's *there?*'

They didn't answer.

There was something terrible about this place, Joanna felt. Strange, mixed up smells, some sickening, some pleasant, almost fragrant . . . Sandalwood, she recognized, and something else, familiar, she thought, though she couldn't quite place it. There was ugliness, too, invisible yet thick as fog, an atmosphere Joanna had never encountered before in her entire life, not even in hospital when Philip had been dying, nor in the room in which she had visited him afterwards.

Something worse than death.

The breathing in the room became uneven, and the unseen person moaned.

Joanna's terror soared beyond anything she had ever

known. She could not move, she could not see. All she could do was wait.

Silently, she prayed. For Jack to come, or Oates, or Agent Poole. For deliverance.

And then, suddenly, she knew what the familiar scent was. Mitsouko.

53

'We're here.' Chen watched Donovan release his seat belt. 'You'd better wait for me.'

'Okay.' His jaw was clenched tight.

She drew the key out of the ignition and opened her door. Donovan turned around to fondle Sophia's ears, still trying to keep his own impatience under control. Whatever was up with Chris might just be huffiness, but his antennae were warning him that there was more to it than that. He didn't understand – wasn't sure he *wanted* to understand – what was going on, but if Mel was right and Joanna was in danger, he was damned if he was going to take any risks right now.

Chen opened the passenger door. 'Ready to go, Jack.'

He stepped out into snow, felt the fresh stuff falling thick and fast, unfolded his cane, then took her arm. 'Come on, Sophia.' The dog jumped down and he felt her press comfortingly against his left leg. He wished now that he'd taken the time to fetch her harness. *Too late.*

'Straight ahead,' Chen said, 'No steps.'

He held back. 'What's it like? The house?'

'Two storeys, grey stone, not too big.'

'Any cars?'

'No.' She didn't mention a white panel truck parked beneath the branches of a birch tree a little distance away.

'Does it look lived in?'

'Not so's you'd notice.' She sounded brisk.

283

'Any smoke from the chimney?' Donovan asked. 'Lights? Shutters? Drapes?' If Lamb were with him, he'd have an instant picture of every significant feature. But then, Lamb was the reason they were here.

'No smoke,' Chen said, 'I thought you were so keen to get inside.'

'Let's go,' he said.

She guided him to the door. Sophia dipped her muzzle briefly into the snow, then lifted it, shook it dry and followed.

'Door,' Chen said. 'You want to knock or shall I?'

Donovan raised his right hand and rapped twice, smartly, on the wood. He waited three seconds, then banged harder.

The door opened.

'Donovan.' Lamb stood on the threshold, dressed in black roll-neck and trousers, staring at Chen. 'How did you find me?'

'What's going on, Lamb?' Donovan asked. 'Where's Joanna?'

Lamb was still focused on Chen. 'Chris, why are you here?'

'Mel called Donovan,' she said. 'Something about Joanna and a sedative.'

'Where is she?' Donovan demanded.

'You'd better come in.'

They stepped inside. Donovan let go of Chen's arm, and Lamb, out of habit, took her place and led him through a dim hallway into a medium-sized living room with plank flooring and stained white walls, sparsely furnished with two straight-backed chairs and a small wooden table. Anxious as he was to get to Joanna, Donovan registered thanks for the absence of carpeting, heard Sophia's claws on the floor, felt the hollow emptiness of the place, smelled damp, picked up a disturbing sense of desolation, and had to fight to remember to count paces and mentally log changes in direction. *Forget that, and you're really lost.*

'Have a seat.' Lamb steered him to one of the chairs, placed his left hand on its back and moved away.

'Where's Joanna, Lamb?' Donovan did not sit. Sophia halted beside him, ears twitching.

284

'She's resting.' Lamb watched Chen walk to the windows, look briefly outside, then turn back to them and check her watch. 'She's fine.'

'What are you doing, Chris?' Donovan's head tilted in her direction. She didn't answer. 'Chris?' His voice was sharper.

'Relax, Donovan,' Lamb told him.

'Mel says you gave Joanna a sedative.' Donovan turned back to the other man. 'Mind telling me why you would do something like that?'

A vein in Lamb's right temple twitched. 'I had to. She was hysterical.'

'Why bring her here? Why didn't you leave her at Mel's, or bring her to the farm?' Donovan paused. 'She is here, isn't she?'

'She is,' Lamb said. 'I brought her here because I thought that the fewer people involved, the better for all of us.'

Donovan remembered every word of Mel's impossible story, and felt nauseous. 'Pete's not involved in this then?'

'No,' Lamb said. 'I would have come to fetch you, you know. There was no need for Chris to bring you over.'

'What do you mean, no need?' Donovan's outrage was growing.

'I didn't want you unnecessarily upset.'

Donovan heard and felt the other man's unease. Murdoch Lambert was so seldom uneasy, rarely showed anxiety of any kind, except perhaps when their work was going badly. *Our work*, he thought, and shuddered involuntarily.

'I want to see Joanna now,' he said again.

'She's sleeping,' Lamb said. 'There's no hurry.' He paused. 'There was no need for Mel to drag you into this either.'

Donovan waited a moment, struggling for composure. 'She told me some things, Lamb. Things I'd much rather not believe.'

'That's Joanna's fault,' Lamb said. 'I told you, she was hysterical.'

'She's not the hysterical type.'

'No.' It was the first time Chen had spoken since entering the house.

Donovan turned towards her voice. 'What do you know about this?'

'Everything,' she answered.

'Jesus, Chris!' Lamb stared at her.

'I don't understand.' Donovan turned from one to the other. 'One of you has to explain this to me.'

'All in good time,' Chen said.

'Stop jerking me *around*!' Donovan turned back to the other man. 'Take me to Joanna now, Lamb. *Now!*' He thrust his cane out and started towards the door, Sophia at his heel.

'Don't be an idiot.' Lamb stepped into his path. 'You won't find her without help.'

'So *help* me.' Donovan jabbed the cane at him and it struck Lamb on the left thigh. 'Take me to her or get out of my fucking way.' He paused. 'Sophia, go find Joanna.'

The German shepherd barked.

'What do we do?' Lamb asked Chen.

'Sophia, go find *Joanna*,' Donovan urged the dog again.

For one more second, Sophia wavered, then went to the door and scratched at its base.

'For God's sake, Chris' – Lamb was suddenly agitated – 'we have to do something.'

'We're going to.' She walked past Donovan to the door and opened it, and the dog shot past her out into the hallway.

'Sophia!' Lamb went after her, grabbed her collar.

'What's going on?' Donovan followed uncertainly, swishing his cane.

In the hall, by the front door, Chen took a key from the pocket of her slacks, fitted it into the lock, turned it, removed the key again and slipped it back into her pocket. Any lingering hopes Donovan had been harbouring that Mel's fears might have been groundless, flew into the cold, damp air and disappeared.

'What the hell is going *on* here?'

'Sure you want to know?' Chen asked.

'*No*, Chris!' Lamb was urgent.

'Shut up, Murdoch,' she told him coldly. 'Hold the dog and keep quiet.'

Donovan's chest constricted with fear. His world was being

286

turned upside down, the people who'd inhabited it suddenly not what they'd seemed to be.

'Well, Jack?' Chen said. 'Do you want to see Joanna now?'

He had a sudden urge to punch her. 'Yes.'

She came to his side. 'Give me your cane, please.'

'I need it.'

'No,' she said. 'You don't. I'm going to guide you.'

Donovan gripped the cane harder.

'You want to see her or not?'

He let her take it. She folded it, laid it quietly down on the floor, then straightened up.

'This wasn't part of the deal, Chris.' Lamb's agitation was growing.

'I told you to be quiet.' She paused. 'Take my arm, Jack.'

Donovan took it, let her lead him away from the front door towards the back of the house. The feeling of hollowness was all around them as she stopped at a door, turned the handle and opened it.

'We're going down some stairs now, Jack,' she said. 'Usual routine?'

He said nothing, just let go of her arm, waited for her to step in front of him and laid his right hand on her shoulder.

They started down.

54

She heard the sound of the door opening first, then the woman's voice, too indistinct to recognize from where she lay. Then, suddenly, from out of the darkness: 'Joanna?'

Jack's voice.

'I'm here!' She tried to move but couldn't, thought her heart might burst from the effort, but he was *here*, and that was all that mattered.

'Joanna, where are you?'

Coming closer. She could smell the faint aroma of cigar. 'Over here!' She heard scuffling, snuffling, scratching – then a bark. 'Sophia! Oh, thank God!'

The lights came on, dazzled her with their brilliance as the dog reached her, jumped up at the gurney, whining and licking her face.

'Jack, I can't move,' she called out. 'Mel and Lamb drugged me and they brought me here, and I can't *move*.'

'I know,' Jack's voice said. 'I'm here now. It's going to be okay.'

Her blindness started to go away. He was coming towards her – he looked shocked, he looked *angry*. Joanna blinked, saw that Chris Chen was leading him and felt gratitude soar. 'Chris, thank heaven!'

Chen didn't answer. She was looking beyond the gurney at something else, and abruptly Joanna remembered those other sounds, the breathing and moaning, and it was an effort to turn her head the other way, but she had to . . .

Tom Oates lay, about eight feet away, on a table, bound and gagged.

'My God.' Joanna's voice was reduced to a whisper. 'Tom.'

'Tom?' Donovan echoed, confused.

She turned her head back and now he was beside her, reaching out to touch her, to find her face, but Chris (whose perfume she had smelled in this place) had left him – just *left* him without his cane, and Sophia – not wearing her harness – was sniffing around the gurney, and there, coming down some steps, was Murdoch Lambert. And suddenly Joanna was more afraid than ever.

'Murdoch's here, Jack,' she alerted him. 'He drugged me!'

'I know. Tell me about Tom.'

'He's *here*. He's tied up!'

Donovan twisted his head back and forth, holding onto Joanna's right arm for balance, trying to locate the man but stay oriented. 'Tom, where are you?'

'He can't answer you,' Chen told him.

'He's gagged. On a table, to my left.' Joanna longed to grab hold of Jack's arm, but she still couldn't manage the movement. 'I don't think he's conscious.'

Donovan's mind was flying, his nasal receptors picking up odours and trying to decipher them. *Chen's Mitsouko, mixed with sandalwood and other things, awful things.* His spine prickled and his stomach ground with dread. Beside him, Sophia whined and scratched at the wheels at the base of the gurney, and behind him, at the foot of the stairs, he was aware of Lamb, silently watching.

'What's going on, Lamb?' Donovan fought for composure. 'Is this your house?'

'It's mine,' Chen said. She took off her coat and hung it over the back of a chair. 'Let me fill you in, Jack. You've already found Joanna, who's been drugged, as she said, but who's not really been harmed.'

'Not harmed!' Donovan searched for Joanna's arms, felt their dead weight. 'Are you *nuts*?' He pushed back the silky fabric of the pyjamas, stroked her forearm, felt the coldness of her skin. 'Joanna, try and move your arms.'

'I can't.' She swallowed down the urge to cry, to let go. 'Not properly, but I can feel your touch, so I'm not paralysed.'

'See?' Chen said. 'She's just fine.'

Joanna was staring at the other woman. She looked the same as she always did: beautifully dressed, glossy hair pinned up, mother-of-pearl locket around her neck. *Yet not the same*. Her eyes were different, glittering, their pupils large, and there was an almost palpable aura of nervous energy radiating from her.

'Agent Oates is unconscious right now, as Joanna told you,' Chen went on, 'but he's alive.'

'Are you out of your mind?' Donovan let go of Joanna's arms, bent down, found Sophia's collar and held on to it. 'Have you lost your fucking *mind*?'

'Not at all, Jack,' she said.

Lamb took a step forward. 'Chris, what are we going to do? This is not—'

'Shut up, Murdoch.'

He did as she said. He was different, too, Joanna realized, hardly able to take in the change. The confident, arrogant man was gone. He looked dazed, shocked, almost as afraid as she felt.

'I found this house a while ago.' Chen was talking to Donovan. 'It wasn't much to look at, but it was the perfect location. Between Opus 40 and Gilead Farm – two sculptors' sanctuaries. And I needed a place for my own work.' She paused again, looked at Lamb. 'For *our* work, I should say.'

Icy comprehension began to dawn on Joanna. 'The bones . . .'

'The bones,' Chen confirmed.

Joanna looked back at Tom and found that she seemed to have a little more movement in her neck, could crane it further and more easily.

'Feeling starting to come back?' Chen noticed.

Joanna kept silent, not daring to speak. Pinpricks of sensation were travelling up and down her legs, but she kept very still. Chen walked away, into a far corner, her movements sleek but brisk, very much in control. She picked something up from the table, walked back towards the gurney.

'What's that for?' Joanna's voice was higher with new fear.

'What?' Donovan turned back and forth. '*What*?'

'She's got rope!' Joanna told him. 'She's going to—'

'Be quiet, Joanna.' Chen walked round to the far side of the gurney, clear of Donovan and Sophia. 'You'll have full movement soon, and I don't want you going anyplace.'

'Chris, there's no need,' Joanna protested. 'I won't move.'

'Leave her alone.' Donovan's voice was almost a snarl.

'Or what, Jack?' Chen was efficient as she used one length of thin rope to restrain Joanna's legs. 'What will you do, blind man?'

'Lamb?' Donovan turned around, trying to locate the other man. '*Do* something!'

'I can't,' Lamb said. 'I'm sorry, but I can't.'

Sophia started to growl.

'Get them both away from the gurney,' Chen snapped at Lamb.

He didn't move.

'Get them clear, or I'll kill the dog.'

'*No*!' Joanna cried out.

Chen used the second length of rope to pin down her arms, the glittering eyes fixed on Lamb, her air of command increasing. 'Put Jack in that chair.' She nodded towards a straight-backed chair against one of the walls. '*Do* it!'

Lamb stepped forward hesitantly. 'Come on, Donovan.' He put out one hand, touched his arm.

'Don't *touch* me!'

'Sit down, Jack, or I'll hurt Joanna,' Chen threatened.

Sophia, staying close to Donovan, was still growling, ears folded back.

'I will do it, Jack,' Chen said sharply.

Donovan knew that, without any kind of weapon – not even his goddamned *cane* – he had no alternative. 'All right.' He allowed himself to be led, felt for the seat of the chair, did as he was bidden. Sophia was running back and forth in front of him, he could feel her hot breath, hear her agitated panting.

'We'll be all right, Jack.' Joanna saw how stricken he looked, knew the fear was for her. 'Gary Poole – Tom's partner – knows all about this. He'll find us.'

'Tie him to the chair, Murdoch,' Chen ordered. She looked at the German shepherd, still running back and forth. 'Tell Sophia to lie down, Jack.'

'Come on, girl,' Donovan called, and the dog came instantly, as Lamb found another length of rope on the table and returned to tie his arms, tethering him to the chair. Sophia growled.

'Cut that out.' Lamb backed off a little way.

'It's okay, hero,' Donovan told him disgustedly. 'She won't hurt you.' He waited as Lamb bent back to his task, waited until his face was just an inch or two from his, then spat with perfect aim into the other man's left eye.

Lamb shuddered for an instant, then tied his last knot and stepped away. 'Everything I've done' – his voice cracked with tears of humiliation and anger – 'has been for you.'

'Oh, *spare* me,' Donovan said. 'I know about the bones.'

'*All* for you.' Lamb was trembling. 'If you're honest with yourself, you'll know that.' He turned away, dashed the back of his right hand across his eyes.

'Actually' – Chen moved away from the gurney – 'Murdoch's part in all this has been much smaller than you may think, Jack. Fact is, I was the one who showed him how best to help you – and he *did* want to help you, more than anything, that's true enough.'

Lamb made a choking sound and leaned, half-fell, against one of the walls.

'Murdoch had his talent – you had yours.' Chen began to walk back and forth, using the whole width of the room, and Joanna fancied she could almost see the force field of her energy expanding. Suddenly, the administrator reminded her of a cat on the prowl, eyes taking in everything around her, mind focused.

'He was fixated by bones,' Chen said. 'He was good at making replicas. But I saw possibilities he hadn't dreamed of and showed him the way. And he couldn't refuse me because he was in love with you – and you did know that, Jack, whatever you say.'

'Oh, God,' Lamb said, face to the wall.

'It was child's play, sucking him in, because he was so crazy about you.' Chen's pace and speech speeded up. 'He soon found out what I could do for him, the things I was prepared to do for both of us – things he'd never have had the courage to do alone.'

'I didn't know.' Lamb's voice was muffled. 'I didn't *know*.'

'Not at the start, maybe, but soon enough.'

'For the love of *God*,' Donovan exploded from his chair, making Sophia jump, 'will someone tell me what the fuck it was you *were* doing?' He was turning his head, trying to keep up with Chen's constantly changing position. 'You're saying the bones weren't resin.'

'Give the man a prize,' Chen said.

'But he showed them to me. I *felt* them. They were resin.'

'The ones he showed you were resin,' Joanna told him, hating his wretched bewilderment. 'Murdoch made his models for your approval, but the next time you handled them they were wrapped, weren't they?'

'But *why*?' Donovan felt as if he'd fallen into quicksand. He turned his head towards Lamb, over by the wall. 'You had such a gift – that was the whole *point*, the miracle of your craft. Why did you have to cheat?'

'Fear.' At last, Lamb turned from the wall and faced Donovan.

'Of *what*?'

'Of losing you.' Lamb's thin lips were so pale they seemed almost to have vanished. 'Of losing your respect.'

'He was scared he wasn't good enough,' Chen took over again. 'He was good, but he didn't get it right all the time.'

'Who the hell *does*?' Donovan said.

'We did,' she bragged. 'Perfect results every time.'

'She brought me the bones.' Suddenly Lamb was desperate to explain. 'She told me she'd obtained them for me at great cost and risk. I was unhappy about it—'

'*Unhappy*?' Donovan erupted again.

'I'd always used human remains for my studies – you knew that, Donovan, and it never troubled you. This didn't seem so different. It wasn't strictly legal—'

'Legal?' Joanna echoed disgustedly.

'It made no difference to anyone – the people they belonged to were dead and gone,' Lamb went on. 'And in a way, it was a new challenge.'

'Jesus.' Donovan shook his head in disbelief.

'You think it was so easy? Making those perfect resin bones first, then having to throw them out and work on what *she* brought me? They were *lifeless* –' He gesticulated with his hands. 'I had to find the means to link them, to replace the musculature that had held them together before—'

'But they weren't just bones!' Joanna had to make Donovan understand while she could. 'Jack, they *killed* people to get them! That's what they've been doing all these years. They kill people and mutilate them!'

'But I didn't *know* that!' Lamb screamed at her.

'Not the first time,' Chen said. 'But you had a pretty good idea the next time, and after that you knew everything, but you didn't pull out.'

'Because I was too terrified of what I'd already done.' Lamb's voice was cracking, his expression agonized. 'Because you swore you'd say it was all my idea.'

'Because you loved the success.' She was blunt, cruel. 'You couldn't cut it as an artist working alone; the only person who thought you had talent was a blind man. And then suddenly, because of him – because of *me* – you had it all.' She came to a sudden halt in front of Donovan. 'He even picked them out, Jack. Those people he described to you so vividly – *remembered* so clearly, weeks, months later. He remembered them because he'd chosen them.' She allowed herself a pause, wanting the full impact of her words to strike home. 'Because he was the one who'd drugged them and brought them to me.'

'I don't believe you.' Donovan's face was ashen.

'I do,' Joanna said. 'Remember Ellen Miller, the dancer from Red Hook? Tom told me—'

To her left, over on the table, Oates stirred a little and

294

Joanna paused to look at him. He seemed, she thought, to be slowly coming to, and as she turned her head she realized that freer movement was starting to return to her own body as Chen had predicted it would – much good it did her now.

'Go on, Joanna.' Chen's voice startled her. 'Tell him what we did.'

Joanna felt very sick. 'They cut off her right foot, Jack.'

'Whose foot do you think you've been sculpting for the last few weeks?' Chen smiled viciously. 'Whose bones do you think you've been working around?'

Donovan made a terrible moaning sound and let go of Sophia's collar. The dog gazed up at him, whining again, ears folded back against her master's distress.

'Oh, God, Jack, I'm so sorry,' Joanna said softly.

'Joanna's sorry,' Chen echoed. 'She loves you, Jack – but then, doesn't everyone?'

'Go to *hell*!'

'We're both going there, Jack,' she said.

Joanna glanced at Oates again, then back at the Chinese-American woman. 'You must know Tom wasn't working alone, Chris,' she said. 'You must know it's only a matter of time till someone comes.'

'Of course.' She came to the foot of the gurney. 'That's why I chose this house – workshop here, dumping ground not far away.' She turned back to face Donovan. 'Opus 40, Jack. Whether anyone finds us here or not, Opus 40 will reopen in June, and then it won't be long before some visitor stumbles on our . . .' She glanced across at Lamb. 'What did you call it, Murdoch? Our detritus?'

'*Detritus*!' Donovan exploded again and Sophia cowered at the rage and revulsion in his voice '*Damn* you, Chris!'

'I know about waste,' she said. 'I grew up over a whorehouse, Jack. I don't think I put that on my CV, did I? It did qualify me, though, taught me all about the cheapness of the human body.' She shrugged. 'At least, in a way, we've given these people some value; a kind of immortality. And pretty soon, everyone's going to know that.'

'You want to be found out?' Joanna was incredulous.

'I want Donovan to be found out.'

'*Why?*' Joanna asked, softly.

'I want to destroy him.' It was simply said.

'But it'll all be over for you, too.' Lamb, too, seemed genuinely baffled. 'The success, the money . . .'

'Money?' Joanna queried.

'Blackmail,' he said bitterly. 'Enough to feather herself a nice nest. To stop her telling Donovan what I was doing.'

'The apartment on Madison Avenue,' Joanna said to Chen. 'Yours, not Murdoch's.'

'Money was just a by-product for me.' Chen ignored her. 'The important part's still to come. Ruining you, Jack. That's what matters.'

'But why?' Donovan asked, newly bewildered.

'You're a user, Jack Donovan,' she answered. 'You like having people think you're brave and brilliant and generous, but you don't really give a damn about them. You're a taker.'

'That's not true,' Lamb protested.

'Of course it's true.' The honey-coloured oval face looked suddenly pinched and uglier, the exotic eyes colder, older. 'He takes, over and over again. Love, help, service, loyalty.'

'I never took you for granted, Chris,' Donovan said.

'You take *everyone* for granted. And you don't care what happens to them.'

'That's not *true*.' Lamb defended him again.

'He didn't care about my brother,' Chen said.

'Your brother?' Donovan's bewilderment grew.

'See?' Chen looked from Lamb to Joanna. 'He doesn't even know who I'm talking about.' She turned back to Donovan. 'Think about it,' she snapped suddenly. 'While we move on.'

Joanna felt her stomach lurch.

'A small demonstration.' Chen took two steps closer to Donovan, and the dog began to growl again. 'Take Sophia's collar, Jack, please.'

'How?'

'You can move your hand enough to hold her collar. Good.' She paused briefly, her voice showing faint signs of strain, her breathing quickening. 'You've helped choose a few of your

296

own subjects, you know, Jack. Remember a young man in New Paltz, out walking with his parents a month or so back? Murdoch told you how beautiful he was – said his hair was short and soft, like mouse fur. Remember?'

Donovan couldn't speak.

'His name was Luke Schuyler and he had great legs, as it turned out. One of them's ready for you now, Jack, any time you feel up to it.'

Lamb gagged, covered his mouth with both hands, and slumped back against the wall nearest him. Chen ignored him, kept her attention on Donovan.

'Cat got your tongue, Jack?'

'Fuck you,' he said, softly. 'Oh, *fuck* you.'

'Then there's our friend here, Agent Oates.' Chen's breathing was noticeably more rapid, forming a film of sweat on her forehead and over her upper lip. 'Remember how Murdoch described Tom to you the first time he came to the school?'

Joanna's stomach clenched again. She turned to look at Oates. He was conscious now, she thought, aware perhaps of all that was going on around him, yet he was showing no signs of movement, no trace of the terror he had to be feeling.

'Those Native American cheekbones?' Chen asked. 'The nose?' She turned around suddenly. 'Let's go take a look?' She moved swiftly to the table, bent over the agent and pulled the gag out of his mouth. Oates gasped reflexively for air, choked and coughed. 'Come here, Murdoch. Tell Jack what you see.'

'No,' Lamb said, staying at the wall.

'Joanna, what's happening?' Donovan was desperate. 'What's she *doing*?'

'Shut up, Jack.' Chen seemed to be gathering momentum, her speech patterns growing faster, more aggressive. 'Murdoch, you should talk Jack through this process – you're his eyes, after all, aren't you?'

'You're insane,' Lamb said.

'Time you faced up to your role in our creations. Time you saw what really happens down here when you've finished making your deliveries.'

297

'Joanna, what's *happening*?' Donovan beseeched her.

'I don't *know*!' She was terrified.

Donovan let go of Sophia's collar again, rocked in his chair, strained against the rope holding him and failed to budge it.

'Don't want to help me, Murdoch?' Chen taunted. 'Okay, then we'll stick to the old routine, shall we? Me doing it my way, except this time you'll be my audience.'

She turned abruptly, violently, on her heel, walked to the foot of the staircase, reached for a switch on the wall, flicked it.

And the lights went out.

55

Gary Poole had given up on hearing from Joanna Guthrie a while back. He'd called Donovan's apartment repeatedly, left a bunch of messages, checked with his own office to make sure she hadn't spoken to anyone else there. And then he'd begun focusing all his energies on the issue that concerned him more: finding out where the hell Oates had disappeared to.

The guy had been so gung-ho to restart work that morning, and there was nothing Poole could imagine that might have distracted him from that commitment – unless he'd learned that Guthrie had gotten herself in some kind of a jam. But even then, Oates would never just go off half-cocked without telling anyone.

Poole knew he'd never had his colleague's flair for hunches, but the fact was, he didn't *need* great instincts to know that even if Joanna Guthrie was not in trouble, Oates almost certainly was. And if that was the case, then it seemed probable that his trouble was connected with Guthrie, who was linked to Donovan, who was in turn, so far as Poole could tell, joined at the hip to Murdoch Lambert, the bone guy Oates had been suspicious of.

Which was why he was on his way down to Kinderhook now, to check his pal's house, make sure he hadn't taken a fall or had some other kind of accident. After which he was going to drive further south. To Gilead Farm.

56

People talked about minutes seeming like lifetimes. Joanna had been through times like that; when she and Philip had waited for the doctor to tell him if he was going to live or die; when one of Bella's first litter of puppies had waited several seconds longer than the others to start breathing on its own.

Nothing like this.

Nothing.

They all waited. She'd told Donovan, swiftly, tersely, that Chen had turned out the lights, but since then no one had spoken.

All in the dark now. All blind.

Joanna prayed, *thought* she prayed, though her brain seemed to have numbed. She was trying her hardest to hear, or just to intuit, whether or not Chen was still there in the basement with them, but she could neither hear nor feel her. That was Jack's province, and since he was keeping his own counsel now, she had no way of knowing if he knew more than she did. Over to her left, she heard the sound of Tom's breathing, shallow and fast. Somewhere to her right, Lamb was muttering under his breath, maybe praying, too, maybe cursing. She didn't care *what* his personal terrors were at this precise moment. She cared about Tom, and about Jack – but she couldn't hear anything from where Jack was sitting in the blackness.

And then Sophia whined, and now she did hear his voice again, heard him speak softly and gently to the dog, reassuring her, the way he often did.

What was Chen *doing*?

Lamb let out a moan.

Sophia whined again.

And the lights came back on.

Joanna heard Lamb's choking gasp before she turned her head and saw for herself.

And then she, too, cried out in terror.

It was impossible not to.

A monster was staring back at her. A hideous demon with enormous, protuberant eyes, with horns and a crest over human nostrils, and an upper lip that curled obscenely, horrifyingly, above fangs sharp and long enough to impale a human throat.

'*What*?' Donovan called out desperately. 'Joanna, what's happened?' Beside him, Sophia went into another low, growling crouch. 'Joanna, are you *okay*?'

She could hardly breathe. 'It's Chen.'

It *was* Chen – of course it was Chen, she knew that full well – and yet at the same time it was someone else entirely, some*thing* else. Her body, from the mask down, was now clad in black, close-fitting overalls made of some synthetic fibre that gleamed in the light.

The mask was there to terrify. The overalls signified work.

That was infinitely more terrifying than the mask.

'What's she doing?' Donovan's helplessness was driving him crazy. He rocked his chair violently, sending Sophia into a fresh frenzy of panicked growling. 'Joanna, for God's sake, you have to tell me what's going *on*!'

'She's wearing a mask.' Joanna fought to keep her voice steady. 'It startled me, that's all.'

'It's a very ugly mask,' Chen's voice said from behind the monster's face. 'It's called a *t'ao-t'ieh*.'

'She's insane,' Lamb said. 'I told you.'

'Not insane,' Chen corrected him. 'Just playing a game.' She turned to face Donovan. 'It's a game I used to play with my brother.'

'Am I supposed to know your brother?'

301

'No, Jack. You never knew him.'

'But you said before that I didn't care about him.' Donovan knew now that he was fighting – they were all fighting – for their lives. 'That makes no sense, Chris.'

'I'm not Chris now,' she said from beneath the curling upper lip.

'Who are you?' Oates asked from the table. It was the first time he had spoken since the gag had been pulled out of his mouth, and his voice was hoarse, but not as weak as might have been expected.

'My name is Lei Kung – in English, the Duke of Thunder.' Chen turned from Donovan and walked to a spot between the table and Joanna's gurney. 'When my brother and I were kids, living over the whorehouse, we played some pretty great games together. Fantasy games, I guess you'd call them, but all Kai and I knew was they helped us to escape. I was the Duke of Thunder, who could punish evil mortals by gouging their bodies with a chisel, and Kai was Yün-T'ung, the Cloud Youth, who could whip up storm clouds when the Duke ordered him to.'

'Cute,' Donovan said.

'Shut up,' Chen said, whipping around.

For the first time, Joanna realized that she was holding something in her right hand. 'Jack, she has a knife.'

'My chisel, you mean,' Chen said.

'It isn't a chisel, Jack,' Joanna said, clearly.

'Want to know my name for you, Jack?' Chen asked.

'Why not?' he said.

'Tsao Chün. The Furnace Prince. He used to make dishes of gold, and the people that used them became immortal.'

'If you say so.'

'You like your name, Tsao Chün?'

'Sure,' he said. 'Why not?'

'Good.' Chen turned around abruptly, moved to the table where Oates lay. 'Let's get on, shall we?'

'She's gone back to Tom,' Joanna told Donovan, terrified again.

'Not she,' Chen corrected. 'He. The Duke, remember?'

'Yes,' Joanna said, and noticed for the first time that

302

Chen's movements had become brisker, less fluid, less feminine since she'd reappeared.

Oates didn't speak as she bent over him, just closed his eyes.

'Tom has a collection you'd be interested in,' Joanna said, *Distract her*. 'Have you heard of shamanism, Chris?'

Chen didn't look up. 'If you can't remember my name, Joanna, please be quiet.' Even her voice was a little deeper.

'Tom has some remarkable masks, too,' Joanna persisted.

'I don't think she wants to know,' Oates said huskily, opening his eyes.

'I'd like to hear about them,' Donovan said from his chair.

'Be quiet, Tsao Chün.' The mask looked up. 'Still don't want to help out here, Murdoch?'

Lamb, over by the steps, leaning against the wall for support, looked sicker than ever. He shook his head, apparently beyond speech.

'Fine.' Chen paused, then went on. 'Normally, the Duke likes doing this part in the dark. It helps him *see* the subject from your viewpoint, Tsao Chün.' She touched Oates's face for the first time and he cringed involuntarily. Chen laughed from behind the mask, stooped to place the knife on the floor, then straightened up again and ran her right index finger over the FBI man's curved nose.

'Please,' Joanna begged softly. 'Leave him alone.'

This time Donovan didn't ask to be told what was happening. Joanna thought, looking at his expression, that he knew more than he wanted to.

'Murdoch taught the Duke much of what he needed to know about the human skeleton,' Chen said. 'But I think by now, he's learned more than Lamb ever knew.' She paused, concentrating. 'The nose *is* fascinating.' The fingers of her left hand traced the lines of Oates's right cheekbone. 'All the bones are very fine.' Another beat. 'The whole head is almost perfect.'

Joanna saw Oates's chest contract, saw that his right arm was quivering. She wanted to scream.

Chen straightened up, let her hands drop to her sides. 'Lei

Kung, the Duke of Thunder' – she looked around the room from behind the mask – 'was a Chinese Taoist deity. He was considered a fearsome god, with claws and bat wings, but his role was ordered by Heaven.'

'What role?' Joanna asked, still desperately hoping to distract her.

'He punished mortals who'd committed secret crimes.'

'What secret crimes have I committed?' Oates asked.

'Not you,' Chen answered him. 'Tsao Chün.'

'If it's me you're punishing,' Donovan said, 'why not let the others go?'

Chen took a few long, unnatural, striding paces away from the table and stopped. 'Taoism has a lot of myths about immortality, you know, Tsao Chün? There's one that Kai and I used to enjoy about Hsi Wang Mu – that's the Queen Mother of the West. She used to hold banquets for the Eight Immortals. One of them rode a donkey that he could fold up when he wasn't riding it. Another could eat mother-of-pearl and then float away.'

The mother-of-pearl locket, Joanna remembered. And the soft, pastel, feminine colours. In absolute contrast with this new, terrifyingly altered identity.

'Ah, well,' Chen said from behind the *t'ao-t'ieh*. 'Back to work.'

'I asked you a question,' Donovan said sharply. 'Why not let Oates and Joanna go? If it's me you're trying to punish.'

'What better way to add to your punishment than by using your friend and your lover?' Chen paused. 'Come and help me now, Murdoch.'

'Forget it,' Lamb said.

Chen – the Duke – made another abrupt turn, walked back to the table where Oates lay, bent to retrieve the knife she'd laid on the floor, walked over to Lamb and pointed the blade at his throat. 'Do you need reminding,' she asked, 'about the people you've helped kill this far?'

'I've never killed anyone.'

'You may not have done the cutting, but don't you suppose a jury might think what you did was even worse? You chose

304

them. You *abducted* them. You brought them to me, so I could take care of all the ugly stuff, and then you played your own games with their bones. Didn't you?' She touched his neck with the blade, watched him squirm. '*Didn't* you?'

'Yes.' Lamb's voice was a whisper.

'Without me, you have no future,' Chen went on. 'You understand that, don't you, Murdoch? *Don't* you?'

'*Yes.*' His face was so chalky Joanna thought he would faint.

Chen lowered her knife hand. 'Then get over there and help me.'

She walked to the table in the far corner of the room and unfolded something – a pouch, Joanna thought, craning her head. Two more knives were lifted out, blades glistening in the light.

'Oh, Christ.' Oates had seen, and knew.

'Oh, no,' Joanna begged. 'Please, *no!*'

'Oh, *Jesus.*' Oates closed his eyes tightly, and his lips began to move in some kind of silent prayer.

'Jack, she's got more *knives!*' Joanna strained against the ropes tethering her to the gurney, and Sophia began barking, high-pitched sounds of distress that were painful to the ears.

'For God's sake, Chris!' Donovan yelled, rocking and pulling against his own restraints, shaking with the impotence of his anguish and rage.

Chen set the knives down again on the table and took something else out of the pouch – something too small to see from a distance – and now she was walking back, moving more slowly – the monster in black – *the Duke* – towards Oates.

Oates opened his eyes, saw what was in her right hand. For just one more second he didn't understand. And then he screamed.

'Oh, my *God!*' Joanna saw something tiny and round in Chen's fingers, saw her bend over the helpless man, saw him start to rock his head wildly from side to side. 'Oh, my God, Jack, she's trying to *suffocate* him!' She was sobbing in despair. 'She's putting something into his *nose!*'

Chen used her left hand to hold Oates's head still – she was strong, small, but so *strong* – and as the little rubber plug slid

305

into the left nostril, Oates screamed again, and Joanna gagged from shock and revulsion and began to cough.

'Joanna!' Donovan was frantic. 'Joanna, are you okay?'

She couldn't answer, her throat was too constricted, the horror too terrible, her inability to help Tom, her terror for him and for Jack and for herself . . . She couldn't seem to stop coughing . . . she was *choking* . . .

'Someone *help* her!' Donovan roared.

'Fuck's sake,' Chen said, hardly glancing up. 'Help the bitch, Murdoch.'

'Go on, you bastard, *help* her,' Donovan yelled, and Sophia, even more distressed now by her master's rage, darted away into the corner, head down, shoulders hunched, growling.

Lamb stared at Joanna. 'She needs water.'

'So *get* her some fucking water, moron,' Chen told him.

Through streaming eyes, still racked by her coughing fit, Joanna saw Lamb back away, then turn and run up the steps. He reached the top, opened the door and vanished from sight. Joanna saw Sophia, still hunched in the corner near the steps, and realized suddenly that the dog was their only hope, and despite the coughing fit, she forced her mind rapidly back to the weeks of the German shepherd's training and working trials with Fred's friend in the police force. They'd used a command for sending the dog away. Maybe, just *maybe*, if she combined that with her guide dog training . . .

The door was still open. *Now*.

Joanna tried to get her breath.

'Sophia, away. Find help!'

Her voice was cracked and weak. Sophia heard her, looked in confusion across to Donovan, then back to Joanna.

'Sophia, *away*. Find *help*!'

Chen turned to look at the dog, saw her ears cocked. 'Shut up, Joanna.'

Joanna strengthened her tone. 'Find *help*, Sophia!'

'I said, shut *up*!'

'Sophia, *away*!' Donovan roared the command. 'Find *Pete*!'

For one more instant the dog hesitated, and then she was on

her way, racing up the steps and out through the door.

'Stop her!' Chen yelled furiously from behind the mask. 'Murdoch, the dog's loose! Stop her!'

'*Away*, Sophia!' Donovan yelled. 'Get help!'

From above, they heard Lamb's running feet, then his voice, shouting at the dog – then the sound of smashing glass and a bellow – and then Lamb appeared in the doorway at the top of the steps. 'She went through a *window*!'

'Good *girl*,' Donovan said.

'You think?' Chen turned on him, hands clenched into fists.

'Yeah, I think.'

Lamb hovered at the top of the steps. 'Do you want me to go after her?'

'No need.' Chen's cruelty was undiluted. 'She'll have cut herself going through the glass. She'll probably bleed to death long before she gets anyplace, let alone the farm.'

'She's police trained,' Joanna defied throatily. 'She'll make it.' The need to cough was returning, but she scarcely dared. She darted a swift glance across at Oates. His colour was greyish, but at least Chen had only managed to put in one of those awful rubber plugs before she'd been distracted.

The monster – *the Duke* – turned around again. Joanna froze, heard Oates's breathing quicken again, shallow, terrified.

'I've had about enough of you, Joanna Guthrie,' Chen said slowly.

Oates understood the switch in attention. 'Is that you or the Duke speaking?' he asked her, attempting to draw fire back to himself.

Chen stepped closer to the gurney. The mask bobbed a little as the human eyes behind the protuberant demon ones scanned Joanna's whole body. 'What do you think, Tsao Chün?' She didn't turn towards Donovan, just raised her voice a little. 'We know you find Joanna beautiful – those long, fine, English bones . . . Wouldn't you just love to sculpt them?'

'He already has sculpted me.' Joanna's voice remained hoarse, trembling a little. *Someone will find Sophia . . . You just need time.* 'It's as wonderful a piece as anything you and Lamb ever helped him create.'

307

'But not as accurate,' Chen said, and rolled up Joanna's left sleeve. 'A little thin, perhaps, but that's hardly going to matter, is it?' She stroked the forearm, and all Joanna's nerve endings were functioning again, the touch making her shudder. 'I'm sorry – am I scaring you, Joanna?'

'Leave her alone.' Donovan's voice was filled with hatred.

'Jack never needed you to make him great.' Joanna was trying to buy time. 'He's just generous – he liked helping people he thought were his friends.'

The slap came without warning, and Joanna cried out. Oates jerked in furious reflex and Donovan rocked violently back and forth in his chair.

'Murdoch, get down here,' Chen screamed suddenly.

Lamb, wavering halfway down the steps, started down reluctantly as Chen strode back to Oates's table, tugged the small piece of rubber out of the man's left nostril and came back to the gurney, holding it up in her right hand.

'What are you doing?' Lamb stopped again at the foot of the steps, face more blanched than ever. 'Just what do you think you're *doing*?'

'You're not thinking straight,' Oates yelled, panicking for Joanna. 'Chen, *listen* to me—'

'Not Chen, remember?' She didn't look at him. 'Lei Kung.'

'Okay,' Oates said, '*okay*.' He had to pause to swallow, to draw breath. 'Listen to me, Lei Kung. The dog may not make it, but Gary Poole will – like you said before, it's just a matter of time.'

'Quite right,' she agreed. 'Better not waste any more.'

'Better make a deal,' Oates said.

Behind the mask, Chen made a sound of derision and bent over Joanna.

'*No!*' Oates yelled. 'Joanna, fight her – keep turning your head!'

'Chris, for God's sake!' Lamb started towards the gurney, then halted again.

'Lamb!' Donovan's voice called out to him. 'Lamb, undo this rope.'

'I *can't!*'

308

'He can't,' Chen said mockingly, grasping Joanna's long hair and holding her still while she pushed the evil little plug into her right nostril.

'Jesus!' Oates cried out. 'Lambert, stop her! You have to *stop* her!'

'I *can't*!' Lamb screamed back. 'She'll kill me!'

The monster straightened up, and Joanna, gasping and terrified as she was, saw that the effort had taken its toll, because Chen's hands were shaking and her breathing was rapid and shallow.

'What about us, Lamb?' Donovan was fighting for Joanna's life. 'All those years of friendship? Everything you've done for me – do you think I could forget that? Can *you*? Honestly?'

'Be quiet, Tsao Chün.' Chen's voice was still harsh, but it, too, was shaking now.

Donovan ignored her. 'Untie me, Lamb, and you stand a chance. I'll tell them you helped us – we'll all tell them.'

Oates had spotted the changes in Chen. 'What's up, Duke?' he asked, gambling on a sudden hunch. 'Need some help of your own?'

'Shut up,' Chen said, but the trembling was getting worse.

'What do you need?' he asked. 'To go on being Lei Kung – to go on being the Duke?'

'I told you to shut *up*.' She turned on him, but had to hold on to the edge of the gurney.

'What are you on?' Oates wasn't letting up now. 'Coke or heroin? What do you need right this minute? Blue sky or blow – or maybe you like both – want a Belushi cocktail?'

'Shut the fuck *up*!' Chen screamed, then turned to Lamb. 'Go on then,' she yelled at him. 'Fetch it!' Lamb didn't react. 'Fetch my stuff! *Now*!'

Lamb still wavered.

'I'm right, aren't I?' Oates asked Chen. 'You need it real bad. Or is it the Duke? Can't he do the job unless he gets his fix?'

Chen ran to the table over by the wall, grabbed a fat roll of sticking plaster, ripped off a length, ran back to Oates and slapped it over his mouth.

309

Across the room, still trapped in his chair, Donovan knew they were running out of time. He went on flexing his arms against the knots – they seemed to be giving a little – and he'd built himself a pretty good picture of the room by now, knew where everyone was positioned, just in *case* he got a shot at Chen. He thought he knew exactly where Joanna was, and where Oates was lying, and he *thought* he knew where those big fucking knives were . . .

Lamb was still standing in the middle of the room.

'Are you going to do what I say or not?' Chen shrieked at him.

For another moment he seemed to sag a little, then turned back towards the steps.

'You even *think* of getting out of here without me, Murdoch, you'd better think again, because I'll slice the heads off these three bastards and I'll make sure *you're* the one they blame for it . . .' Suddenly Chen ripped off the *t'ao-t'ieh* – her face beneath was pale and grimacing, her mouth contorting with pain.

Lamb was halfway up the stairs.

'Better not forget it's your handiwork Donovan's always praised to everyone!' she screamed after him.

'Not too many people know about that, Chris,' Donovan pointed out, still flexing his arms, and the goddamned knots *were* giving, he could *feel* them loosening. 'Lamb never wanted credit, remember?' He paused. 'Not remembering too much right now, are you? Need your fix too badly?'

Chen threw the mask on the floor, felt in the right-hand pocket of her black overall, produced a second plug and went back to the gurney.

'*No!*' Joanna thrashed her head back and forth. 'Oh, God, *no!*'

'Shut up!' Chen shrieked at her. 'Shut the fuck *up!*' She ran back to the table by the wall, ripped another length of sticking plaster from the roll, ran back to the gurney and slapped it hard over Joanna's mouth. 'Murdoch!' she yelled. 'Where the fuck are you?'

'Joanna?' Donovan grew more frantic than ever. '*Joanna!*'

310

Chen grabbed the long red hair again, struggled to get the second plug into Joanna's left nostril, dropped it, bent to retrieve it, seized the hair again, pulling it even tighter, and drove the plug home.

Joanna's muffled scream was all Donovan needed. He focused every ounce of strength, all his power, all his rage, on beating the ropes around his arms – and this time, the knots *gave*, and he was on his feet – and now he was directing his energies to locating those knives . . . *There*, on the table . . .

'Murdoch!' Chen shrieked again. 'Donovan's free!'

She hurled herself at him. Donovan turned and slammed into her with his left side – *'Bastard!'* she cried in pain as he turned back to the table, frantic to find the knives before she could recover.

Joanna could hardly breathe at all now. There was a *whisper* of air bypassing the plug in her left nostril, but it wasn't enough, it wasn't *enough* . . .

Oates's shout, stifled by sticking plaster, came too late to warn Donovan. Chen, agile from years of *t'ai chi* despite her addiction, kicked Donovan hard, finding his left kidney. Grunting with pain, he grabbed for her – they crashed to the floor, the knives tumbling too, blades flashing – Chen reached for one of them—

'Donovan, watch *out!*' Lamb yelled.

Chen wheeled round and saw Lamb too late. His right boot connected with her chest, thrusting her on to her back, making her scream in agony and drop the knife. *'Snake!'* She stared up at him in rage and disbelief as he snatched up the knife, then swiftly kicked the second one clear, sending it skidding over the floor and under the table near the far wall. 'What are you going to do now, *snake*? Kill me?' Even in pain, she was still mocking him. 'If I die, where does that leave you?'

'Where's Joanna?' Donovan scrambled to his feet, disoriented and desperate. 'Lamb, she's going to *die!*'

'Go left,' Lamb told Donovan, not daring to take his eyes off Chen.

'*Where?*'

'Further – that's it – there's tape over her mouth.'

Donovan felt for Joanna's face, found the gag, ripped it off, heard and felt her sucking in air and starting to weep reflexively. 'It's okay, baby, it's okay.'

'Her nose,' Lamb shouted, still wielding the knife. 'Plugs in her *nose*!'

'*Bastard*!' Chen gasped, her trembling growing worse, her oval face ugly now with hatred and sweat and pain. 'Why are you helping *them*?'

Donovan got out one of the plugs, heard Joanna's breathing getting easier, then found the rope tethering her arms, and unfastened it.

'Tom – to my left,' she gasped.

'No!' Lamb called sharply. 'Leave Oates!'

Donovan ignored him, feeling his way.

'Stay where you are, Donovan.' Lamb was strained to his limit. 'I don't want to see you die – I don't have any reason to want Joanna harmed – but I can't let you untie Oates.'

'That's good,' Chen said from the floor, one hand to her chest, still in great pain but starting to recover. 'That makes sense, Murdoch, keeping control. We have to keep control.'

Lamb didn't look down. 'I should never have listened to her.' He kept his eyes on Donovan. 'I wish to Christ I'd never met her.' He was imploring now. 'The bones seemed to make sense – working from them, just that, nothing more – not the *killing*.'

The circulation was returning to Joanna's arms. Moving slowly, carefully, praying she wouldn't be stopped, she bent forward at the waist to unknot the second rope around her legs.

'Where's my stuff, Murdoch?' Chen made an attempt to sit up, winced, fell back again. 'Did you bring it down?'

Lamb didn't answer, still refused to look at her.

Her face contorted briefly in a spasm. 'It's okay,' she said, controlling it. 'We'll both be okay, Murdoch, so long as you help me.'

Joanna flexed her legs, wriggled her toes, noticed for the first time that she was wearing turquoise silk pyjamas, almost her own size. *Sandra's*, she guessed, irrelevantly, *with Mel so much shorter*.

'We'll be fine, Murdoch.' Chen managed to sit up, strengthened her voice. 'So long as we stick together.'

'I won't let you kill them,' he told her.

'I'm not asking you to.'

Joanna looked at Oates, knew that if she didn't do something now – *right now* – Chen might recover fully, and then there was no knowing what might happen. Moving slowly again, still carefully, she twisted her body to the left and began lowering her legs to the floor.

'Joanna's moving,' Chen pointed out to Lamb.

The monster's recovering. Joanna froze. 'I'm not going anywhere, Murdoch,' she said, 'but I'd keep my eyes on her, if I were you.'

'Despise me all you like,' Chen said, staring up at Lamb, 'but you're still as guilty as I am.'

'You just saved my life, Lamb,' Donovan said. 'Stay on track now, and we'll testify that this was all down to her, not you. But you have to stay *with* us now, all the way.'

Joanna took a swift, deep breath, said one more prayer, and walked shakily to Oates's side . . .

'Don't untie him, Joanna,' Lamb warned.

'Stop her, Murdoch!' Chen got herself onto her knees. '*Stop* her.'

Lamb took a step towards Joanna then halted, his eyes on Chen now.

'Who's more dangerous, Murdoch?' Joanna found the knot for the rope around Oates's arms. 'A drugged man who's been tied up for God knows how long? Or a junkie killer who thinks she's a Taoist god?'

'Bitch!' Chen spat. 'Stop her, Murdoch, for your *own* sake.'

'Who're you going to put your faith in, Lamb?' Donovan demanded.

For one long moment – while Joanna pulled the sticking plaster from Tom Oates's mouth and rubbed his stiff, icy cold arms through the fabric of his white shirt – Murdoch Lambert stood between Chris Chen, his very own devil, and the black depths that the law would certainly drag him down into if he listened to Donovan.

313

And made up his mind.

He glanced over his right shoulder, very swiftly, then back down at Chen – a monster now, he registered, even without her *t'ao-t'ieh* mask – then at the blind man he had loved for years, done everything for – *everything* . . . looked across at the redheaded Englishwoman in the ill-fitting pyjamas, and at the weak-looking – *temporarily* weak, he reminded himself – FBI man.

He began to move backwards, holding the knife in front of himself – and it was too damned *big* a knife for them to risk arguing with – towards the steps, until he reached the foot.

'What are you *doing*, Murdoch?'

If Chen had looked like a cat prowling around before, Joanna thought standing beside Oates, now she was more like a panther with a human face as she knelt on the floor, ready to spring. She was still sweating, still trembling, but there was real power left in there too, real danger.

'Leaving,' Lamb answered. 'Getting out.'

Joanna stared questioningly into Oates's face as she untied the second rope and began to rub life into his legs. His nod was scarcely perceptible, but enough to reassure her that he was getting there – far from his fittest, but *getting* there.

'What chance do you think you have out there?' Chen asked him. 'Without me to help you?'

Lamb began to edge backwards up the steps. 'Whatever chance, I'll take it.'

Joanna went on rubbing Oates's legs. He nodded again, began to sit up, forcing back a groan of pain, and she helped him get his feet down on to the floor.

Donovan, standing between them and Chen, silent and still, was struggling to do the only thing he usefully, sanely, *could* do without his dog or cane. He was calculating distances, commanding his mental computer to try judging exactly where the weapons were . . . *One knife in Lamb's hand* . . . *One hit the wall at the end of its skid* . . .

'Okay,' Chen said. 'You get out if you want.' She was having trouble breathing. 'But give me my stuff before you go.'

Lamb ignored her, went on edging up the steps.

'I'll die without it.' Chen's eyes darted back and forth between them all. 'Give me a fighting chance – Murdoch, *please*, that's all I'm asking. I *need* it!'

It was almost painful for Donovan concentrating so hard now, in the midst of all the craziness, all the danger. *There were three knives – Chen had another one when she turned herself into Lei Kung – the one she called her chisel . . .* Oh, Christ, where *was* that?

'Throw it to me.' Chen was in a crouch now. 'For pity's sake, Murdoch, you owe me *that* much!'

Lamb stared down at her from the top step, saw the frenzied need in her face, pulled a small plastic bag from the right-hand pocket of his trousers and tossed it down to her. It was a fine throw, the bag landed less than two feet away and Chen scooped it up greedily, pocketing it safely in her black overalls.

'Now the knife!' she shouted.

'No!' Joanna yelled. 'Murdoch, *no!*'

'I can understand you running out on me, Murdoch.' Chen was almost gabbling now, panting. 'But you won't need the knife out there!'

Lamb was wavering again.

'There are *three* of them, Murdoch,' she appealed. 'Three against one! Throw me the knife!' She half straightened, held out her hands ready to catch.

'Are you a good ball player?' Lamb asked her.

'What?' Chen was way beyond irritation. 'Just *throw* it!'

Donovan stopped concentrating on where things were and focused all his attention back on Lamb. He wasn't sure, but he thought . . .

'You have to catch it carefully,' Lamb called, 'or it'll cut you.'

Joanna and Oates felt it too, stood very still, waiting.

Chen couldn't bear any more delay.

'*Throw* the fucking thing to me!'

Lamb's arm curved out to the right, extended fully, like a man about to skim a Frisbee to a friend. 'To you!' he yelled suddenly, and let it fly.

Donovan was ready, had played the game with Lamb often enough, albeit with balls. The knife blade collided with his right palm, slashing it, but he held on to it, too hyped even to feel the pain, and now he was armed. *Blind as a fucking bat, but* armed!

With a scream of fury, Chen launched herself at the table by the far wall, got to the pouch and withdrew something – larger than any of the knives, its squarish silvery blade flashing as the light from the overhead bulbs hit it–

'A cleaver!' Joanna started towards Donovan, but Oates grabbed her right arm. 'Tom, what are you *doing*? Let me go!'

Chen was moving slowly, weaving a little, swinging the cleaver ahead of herself, her decision-making and balance suddenly fogged.

'Jack, Chen has a *cleaver*!' Joanna warned.

'You have to get out of here, Joanna.' Oates was still holding her.

'I have to help Jack.' Joanna struggled to pull away.

Chen turned towards Donovan.

'I'll help Jack.' Oates started pushing Joanna towards the steps. 'You get out any way you can, call someone.'

Chen switched direction again, swung the cleaver at Oates with a great grunt of effort. He shoved Joanna clear, ducked. Chen missed, half fell, propelled off-balance by her own energy, and Oates dived for the knife under the table on the far side.

Joanna ran to Donovan, took his arm. 'Give me the knife, Jack.'

He gave it to her, its handle wet from his blood. 'You okay?'

'Joanna, watch *out*!' Oates shouted.

Chen was advancing slowly, swinging the cleaver.

'Jack, she's coming this way!' Joanna clutched Donovan's arm more tightly with her left hand, held out the big knife with her right. 'Backwards – let me guide you.'

'No *way*!' Chen screamed, swung the cleaver again, catching Donovan on the shoulder. He fell against Joanna,

316

knocking her sideways and making her drop the knife.

'*Jack!*' Joanna saw him staggering, saw more blood, struggled to get back on her feet, get back to him. 'Jack, hold on!'

Oates drove into Chen from behind, but she twisted, suddenly agile again, and the cleaver's blade sliced into his left side. He screamed and fell heavily, taking her down with him, winding her.

'Jack, take my *arm.*' Joanna was back on her feet, staring around for the knife, but not finding it, knowing they had to get out *now*, with or without it. 'Can you walk?'

'I'm not leaving Tom.'

She grabbed his good arm, started pulling him towards the steps. 'He's bleeding badly.' She pulled harder as he resisted. 'Chen's down, but she has the knife and the cleaver. You and I have to get *out!*'

'Go without me.'

'We're going *together.*'

'Don't be a damned idiot, Donovan!' Lamb, still there at the top of the steps, held out his hand. 'I'm not going to let you die.' He came halfway down, took Donovan's arm with a force Joanna had thought him incapable of. 'Stop fighting me!'

'Let go of me, Lamb!'

'You can't fight me, Jack, not with that shoulder.'

'Go *on!*' Joanna was right behind them.

'Jack stays!' Chen's voice came suddenly, stridently, from below. 'Or I cut this bastard's throat!'

They all halted in their tracks, stared down, saw Oates still slumped on the floor, barely conscious, bleeding from the wound in his side, and Chen holding him from behind, the knife blade against his jugular vein.

'Murdoch and Joanna can go,' Chen said. 'But you owe me, Jack.'

'I owe you *nothing!*'

'You owe me for Kai.'

'Kai?' Donovan's head was spinning, from blood loss and disorientation. 'Your brother?' He pulled away from Lamb.

'Donovan, what are you *doing*?' Lamb was distraught.

317

'I'm sorry,' Donovan said to Joanna softly. 'I'm so sorry for everything.'

'You're not staying, Jack. You *can't*.'

'I can't let her kill Tom.' He pushed her gently to one side, found the handrail and started to feel his way down.

'Jack, *no*!'

'Donovan, please!' Lamb begged.

'Running out of *patience*.' Chen pressed the knife closer to Oates's neck.

'You want my forgiveness, Lamb?' Donovan's voice was harder again. 'Then get Joanna out of here – do *that* much for me.'

'All right.' Lamb's voice was anguished, his face chalkier than ever. 'All *right*.' He took two steps down, took hold of Joanna's right arm.

'*No*!' She tried to fight him.

'Running out of *ti-ime*.' Chen traced the blade over Oates's throat.

'Come on.' Lamb dragged Joanna up the steps.

'We can't leave Jack!'

'We have no *choice*!'

At the top, in the open doorway, Joanna dug her bare heels in one last time, looked back down at Donovan at the foot of the staircase, right hand on the rail. She turned to look at Lamb to implore him, but all she saw mirrored in his eyes was her own agony.

'We're going to have to go through the window,' he said, softly. 'My keys are down there with my coat.'

Joanna took one more glance down while Lamb moved away, thrust out his sweatered arm to smash and clear away the glass still in place after Sophia's exit.

'No more time.' He held out his arm to help her through.

'Oh, God,' she said.

'I know,' he agreed.

She followed him.

318

57

Donovan knew that Chen was giving herself a fix. He'd heard her opening the bag Lamb had thrown, wrapping a tourniquet around her arm to expose a vein, and slapping her own flesh ... Now, after a pause, he could hear her long, shuddering, ecstatic sigh of relief, and he knew it was happening. He waited, hoping against hope that she might have miscalculated and overdosed, wondering if he stood any chance of getting to Oates before she recovered from the initial rush, wondering how long her euphoria would last, knowing it depended on too many variables. Without vision, there was no way of knowing. *No eyes, no cane, no dog.*

He didn't have long to wait.

'Still here, Jack?' There was satisfaction in her voice.

'So, are you going to tell me now?' He gritted his teeth and held on to the handrail. 'About Kai?'

'Oh, yes,' she said from the floor. 'I'll tell you.'

She'd taken the gamble of letting go of Oates while giving herself the fix – no gamble, really, not with these two: one unconscious, the other blind. Now she had hold of the FBI man again, had tightened her grip around his neck, keeping the knife close to his jugular. The whole left side of his shirt was flowering crimson, but the blood flow appeared to have slowed as her strength had returned.

'I'm sure you remember the fire,' she said. 'In Chicago.'

For one more moment Donovan's mind scrambled frantically.

319

And then understanding dawned, and with it new horror.

'The man who died,' he said.

Chen's honey-coloured face, ordinarily smooth, seemed suddenly coarser, eaten through with hate. 'The man you told the *Sun-Times* was less important than your dog.'

58

Joanna and Lamb stood outside the house, temporarily disoriented by the monochrome night, the landscape stinging white with snow, trees and bushes laden with it, but above and beyond, nothing but blackness. No moon, no stars, no lights.

'Are you all right?' Lamb looked at Joanna.

She nodded, not yet able to speak. The shock of cold had sucked the breath out of her. She wanted to yell with the pain of it all – silk pyjamas, bare *feet*, Jack and Tom back down there in that basement with a crazy woman . . .

She moved, as fast as she could manage, to Chen's Volvo.

'No keys,' Lamb said behind her.

Joanna sagged, noticed the white panel truck parked on the other side of the house near a slender birch tree – the truck, she guessed, in which she'd been driven from the city.

'All the keys are in the house.'

'Great.' She folded her arms around herself. Breathing was possible again, though it hurt – *everything* hurt. She peered towards the road, her eyes growing accustomed to the uncanny light. 'Which way?'

'To where?' Lamb asked, stamping his boots in the cold.

'Where's the nearest house? Anywhere we can call from.'

He hesitated before answering. 'That way.' He gestured with his chin.

'Are you sure? Murdoch, are you *sure*?'

'If you don't believe me, go the other way,' he said, and started walking.

Joanna stood by the Volvo for one more moment. The night was so eerily *silent*. No sounds from the house, nothing except the creaking of snow-laden branches out here.

Stand here for much longer and you'll freeze to death.

She followed Lamb.

59

'I didn't know anyone had died,' Donovan said, still gripping the hand rail. 'The reporter showed up in my hospital room, asked me a bunch of damn' fool questions. I didn't know that anyone except Annie and Mike was in the house with me and Waldo.'

'No one knew then.'

'So how could I have talked about Kai to the newspaper?' His shoulder was throbbing, but he thought the bleeding had stopped.

'You could have talked about him later, when you did know.' Chen's voice was growing tighter, higher, more strained again. She hadn't had enough, she realized, hadn't taken all the strain and exertion into account – her body was already crying out for more.

'I didn't know who he was,' Donovan said.

'Did you try and find out?' Chen asked.

'No.' *Stay honest.* 'I was told the ME couldn't identify him. The cops thought he might have been a vagrant, or—'

'Or a burglar,' Chen said.

'Yes.' Donovan could hear Oates's breathing, but had no way of knowing how seriously he was injured. *'Bleeding badly,'* Joanna had said. 'How's Tom doing?'

'Okay, so far,' Chen said. 'My knife's still pointed at his throat.' She shifted, the FBI man's weight heavy against her. 'Kai was a burglar that night, but he was also a human being, you know. You *know*?'

'Of course I know.'

'He was *young* – he had a sister who *loved* him, but to you, Mr Big-Shot-Artist, he was no one. *You* were someone, even back then. Famous enough for the *Sun-Times* to want to talk to you about the fire.' The bitterness was more violent than ever. 'But all you cared about was your dog.'

'I loved my dog,' Donovan said. 'I won't lie about that.'

'I loved my *brother*! I knew Kai had been in that house, and I hadn't heard a word from him, so I knew he had to be dead. I read your interview and told myself you didn't know – "The sonofabitch doesn't *know* about Kai," I said, "it's not his fault. When he finds out, he'll talk to the newspaper again, maybe the TV people, and he'll say he's sorry."'

'I should have,' Donovan admitted.

'Is that all you have to *say*? You *should* have?'

'I don't know what else to say. Sorry just wouldn't cover it.'

'No,' Chen agreed. 'It would not.'

60

'You need help?' Lamb asked, a few hundred yards down the road.

'I'm all right.'

Joanna was far from all right. She couldn't feel her feet and it still hurt to breathe, and she knew that if she didn't get out of the snow and wrapped up soon she might be in serious trouble, knew a little about hypothermia and frostbite, but not too much. *That's good*, she told herself, forcing herself on up the road. *The less you know, the better right now.*

'Distances are hard to figure sometimes,' Lamb said over his shoulder, slapping his arms around himself as he moved. 'I don't know how much further.'

Liar. He'd probably chosen the longest route on this godforsaken, pavementless, unlit road – she'd seen that hesitation on his face when she'd asked him which way to go. He loved Donovan, she thought, tramping on, that was almost certainly true enough, but he was even more terrified by the ramifications of what he'd been a part of.

'I'd offer you my boots,' he said, not looking back, 'but they wouldn't fit you.'

Your sweater would, Joanna thought, but didn't say.

'We could stop – I could give you my socks.'

'We can't stop,' she said. 'There isn't any time.'

Not for Jack or Tom.

325

61

'You could let Oates go now,' Donovan said.

'No point,' Chen told him.

'What do you mean?' Donovan froze.

'He's unconscious,' Chen said. 'He can't go any place.'

'So what's our plan? Stay here forever? Or until the cops come?'

'No,' she said. 'We're not going to do that.'

Fresh dread grabbed hold of his insides.

'Come here, Jack.'

'I'd rather stay here,' Donovan said from the foot of the steps.

'I'm sure you would.' Chen was sounding weirder by the second. 'Come *here*, Jack. I want you to do something for me.'

'What?'

'You'll find out.'

'This isn't a fair contest, you know?' He tried to sound light, to rekindle something of the years they'd spent working together. 'You've had your stuff. You could at least get me my cane.'

'Kai died in the dark. It must have been so dark in that crawlspace.'

'None of us knew he was there, Chris.'

'He burned in the end, but the smoke killed him first. He must have been so *scared*. Poor Yün-T'ung. Trapped in that black hole, no one to help him.'

Oates let out a soft groan.

'Come *here*, Jack.' It was a command. 'I'll kill him if you don't.'

'You'll have to guide me.'

'Down one step.' She wasted no time. 'Let go the rail and follow my voice.'

'What's between us?'

'Space,' Chen said.

Donovan kept his arms by his sides. All his blind life, he'd hated having to grope around in the blackness. He hadn't minded the canes so much, they were marvellous tools, there to be used, and his dogs had given him back his pride. He'd even grown to tolerate the help of humans, but wandering around with outstretched arms like some little kid playing blind man's buff made him sick to his stomach, and he was damned if he'd give Chen that satisfaction now.

'Here I am,' she said. 'Here we both are.'

Donovan stopped about two feet away. 'Now what?'

'Now we finish this.'

62

Joanna heard the barking first, and thought she was hallucinating. *Wishful thinking*. Maybe semi-delirium was one of the symptoms of freezing to death, she thought, trying to remember to pick up her feet rather than shuffle them through the snow.

She heard it again.

'Did you hear that?' she called to Lamb, ahead of her in the road.

He stopped, stood rigid and silent. The barking was coming from up ahead, and there was another sound, too – an engine, and men's voices, yelling – and now, out of the inky void she *saw* something . . . *Headlights*.

'Hey!' she shouted. '*Hey*!'

'Shut up,' Lamb told her over his shoulder.

'We're *here*!' She yelled even louder, hadn't believed she had that much strength left. 'Hey, we're *here*!'

'Be *quiet*!' Lamb hissed.

The headlights came closer, then stopped, the vehicle too far away to see clearly, but the doors were opening, and two shapes . . . two men . . . were coming towards them on foot, and they had flashlights, their beams bobbing around in the dark . . . The barking intensified . . .

'Sophia!' Joanna yelled in ecstasy.

She saw the dog first, loping through the snow towards her, then the two men running, and at last she could see their faces – one a stranger, the other Szabo.

'Murdoch, it's Pete!'

Lamb came back to her, stood close by her side. 'Mind what you tell them.'

The dog reached her, jumping up, still barking, tail thrashing, whining passionately. 'Sophia!' Joanna crouched to hug her, saw traces of blood and fragments of shattered glass still visible on her muzzle, head and upper body from her leap through the window. 'Thank God you're all right.'

'Jo, are you *okay*?' Szabo came skidding to a halt. 'Sophia came to the farm. She barked till we followed her – right over the Rhinecliff Bridge – I can't *believe* how clever she is!' He was staring at her pyjamas and frozen face. 'Dear Lord, what's *happened* to you?'

'We have to get help!' Joanna stood up, the dog still dancing around her, and stared at the second man. He was big and solid in a dark brown jacket, with tufts of brown hair sticking out from under a black woollen hat.

'Gary Poole, ma'am,' he said. 'You look about to freeze to death.' He started to unzip his jacket, and there was a holstered gun on his side. He cast a swift, probing look at Lamb. 'FBI, sir. Are you Murdoch Lambert?'

'I am.' Lamb stepped even closer to Joanna, close enough for her to feel his warm breath on her ear. 'Pete, I was never so glad to see anyone!'

'You have to go to a house a mile or so back!' Joanna burst breathlessly. 'Chris is there, with Jack and Tom Oates. She's out of her mind.'

'Chris?' Szabo looked stunned. '*Our* Chris?'

Poole was taking off his jacket for her while Sophia ran back and forth in front of them.

'She's crazy – really crazy,' Joanna told him. 'She's got knives and drugs. She's the one who's—'

'Shut *up*!' Lamb made a sudden grab for her, dragging her back several feet, and there was something in his hand, Joanna could see it in front of her face – a shard of broken glass from

329

the window, lethal as any knife.

'Hey, man, take it easy.' Poole dropped the jacket and started to go for his gun.

'*Leave* it!' Lamb pulled Joanna closer to the edge of the road, the glass at her neck. 'Stay away, and no guns!'

'Okay,' Poole said, and glanced sideways at Szabo. 'Stay very still.'

'I'm not going anyplace,' Szabo said.

Sophia, recognizing fresh danger, began barking furiously.

'Get hold of her,' Lamb ordered Poole. 'And stay back.' The dog went on barking and growling. 'I said get *hold* of her.'

Szabo stepped forward, grasped Sophia's collar. 'Come on, beautiful.'

'For God's sake, Murdoch,' Joanna gasped. 'This is mad. Let me go!'

'I can't. I wish I could, but I can't.' Lamb looked over his shoulder at the black and white open land behind them, keeping the jagged shard close to her neck. 'Anyone follows us,' he told Poole and Szabo, 'I swear I'll kill her.'

'You don't want to kill anyone,' Szabo said.

'He's been in this whole thing with Chen.' Joanna had to get it out, couldn't *endure* the possibility of them not finding out. 'He chose the victims, drugged them – he drugged me and Tom, too, and—'

'Shut *up*!' Lamb started pulling her off the road into deeper snow.

'Give it up, Lambert,' Poole called to him. 'You can't get far in this.'

'As far as I have to,' Lamb yelled and tightened his grip on Joanna.

'Murdoch, you have to stop this now!' she pleaded.

'You know I can't.'

Joanna stared at the two men and the dog, getting further away, saw that Poole was holding his gun now, clasped in

330

both hands, outstretched, but she knew he would never risk taking a shot with her in the way. 'Forget about us!' she shouted. 'Follow our tracks – get to the house and help Jack and Tom!' The cold air hurt her throat, made her voice hoarse. 'Murdoch won't hurt me if you leave him alone!'

'That's right,' Lamb yelled. 'Give me time to get clear, and I'll let her go!'

'Get to the *house!*' Joanna screamed.

63

'Don't be scared,' Chen told Donovan. 'I'm not going to hurt you.'

'I'm not scared of you,' he said. 'But I'm not going to help you kill Oates, if that's what you're after.' He could hear the agent's breathing more distinctly now he was closer, but all that told him was that Oates was alive.

'I'm not asking you to do that, Jack.' Her voice was pitching up and down bizarrely. 'I'm going to give you a very special gift.'

'What kind of a gift?'

She put out her hand. 'It's the cleaver, Jack. The kind butchers use for chopping through bones.' She held it out to him. 'Take it.'

'What for?' He felt sick.

'*Take* it.'

Donovan let her put it into his hand.

'Remember I still have the knife,' Chen reminded him. 'And Tom.'

'I'm not forgetting.'

Quickly, but very quietly, she put the knife down on the floor and rolled up her right sleeve. She looked around the room. 'The floor's not the best place to do this, but I'm not moving. Our friend here's pretty much a dead weight.'

'Let me take him.'

'I don't think so.' Chen leaned sideways and stretched out

her right arm experimentally until it was flat on the ground.
'You have the cleaver, Jack?'

'Yes.'

'Kneel down.'

'Why?' Dread was expanding in his stomach.

'Kneel down, right here. *Now*, or I kill Oates.'

He knelt.

'Put the cleaver down for a second and give me your hand.'

He extended his right hand.

'Other hand,' Chen said.

He felt her take hold of his left hand. Her fingers were hot to the touch, almost vibrating with energy, pulling his hand down.

'Feel that? My right arm. It's flat on the ground – feel it?'

He couldn't tell if the knife was in her other hand or not. 'I feel it.'

'Now pick up the cleaver again with your right hand.'

Realization hit him like a juggernaut.

'*No!*' He snatched his hand away.

'It's my last gift to you, Jack. It's *perfect*.'

'You sick bitch,' he said.

'Only right you should get to keep my right hand. Use my bones for one last, perfect Donovan.' The pitch of her voice was very low again, intensely, sickeningly compelling. 'Considering what my hands have accomplished in your name.'

He stood up, shaking violently. 'If you think I'm going to do this, you're even crazier than I thought.'

'You *are* going to do it.'

'No way on earth.'

'Then I'll kill Oates.' She picked up the knife.

The agent moaned.

'That's the blade nicking his flesh, Jack. He can feel it. Listen.' She moved the knife, cut his skin lightly, clear of the main vein but drawing blood. Oates moaned more loudly. 'Hear that, Jack?'

'Oh, Christ.'

'Get back on your knees, Jack.' She was growing more

333

strident now, more powerful.

Donovan didn't move.

'Surely you want to kill me?' Chen said. 'This is your big chance.'

'I don't,' he said. *Liar*.

'Think what I did to Ellen Miller,' she said. 'Think of the foot you've been working on. The young man in New Paltz. The old farmer – that fabulous forearm the critics raved about.'

'Shut up.'

'Think of the young boy's spine in MOMA.'

'Jesus. *Jesus*!'

'There was an old lady – one of Murdoch's students. I cut off her hand just a week or so ago. It was a great—'

'Shut the fuck *up*!' She was right – he wanted to *strangle* her.

'Of *course* you want to kill me, Jack.' Shriller now. 'And I know I have to die now, or go to jail – I've known it for a long time. And at least this way, I know you'll never, *ever* forget the way it happened. You'll remember the feel and the sound and the smell of it till the day you die.' She paused to breathe. 'Now kneel *down*.'

'Jesus,' Donovan said again, weakly, knowing now that she was completely, irretrievably insane.

Oates stirred, groaned again, a little more loudly.

'His life or mine, Jack.'

Donovan stumbled down on his knees.

'Now pick up the cleaver.'

He felt for it, got it in his hand, wrapped his fingers tightly around the handle, hardly able to breathe, the blood roaring in his head.

'Make sure you get it right, Jack,' she said. 'The cut needs to be clean, or you can't use it for your work.'

'God damn you to hell for this!'

'Like I said before,' Chen told him, 'we're both going there.'

64

Joanna prayed that Poole and Szabo had reached the house. She couldn't see them any more, and even the sound of Sophia's persistent barking had faded away into the night silence; and they were some way from that road now. She hadn't realized before, had been too disorientated to realize, how close they'd been to other people's houses, to front doors they could have knocked on, to telephones they might have used to call for help. But Chen had talked about her house being near Opus 40, and she remembered now what that area had looked like in daylight. Nice houses, mostly clapboard, with neat lawns and forest around them. She realized now that Lamb had probably been dragging her across private properties, and maybe if she had begun screaming, someone might have heard, but she hadn't *known* that decent, normal people were around, because everything looked the same, *felt* the same: black and white and deathly cold.

'You could let me go now,' she told Lamb, who was dragging her by the hand now.

'Not yet.' He was as breathless as she was, the shard of glass still clutched in his left hand, his short hedgehog hair growing whiter with the snow that had started falling again.

'They're not following us.' She was perspiring from effort, thought the sweat might be freezing on her face, wondered how much longer she could survive like this if they didn't find shelter. 'You could go any way you wanted and I wouldn't tell anyone.'

He kept moving. 'Save your breath, Joanna.'

They were heading into forest now, snow-laden maples and pines closing in on them, moving further away from civilization. It might, she hoped, be a little less cold under the cover of so many trees, but it was also going to make it harder for them to be found. She looked back over her shoulder, saw that the fresh snow was already covering their tracks, looked ahead again at the panicked man still towing her along.

'Murdoch, this is so pointless,' she tried again.

'I told you, save your *breath*.'

His grip tightened, wrenching her arm and hurting her back, the old pains from the mugging returning with a vengeance. *Who mugged me?* she wondered suddenly, crazily, wondered if that had been Lamb, too, stealing her photographs, trying to get her to leave the country.

And then she noticed that his left hand, still clutching the broken glass, had been cut, and a little blood was sprinkling on the snow as they ran, and maybe, just *maybe*, someone might see that . . .

Not if it goes on snowing.

65

Coming to, Oates thought he was dreaming. A dream of pure horror, filled with blood and gore, worse than any nightmare he'd ever had. A picture flashed through his mind of an old painting his grandmother had once shown him to warn him about myths perpetuated by racists about the 'savagery of the redskin': man covered in blood, kneeling over slain woman . . .

Not a dream.

'Holy fuck.'

The blood-soaked man didn't move, seemed rooted to the spot.

'Donovan?' Oates's voice was weak. 'Jack?'

'Is she dead?' Donovan's words were uttered so softly, with so much sickness behind them, that they were barely audible. 'I tried finding a pulse, but I couldn't.'

'She's dead.' Oates glanced down at himself then, saw that his own blood was drying, looked back up at Donovan. 'Are you hurt?'

'No more than before.' Still that same sick softness.

Oates didn't want to look at Chen again, but he forced himself to. The cleaver, the tourniquet on her left arm, the hypodermic still in the vein. *The rest.* He retched, closed his eyes, fought for strength, opened them again.

'She did that herself?' It was almost clear. The position of the cleaver seemed to indicate that it had fallen from Chen's left hand. *Almost clear.*

337

'She wanted me to do it.' It was hard for Donovan just saying the words. 'She told me she'd kill you if I didn't do it, but I couldn't, Tom – not even for you – so she gave herself another fix – I heard her – and . . .' He couldn't go on.

'Must have been sky high,' Oates said.

Pain swamped the FBI man again, and the sound of his shudder seemed to force Donovan back from the purgatory he'd felt trapped in. 'Christ, Tom, I'm sorry – how're you doing?'

'I'll be okay. Where's Joanna? Lambert?'

'They got out.'

'Together?' Fear was implicit in the word.

'Yes.' Donovan paused. 'Don't imagine you're up to going after them?'

Oates tried to sit up and fell back. 'No way.'

'She – Chris – left my cane upstairs. Maybe if I—'

'Don't be crazy, man,' Oates told him.

'She brought me here in her car.' Donovan wasn't ready to give up. 'Could you drive, Tom, if I helped you up there?'

'I don't know.' Oates grimaced. 'Not exactly a great team.'

'Oh, Jesus.' Donovan thought of the thinness of the fabric he'd felt on Joanna's arms. Silk, out there in the snow. *Out there with Lamb*. A man capable of doing what he had.

'He threw you the knife.' It wasn't hard for Oates to read the other man's thoughts. 'He won't hurt her. He has no reason to now.'

'We can't just stay down here.'

Oates cast a sideways glance at Chen and felt another wave of nausea. 'I'm game to try if you are.' Anything was better than staying here.

'I'll help you,' Donovan said, 'but you'll have to guide me.' He crouched low, got one arm around the other man's shoulders, started to lever, but Oates yelped involuntarily, and he lowered him back. 'It's no good.'

'Just give me a second,' Oates said.

'You're *injured*, Tom' – Donovan raked his hair in frustration – 'and I'm worse than fucking useless. And Joanna's out there with a sonofabitch who's spent years pimping for a crazy

338

butcher.' He sank back down onto his haunches. 'For me.'

'Cut that out, Jack,' Oates said.

'For *me*, Tom. There's no way around that.'

They both heard it at the same time.

Barking. Voices. Men's voices.

Donovan's head went up. '*Sophia*!'

Oates listened an instant longer, recognized Gary Poole's deep voice.

'Thank Christ,' he said very softly.

And then he, too, began to yell.

66

Joanna hadn't recognized it immediately. It looked so different from that other time at the beginning of the month. Then, she'd entered by car from the road, through a gate, and it had been daytime, the weather fine enough for her to shoot rolls of film and wander around, taking her time. Now, emerging from the woods that surrounded it on three sides, she felt almost as if she were stepping on to some 1950s black-and-white sci-fi film set; Opus 40 on a snowy night looked like a third-rate director's idea of an alien planet after all its inhabitants had been sucked away by a cosmic vacuum cleaner.

'Not so fast, Murdoch,' she pleaded. 'It's dangerous here.'

Harvey Fite's great expanses of smooth bluestone slabs were brilliant white and treacherously icy beneath their feet – her dying, frozen feet. The pools that formed a part of the sculpture were iced over, too, and even the trees looked as rigid as the central stone monolith, like tall, skeletal humans too hypothermic to ever move again.

'We have to slow down.' She pulled right back, forcing him to slow almost to a halt. 'We have to get help before we freeze to death.' Her fingers were clawed, but there was hardly any pain now, and she knew its absence was not good news. 'I swear I'll help you get away.' Her voice was frailer than it had been. 'We can find a house, tell people we've broken down and—'

'And what?' Lamb's lips were blue. 'You think they won't

340

ask any questions, won't want to know what you're doing out on a night like this wearing *pyjamas*?'

'We'll say I'm ill and you were taking me to a hospital. We'll ask them to call an ambulance, and—'

'And what? And *what*?' Despite his exhaustion, Lamb was almost screaming. 'I might have been crazy enough to go along with Chris, but I haven't lost *every* ounce of my brain yet – I'm hardly about to let you go to a nice, cosy house so you can whisper to some Samaritan to call the cops.'

'I wouldn't do that, Murdoch. You're Jack's best friend.'

'Don't be so absurd.' He started moving again, dragged her with him, slipped, righted himself and kept on going. 'Just keep your mouth shut and let me think, can you *do* that?' He lifted his left hand to wipe his eyes clear of snow and stopped again, staring at it, as if he'd forgotten the piece of jagged glass clutched in it. 'I'm bleeding.'

Joanna didn't speak.

'How long have I been *bleeding*?'

'I don't know.'

Lamb looked back the way they'd come. 'I've left a trail of fucking *blood*.' He stared at her. 'You knew, didn't you, you stupid bitch? You knew I was leaving a trail and you didn't say anything.'

'Whatever you say,' Joanna said wearily.

'I should kill you for that.'

'I'd say you're doing a pretty fair job of that already, wouldn't you?'

67

Poole had wanted to leave Donovan and Oates at the house to wait for the paramedics, but both men had refused to stay there a second longer, so he and Szabo had helped them into his Chevy so they could all get back to the spot where they'd last seen Murdoch Lambert dragging Joanna off the road.

'What now?' Donovan had asked with desperate impatience right after Poole had radioed their new position.

'I'm leaving the motor running,' Poole had said. 'You'll stay here with Oates till help arrives.' He'd looked at Szabo. 'I should leave you, too, but you seem to know what you're doing with the dog.' He'd hesitated. 'Any objections to my taking her, Donovan?'

'Sophia's more likely to find Joanna than anyone,' Donovan had said.

'Don't get your hopes up too high,' Poole had warned him. 'It hasn't stopped snowing for quite a while. Their tracks'll probably be covered, and I don't know how well dogs pick up scents in the snow.'

'Sophia's smart,' Szabo had said stoutly.

'Even Rin-Tin-fucking-Tin wouldn't have found anyone if he'd been left behind in a goddamned *car*,' Donovan had said sarcastically.

And so the two men and the dog had gone.

68

Joanna and Lamb were still inside Opus 40 when the first sounds penetrated, breaking through the rasp of their breathing and the grunts of their continuing effort: Sophia's barking first, then the crunching of boots.

'They're coming,' Joanna said unnecessarily, as Lamb's panic drove him to try to accelerate, dragging her even faster over the ice.

'It was the blood,' he gasped. 'You bitch, it was the *blood*.'

'You're going too fast, Murdoch.'

The frightened man had been forcing them to weave back and forth around the gigantic sculpture area, moving in and out of the trees, keeping well away from the lip of the quarry at the centre. Now they were on some kind of plateau, and Joanna's numb, dead feet were barely skimming the icy surface, her strength almost gone.

'Can't we please just *stop*?' she begged him now. 'I'll tell them you saved me from Chen – you *did* save me and Jack, didn't you?'

The snow was falling more thickly than ever, making it harder to see, but Lamb kept on going. 'You could tell the FBI I'm Jesus Christ reborn,' he panted, 'but I'd still go to prison, and you know what they'd do to me in there. I couldn't survive that.'

'They might *not* send you to prison,' Joanna gasped, 'if I testify . . . if Jack and I both testify.'

'Jack's probably dead.' Lamb plunged blindly.

'He *isn't* dead,' Joanna screamed at him. 'Please, Murdoch, let me go – you'll be faster without me.'

'You're my only hope of getting out of this, Joanna, and you know it.'

'That's just stupid – I didn't know you could be so *stupid*.' Tears of sheer frustration were freezing on her cheeks. 'Jack thought you were brilliant.'

'Then that's another thing that's gone forever!'

Neither of them saw the edge of the plateau until it was too late. Lamb skidded, tried to recover, failed and dragged her down with him. They fell, almost soundlessly, hands still linked until they landed with a hideous, numbing crash, on the frozen surface of a large, square-shaped pool, their eyes wide and staring, their mouths open in horror.

'Oh, Christ,' Lamb said quite softly, almost with a note of surprise in his voice. 'Oh, dear Christ.'

And then the world folded beneath them.

Joanna's scream, blending with the ice's cracking, soared vainly into the night. She was free of Lamb's grip, but now, instead, she was *drowning*, fighting for life again the way she had when Chen had plugged up her nose and mouth, only this time there was no whisper of air to save her. The water was so *heavy*, like iced black lead dragging her down, the blackness inkier than anything, darker even than the basement before the lights had been switched on, and maybe *this* was what it was like for Jack . . . Dear God, she prayed not.

I'm so tired, she thought. All the pain had gone now, even the fear was receding, and she thought she was ready to let go at last, hoped that Jack would not destroy the rest of his life with guilt . . .

Something brushed against her in the black water.

A face, looming close to her own.

Not Lamb's. A corpse's face, bloated and ghastly.

Joanna almost opened her mouth to scream, but self-preservation stopped her, and the new horror brought her back to the realization that she was *not*, after all, ready to die yet. She kicked her feet, lungs threatening to explode, kicked her legs madly, and she'd thought all her strength had gone, but there were still these last few ounces of reserve, and she used them all now, pushed up hard towards the surface, towards *life* . . .

Something was pulling at her, at her *hair*, dragging at it . . . then at the collar of her pyjama top. Her head broke through the surface, her face was clear of the black water, and she was choking, she couldn't get any air into her lungs . . . But whatever was pulling at her wasn't letting go, and there was warm breath on her face, and she opened her eyes. And there was Sophia, her beloved *Sophia*, in the water with her, dragging at her pyjama jacket with her jaws . . . And then something else – *hands* – pulling her clear, out of the pool, turning her over, covering her, warming her.

By the time they found Murdoch Lambert, he was dead.

69

The deep, murky pool at Opus 40, and two small glades in the forest beyond, had yielded further remains – what Chen had referred to as the 'detritus' of her and Lambert's work – and the house, too, had provided a steady stream of horrors for the investigating teams that had poured in after the night of December 22nd-23rd. A cast-iron bath in which Chen had washed her victims prior to and after death with sandalwood-scented soap. An expensively ventilated room with a stove and two catering-sized cooking pots (one forty-quart, the other twenty) used for the incomparably gruesome task of loosening flesh from bones. More cleavers, knives, chopping blocks. More black overalls.

And, of course, the discarded *t'ao-t'ieh*. The Duke's mask.

Of Chris Chen, a little more became known. That she had been a neonate heroin dependant born to an undiagnosed addict mother in San Francisco, and that, by the age of eleven, she had been prostituting herself to pay for her own addiction and that of her younger brother, Kai.

'They found an old book in a drawer in her Manhattan apartment,' Oates told Joanna and Donovan during a visit to Fifty-sixth Street on the second Sunday of the New Year. 'An old book of Taoist mythological deities that Chen and Kai probably kept since they were kids living over the whore-house. There were drawings in the margins, with scribbled

346

captions, of Kai flying on his donkey and Chris eating mother-of-pearl and floating over San Francisco.'

'And the Duke?' Joanna asked.

'Oh, he was there, complete with his chisel, and young Kai as the Cloud Youth, whipping up his storm clouds.'

Donovan said nothing.

'These weren't students of mythology,' Oates said, quietly. 'They were the children of a brothel-keeper and an addict. It didn't matter to them how much they blurred the edges of those myths – maybe all that mattered was trying to escape into a better world.'

Chen had left California in her teens, taking Kai with her, Oates told them; had moved to Chicago, put herself through a secretarial course, paying her way as before but taking care of her brother.

'Yet Kai became a burglar,' Joanna pointed out.

Oates nodded. 'And so far as we can figure it out, Chen probably encouraged that, maybe even sent him out on jobs. She said she knew Kai had been in your friends' house in Chicago, Jack.'

'So it was her fault he was there,' Joanna said, softly.

'And the fire was just an accident,' Oates added.

'But then I talked to the *Sun-Times*,' Donovan said, 'and as good as told the people of Chicago that my dog was more important than Kai.'

'You didn't know, Jack,' Joanna said, not for the first time.

Kai had died, and Chen had chosen Jack Donovan to focus blame on, had watched and waited, familiarized herself with his world, seen the vacancy at the school and taken the job.

'She couldn't have done any of it without Lamb,' Oates went on. 'She'd probably never have come up with the idea if it hadn't been for his fascination with bones.'

'And the fact that he loved Jack,' Joanna said quietly.

'Want to know what I think about Lamb?' Oates asked Donovan.

'Why not?'

'Maybe he did love you, but he also wanted what you had.

347

And you gave it to him. You welcomed him, you let him share your art and your home and your friends, and then Chen brought him those first bones, and you believed in him, and the sculptures turned out great—'

'Because of the bones,' Donovan said.

'Because of *you*,' Joanna said.

He shook his head.

'I'll bet *Lamb* believed it was because of the damned bones,' Oates said, 'and that must have driven him even crazier than he always was, because you were getting the acclaim and the praise.'

'You thought he was modest for turning down your offers of credit,' Joanna said, 'but he was just terrified of getting caught.'

'And Lamb's fear only made him more useful to Chen,' Oates added.

Joanna had been staying in the apartment since Kingston Hospital had released them all, Donovan and Sophia coming down to Manhattan whenever the ongoing investigation allowed. Gilead Farm, the school and the apartment, too, had been taken apart by agents, detectives and forensic experts, and each one of Donovan's original clay and plaster works in the basement storage-room at the Fifty-sixth Street building had been broken up in the search for remains and evidence.

There was no one left alive to try for the murders, and there were more than enough witnesses to testify on Donovan's behalf, yet there had been no respite for him as he'd been forced to face the hideous inspection of his life and works of the last several years. In a series of seemingly endless interrogations by police and agents, he had been asked to detail precisely how each of the sculptures built on human remains had come about, from inception to completion. Even more distressingly, Donovan had come to learn about each one of Chen's and Lamb's victims, had made a point of meeting their families, and attending religious services when their remains had at last been laid to rest.

*

'Not one of them blames you,' Joanna said the night after the last of the services.

'I blame me,' Donovan said.

They were in his bed at the apartment, Sophia on the floor close by. It was almost four in the morning, and none of them was sleeping.

'I understand why,' Joanna said, 'but you're wrong.'

'I'm not wrong,' he said.

Joanna had decided not to press charges against Mel Rosenthal for her semi-inadvertent part in the kidnapping – the agent, she realized, felt wretchedly guilty enough without dragging her into court for something she'd done in a moment of panic – but on the rare occasions they had met since that night, Mel had found it almost impossible to meet Joanna's eyes.

'So she should,' Oates said.

As angry as Donovan had been at Mel during and immediately after the events, that, too, had shifted to more self-blame. His agent was a victim, too, was yet another individual suffering because of him.

They had all tried repeatedly to drum home his innocence to the man himself, but he believed none of them. Ignorance of what had been perpetrated in his name, he said, did not make him innocent. Before Lamb and Chen, he'd been a fine, respected sculptor, but once Lamb had begun bringing him their sickening offerings and he'd found himself suddenly launched into the stratosphere of the art world, he had never once stopped to *question* that meteoric rise. Just as he'd never questioned the fact that he had surrounded himself by people who had seemed to adore him.

'I may not be guilty of murder,' he had told Joanna and the others. 'But I'm guilty as hell of what made this whole nightmare possible.'

'And what's that?' Mel had asked, not sure she wanted to know.

'Vanity,' Donovan said. 'Greed.' He paused. 'And the kind of blindness that has nothing to do with my eyes.'

*

Joanna had waited for him to sink himself into alcoholic oblivion, but that had not happened. If anything, it seemed to her, Donovan drank *less* than usual.

'Too easy,' he'd told her.

'You have so much more strength than you give yourself credit for.'

'Strength?' he said cynically. 'Is that what you call it?'

Lengthy legal and ethical debates began, on television and in the press, as to what should now happen to the bronze casts of the tainted sculptures that had been sold worldwide for large sums of money; but the awful truth was that the grisly element would, in time, simply add to their investment value. So far as Donovan was concerned, his work had become an abomination, but Mel was already reporting a disturbing swell of a sick element in and beyond the lower reaches of the art world apparently clamouring for more of the same.

The school had been closed, Donovan's personal studio had been gutted, and Gilead Farm was up for sale. Knowing now that the place he'd believed a creative sanctuary had, in reality, been a corrupt and evil microsociety of which he had been the hub, the sculptor could no longer bear to set foot on the land.

'It's time you went home,' he told Joanna when she found him drinking tea in the sitting room during another of their sleepless nights in the last week of January.

'What do you mean?' Shock thinned her voice.

'You were set to go before New Year's.'

He was on the sofa, Sophia beside him. The dog twitched her ears and thumped her tail, waiting for Joanna to come and join them.

'Do you want me to go?' Joanna remained standing.

The answer was three full seconds coming. 'Yes.'

She sat down in the closest armchair. 'Why?'

'You know why.'

She did know, had known it for weeks, ever since she'd finished giving her account of her own involvement to the investigators and had been told she was free to leave the country. More than ever Joanna had wanted to stay close to Donovan, to try to console him, help bring him through the horrors, but all he had done was push her away. They had shared the apartment and his bed, but they had not made love. They'd spoken about many things, important and trivial, but he had steadfastly refused to communicate at any really deep level.

She'd asked Mel to have lunch with her one day.

'I'm just not getting through to him.'

'No one is,' the agent had said.

'I'm afraid for him, Mel. He's so isolated.'

'He's desolate, Jo.' Mel, too, was growing desperately worried. 'He's sickened and bitter – he's too guilt-racked to work.' She shook her head. 'I don't know what to do for him.'

Joanna was coming to realize there was nothing significant that Donovan was going to *allow* Mel, or her, or anyone else, *to* do for him.

Not even love him.

'You can't have normality with me,' he told her a week after he'd first shocked her by suggesting she leave. 'And that's exactly what you should have.'

It was February now, and the world outside was drab and cold. They had been breakfasting – *trying* to breakfast – but neither felt capable of eating. They had both known for days that this conversation was coming, knew that it was now unavoidable, and even Sophia, lying close by, nose down between her paws, was depressed.

'I need *you*,' Joanna said.

'What you need,' Donovan said, 'is to get as far away from me as possible.'

'You don't know what I need.'

'I think I do.' He was sad but calm. 'You need to go back to England, back to a little sanity and some decent values.'

Joanna tried to lift her coffee cup to her lips, but her hand trembled and she gave it up. 'Don't you think you might need me, Jack?'

His smile was bleak. 'It's not as simple as that, Joanna.'

'Perhaps it should be.'

'Perhaps it should.'

For a long moment she watched him. Physically, he was looking better than he had for a while after the horrors, had put back a little of the weight he had lost, had even got around to visiting his barber for a haircut.

The real wreckage was still there though, on the inside.

'Maybe we could take a trip?' she suggested.

Clutching at straws.

'I wouldn't be fit company.'

'Mel says they're always asking you to tour Europe.'

'I might do that someday.'

But not with me.'

'Push me away enough times, Jack, and I will go.'

His face was implacable.

'That's what I'm aiming for.'

Mel told Joanna that he didn't mean it, that both she and Sandra were sure he needed her more than ever. Pete Szabo told her that, in his experience, when Donovan had pushed people away in the past (not that there had ever been a time anything *like* this) it had usually meant that he needed space, a little time on his own.

'Which was when he'd come to the city,' Joanna said.

'That's right,' Szabo agreed.

'But with me here, there's no place for him to lick his wounds.'

'I'd say that was about it.'

She took a while before she spoke again.

'I don't have to ask you if you'll look after him.'

'No,' Szabo said. 'You don't, Jo.'

She called Tom Oates before she left.

'I guess I'm glad you're leaving,' he said.

'You too?' she asked drily.

'Selfish reasons,' Oates said. 'I hate you being this unhappy.' He paused. 'Truthfully, I'd love nothing more than to think you could stay in this country and start feeling good again – maybe even start seeing more of me instead of Donovan.'

Joanna didn't answer.

'But I know none of that's possible, and that's okay, Joanna. So long as you go home, find your feet again, start feeling *happy* again.'

'I'll miss you, Tom,' she said.

'Not a tenth of how much I'll miss you.'

She reserved a room for her last night at the Peninsula, where she had begun, determined to say her farewells to Donovan and Sophia as swiftly as possible on the previous afternoon, knowing they would be too unbearable to prolong.

She had been right.

'This still feels wrong to me, Jack,' she said, at the door, before leaving his apartment for the last time.

'I know it does,' he said. 'But it isn't wrong.'

She looked at his face, saw the cracks beneath the surface, longed for him to touch her one last time, knew she might fall apart if he did.

'If you need me,' she said.

'I won't call.'

'And if I need you?'

His resolve didn't waver. 'Do yourself a favour and don't call me.'

She wanted to hate him then – and not for the first time – but she knew it was a hopeless, pointless wish. She understood him far too well for that.

'Would you like a minute alone with Sophia?' Donovan asked.

'No,' she said. 'Thank you.' She'd said goodbye to her dog once before at Gilead Farm, but that time there had been a glimmer of hope that she would see her again in Manhattan. 'More than I could bear, you know?'

'I know,' he said softly, and then: 'I'm sorry, Joanna.'

'Me, too,' she said.

'Mel thinks I'm a damned fool.'

'I know she does.' *One final attempt.* 'Maybe, some day,

you'll come to visit us. They're talking about lifting quarantine – you could bring Sophia.'

'Maybe,' he said, and opened his front door. 'I doubt it.'

He went out ahead of her into the small, square hallway, summoned the elevator and stood in silence, waiting, the dog by his side. Joanna was silent, too. Neither of them, she knew, could take any more.

'Stay safe, Jack,' she said as the door slid open and she stepped inside.

'You, too, Joanna,' he said.

They were both dry-eyed as the doors closed.

They both knew that would not last.

70

Time did heal.

It also changed some things.

Donovan was coming to England tomorrow.

His call in September had hit Joanna with all the impact of a sledgehammer. Every atom of her hard-regained composure had disintegrated in seconds. His voice had seemed to strike home somewhere deep inside her, swamping her instantly with longing.

He was coming with Szabo, Donovan had told her; he tended to go most places with Pete these days, he said, relied on him even more than he had in the old days. Sophia would have to stay home, of course, with no changes yet to British quarantine restrictions, but Mel and Sandra were happy to take care of her while he was travelling.

'Is she all right?' Joanna had asked, knowing that she was.

'Sophia's wonderful,' Donovan had answered.

Silence had crept between them then.

'So,' he had said, at last, 'may we come?' He paused. 'Or am I too late?'

Her answer had been one word.

'Come.'

'Are you sure this is a good idea?' Sara had asked when Joanna had gone to visit her that same afternoon to give her the news.

355

'Not really,' Joanna had said and signed.

'But sure enough to tell him to come?'

'Yes.'

Little had changed in the cottage near Shipton-under-Wychwood since Joanna's departure last autumn. The narrowing of Sara's tunnel vision had continued, but there was still enough to allow her to go on drinking in the visual features of her Oxfordshire world with the same thirst she always had.

'You know how I feel about Donovan, Jo.' Sara had looked troubled. 'But it's taken you so long to recover from it all. I don't want him to hurt you again.'

'Nor do I.'

'You know he may do just that? Not deliberately – I don't think that for a second.' Sara's dark eyes were pained. 'But he may not be able to avoid it.'

Since leaving New York, Joanna had received occasional photographs of Sophia, taken by Pete, and Mel had kept her informed about Donovan's state of mind every now and again. He had been working sporadically, she said, from a downtown loft, but his heart had not been in it and there had been no end results for her to sell on his behalf.

Life for Joanna, after the initial shock of her return, had gone on with remarkable normality. Kit and Miriam and Fred Morton had all welcomed her back with open arms, and Merlin Cottage – comfortingly unaltered – had seemed to do the same. Work, too, had been a blessed relief: more photographic commissions, another part-time job back at the Oxford hotel, and a new pregnancy for Bella, had all served at least partially to take her mind off what was missing in her life.

Jack had told her that normality was what she needed, and Joanna was beginning to think that perhaps he had been right.

But now, all that *apparent* normality, that superficial equilibrium of hers, was to be blown away.

Because he had asked if he could come, and she had agreed.

And tomorrow he would be here.

356

71

He looked older, fit enough, attractive as ever, but strained.

'You should have let us go to a hotel,' he said after they had finished their dinner and Pete had retired to bed.

'I told you I had plenty of room,' Joanna said. 'Kit and Miriam are backpacking in Cuba – they don't plan to come home till they've seen in the new millennium there.'

'Still,' he said, lighting up a cigar, 'it's extra work for you.'

'Would you prefer to be in a hotel, Jack?' she asked him. 'If so, I wish you would just tell me straight out, and I can telephone one for you.'

Donovan smiled. 'No,' he said. 'I'm glad to be here.'

'That's all right then, isn't it?' Joanna said.

She'd made up her mind about that before his arrival. There would be no fudging the truth, no burying her head in the sand. If Jack had come to England as her friend and nothing more, she would cope with that, and they would sleep in separate rooms for the duration of his visit. If he had come in the hopes of continuing their relationship as lovers, that was something she was prepared to think about too.

'You asked me,' she said now, 'when you first called a month ago, if you were too late, and I told you to come, which implied that you were not.'

'I remember.'

'Did I read something into that I shouldn't have, Jack?'

357

His smile this time was less certain.

'I don't think so,' he said.

Joanna knew, within a week, that he had more than a straight-forward visit in mind. This was for him, she now realized, an attempt at cutting off from the past and, perhaps, the launch of a new beginning. On the surface, at least, time seemed to have helped Donovan come to terms. Neither guilty, nor guilt*less*. So be it. Time to move on. And if he was going to try to start again, he told Joanna one afternoon in the Nursery as they fed Bella's pups together, he had decided to go for full-blown self-ishness and hope that she still felt the same way about what they had begun in New York.

'So I guess I'm asking you again: Am I too late?'

The sound of large dogs noisily eating from steel bowls filled the air.

Joanna took a deep breath, and reached for his hand.

'I don't think so,' she said.

Szabo had changed, had grown his white-blond hair longer, begun to smoke the occasional cigar, grown accustomed to being Donovan's right hand *and* eyes. He had more self-confidence, Joanna observed, had become swifter to speak his own mind.

'Is Pete okay about us?' she asked one night during the second week.

'Of course he's okay. Why do you ask?'

They were in the bed that Philip had carved for their marriage, and Joanna had no doubts about that at all. Being here with Jack felt right to her, just as making love again after all those long, empty months had felt wonderfully right.

'I was just wondering how he might feel if we go on.'

'What do you mean *if*?'

Joanna curled against him. 'So you do want to go on?'

'Don't you?'

No more fudging, Jo.

'Yes, I do.'

'Good,' he said.

358

'And you think Pete will be okay with that?'
'No question of it.'

In some ways, those early weeks in the English countryside seemed to Joanna to mirror her first month at Gilead Farm the previous year. She and Donovan and Szabo driving around the countryside, into Oxford and the smaller towns and villages; she and Pete sharing Lamb's old role, she more qualified to describe her home territory but the other man observing with a freshness and energy she could hardly compete with. And Donovan, as always, taking in everything, listening, feeling, sensing, memorizing.

'Like computerized human blotting paper,' Sara described his technique one day to Joanna. 'I envy him that skill.'

'You have your own skills,' Joanna said.

She told Sara that Donovan had asked if he might use the big disused outhouse on the perimeter of Merlin Cottage's land as a makeshift studio for the duration of his stay.

'That's wonderful news,' Sara said. 'If he's ready to work, that must mean he's really on the mend, and if the work goes well . . .'

Joanna didn't need her to complete the thought. If his work went well, Donovan might just decide to stay in England long-term. And if, by chance, that did come to pass, Joanna knew that her only major concern would be for Sophia's well-being. Speculation about ending quarantine continued, and one of the promised European 'pet passports' had already been granted in a special case, but hopes of relaxed rules for dogs from the United States were slim.

It was, in any case, too soon to worry about that. Now was for peace and happiness, for lovemaking and mutual discovery, for looking after one another's needs. And for letting time and fate take care of the rest.

The weeks passed. Mel called regularly, starved for positive news on the artistic front, and to reassure them that Sophia was fine.

Some things, Joanna was coming to realize, were not

destined to change. Jack had not yet taken to vanishing into the studio for days on end, but his work was still a closely guarded secret. Only now, of course, it was Szabo rather than Lamb who was allowed into the sanctum; Szabo who drove with Donovan to the foundry in Oxford for discussions about the casting of his first English-made sculpture.

'Doesn't it bug you?' Fred Morton asked her one late-November morning.

'I don't think so,' Joanna answered. 'Not too much, anyway.'

'It would piss me off if one of my blokes kept me in the dark that way.' Fred had long since got over her Donovan-as-Harrison-Ford period. Nowadays, he was just another man, with all the inherent flaws of the gender.

'Maybe it's because I'm so much busier here than I was at Gilead Farm.'

'So long as it's not denial,' Fred said with her Australian bluntness.

72

TUESDAY, DECEMBER 7

Nothing, as they passed – still in their pleasant, if unsettled, state of limbo – into the last month of the century, had made Joanna really uneasy.

Not the item of news reported in the *Oxford Mail* about the ongoing mystery of a young advertising executive from Horton-cum-Studley who had disappeared from his home in mid-November.

Not even the fact that Joanna, Donovan and Szabo had gone for afternoon tea to Studley Priory two weeks before that, and that, prior to going into the hotel for tea, they had strolled in the grounds of the former Benedictine priory and Szabo had described a young man with friends nearby. He had remarked, she remembered, that the man had the kind of looks that Lamb had liked. It had chilled Joanna at the time, she recalled that, too; the casual dropping of that name . . . Lamb, the abductor, Chen's procurer . . . Yet the moment had swiftly passed – had been nothing more than just that – a moment – and she had put it out of her mind, had walked with both men into the hotel and had enjoyed their tea.

It all changed one cold, crisp Tuesday afternoon when she was out walking Bella near the river and thought she saw Szabo, on the far side of a rough hedgerow of hawthorn, walking into a small wood close by.

Joanna waited a moment to be sure that it was him, lifted a

hand to hail to him, about to call his name – and then she changed her mind and stepped back behind the hedgerow. 'Bella,' she called softly, and the animal came directly to her, stood patiently while her lead was clipped on to her collar. Bella had been a wise, calm dog almost from puppyhood.

Joanna did not know why she was waiting or watching. Or hiding.

She could see Szabo through the trees. He had a bag with him, she had noticed, just an ordinary plastic carrier from John Lewis. Twice, he looked around. Not especially *furtively*, yet she felt, nevertheless, that he was looking to see if anyone else was close by.

He did not see Joanna.

Bella whined. She told her, softly, to stay.

Szabo bent down, was crouching low, and all Joanna could see of him now was the top of his flaxen head bobbing up and down.

She held her breath, listening intently, but the breeze was rising stiffly, and the bare winter branches of the trees in the wood were creaking and rustling, and she could not tell exactly what Szabo was doing.

She thought he was digging.

'How's the work going?' she asked Donovan that night in bed.

'Knock on wood,' he said, and gently tapped two fingers on her forehead.

'Anything for me to see soon?'

'I hope,' he said.

And then he began to kiss her breasts, and tangle his fingers in her hair.

And she asked no more questions, and was surprised that her body was able to respond to his lovemaking as it did, for her mind was several miles away, and her heart was cold with fear.

73

Every day, in spite of her fervent desire to forget, Joanna read the newspaper, listened to news bulletins on the radio and found herself paying extra attention to the regional television coverage in the evenings. She suspected that what she most *wanted* to hear – that the young man from Horton-cum-Studley had come home safe and well – was unlikely to make the news.

The finding of his body would hit headlines.

Or the finding of a clay sculpture with human bones inside it.

She told herself repeatedly, that she was being foolish and irrational. If Szabo had been disposing of something shameful, let alone monstrous, he would surely have gone deeper into the woods in the dead of night, not just glanced over his shoulder before digging his hole.

Yet he had, she was almost certain, buried *something* there; whatever, she presumed, he had been carrying in his John Lewis plastic bag. And he had, she thought, believed that there was no one around to see him.

I could go back, she told herself, not for the first time. She could go with a spade, or perhaps with Rufus, the best digger of her bunch. She could find the contents of the bag. Learn the truth, once and for all.

But the real truth was that she did not want to know.

An e-mail from Sara brought her to her senses. Sara said that she had been disturbed by another of her abstract '*Joanna*' nightmares and she wanted her friend to e-mail her back right away to let her know she was safe and well, and to come and visit her again soon.

Joanna composed her reply immediately and determinedly.

I am both safe and well, dearest Sara, and I will come to see you as soon as possible. As to your dream, I don't need to hear about it, and you don't need to trouble yourself about it. I am dealing with it already, as best as I can.

She went back to the woods after dark that afternoon, while Donovan was still working in the outhouse studio and Szabo was in her kitchen, preparing dinner. She wore dark clothes, took Rufus, a torch, and a trowel in an old canvas bag. If a policeman stopped her, she thought, it would be hard to explain what she was doing.

No one stopped her.

No one, to the best of her knowledge, even saw her.

For the first several minutes after she had brushed the dirt from the John Lewis bag and opened it, she wished, more than anything else in the world, that she had stayed with her first instincts and left well alone.

Bones were what she had been terrified of finding.

Bones were what she *had* found.

She sank heavily on to the ground, trembling and shivering. Rufus whined and sniffed at her face.

'It's all right,' Joanna told the dog automatically.

Not all right. Never again.

Close by, a twig snapped. Up in the trees, a night bird flew out of the branches into the dark sky. Joanna froze.

If Szabo had followed her . . .

With Jack, perhaps.

Her heart was pounding, her arms were goose pimpled. She had not felt such fear since that night almost a year before.

But Rufus never growled or raised a hackle.

No one there.

364

Just Joanna Guthrie and one of her dogs and the contents of a plastic carrier bag she'd dug out of a hole in the ground.

It could just be Szabo, she told herself, *acting alone.* Thriving on his elevation to Lamb's former status, infected by the dead man's and Chen's sickness. *Nothing to do with Jack.*

It didn't ring true.

But neither did guilt; not after so much anguish and heart-searching and self-blame.

Numbly, she picked up the torch and shone it back inside the bag.

The bones gleamed whitely.

Three of them, unjointed.

Joanna looked more closely, a different kind of curiosity starting to grip her, displacing just a little of what had over-whelmed her when she'd first opened the bag.

The bones looked strange.

Touch them.

She balked, feeling sick.

You have to touch them, Jo.

She put her right hand inside the bag and touched them.

'Oh, my God.'

A rush of hope sent her system into overdrive; a flush of heat, despite the cold of the night air, a tingling through her limbs.

They were not human remains. They were not bones of *any* kind.

They were resin.

'Oh, my *God.*'

Joanna began to laugh. Sitting there on the cold, disturbed bed of decaying leaves and good, old Oxfordshire earth on the edge of a wood in the dark early evening. It rose up inside her like irresistible bubbles venting out of a semi-sealed boiling pot; all the tension, dread and fear finding an outlet.

Until Rufus gave a single bark, bringing her back down.

She had to make sure – she was *almost* certain, but she needed absolute conviction. And there was only one way.

The basement storage-room of Fifty-sixth Street flashed back into her mind: the young woman's arm beneath its plastic casing.

The laughter was gone again.

Do it.

She took out one of the bones, held it in both hands. And snapped it.

It crumbled, fragments and dust powdering her dark clothes.

'Thank God,' Joanna said.

She stayed there for a long while. Thinking. About what to do with them. About what they were and what they meant.

They were sculpted resin bones. And they were no damned *good*.

Which was why Szabo had buried them.

She remembered coming across him in a tiny workshop at the school at Gilead Farm, remembered complimenting him on his sculpture, remembered him dismissing the praise, telling her he was no good. Strictly amateur.

She saw now that he had been right. Compared with Donovan – compared with Murdoch Lambert – he *was* a poor, amateurish sculptor.

She knew what she had to do with them.

She buried them again.

And then she went home.

She left the trowel and old canvas bag in the greenhouse between the Nursery and the garden, washed her hands under the outside tap, shook them dry – feeling chilled through now, but jubilant in spite of the discomfort – and went into Merlin Cottage.

No one noticed her hang her jacket on the hook in the hallway, or bend down to pull off her muddy boots and leave them on the rubber mat where all dirty boots and shoes were left until they could be cleaned. No one noticed her give Rufus a big, emotion-filled hug before the dog shook himself and trotted on ahead of her towards the Aga-warmed kitchen.

Home free and clear.

Joanna followed the dog.

'Hi, there.' Szabo was still there, pottering around.

'Something smells wonderful.' Joanna said.

'Been for a walk?' He glanced down at her stockinged feet.

'Yes,' Joanna said.

'Must be getting cold out there.'

'Starting to,' she said, and sat down at the table.

The jubilation had gone.

Only guilt remained.

74

MONDAY, DECEMBER 20

She had said nothing that evening, either to Pete or to Jack. What *could* she say? There was so much that she didn't know. First and foremost, the reason Szabo had made those bones. Had he believed that by trying to emulate the legitimate work Lamb had performed so brilliantly, he might be able to help restore Donovan's career to its former glory? And if so, was Jack aware of that, or had Pete been working secretly? That seemed the most likely scenario to Joanna, since otherwise there would have been no need for the burial of the unsuccessful attempt. Burying those resin bones had to mean that Pete Szabo had felt either deeply ashamed or embarrassed – and all Joanna would have achieved by talking about it would have been to make him feel worse. *And* she would have been throwing a spotlight on the fact that Szabo felt Donovan needed help.

She had kept silent for three whole days and nights.

Everyone had noticed that something was amiss with her. How could they not have, with her so quiet and jumpy?

'Shouldn't we be planning Christmas?' Fred had asked that Saturday.

'I'm not sure,' Joanna had answered.

'Why not?'

'Because of last year.'

'Oh.' Only Fred could have loaded that single syllable with so much scepticism and disapproval.

At least, Joanna had thought, that had only been *half* a lie. In less than three days' time, it would be the anniversary of that night of horror – and after that, for more than a month, every day for Jack would be a remembrance of some degree of hell.

'Are you going to tell me what's wrong?' Donovan asked, at last, on Monday evening after dinner. They were in the sitting room at Merlin Cottage, alone in the house but for the dogs, since Fred and Pete had gone to the cinema together.

Nothing's wrong, she wanted to say, as she had responded to every similar question asked over the past several days. But the time had come for the prevarication and lying to stop, once and for all. *For better or worse.*

She looked across at the fireplace, into the flames, thinking how ludicrous it was that finally she was the only one keeping a secret, and that it was the *keeping* of that secret that was making it darker than it was. The only truly dark aspect to all this had been her suspicions.

'You've seen all Hitchcock's films, haven't you?' she asked, suddenly.

He was puzzled by the question. 'Sure.'

'I've been trying to remember the ending of one of them.' She paused. 'Cary Grant and Joan Fontaine were in it.'

'"*Suspicion*",' he said. 'What did you want to know?'

'Was it a happy or sad ending?'

'Happy, I think.' He waited a moment. 'Does that help?'

'Not really,' she said. 'It was just a film.'

In the fireplace a log shifted. The flames crackled and a small shower of sparks flew up the chimney.

'So?' Donovan asked quietly. 'Are you ready now?'

'What for?'

'To tell me what's been making you so unhappy.'

She had known all along that she would have to tell him in the end. Not because of anything Pete had done – not because of the bones. Because of what had happened to her after she'd witnessed Szabo burying the bag. Suspicion. Not just of Pete, but of Jack himself.

369

For more than a week after she'd watched Pete dig that hole in the wood, Joanna had tormented herself with doubts and fears.

She had not trusted Jack.

That was, when all was said and done, the worst of it. The wreckage was still with them. Not just in Donovan's soul, but in hers, too.

She had doubted him.

And that was what she had to tell him.

75

He drank himself into oblivion that night. As he had that Thanksgiving Day the previous year, he gave Joanna advance notice he was going to do so, even telling her that he would replace whatever he drank.

That was the closest to cool he came with her. If Joanna had expected recriminations or long wounded silences, they were not forthcoming.

'You want me to blame you?' he asked her just before he told her he was planning to get drunk.

'I don't know,' she'd said. 'I blame myself.'

'You shouldn't,' he said. 'You're a strong, brave woman, Joanna, and you went to hell and back last year because of me. You saw what you saw, and you weren't coward enough to pretend you hadn't seen it.'

'But I thought—'

'You thought I might be a killer.'

'No.' On that, at least, she could be adamant. 'Not that.'

'You thought Pete had turned killer for my sake, and I'd grown sick and twisted enough to overlook it, just in case that was the only way I was ever going to sculpt successfully again.'

His mouth had quirked then in a kind of smile, as if he had been able to find a measure of humour in the situation, but Joanna had known how far from the truth that had to be.

'I'm so sorry, Jack. I don't know what else to say.'

'I don't think you have anything to be sorry for.'

'Except that I've hurt you deeply,' she had said. 'When you've only just begun to get over last year.'

'But you didn't do it deliberately.' Donovan had been very gentle. 'And I think that *not* telling me might have hurt me more deeply, in the long-term.'

'Perhaps,' Joanna had said.

He had asked her then if she had enough whisky for him to get drunk on – and that, surely, was proof, if nothing else, of how much she *had* wounded him.

'I bought a case of Jack Daniel's when I knew you were coming.'

He'd given another of those sad smiles then.

'Must have figured I'd be needing it.'

76

'I've made a few decisions,' he told her the next afternoon.

They were in the kitchen, entirely alone, even the dogs elsewhere.

'I think it's time we headed home.'

Joanna felt something old but painfully familiar clutch at her heart, and recognized it immediately. Grief.

'Is that what you and Mel were talking about?' The agent had telephoned just after two, aware that it was a year on from the horrors.

'I mentioned the possibility.'

Joanna waited a moment.

'How's Pete?'

'He's okay.' Donovan paused. 'I haven't told him. I don't plan to.'

'I'm glad,' she said. 'When will you leave?'

'That depends on you.'

'Me?'

'Christmas is just a few days away. I'd like to spend it with Sophia.'

The grief magnified. 'I think that would be lovely.'

'I'd like to spend it with you, too, Joanna.'

She shrugged. 'Can't be in two places.'

'I know it's short notice,' he said.

She noticed, for the first time, that he was leaning forward across the table, and that the hunch of his shoulders matched the intensity on his face. Some of the grief went away.

'I don't understand,' she said.

373

'Which part?'

'How you could still want to be with me,' she said. 'After yesterday.'

'I thought we covered that last night,' Donovan said. 'You're strong, you're courageous, and you were honest with me. Not to mention the fact that you're a beautiful, intelligent woman and I've been in love with you for a long time.' He paused. 'How could I *not* want to be with you, Joanna Guthrie?'

Now she could not speak at all.

'Will you at least think about it?'

'Yes.' Her voice was faint.

He told her then that he wanted her to fly over with him for another reason. Mel had told him that she'd found some property in Connecticut she thought might suit what he'd had in mind for a while now.

'What's that?' Joanna was intrigued.

'I want to open another school,' Donovan said. 'For blind and disabled artists. All ages.'

Grief had vanished completely. Excitement gripped Joanna.

'Oh, yes,' she said, softly.

'Plenty of space for dogs,' he added.

'Sophia would love it.'

'It wasn't just Sophia I was thinking about.'

Standing silent and motionless out in the hall, Szabo listened to them and felt a dull ache in his heart. He'd realized this was coming, had resigned himself. They would probably talk for a while now: about the tough road that lay ahead of them both, about how hard it would be for Joanna to leave home. But he knew now that she would agree to do just that. It was the absolute opposite of what he'd hoped and planned for, had rendered all his recent hard work null and void.

But he was a patient man.

He had made those resin bones just for *her*, that was the irony of it; had made them specifically in order to dispose of them. Ever since the November afternoon outside Studley Priory when he'd passed that remark about the young man having looks Lamb would have liked, Szabo had felt Joanna's unease around him and had realized that she would never understand what had to be done.

That was why he had made the resin bones. That was why he had followed her and the dog on their walk to the woods a week ago and had made certain she had seen him burying the bag. He'd *known* she'd be unable to resist digging it up and taking a look. And after that, he'd thought it a safe bet that she'd feel she had to confess her doubts to Donovan.

She was that kind of woman. She had *integrity*.

He had been so sure it would finish them, so certain that her lapse of faith would destroy their fragile relationship forever. But that had not happened, and now he saw that he was going to be saddled with Joanna Guthrie for a while longer.

It wasn't that he didn't like her. On the contrary, Szabo had liked and respected the red-haired Englishwoman from the beginning. But now, alas, she was in his way.

He'd been as horrified as anyone when they'd first found out what Lamb and Chen had done. The thought of so much gratuitous cruelty and evil still made him sick to his stomach. But then again, he had come to learn that, when it came to love, there were few things one could not do if one had to.

If anyone knew what Donovan had endured since that terrible time, it was Pete Szabo. He'd seen the pain and anguish and guilt at first hand, seen it drag that brilliant, remarkable man down to below rock bottom. He'd cared for Donovan as best he could, had taken over from Lamb in many ways, had become his right hand and trusted eyes. The sculptor had needed him more than he ever had before, and it had been Szabo's privilege, his *joy*, to serve him. He'd been so thankful, so *proud*, when Donovan had tried to return to work. But the work had not been the same. Could not be the same. And Szabo had ached for him, had longed to help him.

That was why he'd begun preparing for their future. He was no fool; he knew he'd never have Lamb's gifts, but that was hardly going to matter in the long haul. When Donovan's guilt and horror became submerged beneath the worse agony of losing his talent.

375

When he was finally ready to admit he needed help.

It was tragic, in many ways, but there simply could be no denying that Donovan's true genius had only soared because of Lamb and Chen. Now, without them, he was almost mediocre by comparison. *He* knew it, and Mel knew it, and when Joanna saw his work – when Donovan was finally ready to show it to her – she would know it too.

The problem was, it might not matter to her. Joanna Guthrie was an ordinary, respectable woman, with ordinary values. She would love Donovan, brilliant and successful, or not. She would not understand how vital greatness *was* to an artist like Donovan. She might even consider mediocrity better than excellence – if the cost of excellence was another person's life.

Szabo had come to learn that wasn't so.

Donovan would, in time, come to see that too.

Joanna would probably never reach that conclusion. Because, when all was said and done, she did not love Donovan as completely as Szabo did. The simple truth was that if the bones he'd buried in the woods had been real, had been *human*, Joanna would have turned her back on Jack Donovan.

Szabo would never do that.

Which was why he intended to go on practising his new craft – Lamb's and Chen's craft – for the time being. They were young enough, he and Donovan, they had time on their side. He would bide his time, quietly and patiently. He would wait and watch as Donovan became increasingly dissatisfied, as resignation turned, first, to frustration, then spiralled back down to dark, unbearable depression.

And then Szabo would bring him his first gift.

And if Joanna Guthrie was still around when he was ready to do that, then she would simply have to go.

Because greatness in art was more precious than one woman.

Even Donovan, ultimately, was bound to understand that.